Absent Children

Absent Children

◆

Tim Wenzell

Writer's Showcase
presented by *Writer's Digest*
San Jose New York Lincoln Shanghai

Absent Children

Writer's Showcase
presented by *Writer's Digest*
an imprint of iUniverse.com, Inc.

For information address:
iUniverse.com, Inc.
620 North 48th Street, Suite 201
Lincoln, NE 68504-3467
www.iuniverse.com

ISBN: 0-595-12142-X

Printed in the United States of America

for Ryan

Grief fills the room up of my absent child

Lies in his bed, walks up and down with me,

Puts on his pretty looks, repeats his words,

Remembers me of all his gracious parts,

Stuffs out his vacant garments with his form…

Shakespeare, *King John*

Contents

The Closet Box

◆

I

After the masked hoodlums broke in on a stiff winter night and took his little brother Benjamin from the crib, Eddie Shemanski built a room behind the wall of his closet that fit him precisely and hid him quiet behind the hanging sweaters. He built the box out of the two by fours and the drywall scraps his father had left in the attic. Eddie would hide in the box, retreating there every time he heard a knock at the door, and sometimes when the phone rang and sometimes when he thought that his father wasn't really his father. He would look out from his breathing holes and wait for the answer at the door, wait for the reply to the phone call, wait to see his father's loafers squashing his shag carpet as he opened the closet door, calling his name and asking: "where did you get to you little son of a bitch?"

One night, Eddie saw a customer in the restaurant who looked exactly like his father. "Well, they say everyone in the world has someone that looks exactly like him," some of the employees whispered. The striking similarities, right down to the crooked teeth, gave Eddie the same dream night after night: he was fishing on a river, playing catch with a man sitting at a table. A candle burned in front of him as he sat holding his fishing pole. watching those crooked teeth bob up and down in the water.

Sometimes early in the morning just after he awoke, or when his father walked down the hall between innings to go to the toilet, Eddie became convinced it was that same restaurant customer (whom he thought might have been named Clem), and now he had barged into his house to reclaim his long-lost son.

After the dreams stopped and he forgot about his father's look-alike, Eddie started smoking his mother's Kools in the closet box. He found a way to take them there four at a time along with one of her Bic lighters. He'd be careful to plug the holes and close the door tight. Once, when he he left the door open, a graveyard of smoke drifted and settled on the floor of his room. He tried desperately to vent the smoke out his raised window with a pile of papers. Then he heard the squeak of the floor-boards in the hallway and his mother's voice calling for laundry.

"Set the lighter on low," Eddie told himself as he entered his chamber. He remembered the accident with the tall flame and the top of his box and the severe burns that encrusted the palms of his hands with blisters. He had told his parents that the blisters came from a coffee pot at the Scout outing.

Eddie stashed an empty tuna can in the far corner of the box. He enclosed it behind a cardboard flap and his menthol butts filled it up each week. He'd slide the stuffed Starkist can into his trousers and take it down two flights to the kitchen on trash night, and then he would quickly empty it beneath wads of wet paper towel or coffee grounds or shaved apple slices from another one of his mother's charred pies. Sometimes a butt or two would lodge in his underwear and make his crotch smell like tobacco. Sometimes they slid down a trouser leg and fell to the floor. Eddie would flash his fingers to the floor and grab the stray butts before his father looked up from the box scores.

"Eddie's clothes…they smell like ciggies, honey. They smell like ciggies, lots of them," he heard his mother say to his father from their bed one night. She had just come up from the basement, and Eddie closed his windows and the sound of the crickets off and rested his ear lightly upon the air vent as their voices echoed up.

"I smoked on the corner of Tenth and Reed for twelve years," his father said. "Eddie knows that from all the Pete stories. He would just tell me I had no room to talk if I confronted him about it."

"At least let him know about the dangers of smoking…show him pictures of emphysema patients or something…"

"Why don't I just show myself the pictures? I have no room to talk. I smoke two packs a day, honey, and I have no room to talk." Eddie heard the light click off as he watched the reflection die off the vent wall. He calculated that his mother smoked three packs a day. He crawled into bed after he flicked off his own light. For almost seven hours he laid awake thinking about what he could do to correct the problem, finally deciding he would begin to smoke nude. Eddie figured the smell could simply be washed away. "Besides", he thought, "I won't give dad the satisfaction."

Eddie's smoking ritual became like taking a shower from that moment on; he left his clothes in a folded pile in front of the box, then stepped in, chain-smoked four Kools, and sealed the door behind him. He usually waited until his Uncle Pete came over to light up, waiting for the moment of the knock and for his uncle's voice to trail off down the walk. Then he'd sneak into his parent's room during the commotion at the door, put his hands into the pockets of his mother's windbreaker, and rummage through the pack that was always there. He would unzip his fly and fill it with stolen cigarettes, five or six of them. (When he would get greedy and go for seven or eight, he would always manage to tear up a cigarette in the teeth of his zipper and leave a trail of tobacco leaves.) Each night, the time of his thefts came just before seven-thirty, when baseball was coming on, the event his father lived for. Baseball: Eddie's recurring hell, coming out of the television six nights a week.

Eddie hated summer. He hated the heat and the humidity and he hated the insects. He despised the noisy ones, crickets and cicadas and such, anything that gathered together and kept him up worrying about bugs crawling into the room. But mostly, Eddie hated baseball. When his Uncle Pete would come over with his Baseball Encyclopedia, he knew all the ear plugs in the world wouldn't shut out the trivia questions booming back and forth across the living room between his father and his uncle, deep into the night. McCovey, Ruth, Maris, Gehrig, Greenberg, Campanis, Fingers, Robinson, Frisch and Williams; the names tumbled on and on, one after the other. Only, league, consecutive, and most. Years and careers, games and hits, losses and wins. The words merged and echoed in foreign syntax, down the hall and beneath Eddie's door, leaking through the pillows he had mashed in failure against his ears. "Give me something I haven't heard", they dared each other, vibrating the drywall. "Give me something I haven't heard."

II

Eddie brought in a boom-box for one of his dishwashing shifts at the restaurant, after Jeff Poindexter the drunk cook had dropped his radio into the gravy. He brought it in because Lou the owner had said "no more radios behind the line" and for Jeff to get himself together or else. Lou pointed out that Eddie was perfectly free to put something on the plate shelf and he made a little space for him next to the foil. Eddie brought the boom-box in to soothe his night with some reggae. He brought the boom box in to show up the night cooks.

"Put the game on," the drunken cook demanded. "Let us hear the game." Eddie looked up at the clock and it read seven-thirty. A chill ran through him and he thought of his closet box.

"I hate baseball, it's my radio, fuck you," Eddie replied. He sprayed down a rack of soup bowls and slid them into the machine.

The nice cook approached him around nine o'clock and asked if he could simply get a score, with the promise that he would put Marley immediately back on.

"Sure, but only if you make it quick," Eddie replied.

The nice cook cranked the dial with his wet hand and then stood in Eddie's way and listened to the buzz injected through the boom box by the dish machine. The baseball announcer fought through the buzz and called a ball and then another ball and then a strike and then a foul, a foul, a foul, a ball, a pop-up for the second out and then three strikes in a row for the third out. "We go to the top of the seventh," the announcer said out of the rinse-cycle static, "with the score Reds eleven, Phils one."

The nice cook gave a groan and walked away without changing the station back, drying his hand on his apron, his gait slow and hunched.

"Something wrong?, Eddie asked. "Eleven to one…is that bad?"

The nice cook looked back, puzzled like a mathematician with a piece of chalk. "Bad?" he replied. "Bad?"

Eddie pulled a hot rack out of the other end of the machine, slipping the plates quickly into a stack with the tips of his fingers.

"Dude, they're down by ten runs," the nice cook said. "Wadya mean, bad…that's as bad as it gets."

"Well, how many points is a run?" Eddie asked at the shelf, not caring for runs or points or anything at all to do with baseball (uncles or fathers.)

The nice cook straightened up and widened his eyes in disbelief and then retied his apron strings by the sink. "A run is a run, there's no points in baseball."

"You mean you don't get any extra points for sliding in fancy or anything?" Eddie asked.

"Where the hell did you grow up,?"Jeff slurred as he eyed him between the hanging tickets. "What are you, some kind of sports idiot?" He turned and held aloft a New York strip with a pair of tongs, smoking and well-done on its way to a platter. "Didn't you ever play baseball?"

Without an answer, Eddie switched back his station and turned the volume up, as the reverberating cadence of a reggae song divided him into his solitude. Jeff began to laugh and the nice cook chuckled his way back into his fold. "Unbelievable," he heard them say to each other, as they reached together and pulled off a bundle of tickets from the wheel. "Unfuckingbelievable."

Eddie never told the cooks or the waiters or Benny the week-night dishwasher of his confessional, of his peculiar habit of retreating into his closet box. He didn't tell them what he did when he went home, how he closed the door to his room, locking it and listening. He didn't tell them about his journey through a forest of hanging sweaters to smoke his cigarettes. No, he never told them about his private little problem.

Never in his darkness did he bother long enough to think: "Why don't I just sit on my radiator and blow it out my window? Crawl out on the roof? Walk out to the woods, sit down on a log, smoke it in one of the clearings?" Eddie smoked mostly because he was angry at the prospect of another long night of baseball and the loud slurring of drunken trivia and the clinking of empty beer bottles on their way to the recycling tub. The dark interior of that box would embrace him. The glow of the cigarette that lingered there between the walls would mesmerize him. The walls muffled away the outside world like the encroaching air of a coffin. Eddie sealed himself in a stagnant little universe, comfortably trapped, comfortably alive and alone. "I love to take big drags in here," Eddie thought. " I love to blow them away invisible." But he also smoked because he was nervous, and that was why he went to his closet box, because he was nervous.

III

Eddie's mother answered the door one night and found no one there. He heard her from the box as she opened the door, guessing that she was peering about the bushes, hearing the click as she flicked on the porch light. Then she screamed and Eddie's heart grew rapid as he awaited the sound of a stranger's footsteps on the stairs. He anticipated the planned trip unfolding into his bedroom to steal him away with scarves and blindfolds. (His mother had jumped back at a Luna moth that had crashed into the screen, though there was no way Eddie, in his darkness, could know this). He listened as she went sobbing from the front door to the bedroom in hurried steps, and then as his father sighed deeply and got up from his game. Feeling safety, Eddie slid out of the wall and over to the vent. She began talking, in waves of wails, about Benjamin.

"It's been well over two years," she said. "They never found the men and I can't help thinking what they've done to our little baby or where he might be. I can't help thinking they planned it all out. If only we could have seen behind those masks.... we might know who they were."

She sobbed for a while. It came up the vent and Eddie laid down on his shag carpet and looked up at the stained ceiling, waiting for her to stop. He heard the cheering coming out of the television in the other room. His father was missing something exciting, maybe a home run or a double-play grounder, maybe a bench-clearing brawl.

"Remember how they came in, Harv?" she sobbed with more control. "Remember how they put us face-down on the floor at gunpoint and marched right up the stairs and into his room?"

"Yes, honey, we've been over it. Remember what the counselor said, we should try to put it behind..."

"I'm screaming at moths, for Christ's sake," she said. "Two and a half years later and I'm jumping at bugs on the screen."

"I'll bet that Burke kid is up to his knocking pranks again," his father said. "Damned son of a bitch kids have no regard, no regard."

"The detective couldn't find a motive. I can't believe there was no motive," she continued in her sob state. "Someone was spying on us and knew where to go. They wanted Benjamin, somebody wanted Benjamin in the top room. They came in and stole him like he was a television or a VCR or an expensive necklace."

His father gave a sigh that hissed up the vent. Eddie figured he wanted to get back to his chair in the living room, because somebody was mounting a rally.

"There's nothing left we can do, honey, you know that," his father said. "What's the point any more?"

Eddie's mother sobbed long and low and his ear hurt from resting it on the louvers of the vent plate. So he got up and went down into the kitchen to survey the garbage situation. His father came walking out from the bedroom, a brisk walk past the kitchen door, pulled like a magnet to the cheers coming out of the living room television. Baseball: he clapped his hands three times and hollered "Yeah!"

Eddie watched him as he stood next to his chair when the score came up and as a commercial flashed on and then as he finished his backwash. Eddie looked over to the corner of the kitchen: his father had already taken out the garbage. Damnit—he would need to find another way to get rid of the butts in his tuna can. He considered smuggling them out in his underwear on his way to the restaurant. Instead, he stuffed them in an old sock, one of the ones with the holes and the permanent sweat stains off the survival weekend. He dropped the sock between the beams of the wall, figuring he would be fully grown and his parents long gone by the time it was finally unearthed.

IV

Eddie bought some joints from Benny the week-night dishwasher one afternoon in the lot, just after Lou left for the liquor order. He had smoked some pot at the Lenape Valley Jamboree with some of the Life Scouts that spring, and, upon getting stoned, he had liked the way the fire leaped to the lighter fluid. He had watched the trees flashing in and out of his sight and he had liked the way the black leaves moved like quivering jellyfish...and he had liked the way the eyes of the scouts wrapped in a circle around the flames, dark socket to dark socket, connected. So he said "yes" when Benny asked him if he got high, and then he bought some joints from him out of the ounce Benny pulled from his duffel bag. Eddie unzipped his fly, slid them in, and zipped slowly back up a notch at a time.

"What are you doing?" Benny asked him. "They have these things now called pockets."

"Yeah but you don't know my parents. It gets like a Nazi police station going home sometimes."

"You mean they actually search you?"

"Oh, no. But the way they look at me, especially back when I was snagging Mom's cigarettes from the junk drawer and putting them in my pockets, it was like they knew." Eddie patted his crotch. "I don't want to chance it. God knows what would happen if they found out I smoked a drug."

Eddie went home and searched for his mother's lighter in the box. He had tossed his tuna can and now there was nothing behind the cardboard flap: no butts, no can, no lighter. The lighter might have dropped down between the beams with his sockful of butts, the way his hamster Elvis had done five years back when it escaped through the hole in the aquarium. He would have to get another lighter or maybe some packs of matches. He would need another container, too—maybe a cleaned out soup can this time around.

Eddie disrobed and smoked his first joint the night of a double-header, the night his Uncle Pete had just come from an argument with his wife Rita. He listened to the scraping of his uncle's shoes on the walk before he went in (scraping shoes meant his uncle had started early on the beer-drinking, probably at Fitzgerald's Pub, and he would spend the night on the cot). Sure enough, he heard his father tell him to park his car up on the grass. "You don't want a ticket like you got the last time you stayed," he said.

"Never paid the son of a bitch, either," his uncle said. "A man should be able to park on the street." Eddie heard the hum of the refrigerator motor as it rattled the bottles. Uncle Pete was hunting for the imported beer.

"Are you ready for six hours of baseball?" his father asked. Then he heard their echoes from the kitchen, laughing mostly, talking about Rita "the bitch" and how Uncle Pete was going to take her poodle out to the woods and let it loose. The television had not yet been turned on and their voices carried up through the silent house like prayers in a church, penetrating his black universe.

"Damned thing will starve to death, too, because there'll be nobody out there to feed it filet mignon and spring water," Uncle Pete said. "And you know what I'll tell Rita…I'll tell her I tied its little paws together and laid it in the driveway and backed over the damned thing…crunch, crunch, crunch with the tires back and forth over and over until I pulverized it and I buried the pieces in sandwich bags down by the creek or something. I'll tell her that and then sit back and watch how riled up she'll get after she can't find the miserable little thing under any of the beds. I'll laugh like Jesus all the way to Fitzgerald's."

Eddie flicked the match and the flame lit up the blackness of his box, and he nervously touched it to the end of the joint. He held in the wicked smoke, held it long enough to spit it out in a quiet cough, just the way the Life Scouts had instructed him. He did it again and then he did it again and then he imagined the smoke hanging by circular wires around his chest, halos unseen. I am like the planet Saturn, he thought.

V

1971. The first ball game Eddie ever went to and the first year of the new stadium, Veteran's Stadium. It was state-of-the-art because you were never going to need grass again. "Astro-Turf is the greatest invention ever conceived in the history of man," his father told him, patting Eddie on his wet hair and directing him to the station wagon. "No more lousy-paid maintenance people having to cut the grass all summer." He backed down the driveway, stopped, looked out at his own crabgrass. "Wish I could afford the stuff for our yard, what with the way the mower's been acting."

Eddie sat in the yellow seats of the big new stadium holding a tub of Coke, between his father and William. William, his older brother, had just given up a guinea-pig breeding business and had started selling cancer insurance to stricken families. William would get customers names from the hospitals, knock on their doors, and get himself inside to open his brief case and talk payment plans. Sometimes he'd hang out at The Cemetery Stop and interrupt people while they were headstone-shopping, throwing out a line or two of condolences. Then, he'd rattle off his memorized speech, the one that guaranteed a sell.

Five years back, William had left the house on a Harley headed for the Northwest Territories, the night after he'd given Eddie a pet hamster for his sixth birthday, asking only that he name it "Elvis". Eddie wondered how a guy such as his brother, at one point of his life headed for the Northwest Territories on a Harley and then later breeding guinea pigs, could come back home and peddle cancer insurance to grieving families. He wondered where along the line he converted himself into a money-worshiping grub and how he could put on those false faces, cemented with remorse and covering the cracks of his rotting greed.

His father was explaining the significance of the third-base coach bringing out the line-up card to the umpires, talking over Eddie and his tub of soda to William. William wanted, in his wiser state, to learn more about a game he never had an interest in as a child. William had grown closer to his father since he'd moved back. He'd taken his old room on the bottom floor and had his long hair cut off. But he had grown closer mostly because he had brought home a load of money and helped his father out with mortgage payments and bought a new set of sliding doors and ratchet sets and such.

"You see, the Phils have been on a long losing streak, eleven in a row now," his father said. "Eventually, after you can't find any good excuses for losing any more, you begin to think it's bad luck that's nailed your whole team. You get superstitious, you try to do things differently. Now, look down and see what we have going on at home plate…a manager telling his third base coach to go out to the mound instead of himself. Maybe we'll win if I send someone else out, he's thinking. Maybe I'm bad luck, maybe some witch-doctor put a curse on me. I've got to do something now, in a hurry, before it's too late, before they decide to fire my ass."

Eddie only remembered their voices suspended above him, like a high wire act just out of reach; they were talking about line-drive double plays and when to sacrifice and should they use the suicide squeeze, and he lost himself in the black swirl of ice cubes dancing in his Coke. They talked on and on, into the game and above the rows of voices that shot out in a recurring spasm of boos and catcalls, as the Phillies dropped fly balls and got tagged out at home and struck out, batter after batter in the dead heat. His father reached over Eddie with his scorecard and his little yellow pencil and showed William the numbers assigned to each position. Then his father sighed in irritation at this cumbersome arrangement and finally asked Eddie to switch seats because it would be easier to explain things. Another rain of boos descended from above.

Sitting on the end, Eddie watched a program flutter down from the upper deck, the pages wing-like in its downward flight, a paper bird. Eddie looked at his father and William gathered around the numbers. He could have gotten up and lost himself in the upper deck between the legs of ushers and vendors and they would never have noticed. He looked at the remaining ice cubes melting at the bottom of his tub and flung the container into the air in one clean jerk. He watched in his anger as the tub sailed high above the heads of the crowd, a crowd now standing and pumping their arms furiously over a misplayed ball, anger and contortion spread like butter over their collective faces. His projectile caught a momentary breeze that carried it ten rows out, then turned for its rocket-ride downward, ice cubes weighing the bottom of it and dropping it like a bag of bricks directly onto the head of an old woman. The hard edge of the cardboard sliced full force against her fragile forehead. Eddie got up and watched from the railing as it opened up her up like a surgical instrument. The blood ran down over her lava-rock face, streaming across her eyes as they shot about in terror and then flickered shut. The entire row, whom Eddie guessed were grandsons and sons, converged upon her in terror, calling for medical help and looking back into the crowd for the perpetrator of the unspeakable act. An older boy in a green jersey looked directly at him; he stared up at Eddie as his father called him back to his seat. The green boy was swept away down the row in a furious melee of security people and emergency help. Eddie eyed the old woman's trembling hands as they passed on the stretcher, as they moved beneath the quieted crowd and away from the oblivious ballplayers hundreds of yards down. He watched her disappear into the tunnel, followed by her grandsons, then her sons, and he weighed the significance of the empty row.

His father looked up from his scorecard and wrinkled his nose. "I wonder what happened over there."

1971. The last ball game Eddie ever wanted to go to.

VI

Even now, stoned in his box, Eddie recalled the old lady and the hurried medical men and all the family members swallowed as a parade into the tunnel. He feared that the old lady had died, maybe on her way to the emergency room. They had bandaged her up and had sewed her old skin together during the bumpy ambulance ride, but the shock of the blow had seized her heart and didn't let go until it had stopped beating. Maybe she was the nicest woman on her block,with flower boxes and cats and home-made biscuits. Her sons and grandsons adored her and took her to ball games and listened to her talk about the old-timers, Babe Ruth and Jimmie Foxx and Rogers Hornsby. She would tell them about the ticker-tape parades for the A's down Broad Street on chilly October week-days. But now the sons and grandsons were left with only an obituary reading 'Very Remarkable Lady' after Eddie's pointless act. They were left in a somber waiting room to question the absurdity of her stadium death. Angry, crying, bewildered, the sons raised their voices into shouts down empty hallways, vowing that whoever did this to their mother would be hunted down.

The boy in the green jersey: the look on his face returned; it came out of the brilliant sun of that afternoon game and entered into Eddie's sealed chamber as he sat there stoned as could be. That boy must have seen him throw his empty tub into the air; he must have looked closely at him and remembered where he was sitting and blurted it out in the waiting room. "It was a kid that did it, a little kid. I saw him throw the thing into the air, pop. I saw him come over to the railing and watch grandma bleed. I'd recognize the kid anywhere, pop. He thought the whole thing funny."

A sudden revelation seized Eddie and pulled him down to a seated position in his box and constricted him as he snuffed his roach against the wall. Green jersey, green jersey, green jersey: one of the men who abducted Benjamin had worn a green jersey, a green jersey with white numbers, the number sixteen (he recalled the testimony of his wailing mother). Eddie tried to remember if that was the number on the boy, because it was the number on the man, the man who had made his parents lie face-down on the rug. Yes, he pictured the sunny day seven years back, the crowd rising to its feet and the scramble down the row to attend to the fallen women. The boy had stood up on his seat and glared back at Eddie with those furry eyebrows, that hairy anger. No doubt remained: the boy had seen him throw his empty soda. He had witnessed his grandmother's executioner with one long and unforgetful stare. The number sixteen was there, spread across his chest; there was no other number. Eddie looked into the blackness: sixteen.

But it couldn't be, it wasn't possible. How could the boy track him down, a little boy's face in a crowd a level up? Why would he wait to seek his vengeance, five years after the fact? The boy was in his twenties by now, bigger than his jersey with a furry moustache to match his furry eyebrows and driving a used car, out on dates and beer-drinking binges past his curfew, no doubt. Surely he forgot, maybe during the summer when he shot up two inches, the summer he grew out of his green jersey. No, there was no way, it was ludicrous to even think it, Eddie thought. It couldn't have been the same person. I am simply stoned and paranoid.

The television was blaring downstairs now and someone was fouling off pitch after pitch. Uncle Pete was asking a question in the foreign syntax of his baseball trivia, slurring it out loud across the room. "Who was the only guy to hit for the cycle in each league?" he asked. It was only the television for a while and Eddie figured his dad was done in,

that the Petester had him down another beer. He heard it go to commercial, and then, in the middle of a lingo, the name "Bob Watson"
came out of his father's throat, from out of the easy chair and across
the carpet. His loud and certain answer caused Eddie's uncle to rattle
the television tray with an "almost had you you son of a bitch." Bob
Watson…what a simple, idiotic name, Eddie thought. This guy does
one freak-of-nature thing in one miserable career and lives forever in
baseball trivia, hailed by drunken losers.

He listened as his father and his uncle got silent for a time, when he
could hear only the game, the faint echo of a sparse crowd clapping, the
steady drone of the man's voice as the pitches came in. Nice, really,
Eddie thought. A soothing and pleasant sound, like a sprinkle of warm
water running over you.

In Eddie's black little universe, baseball was an echo trying to reach in
and grab hold of him, always trying to rattle him. Now, he would try to
like it. He focused on his father's voice, his uncle's replies. "Ball three…if
Hobose gets aboard, it's a sure steal," his father said. "The guy's only
been caught once all year." Eddie wished the guy aboard, and he wished
him nailed at second base.

Eddie wanted to wrap the foreign syntax around him, embrace it, like
it. After all, William had done it, and whenever he called from
Washington, he and his father would spend the first five minutes on the
phone talking about his Congressional pursuits and then the next two
hours talking baseball. (William was involved in a campaign to bring
back the Senators). If Eddie learned to like baseball like his brother, he
could sit down on the couch and watch the game, ask some tough trivia,
make their beer runs. He would just need to come down the steps from
his room and ask his Uncle Pete to slide over.

Eddie tried. He squeezed his temple and pretended to like baseball,
but it didn't matter. Darkness, noise, closed eyes: they couldn't keep out
the number sixteen, and that peculiar color of the boy's jersey, the color

of dying grass. Breaking his link to the voices downstairs and to the drone of the game, he surrendered to the thought gnawing at the edges of his closet box: "I've killed an old lady."

VII

Eddie laid his head against the beam, tired from the long day. He had gotten up at four in the morning after a car alarm had gone off down on Catherine Street, and he could not return to sleep because the cut on his thumb had begun to throb. He had gone downstairs to wash it in the bathroom sink and his father had clicked on the hall light to ask if everything was all right.

"Some plates slipped during a bus pan slam and I tried to catch them before they hit the floor and one of the broken pieces got me...Lou the owner wrapped my cut in band-aids and told me it was too busy to go get stitches," Eddie had told him. Eddie had stayed on and worked late and didn't think about the rinsed sauces and the beet juice and the lamb scraps and whatnot running down the dirty china and getting inside his band-aids and settling into his cut. His father had warned him over the running water that if the throbbing persisted, they should both head to the doctor when he awoke. But Eddie never slept, and now here he was, in his box with the pain returning to his thumb, with the day now gone deep into the night, without a word to his father. The droning of the baseball game injected him like a sedative, and he rested the point of his skull against the corner of the box and fell asleep there.

When Eddie awoke, the game had been clicked off. His father and mother had gone to bed and his uncle had fallen dead asleep on the cot, leaving only the muffled crickets to chirp outside his box. Eddie didn't know where he was during the first few seconds out of sleep; blackness brought no familiar things to place him into the conscious world, so he hovered in transition like a bird on a storm front. His mind worked, trying to grasp any tangible thing so that it could tell Eddie any bit of information. Images came and went, slides on the wall, shadows rising tall from all sides, monolithic overcoats approaching and converging; bars, shadows of bars, left and right, tapering below his feet. A crib, he was in a crib, long and narrow, bars rising beyond arm's length, the shadows of other things above him, the swaying of the tree branches hitting the house, the long and evil fingers of strangers coming out of overcoats, reaching down. "I'm in a crib…I'm in a crib, a crib,who am I?" he silently questioned the unfolding blackness. "Where did I wake up?"

Eddie leaped out at the vast nothingness, thrashed at the imaginary forms swelling and disintegrating before him. He felt out into the blackness. "Solid wall, solid wall…the ceiling, I can touch the ceiling" he thought. "Wait, no crib, I'm not in a crib, there are no overcoats or dead branches or mobiles hanging and twisting on their strings, no faces coming closer. I'm in a box, my closet box, the one that I built with the two by fours and the drywall scraps out of the attic, the place no one knows about." He felt his nakedness, and then his hand felt along the floor for the roach he remembered snubbing. "I should find out what time it is", he thought as he inhaled the remaining hit.

It was five-thirty in the morning when Eddie came out of his box. Fully awake, he laid on top of his sheets and watched the light coming back to the yard. Now he remembered the night they came just about this time two and a half years back. On that night he awoke and heard the pleads from the den, the whimpering of his mother, his father's offer "take what you want but please leave us be."

And then the reply,"Face down damnit." That was all he remembered them saying,"Face down damnit." They came up the stairs, two or three steps at a time, boot to boot. Eddie could remember smelling strangers in the house, watching the shadows coming across the light cracks from the hallway, feeling the draft of the winter night rushing into his room.

He slid under the bed and curled up beneath the balled-up quilt, closed his eyes, tried to shut things out, pretend there was no world out there, no sound of strange footsteps or the sound of a crying baby or the screaming pleads as the front door slammed shut, Benjamin stolen.

Eddie wasn't quite sure, but in the muffled cocoon of his quilt, he thought he remembered the men stopping in front of his room, talking in precise whispers. "Eddie…where is he…he's not in his room…he's sleeping over at a friends, probably the Helmuth kid…damnit now what…." Then the men went and took the baby in the next room, in plan B of their quickening moments. Eddie was sure, as he replayed the events in his mind, sure as he'd ever been of anything: the men had come for him, not Benjamin. After all, Benjamin had done nothing to harm anyone, save an extra-dirty diaper. Neither had his mother or father, save cutting someone off on 676. "I, on the other hand, have killed a woman," Eddie thought. "I nailed her in the head with an empty cup and her family has come to hunt me down."

His green-jerseyed man had now assumed full imaginative reality: scruffy, moustached, tattoos of ships up the arms, vengeance-motivated. He was waiting somewhere nearby in a turned-off van for Eddie to put out his light and fall to sleep. He was getting his ski mask ready and he was going to slip in any night now and abduct him, tie him up and put him into the back of his van, overpower little Eddie with his battleshipped forearms. Too frightening: Eddie started sleeping nights nude in his closet box. With two long nails, Eddie hammered one of his pillows to a wall of his box, marking the place where he would rest the back of his skull and doze off.

VIII

"Please, officer, do what you can," came his mother's wails from the bottom of the house, "he should have been home by now." Eddie awoke in his box, calculating where in the house the voice came from: porch, it was coming from the porch. His mother was talking to a policeman—he could see the flashing lights coming through the breathing holes. He could hear the dispatches entering the closet, out from the speakers on their dashes. His mother was worried about him, because the last she had seen him, he was in his room. "I only fell asleep during 'Jeopardy'," she told the man. "I would have heard him go out with the way he always slams the door. And why in the world would Eddie sneak out?"

Sobbing some more and some more, she went on and Eddie listened and stayed in the box, afraid to come out but wanting to tell her he'd been inside the house the whole time. If he came out he would have to divulge his secret, tell them about his secret little place. He'd have to let them in on everything, the times after school when he sawed and drilled and screwed the closet box into the wall before they both got home from work, and the times he'd carry the hammer back through the living room under his coat to return it to the bottom of the tool box. He'd have to tell them about the panic, when he heard the knocks and the rings and how everything scared him and made him retreat between the walls. "I know I'm the next—they're out there somewhere planning to come and get me," he would finally say, and he'd seek the comfort of his father's hairy arms, where Eddie would lose all control in a fit of unbroken tears. Between sobs, he would tell his father about the game, about the tub of melting ice cubes he sailed in anger into the air. "I killed a lady because I am jealous of William," he would finally blurt out wet-faced into his father's stomach. "And I hate everybody."

Eddie stayed in the box until the flashing lights went away, as the police cars started up and roared away towards 676. He heard his parents sobbing from their bedroom, and this time he didn't crawl to the vent to listen. Rather, he tried to close off their sobs with other thoughts. He put his thumbs inside his ears and he wondered: would the new kid who Lou just hired be able to handle a Saturday night slam? What if he went down in flames? Would Lou beg me to come in in the middle of the night to bail him out? Eddie figured it might be a good time to hit Lou up for a raise. A quarter? Fifty cents? A dollar?

After his parents went to sleep, Eddie sneaked down the stairs and slipped silently out the door. He walked up the road, shirt buttoned wrong, to the Buy-Rite, feeling the cool breeze revealing itself through the trees along the way. He stood under the spotlamp and pulled a quarter from his pocket, and he deposited it into the pay phone. 645-2109: his father answered on the first ring, sounding frightened, a crackling hello that expected some horrible news.

"Dad, it's me Eddie."

"Eddie, Oh my God, Eddie. Where are you, what happened?"

"A long story, dad, a long story. The thing is, I need to get my shit together. I've got some problems that I need to work out, things I don't want to tell you about until I'm ready."

"Where are you?"

"Somewhere close…somewhere distant," he said. "But I'm fine. I just wanted you and mom to know that I wasn't kidnapped. I've got to get away from things, dad." The pause on the other end was long, filled with the heavy breathing of his father deep in thought. "So you're telling me that you're running away?" he asked finally.

Eddie paused, deep in thought with the same father-like breathing. "Yes, dad, if you want to call it that. It's a temporary thing, and I'll be back when I get my head in order."

Eddie hung up and then he stood and stared at the silver buttons of the pay phone. He walked slowly away from the booth, sat down on the curb beneath the spotlamp, and buttoned his shirt the right way. He looked out at Newportville Road as it continued past the last street lamps; the road carried out on a straight line into the subdivision and then dropped into the darkness. He thought briefly about that darkness, how different it was from the darkness of his closet box. It was filled with possibility, and it went on, it really went on.

His brain worked to establish a fixed image of what things would be like if he continued on and never looked back, if things became permanent like this. He looked down to the gravel gathered around his shoes, and he wondered whether the Phillies had won.

Endust

───────────◆───────────

I

Eddie spent his first night cuddled under a lilac bush on a large suburban lawn down Midvale Street. He didn't know much about the owners, except that there was some sort of altercation with the police a few months back and they took away the husband in cuffs in the middle of the night. Eddie remembered his mother and father talking about the incident, saying that the man was drunk off a football game and throwing things, toasters and such.

There were all sorts of bugs that came to bother Eddie in his sleep under the lilac bush, chiggers and mosquitoes and one large black water bug that brushed by the lobe of his ear. Eddie scratched parts of his body most of the night, listening to the incessant buzzing of mosquitoes milling about his ears in search of blood. Of course he couldn't sleep and he wondered what he was doing under a bush and whether he had made a wise decision about things.

Eddie didn't want to spend all of his nights under the bushes of toaster-throwing neighbors. He hated the bugs, that was for sure, remembering the thousand-leggers on his ceiling in the top room as they hurried across the stains. He realized in his half-sleep that he wasn't very prepared for running away-he had his clothes and that was it; no knap-sack, no change of clothes,no money (except for the five-dollar bill), no lunch packed or even a beverage to sip on. And no grand plan.

Eddie was thirsty; all the scratching and the restlessness and the humidity of the night had burned his throat dry. He could see a garden hose hung along the side of the house, barely visible in the shadows of the distant street light. He crawled quietly across the lawn toward the hose. He could hear the faint drip of the water falling to the damp earth, and he scurried on his hands and knees to reach it. He turned the spigot right, clenched his fist around the bumpy knob, and gritted his teeth. Wrong way, he thought. He was always doing that, with spigots and screws, even with gas caps when he worked over at the mini-mart. Eddie turned it counter-clockwise, and the water gushed loudly into a patch of ground cover. Realizing the hose was not connected, he frantically tried to turn it back, but his hand slipped on the wet spigot. Then he was bathed in light from one of the windows above him. Quickly, he reached his mouth over the patch of ground cover and stuck it beneath the spigot. The water gushed all over him, down his throat and all over his face, soaking his shirt. He could hear the voices gathered above him at the window, and then he saw the dark heads looking down on him as he quenched his thirst. It would only be a matter of seconds, Eddie cal-culated, before they took some sort of action. Eddie imagined, in this interlude, a heavy metal toaster heaved at him from above.

He took off across the yard, away from the light of the window and the distant street lamp and into the darkness of another sprawling lawn. He continued on over more lawns until he came to a high wooden fence. The Sharpesons, he guessed, with their carefully maintained pool. He followed the fence until it ended on Delancey and sat down on the curb to think about where he was going to go. He could still hear the gushing of the spigot, and then the slamming of the door, some faint voices, and silence.

Eddie's hand hurt; he had turned the spigot with his cut hand and he had broken open the scab. He could feel the blood mingling with the dirty tap water water, and he rubbed it dry on his pants leg. There was no doubt that the police would be searching for him soon. He figured that they were at his house listening to his father explain the phone call, piecing together where he had gone. They would search the neighborhood first, look with spotlights up and down the streets. His father would be riding with them, sitting in the back seat and looking out over the black lawns.

That was the one thing he did not want, for his father to find him. He'd chase him until he caught him, probably dive right out of a moving car and tackle him like he was playing some game of football—and then drag him home and lock him up. He'd send him to a team of psychiatrists and then everything would come out: the closet box he'd built, the killing of the old lady at the ball game, the jealousy of William. He would be getting mental help for the rest of his life, visit after visit, couch after couch.

Eddie didn't want to cower home, that was for sure. Billy Stigmeyer had run away for a day, back in early autumn, when he took off to the woods and lived in his tree fort. Then he ran out of guts after a wasp stung him on his forehead. Eddie watched poor Billy from below as he cried from behind the leaves. He was in pain, there was no doubt about that; it was a monster sting. Eddie had gotten some bee stings on his ankles, and he knew that the wasp and the forehead were a much more serious matter. The head contained the brain and the face, Eddie surmised at the time, and ankles were nothing. In agony, Billy pounded his fists against the beams of his fort: he knew he was caving in and that he'd be home in his own bed by nightfall with an ice pack over his face, sobbing his apology. So Eddie just walked quietly down the path during his whimpering tirade. He walked on down the path, through the undergrowth and out of earshot. Eddie figured climbing up the chincy wooden ladder of his fort and consoling Billy would just get to be a mess. Billy, after all, might have thrown a tantrum—swinging his fists, burying his face of tears on Eddie's t-shirt. "Better that I keep walking down the path," Eddie said. "You would do the same thing if you were in my position." Eddie told him that off a joint the Sunday after Billy moved back home.

They became the inseparable S boys: Shemanski and Stigmeyer, of the eleventh grade at St. Anselm, sworn to a code of non-conformity. They painted a poster of Karl Marx and hung it in a stall of the third floor Boy's Room. They turned the toilet into "The Socialists Stall" and intimated among friends that the stall was free to be used by anyone, that no one had any rule over it, that girls could come in and use it—teachers, principals, the president of the United States if he decided to swing by on a campaign to the high school. It was there for everybody, so just be economical with the toilet paper and the smell.

Eddie kept thinking about Billy, how things would be when they both saw each other in school again, now that they both had run away. Eddie became frightened just then, precipitated by the fall of some raindrops. Would he whimper home just like Billy? And he, without a wasp sting on the forehead? Could he handle the shame? No, best to keep it up, to keep going no matter what, to keep going. But to keep going means to have some sort of plan.

As the rain came in a fine mist from the darkness, he thought about holing up at Billy's. He remembered the shed where they smoked their joints last summer, how the grass that had turned to straw in the darkness there, how soft it was to sit upon. He could sleep on that straw and hide out in the shed by night. No one would ever see him with all of the bushes they had planted along the edge of the yard.

II

Eddie walked along under the flickering street lamps on Wellsley, watching the fine rain fall and the Luna moths circle in an ellipsis around the tin shields. They smacked the metal with their powdered wings and dropped in and out of the darkness. Wellsley was always having problems with the street lamps, his father had told him when they were driving up the dimmed street one night. It had something to do with the electricity, some sort of wiring problem deep in the ground. "Everyone on the block pays a fortune in electric bills," he had said. "Bill Otterman told me two hundred a month. Had a specialist from the electric company out who told him there's not a damned thing anybody can do about it either."

Eddie reached Interstate 9 just as the rain gushed down in a torrent. There was nowhere for him to seek cover along the six-lane highway; it ran in a straight line without a tree or a bush by the new subdivision they were building. He looked through the downpour at the wooden skeletons lined in a row along the plowed path, envisioning for a brief instant their completion, and then the families, the cars, the trees and the manicured lawns covering the mud on which he stood. Someday these will all be places to keep out of the rain, he thought.

He pulled a sheet of particle board from the muddy field where he stood waiting for the cars to pass. Standing in the muck, he propped the board up against the cinder block wall built to his waist and slid beneath it as the rain pelted down.

Billy's house was still a mile or so away over in Fairlawn, and Eddie figured the walk in the downpour would get him sick, so he'd better stay out of it as long as he could. The rain was coming down just like it had during the football game against Bridesburg when he was on the 80-pound B team. Mud: Eddie stood there on the sideline in the rain, ready to go in, and it kept coming and coming, penny-sized drops bombarding the sideline He watched all of the other boys coming back from the field black with mud, chunks of sod stuck to their face masks, the glow of victory about them, the heavy exhaust of competition clinging to their throats and the cold "number one" of their index fingers. Eddie just stood and felt all empty inside as he waited for the chance to go in, waited to get his uniform dirty just like that. Then the shivering consumed him as the seconds ticked away and the game was in hand. Empty and cold, he watched the rain pour down as his father brought him a dry jacket and the promise of a spaghetti dinner. Eddie went home sick and shivering after that 27-0 victory, and he had to go the the doctor to get flu shots. Later that week, he missed some lessons in Science Class that he was later tested on and failed.

Eddie sat in the mud of the development waiting for the rain to subside, looking out from behind his particle board lean-to and watching the sets of headlights plow down the interstate. Why is it there seem to be so many more cars on the road in the rain? Is it that people just drive slower and the traffic gets more congested? Where are all of them going that makes going out in this weather so important? Eddie's father used to curse all of the rain traffic, emphatically insisting that people,deep down, wanted to drive in miserable conditions. The traffic had nothing to do with slow driving. "Everybody just wants to torture themselves," he had told Eddie over the squeaking wipers. "They have nowhere in particular to go...oh they say they need some milk or paper towels or have to visit some relative...but really they just want to curse the miserable driving conditions, to curse themselves. You see, everybody loves misery, Eddie."

Waiting over an hour for the rain to let up, he could see that it would be a long night under the particle board. He could think of nothing but the warm dry tool shed several streets down. When the wind gusted through the lean-to and made him shiver, Eddie decided that he would walk to Billy's house in the rain. He waited until the headlights stopped coming and then, in a matter of seconds, he dashed out from his cover and tore across the six-lane highway.

Scaling the medial wall, Eddie split his pants. He tried to jump over it in one swoop because he saw a large oil truck in the oncoming lane and he wanted to beat it. But his legs got caught as he tried to straddle the median. After the rip, he felt the draft of the wet night seeping between his legs and the light pain from the skin abrasion as his legs moved quickly to beat the rush of water from the truck. He ran into the bushes growing on the other side and caught his breath as the oil truck sent him the wall of spray anyway. He felt the long rip and wondered how he might stitch it up, if perhaps a pair of Billy's pants might fit him.

Billy's house was down another half mile or so, but with the way the rain was gushing, it became a long struggle. His clothes felt as if they weighed more than his 135 pounds. As the sound of the cars died away and he wormed his way into the heart of the next subdivision, he could hear the squishing in his sneakers…a gallon of water, he surmised. He remembered the same sound coming out of his boots when he would hunt for painted turtles down at the donut pond, in the years before the developments killed all of the reptiles.

When the wind came up, every ten seconds or so, the force of the gale between the houses would spray a wall of water in his face that would take his breath away and knock him to the ground. The rain died to a drizzle as he made his way down Freemont, and he heard the sound of a car coming up from behind him. Eddie became alarmed because he did not see the lights. At night and in the rain, a car without lights couldn't make it very far. It might be someone tailing him, the police or maybe his father. Maybe it was the man in the green jersey finally closing in on him. He heard the car coming closer and he was afraid to turn around. Now, as the sound of the engine began to drown out the falling rain, Eddie realized the car was slowing down. He moved away from the street and walked along the edge of a lawn.

"Excuse me…excuse me, young man," came a voice from just behind him.

Eddie turned to see a long blue Cadillac cruising along with its lights off. He could see the pale face that seemed almost phosphorescent in its composition, falling into an abyss of two dark eye sockets. Two beady eyes reflected out of the abyss, watching him as the Cadillac eased close.

"I say…excuse me young man…could you tell me where I could find a room?"

Eddie turned to see the smile of the man with the full disclosure of his little yellow teeth. He could smell the heavy aroma of pine emanating from the interior of the Cadillac. A pang of panic flared up in Eddie as he eyed the dark cavern of the back seat and the unlocked doors. This guy wants to get me, he thought. This weirdo wants to abduct me and shove me back there and lock the doors and then kill me or perhaps commit some horrible act that I would remember and have nightmares about for the rest of my life.

Without looking back, Eddie sprinted across a corner lawn. His sprint caused a dog to come barreling out of the darkness. Suddenly on the grass, Eddie was trapped between the dog and the pale man. He could still see the Cadillac still creeping along and he could still feel the cold eyes and the white bony face watching him from behind the open passenger window. The dog was a small black poodle and it barked with a certain viscousness that made Eddie believe it was about to attack him. He could hear the rumble of anger inside it and see the little pointed teeth bared as it charged for his legs. Quickly, Eddie raised back and kicked with all his might. He caught the dog at the bottom of its jaw as he flicked his hard wet heel upward in one swift motion. The porch light flicked on from the corner house, the dog yelped and fled in pain, and the blue Cadillac turned on its lights and sped away. In an instant, Eddie was behind the spreading yews and into the next lawn, protected by the darkness. He watched as the dog ran to a fat woman on the step. She picked up the poodle and dried off the rain with a pink towel as she peered into the darkness for the perpetrator. The street, without the

Cadillac, was again consumed by the sound of the rain and Eddie's heartbeats slowed to normal. As he stood behind the spreading yews, he could think of nothing but the warm dry tool shed that would be his benediction.

III

The dimensions of the Stigmeyer's yard startled him. It was almost a year since the last time he visited, but now the house, in the dark and the rain, seemed to have crept closer to the shed. Eddie studied the house carefully for several seconds to assure himself that he was at the right address. He watched the windows carefully for activity, remembering his fiasco at the toaster-thrower's house, and looked up at the dark window to Billy's room. The rain began to let up, and, within the confines of the subdivision, the wind had died considerably.

Moving to the other side of the shed, he approached the metal door in his sopping clothes. He tried the latch and it opened with a little metal click. Then he tried to pull the door open, at least wide enough so he could slip in. The bottom of the door wedged itself into the soft earth, and Eddie noticed the heavy clump of grass that had grown over the bottom latch. He gently pulled the door with all his strength until he could see the tin door bending in the dimmed light. He realized he would have to free the latch with his hands so Eddie got down on his knees in the thinning rain and plunged them into the muddy earth to remove the overgrown sod. He looked up from his knees to the house. The stucco was darkened by the rain, and the house loomed under the thick wet elm leaves like a monolith in a rain forest.

As he dug along the edge of the door, Eddie wondered if Billy was home. He was always staying out with his girl friend Dina and sleeping on her family room couch, especially if there was a Phillies game being played on the West Coast. His girl friend's father was a big baseball fan,

just like Eddie's father and just like Billy. Sometimes Billy would stay at
Rob Wilks when he was having bong parties. He'd take his big bag of
pot over and he would stay the night. Eddie looked up at Billy's darkened window and wondered if he was asleep. Perhaps he was lying
awake, plotting how he was going to run away again, minus the hornet
sting this time. He wondered how he was going to let Billy know that he
was holing up in his family tool shed.

Billy Stigmeyer still kept his nickname from grade school, "Boy
Clean." In the first grade, Billy was the little boy with the allergies who
sat in the last row, away from the windows. Eddie became friends with
Billy because his mother and Mrs.Stigmeyer had become bingo buddies
at the church hall. Eddie would ride over in the station wagon when she
visited. He recalled Billy's room, clean and sparkling with the pungent
odor of furniture polish, when he was shown it for the first time. Billy
brought him in to play with his army men. The room was darkened,
with the shades pulled down, and the shining furniture, his dresser, and
his end tables reflected the lamps burning at three in the afternoon.
Shiny reflections, that's what Eddie remembered the most: the shaded
window and the curtains, the lamp bases, the plastic dinosaurs, the
spelling bee trophies, all mirrored in the polished wood.

Billy had brought some army men from a set of buckets in the closet
and handed Eddie the Germans. "I get to be the Americans, since it's my
house," he had said, and then he dumped a hundred or so soldiers onto
his tightly-made bed. Eddie remembered the rattle of his Germans in
the bucket, thinking immediately that his side did not have near as
many men.

"You know the Americans always win," Billy had said. "You know the
Germans can't win or they'd take over the world. That's what my dad
told me and that's why he bought me mostly Americans."

On the car ride home, Eddie's mother had told him that Billy was
allergic to dust. He had been taken to a hospital when he was only three

because his eyes had puffed up like a guppy's one afternoon and he had scratched his body up with his unclipped fingernails. Doctors studied him and finally discovered that dust was the culprit—that dust had settled into all of the cracks of his floorboards and coated his furniture and his toys.

"They had to take precautions," Eddie's mother had said. "Billy needs a dust-free room, and he can never sit anywhere that dust could accumulate."

Eddie and Billy entered first grade together and during the first week, Billy began to sneeze and itch in his desk by the window. Unseen dust, Eddie thought, dead human skin raining down upon him in a lethal downpour, bombarding his desk, encrusting his eyelids. Billy sat there and said nothing to Sister Joseph Marguerite, consumed by his misfortune and his shyness. He didn't want to tell the nun of his affliction; he didn't want to tell his parents that he was allergic to the first grade. But his puffed-up face alas became too obvious, and his mother sent in a note requesting that he be moved to a more dust-free area of the room. Sister Joseph Marguerite tried moving Billy around like a pawn on a chess board to find the best spot for him. But even in the back of the room and far from the window, poor Billy sneezed and itched, and, by the end of the long day, left for home with swollen eyes.

The doctors told him that he would need to take protective measures. They gave him some extra medication and suggested that he keep his desk dust-free and to clean it periodically throughout the day. So Billy's mother sent him to school with a little bag of pills, a can of Endust, and a soft rag. The sound of the spray: the little particles of polish rose into the air as Billy dusted his desk every day between religion and science; they floated and danced in the stagnant air. Billy would get up and wipe his seat and then the top of his desk into a perfect dust-free universe. Miriam Mackey and Dennis O'Hara, who occupied the seats nearest him, would have to get out of their seats while Billy polished their desks as well. It became Billy's routine all the way through grade school.

Billy became known as "Boy Clean," a name given to him by an eighth-grader in the school yard. The boy had spotted the can of Endust and the polishing rag sticking out of his school bag, and called his clique over to poke fun at it. Billy, however, liked the nickname; he was proud of his "clean" image. He had even intimated to Eddie that he would like to be called the name by his very best friends.

So Eddie called Billy "Boy Clean" in the ensuing years, as his polishing routine continued into the second, third and fourth grades. Billy's mother and father, even his sister Susan, called him the name. One Halloween, his mother went to her sewing machine and stitched together a costume for Billy. She had found the letter she kept from her days at Boston College when she was on the swim team. She took it, the letters "BC," and sewed it onto the front of an old sweat shirt.

"Aren't I clever,?" she asked Eddie when she brought out the costume. "It stands for Boy Clean." She had also torn up an old black evening dress and converted it into a cape. Billy brought his snow boots up from the basement and found a black mask to cover his eyes. Fully dressed while Eddie was waiting, Billy took off down the hall and in one giant swoop jumped from the top of the stairs into the center of the living room. "I am Boy Clean coming to your rescue," he called, and he sprayed the cans of Endust, hanging from his hip, in unison.

Billy wore the costume every Halloween until he entered high school. By the time he had made his last trek for candy across the subdivision, the outfit had become ragged and outgrown. The cape was lost seasons before in a melee with some kids from Thornbrook—the sleeves were torn by his growing body—and the Boston College letter was left hanging by threads after his mother had stopped her sewing and started drinking. He still carried the holster, though. The cans of Endust had been empty for years, but Billy carried them anyway just to talk about how he used to spray and polish every door in the neighborhood on Halloween night, one after the other up Sinkler and Wellington and Quibble and Davis and then down on Holloway.

"Hell, you wouldn't believe all the candy I got out of the deal," he ritualized every Halloween. "As many pillowcases-full as I could carry....I'd have candy until the Fourth of July."

On the night that Billy got rid of his costume for good—three years back—they sat down and smoked their first joint on the corner of Reed and Pelham. Billy, in a loud hoot, stood up and twirled one of his pillowcases of candy over his head. He heaved it into one of the tall trees in front of the Jenicky's house. The sack of candy opened up and rained down Milky Ways and Snickers and Smarties with a mixture of dying leaves, Billy hollering "double live gonzo" all the while. Then he stripped off his costume, tore away the holster, and flung it around a stop sign. He stuffed the torn shirt with the ragged letters down into one of his remaining pillowcases and remarked: "Well, I wore this fucker into the ground."

Billy's allergy to dust had dwindled by the time he entered high school. He clung, however, to the "Boy Clean" image, and maintained his neatness with all his things. He had shed the Endust and the polishing rag, but now everything in his life had order: the way he dressed, the way he combed his hair, the way he maintained his locker, his room, his ten-speed. Even when he rolled joints, Eddie recalled Billy's ritual for keeping things neat and orderly, with the paper lined perfectly, the pot cleaned of seeds, the perfect amount of saliva—not too wet, not too dry. Billy always insisted on rolling the joints because Eddie was too sloppy with his pot. Though the allergy had all but left him, it was as if, by habit and by design, Billy wanted to hold on to his "Boy Clean" image. He was his own boyhood hero; his polishing days would remain the highlight of his life, the reward of all that candy, all of that attention. His legacy would be the memories that returned with the odor of Endust.

IV

As the rain reduced itself to a slow drizzle, the door came free and Eddie pried it open from his knees. The light from the distant street lights was such that he could not see into the darkened shed, so Eddie crawled through the opening on his hands and knees. Closing the door behind him, he could feel the stiff straw in the darkness. He groped for a dry spot long and wide enough for him to sleep on his mattress of sod. He could feel the metal objects on the ground—mowers and rakes and shovels, he guessed. He remembered all of the rakes the last time he was in the shed, hanging by long nails from the wall, green and silver and black. So many rakes, he remembered thinking as Billy rolled the joint.

"Bet you're wondering about the rakes," Billy had said to him during a toke. "My old man works in a rake factory…gets em' by the dozen…all the flawed ones with not enough prongs. "

Eddie had asked Billy what was the point of having so many rakes, and Billy explained his father's annual Rake Day: on the first weekend in November every fall, his father would buy a keg of beer and hand the rakes out to all of the men of the neighborhood. They'd drink the beer and then proceed to rake all of their leaves down the street, down the long path of grass between their curbs and the sidewalk. They'd rake them in unison into the open lot where they'd plowed over the frog ponds, and they'd each bring their share into the mountain of leaves. They'd build the leaf mountain nearly twenty feet high and then bring out some freshly chopped firewood, thick cherry logs that would fill their arms. One by one, each would drop his share upon the pile. Sammy Conway would bring the gasoline, Johnny Stigmeyer the beer, Alex Neadle the stories and poems that he'd read after the leaves were sucked into the mountain of flame.

The mountain of flame. The smell and the thick black smoke constricted the neighborhoods, stagnating in the still-humid air like a storm cloud. It was a haunting image, almost ghostlike in its anticipated transformation as it crept out slowly over the trees along the lot, moving like an entity across the interstate and descending upon the asphalt. On Rake Day, the smell of burning leaves forever imprinted itself upon Eddie's memory cells. The haze of sunlight through the smoke, block upon block, would always be his vision of autumn.

Johnny Stigmeyer was told to stop his event because it became illegal to burn leaves. It had more to do with the environment than any fire problems that might destroy the lot, any dry patches of grass that might inadvertently flare up and spread to the bordering houses. An environmental group out of Fergusonville finally brought some police one year and waved posters of the earth and its widening ozone and shouted quotes from Emerson and Thoreau across the open space. They waved their ozone posters while the police ordered the men to put out their bonfire, and it took a fire truck and two hoses to extinguish their ritual.

Eddie laid down on the dead sod and thought about the men standing around the extinguished bonfire. Where will they be without Rake Day? Most likely, he thought, they will just take that keg from the first Sunday in November and get really drunk off another football game. But where would they be without the leaves?...or where would the leaves be without them? Would Mr. Neadles stories go untold?

He took off his shirt and squeezed the rain out of it, and then balled it up to use as his pillow. Despite the rain, it was hot inside the shed, and he laid down and tried to focus on the things around him—the dark forms of the tools that hung, the mower in the corner somewhere, the cans of pesticide stocked on the shelf. But the darkness was everywhere, without a crack of light to help his eyes along and reveal things; it was not unlike his closet box, the way the blackness consumed him.

Running away from home hung sharply in Eddie's mind, suspended itself like a flare for several moments as he stared into the darkness and tried to focus on a plan. His exhaustion consumed him as his head settled into his damp shirt, and, thankful that he did not decide to stay at the construction site, he rapidly fell asleep.

V

  Eddie had a dream that was like no other, a metal dream filled with sharp pointy garden tools going on and on. In the waning moments following his sleep, the images would drift away into forgetfulness, perhaps only to reveal themselves in some unconscious action days or years hence. But for now, he walked on and on through a large mechanical city filled with towering buildings, all built of hoes and shovels and weed-wackers. In his dream, he had lost the memory of the tool shed in which he was sleeping. In fact, he had lost all memory of his own conscious universe, the real things, the horrible things. He seemed to feel he was at home here under these gigantic garden tools, and as he walked the dirt paths that snaked between the metal con-glomerations, he sensed that he was going to a little metal house off of some smaller path just ahead, as if he'd traveled here a thousand other times and that giant garden tools were a normal thing to behold. He followed the fat path right along the rows of shovels, past the the lawn-mower sculpture and around the gigantic lawn sprinkler that rose a hundred feet above him. There would be a light burning still on the porch, a light awaiting his return. It would not flicker out because Eddie knew, in his dream, that light bulbs in this particular universe never flickered out.

  But then, as when all dreams end, his conscious universe seeped in, just a few drops of reality to poison his dream. Eddie realized as he walked that there would never be a house with a light burning; the fat path kept on with no break, and the shovels, their spades buried half-way into the earth, stretched to unconscious infinity. There was no side path, there was no house—the faint image of what he thought it might be slipped from him until it was no longer there. And where were the rakes, Eddie kept wondering as he looked at the shovel handles going on and on in straight lines. Seconds before waking, Eddie asked the metal city, "Where are the rakes?"

In the waking moments of his shed slumber, he again was faced with the disturbing search for a light in his universe, as the dark forms hung just outside of his recognition in the blueblack light. For a moment, he thought he was back in his closet box and he thought he could hear the voices of his parents downstairs, the television going, the sound of the crickets coming out of the bushes, a distant call of pitches from a baseball announcer. For those suspended seconds, he thought that his runaway was a dream, that he hadn't really done any of it. It was crazy to run away with no plan, with nothing but the clothes he wore, with no money but a five-dollar bill; yes, yes, it had to be one of his dreams.

As the morning light seeped through the cracks along the top of the shed, the forms of all the rakes began to come out of the darkness, and Eddie felt the dampness that enveloped him and then the straw that ran up his bare back. It all came back in a flash of fresh memory—the desperate flee from his house in the middle of the night, the call to his father, the nap under the lilac bush, the walk in the rain, the digging, the thoughts of Billy waking in the house just across the lawn or maybe just his empty room. These memories wiped away the remnants of his dream, snuffed out the mechanical city of spades and hoes and weed-wackers and buried them in the dark earth of his subconscious.

VI

Eddie opened the door to the shed and crawled along the ground to peek up at Billy's window. Billy usually slept late in the summer, so he didn't expect to see a light on. But he looked anyway, in the hope that

Billy might have been restless in the night and awakened early. Eddie himself was quite often restless in the night, especially on nights that it rained. It must be the pitter-patter, Eddie had thought to himself so many times while he buried his ears in his pillow in that bedroom at the top of the house. It must be the way that it breaks the silence. It rained and rained and rained on the nights after Benjamin was stolen. The rain must have gone on non-stop for two weeks, night after night, buckets of baseball-sized drops bombarding the roof. It would be nice during the days, some gray clouds maybe but never anything wet.... but when the nights would come, the sky would mysteriously open and let rip with its contents, pounding sometimes against the glass with the heavy gusts of wind that would make their way through the trees. The slamming of the doors along the hallway, that's what Eddie remembered most....bam bam bam...doors against the wall.

How many times had mom and dad gotten up? How many times had they whispered about people conspiring against them in the night to take their second child? They would wait at edge of their bed for the men to come. They would rush down the hallway in the night after a noise, along the shadowed walls with their bats, waiting for the invading army to appear from behind the couches.

How many times did he plead with his mother and father to sleep in their room? Crying from the slamming of the doors, he would tear from his bed down the bare steps and wail into the master bedroom, asking for some space on the bed.

"Go back to your room, it's only the wind," his father said on one of those rainy nights while leaning against his bat. "No one is here to get you, take my word."

On Billy's lawn and fully aware that he might be spotted, Eddie looked up and saw a shadow cast itself along the ceiling of Billy's room from what looked like a desk lamp. The shadow moved like a flash across the glow and then disappeared. He ran to the base of the window, ready to shout, but then he noticed the screened windows of the neighboring houses appearing in the unfolding light. So he reached to the ground and grabbed a handful of mud from the rhododendron garden and heaved it at the window. The mud made a dull thud along the window mold and it rained down in broken clumps, back from where it came.

He stepped back and watched, hoping for Billy's head to appear at the window. Before he could contain himself, he shouted out "Billy!," as if that was what he was destined to do all along, just the way he had planned it before falling to sleep in the shed. The neighbors open windows were something he never considered in his plan; now the shout was out. Now he figured he might be spotted by someone looking for him, that perhaps he might need to cower in the rhododendrons for a bit or maybe take off down Millside Street. But he wanted Billy to see him, so he waited in the open space where he could easily be spotted.

Billy appeared at the open screen and looked down. "Eddie...jezus, Eddie is that you...up so early? Your clothes are wet...you been out in the rain? What up Eddie?"

"Something's up," Eddie shot back in a loud whisper. "Come down."

The head disappeared from the window and Eddie slid closer to the bushes gathered around the house. He saw another form appear in one of the windows two houses down. It was the old Canicky house, at one time home to the only boy ever to escape from the Fergusonville Reform School, the boy who made his brother drive him around to rob houses and tear up lawns with the snow tires and give the finger to the picture windows of nosy neighbors. Now there was someone new in the house, someone unknown, some shadow watching him from behind the shade. Eddie moved beneath a bush, out of sight from the dark form, just as Billy appeared in his shorts from the front of the house.

"Holy shit dude," Billy said. "Where you been, swimming.?"

"Every street between my house and here," Eddie said. "Listen, I did it.... I took off. I took off last night from the folks and I slept in your tool shed. I need to hole up here for a while. I need to sleep in your tool shed for a while."

Billy got calm in the face, like he was expecting the news, as if he knew in some secret way that running away was Eddie's destiny.

"Yeah but ya gotta keep it neat," he said. "Ya can't leave food layin' around, and beers and stuff. If the rats and mice come and then the moles and the shrews, dad will get over there with the traps."

Eddie agreed to eat all of his food and not leave any to the rodents. He agreed to come home between one and two a.m. along the Wilkenson's hedge after the last of the neighbors had flicked off their lights. He would burrow between the dying patch of evergreen and make his way along the grass with his ass down. He would, in the flash of a raised arm, unlatch the door handle and let himself in along the ground. Wriggling every night into the dark shed, Eddie would crawl to the dead sod and the darkness and lock the world away with the turn of the latch.

His first two weeks spent in the tool shed came with ninety degree temperatures and humid nights. The metal sides of the shed conducted the interior to a good one hundred degrees and Eddie felt the waves of heat bobbing about. He sweated in his darkness as he laid on the dead sod listening to the muffled cicadas that surrounded him in the bushes. Early in the morning, Billy came out before his father got up for work to bring Eddie some toast and orange juice, just before the first of the neighbors bedroom lights came on.

"Damned toasters on the fritz," he said one day through the crack of the open shed door. "Sorry about the char marks."

Eddie didn't mind the burnt toast, even though he never cared for it that way when his mother would do it. He was hungry and he wanted to wait until desperation set in before spending the five-dollar bill.

"Hey, I've got a buddy…Chile Hodgkins if you know him, an assistant kitchen manager over at Bingo's," Billy said one morning over the toast.

"He could get you something, some dishwashing shifts on weekends. Just tell Chile you worked for Lou. He knows Lou, and he'd give you a job because you kicked ass for Lou."

"But I quit without a notice," Eddie said. "Lou's pissed at me, I know it because I just didn't show one night."

"Chile won't call for a reference, Ed. Just tell him you worked weekends there. Just tell him you kicked ass on Saturday night."

Eddie borrowed some of Billy's clothes, a pair of jeans and a t-shirt with a red fist clenched under the letters "Power". The pants were a little too long so he had to roll up the cuffs. He also had to tie the pants around the waist with some twine he found in the shed and he let the t-shirt drape over the belt loops. He slid along the hedge just as the sun was making its way through the trees and headed down Route 2 to the restaurant job he was promised.

VII

Bingo's was bigger than he remembered. He saw the new stucco extension that made him believe the building had been recently enlarged. There were no cars in the newly paved lot, and upon noticing the opening time, eleven a.m., Eddie deduced that the early employees had not yet arrived. He sat down on one of the the freshly painted lines that ran to the back wall to where tall weeds and an old car lay hidden. He sat and watched a red-winged blackbird walk along the edge of the cement. The bird was looking for a meal, a stray bug that might have ventured out of the grass. It reminded him of all the red-winged blackbirds he had always seen hanging off the reeds down at the donut pond.

The sun had baked a fine sweat onto his arms by the time the red Volvo rolled into the lot. He expected a more expensive car from someone who was an opening manager of an expanded restaurant. However, the car was dulled by primer with a bumper that had been remounted haphazardly with several yards of rope. The man who opened the car door was small with a moustache like a woolly caterpillar and a tiny pair of gold-rimmed glasses. Eddie got up from his spot on the lines and approached the little man.

"Excuse me sir," he said. "I'm here to apply for a job."

The man turned and surveyed Eddie. He pulled the edge of his moustache as if to straighten it. "Applications are taken between eleven and twelve and three and four," he said. "It's just about nine now. I'll be happy to talk to you in a couple of hours."

Eddie remembered the scene in The Wizard of Oz where the little man with a moustache told Dorothy to come back later. He suddenly realized the man looked just like that man in the movie.

"Oh, but please sir…I've come such a long way. I'm a friend of Chile's and I'm a good worker," Eddie said, feeling the sun on his knees.

"Oh, you're a friend of Chile's," the moustached man said. "Well why didn't you say so…come on in." He extended his hairy hand. "I'm Scott."

Scott pulled a conglomeration of keys from out of his baggy pocket and selected, in the flash of some fingers, the appropriate key for the alarm. He slid his fingers to the next key on the loop and opened the door.

He saw the restaurant in the dimmed fluorescent of the kitchen lights. Because he had just come from an open lot baked by the sun., the dining room was barely visible It felt painful to his eyes as they worked to establish the identity of things, the size and shape of the tables, the fixtures nailed to the plywood, the bar across the carpet.

"Dish machine was acting up yesterday," Scott said. "Sure hope maintenance fixed it. Had to hand wash the dishes in cold water over lunch yesterday. A bitch and a half."

"I know what that's like," Eddie said. "Had me doing that for a week straight one time over at King Arthurs." Eddie saw the restaurant reveal itself with the flick of the lights: old blue leather seats with silver studs and tables lined along the curtain and then booths that ran to the swinging doors stationed on the back wall. Some of the tables still held their dirt from the night before. Wet puddles and filthy forks lingered and ketchup bottles sat half-empty, the smear of a busy night pasted upon them.

"Damnit," Scott said. "Night crew did it to me again." He flung his keys at the back wall and they hit the wallpaper just below the oil painting of a ship going down at sea. Eddie moved away from him, afraid that his temper had not yet fully flowered, that he might be the unlucky victim of the next hurled object.

"Been having some problems with the night wait staff," Scott sighed. "Seems they all want to get out of here for last call so they leave the work for the day crew." He walked across the carpet and picked up the keys. "I'm easy and they take advantage."

Scott instructed Eddie to have a seat at the bar as he flicked on the lights which brightened the kitchen. Eddie sat there for some time, nearly half an hour, before Scott returned. He carried a clipboard atop a case of Bloody Mary mix. He had a pencil in his mouth and spoke out with with a garble, "The bartenders going to be late. Fill this out...take the pencil."

Eddie awkwardly reached to Scott's mouth and took the pencil. He noticed the bite marks made by his molars, all up and down the yellow paint. He looked down at the empty application and noticed "Hired" written in large letters at the top.

"Is this o.k.?" he asked Scott, pointing at the word. "Someone wrote on it."

"That would be be," Scott said during the clinking of the Bloody Mary bottles. "I need a dishwasher like nobody's business and you can fill that out while we discuss your schedule."

"I'll work six days if you can do it for me," Eddie said.

Scott agreed to hire Eddie Tuesday through Sunday from eleven to five at $2.50 an hour. Eddie figured that he could live in Billy's tool shed a while longer, a month maybe, accumulate some money, and then find a place to live. He would just need to keep things cool and not let anyone know about the closet box and the dead old lady and the runaway. He would just have to pretend that everything was all right.

"When can you start,?" Scott asked. "I need you right away."

"I can start today if you want," Eddie said.

"Fine," Scott said. "I was ready to do the dishes again today. I'll go get you a shirt and an apron and get you started."

Scott brought Eddie some Endust and a pile of rags and told him that the dining room needed some cleaning. "You can start down on those tables beneath the ship," he said. "My waitresses won't be coming in for another hour and I want to get ahead of the game. Got a ten-top at eleven-thirty."

Eddie took the rags and the furniture polish and walked to the darkened area of the room. He looked around at the smeared tables as the light knifed through the edge of the curtains. He sprayed the Endust and inhaled the smell, watched the familiar particles rising. And then, with a sudden pang that reached in and ripped at his insides, he yearned to be back there in his desk—in the third grade with nothing to worry about but the memorizing of some times tables, or what questions he might be asked out of the reader, or which seat he would get on the bus ride home. He could still recite "The Lord's Creed" from memory, so he whispered the words to himself as he polished the tables under the sinking ship.

On the last table, in the back corner, Eddie saw the *The Daily News* spread out with its back page up. "Another Day Another Loss," said the headline of the tabloid. He saw one of the Phillies pitchers in the photograph, with his cap off and held high in the air. The sad man was wiping the sweat from his brow. There was a runner in the background jogging casually around the bases, and, without reading the inscription, Eddie surmised that a home run had been hit. His father must have thrown some things at the set and cursed the opposing player's home run trot, just the way he had cursed all the dropped balls and the strikeout double plays and the missed opportunities. He must have made a remark about the Phillies manager sitting quietly at the end of the dugout, waiting for his demise.

Wiping in clockwise circles, Eddie thought about his mother sitting in the back bedroom. She was crying all the while, that was almost certain. She was crying and praying for Eddie to come walking back through the door. She was going to go out into the living room after her prayer and after she stopped the flow of tears. She was going to get angry at her husband for watching the game, come out into the living room and stand in front of the set. She would tell him about the things that were more important: that he should be on the telephone calling people in search of Eddie or worrying in silence with the set off at least. She would tell him that it was improper to watch baseball at a time like this.

He knew that his father would just tell her to calm down, tell her that he'd done everything imaginable and what was the point of worrying any more. He would walk her back to the bedroom, kiss her on the forehead, maybe pull the covers up, fluff up a pillow for her, walk out, and gently close the door. Then he would go to the refrigerator for another beer.

Turtle Log

◆

I

Just as the rain hit the trees, Eddie started his first shift at Bingo's. The wind, gusting well over fifty miles an hour, burst through the open window above the spice racks and spilled a jug of black peppercorns onto the floor. After he closed the window, but before he could sweep up the mountain of pepper, Scott the manager walked into the kitchen. He noticed Eddie standing in front of the mountain, searching with his eyes for the broom.

"Already?" Scott asked. "That's a hundred dollars worth of peppercorns you just spilled there."

"It's not the way it seems," Eddie said. "The wind, it came through the screen and tipped the thing over. Somebody balanced it on the edge of the shelf."

He found the broom in the sink along with the damp mop from the night before. As he filled the dustpan with peppercorns, he tried to figure out whether or not Scott was serious, and what each peppercorn cost apiece. He estimated, in a manner of a minute, that he had spilled about 600 million, which worked out about a penny for every ten thousand. Miriam Mackey, the little blonde girl in back of him in the fifth grade, had taught him the secret to guessing things in the millions. "Count in tens," she whispered, "Count in tens." She had won a contest guessing jelly beans in a beer barrel over in Fergusonville and she received a free trip for two to the Azores. Her parents took the tickets out of Miriam's hand for safe keeping, and then they flew away themselves, with the promise of souvenirs. Miriam, who was put in the care of her aunt, left her house through an open window during halftime of the NFC Championship game. She broke into her own locked-up home through the rusted basement door, stole the money that her father lay hidden in the lamp base, called a cab to the airport, bought an airline ticket, and flew down to the Azores herself. When she arrived, she went right to the Sheraton, where she had won her hotel room, and sat down in the lobby. Between the sandaled tourists, Miriam waited until her parents came by in their bathing suits. Then she got up and told her parents, as they dropped their gear in shock, that she was ready for a swim. That's the story Miriam told in the schoolyard, and no one believed her, including her four best friends.

Though Eddie didn't believe the story either, he gave Miriam his ring later that year because he was in love with her, falling into a trance and watching her curls every time she went up the aisle for her papers. He still felt bad, not because Miriam never returned the love, but because he'd given up the best ring he'd ever had. He held back tears during morning prayers when he looked down at his folded hands and saw his ring finger bare. Then he broke loose with a gush of wails, and Sister Dominicus made him stand in the hall until he composed himself. After Spelling, he had to come in and say the rosary in front of the Jesus statue. It was only a plastic ring out of the vendor somewhere in a shopping center, and it only had a fake ruby glued to the middle—but it was the coolest ring Eddie had ever seen. As the years went by, and as Miriam Mackey faded into obscurity to the back of one of the other rows (with her curls ironed out), the ring assumed a sublime nostalgic beauty: the plastic stone became a priceless memory, a glassy ember that Eddie would forever want back. (But Miriam Mackey, in love with a seventh grader and not a connoisseur of toy rings, had tossed the ruby away into her kitchen garbage one long-ago trash night).

II

"I've got a food order coming in the back door," Scott said. "I'll need you to help me load it in the walk-in." Eddie opened the swinging doors that revealed the back wall at the end of the lot and the field of weeds carrying out to the junkyard. A fat bearded man stood on the dock with a clipboard, and he shoved his order at Eddie and said "Sign."

"It's my first day, I don't know if I should do this," Eddie said. "Scott will be along."

The bearded man took a deep breath and turned to look at the trees behind him. There were two squirrels biting each other and squawking; one of the squirrels chased the other down a thick branch. "Damned things get in your house and chew your attic to pieces," the man said. He eyed the back of the truck and pulled the frayed rope from the bottom of the door. Rolling the door open and revealing a room of food, he looked down at his clipboard and raised an eyebrow.

Eddie felt an uncomfortable silence as he stood there with the man, a silence much like the car rides with his father when there was nothing left to talk about. He was hoping that the man might say something else to break the silence, because he himself could think of nothing. It was his first day, and he could think of nothing. The man was little and fat, as Eddie found the time to notice. He had a bright scar along one of his forearms and there was a tattoo of some sort hidden mostly beneath a sleeve, the edge of what he deduced was some sort of an explosion. Quiet he was: it must be all the driving. It must be all those lonely hours on the interstate listening to a truck engine and bad radio.

"A little early Frank," Scott said as he walked up. "You been speeding again?"

"I'm right on time," Frank said. "You forget that it's *your* clock that runs a little slow."

With his inventory sheet, Scott stepped on the back of the open truck and counted the cases of tomatoes stacked against the wall. Then he moved to the cases of lettuce and eyed finally the lobsters boxed in the next row.

"Wife kicked my ass out last night," Frank said. "Seems I went on one too many binges."

"Welcome to the club, fuck-up," Scott said. "Happened to me four years back."

"What did you do?" Frank asked.

"What else to do,?" Scott returned. "Johnny, give me a Molson."

Frank doubled over in laughter and he had to balance himself along the edge of the truck. Maybe he wasn't so quiet after all, Eddie guessed, looking at how he stood. He surmised that he must have gotten that gut from a string of nights drinking and carousing in corner booths. He must have gotten that laugh from hearing years of funny punch lines.

Scott asked Eddie to accompany him to the freezer. They would need to put away the waffles and the french fries and the synthetic burgers and count the leftover stock.

"Count the number of cases," he told Eddie, handing him the clipboard. "And count the single heads left in the open boxes." Scott rubbed his arms as the stinging cold reached out from the open freezer door and as a mist enveloped them like a Transylvania fog. There was a light mounted to the wall covered with a thick layer of ice. One icicle, nearly a foot long, came to a sharp point right above Eddie's head as he entered the freezer. Scott reached in with his hairy hand and snapped it from the light. "So you don't have a horrible altercation," he said. Scott heaved the icicle like a javelin toward the sink; it hit the side and shattered all over the floor. "Murder weapon, what murder weapon?" he asked. Eddie could see the bearded man through the fog, doubling over in laughter again.

"Everything's off and I'm movin' on," Frank said, kicking the broken icicle across the tile. "Watch your lobsters, some of them don't have bands."

"Always in a hurry aren't you Frank?," Scott said. "Slow down for God's sakes would you? There are women and senior citizens on the road."

"Don't worry," Frank returned from the open doors, "I only run over furry little animals."

The truck started up and pulled quickly away from the dock. Eddie counted everything in the freezer: the waffles, the shrimp, the king crab claws, the cases upon cases of french fries. He wanted to ask Scott why it was his responsibility to count all the frozen things, especially since he was just a dishwasher. He kept his silence but he could see that there would be much more to his job than just washing dishes—he'd already, in his first ninety minutes, cleaned the dining room tables and mopped up peppercorns and such; now here he was, standing in zero degrees.

"Chile will be here soon," Scott said. "He's just getting off a vacation and I know how he is when he just comes off vacation. He'll appreciate that you did the counts for him. He'll appreciate that you're a friend."

Then the low voice came from the edge of the fog, and Eddie exited the freezer to see the man's face. He knew it was Chile; he remembered the voice from one of Billy's parties. It was the guy with the boots, the guy who talked about Nam.

"Scott you in there?" He fanned his way through the smoke.

"Sorry. Got caught relaxing a day too long. Took the tent back a day late and the sons of bitches charged me an extra twenty."

Scott punched Chile in the shoulder as he stepped to the edge of the freezer. "Got your buddy here doing the counts," he said.

Eddie's eyes met Chile's as he looked in; his brain worked to serve a quick reply. "Remember the big Stigmeyer party last November? Remember the guy who was hanging around Billy all night? Well, hey it's me, Eddie…Eddie Shemanski. Billy told me to come down to see if you needed anybody. I was working at King Arthur's and I kicked ass for Lou….Scott here pretty much hired me on the spot."

Chile stood silent and focused on recognition as Scott waited. "You're the guy with the grapefruits," Chile replied. "You kept coming out from the downstairs curtains with grapefruits over your eyes. Yeah, I remember you. You had the whole room wailing. You said you were an entity named Zorgon from the planet Weed."

Scott dropped his mouth a bit and stared at Eddie and the clipboard. He was figuring out what to do.

"Scott don't get me wrong with the Zorgon bit." He pointed his finger at Eddie. "You can't hire a harder worker. This guy pumped it out for Lou over at King Arthur's. This is the kind of guy managers die for."

Scott shivered at the edge of the freezer and then he turned and looked again. "How was your vacation?" he asked Chile. "You went to Ricket's Glen, no?"

"Week and a half," Chile replied. "Everything went great until the last night."

Chile looked through the fog as Eddie shivered below the cases of waffles. "On our last night…or I should say morning…just after we'd gone to sleep…the park authorities decided that they would spray some insecticide over the campground," he said. "The mosquitoes are building a shitload of nests this year and the park was working to nuke them because all the campers were complaining about the swarms." The freezer motor shut off just then, and Chiles' voice became the center of sound.

"I wake up and I'm still half-sleeping you understand. I must have been in a war dream, because all of a sudden I think I'm back in Nam. I hear the choppers out in the real world, you know, the world where they're just laying the fog down and killing the mosquitoes. But me, I think I'm back on the rice paddies and the choppers are coming in. I'm all in the dark see…half-asleep, half in my dream, and I think I'm in a tent with my platoon buddies and the choppers are coming in."

Scott snickered, then wiped away the smile. Chile's face held some seconds of silence, along with some grim eyes. "I'm not shittin' man, I swore I was back there."

The motor kicked on again and Eddie noticed that the cases of shrimp were swaying along the back wall. Scott had stacked them too high and they were about to tip over; he could see that the top ones would hit the floor.

"I'd better fix the shrimp," Eddie said. "They're teetering."

"You got 31-35's stacked with 21-25's," Chile pointed out. "Every time I boil shrimp for cocktails, I open the wrong damned boxes because they're all stacked together."

"Oh, sorry," Eddie said. "Lou used to buy cooked shrimp from the meat market next door to King Arthur's. I haven't worked with frozen shrimp." Eddie didn't get to the stack in time. The boxes, seven or eight of them, came raining down to the freezer floor. One of them slid like a hockey puck out the freezer door, along the floor of the walk-in refrigerator and out to the kitchen tiles. Chile dodged out of the way as the missile sailed to the sink. "Whoa, captain, are you trying to strafe me?" he asked.

Eddie realized that Chile had forgotten his name already. "Sorry Chile," he said.

"Let me get this straight," Chile said. "You mean Lou over at King Arthur's actually bought his supplies from a supermarket?"

"Most of the time…the last few months, anyway," Eddie said. "He's pretty much broke…he used to give me money and send me over for things."

"Well no wonder the dumbfuck's broke, buying without a purveyor." Chile stepped on a roach. "I heard he wasn't doing so well. Saw him parking with his wife down on Sedgewick…he's got some bald tires on that Caddie of his."

Eddie finished the food order and then began to set up the machine. It was the same type of machine that King Arthur's had: slide the rack in, pull the door down, unload on the opposite side in ninety seconds. Bingo's had a nice rinse hose, though, with a sure-grip handle that jolted the power of heavy water pressure through Eddie's arm like a mild electric shock. Eddie figured that this job wasn't going to be so big a challenge, the lunch rush at least. He could definitely handle the twenty-five tables and the counting of things. He just hoped that Chile could remember his name and forget about the grapefruit incident and that he wouldn't nickname him "Zorgon."

III

Eddie set up the machine and finished stacking the dishes left in the racks from the night before. He couldn't keep his mind off Lou, and on the day that he had seen him last, the weekend before the runaway, the day of his very last shift. Lou was fumbling through some invoices on his desk that day, and there were papers, thousands of them it seemed, scattered on the floor. Eddie was afraid to approach him for his pay-check, but he wanted to get his first. The week before, his paycheck had bounced because the other employees had gotten to the bank before him and they had cleaned out Lou's account. Now, with the hope that Lou had replenished his money enough for him to cash in (and that the other employees were waiting until morning), Eddie approached Lou as he looked up from his spot of light.

"You need something Eddie,?" Lou asked.

"My check Lou if you've got it." And then Eddie stood there in the silence, as if the silence was some sort of slow tide coming in and enveloping his ankles. Lou gave a little sigh as he scratched along his back and squirmed in his chair. "Well, that's going to be a bit of a problem, he said. "You, see, according to these papers, my funds have all run dry."

Eddie stood in the darkened doorway with the wet band-aid hanging from his finger; he was going to ask Lou for a fresh band-aid first, and then hit him up for the pay-check. But now the pay-check was an impossibility, and the air was out of his lungs. He stood and eyed the first-aid box mounted on the wall above the desk. A fresh band-aid would be nice, that was for sure. He could feel the disgusting dish soap encrusting his old one. But the air was out of his lungs and he couldn't bring himself to ask Lou, whose eyes hung sadly over his invoices, for a thing. So he just stood in the doorway for several seconds as his mind worked to think of another place to replace his band-aid: his parent's medicine cabinet, the drug store on the way home (did they sell them in singles?), or maybe he would just keep the same old one and wrap it with some Scotch tape out of the junk drawer. He calculated that he could afford a whole box of band-aids if he was able to get the paycheck.

"I'll have it sometime tomorrow afternoon," Lou said, and gave a smile like Eddie had never seen come out of Lou, a resigned smile that sent him a little chill. "Count on it, gumba."

Lou was at the end, Eddie could tell that. Wallowing in his overdue bills, his eyes were sunken and his shirt was pulled out and he didn't know where to go next with his pen. Eddie bet that every one of those papers on the floor was a bill for something or another, and Lou just didn't have the money. He wondered if Lou had promised all the purveyors the same thing that he'd promised him. "Tomorrow gumba," he was probably saying to them over their phones and to reassure hope. "Tomorrow."

A year earlier, Lou's wife Candy had had her breasts removed. The doctors had gotten the cancer in time, Eddie had heard Lou saying to one of the line cooks, but the breasts would have to go. It took everything Lou had to pay for that. On the day that Candy came back to the restaurant to hostess a Saturday night shift, Eddie couldn't help turning and looking at the sag in her blouse. He couldn't keep his eyes from wandering behind the menus she carried. There were no breasts there—just a flat, scarred wasteland.

Later in the evening, during one of the rushes, Lou sent Eddie to the meat market with a twenty dollar bill and a list that included peanut butter, frozen drumsticks, and Delmontico steak. He rushed back in the side door because the customers were waiting for their food. Lou was busy saying "calm down sir" to a man with blood rushing through his head.

One of the line cooks grabbed the bag from Eddie's hand, ripped open the package of drumsticks, and dropped them into the deep fryer. "Where the fuck's the Delmontico?" he asked, and pulled the wrapped steaks from the bag. "What the hell are these?"

"I asked the guy for Delmontico and that's what he gave me dude," Eddie said. "I'm just a dishwasher, I don't know meat."

The cook tossed the steaks on the grill. "Hey ask me if I give a shit any more," he said. "They might as well toast this place right now for the insurance."

Everyone but Eddie and Jeff Poindexter the drunk line cook were laid off from the kitchen crew the following week. (After some food poisoning did in a Wednesday night crowd, the dining room had become a nightly ghost town). Lou, however, with his untucked shirt and his sagging eyes, stood undaunted by the window. He waited and waited for the cars to pull in, staring at the lot lamps with his eversad twinkle. When some guests would finally stray in, some senior citizens from Hudson perhaps or some passers-by who admired the Medieval scroll of "King Arthur's Steak House," Lou would fawn over them and take them to the best table in the back, engaging all the while in his small talk. His wife brought back the menus from the host stand and the lone waiter filled their water glasses and stood behind him, waiting for him to finish his handshakes and hollow laughter. The customers must have been able to read right through Lou, Eddie guessed. They must have known that his banter was really his cry for help. "Pity me," he was saying in small-talkese. "My restaurant is going under and I'm flat broke."

The customers usually wound up ordering the things that Lou suggested, the items he still had in stock in his near-empty refrigerator. Lou always pushed the pasta and the frozen scallops because he had plenty of those left (Jeff had over-ordered some months back). Eddie would watch Lou's movements from the door: if he started into his pockets, he knew they'd ordered something Lou didn't have in stock, and he would have to take off his apron and make a run over to the meat market.

Eddie never picked up his final paycheck because he ran into Candy the following afternoon as she was pulling a parking ticket from the Cadillac. Crying, she pulled Eddie aside just before he went into the restaurant and asked him was it all right if he waited another week for his pay. He couldn't look at Candy while she cried—not because he was angry at the prospect of waiting for his money, but because he knew that his eyes would inevitably look to the scarred wasteland of her sagging blouse. So he listened to her explain about the cost of the operation, the slow business, and finally the "damned son of a bitch ticket," while he stared away at the expired meter.

IV

Despite the rain, the lunch rush was busier than Eddie expected. The cars kept coming in off the down ramp, and the place filled up and stayed filled up. Some old ladies from Hudson had their umbrellas torn from them by the wind (and their white hair frazzled) just as the doors opened at 11:30. Scott patted them with towels from the rest rooms and told them that the white clam chowder was on him.

"The damned gutter snapped with the extra rain water," Scott told Eddie in the foyer, after the ladies were with their menus. "I need you to go out there and hitch it back up. "

Eddie looked out at the gray slanted lines of rain exploding across the lot. He should have been thinking about how he was going to say "no" to Scott, or at least fashion a request to wait a little while until the rain let up. But instead, because it was his first day on the job, he was thinking about a poncho that he might find and take out with him, and how his worn sneakers would fare on the metal ladder.

His legs slipped a few times on the rungs, but nothing so vital that he might have fallen completely to the ground or perhaps become so injured that he couldn't re-mount the gutters. He grabbed and panted and climbed, though, and over the roof he saw some lightning bolts that reminded him the gutter was of steel. Finally in the thunder, he screwed the gutter back into the roofside—just as the ladder began going down into the mud—and just as he'd had enough. Scott threw him some bar mops and a 'thank you' on his way back in, and then Eddie washed the dishes in his wet clothes, with the promise of a burger at the end of his shift.

Eddie finished a little early because Domingus the night dishwasher came in at three instead of four. He shook Eddie's hand and then pulled him over to the sinks and whispered with wide eyes and a thick accent that the police were chasing him. Apparently, Domingus had tried to sell some frozen shrimp over in Kemper Park to a guy who said he was a sous chef but who turned out to be a detective. The guy flashed his badge and accused Domingus of robbing a seafood truck out on Roosevelt Boulevard. He told Eddie (with cupped hands) that he'd done it and then he told him how he high-tailed it through the lumber yard and ran down the bike path and then across the golf course. "No one will think I here, because I never on time," he said. "This the last place they look."

Eddie clocked out at four and forgot about his burger. He went into the bathroom and pumped up a handful of pink soap and rubbed it into his scalp. Then he forced his head into the small sink, turning the faucets on full as they spilled the water down over his face. He worked the soap to a fine lather as it burned his eyes. Then he patted his head with some paper towels, found a comb on the back of the toilet seat, and parted his hair.

Hungry for candy, he took his money and bought four dollars worth of Snickers and Kit-Kats at the Buy-Rite. He stuffed them into his pockets and then hung out in the record stores along Reed until the sun sank past the roofs. After the stores closed up, he sat on a cinderblock wall, finished his candy, and stared at traffic, keeping his eye out for police cars and his father's possible Chrysler. Had the police come for Domingus? He imagined the front of Bingo's bathed in flashing red lights, the air filled with the sound of dispatches, Domingus cuffed and arrested for shrimp theft.

A clock in the hardware store window told Eddie that in less than three hours he could burrow along the hedge and crawl to his mattress of sod in the tool shed. With the little change he had left, he stopped in the drug store and bought a traveler's toothbrush and a little tube of toothpaste so that he might get out the peanuts and the sugar from between his teeth. He stood on the corner of Reed and Willis and squeezed a little of the paste onto the brush and slid it into his mouth as if it were a lollipop. He thought about the sugar in his teeth and then about his mother's most recent trip to the dentist. She had had the last of her teeth removed the previous summer, twelve rotted teeth extracted in one long sleep-induced sitting. She had just walked around with her bare gums all of July and most of August, waiting for them to heal and for the dentist to fashion her false teeth. Eddie remembered how repulsive she looked eating the soft foods at the dinner table, sipping soupy corn and slurping pureed meats through a straw, trying to hide her bare gums by the stretch of her lips and the shield of her hand. Then the dentures came and she came back from the dentist with a big smile, rows of white teeth, and a proclamation of "the new me." She kissed Eddie and hugged and kissed his father, staring at herself and smiling at various angles into the hall mirror. But her proclamation, "the new me," was short-lived, as she was visited that night by another one of her Benjamin dreams. She sat up screaming again at three a.m., talking about ghostly baby faces and outstretched little fingers "that looked so real I tried to touch them." The voice of Eddie's father beckoned her back to the pillow, after she had paced about the room crying "Benjamin God help you Benjamin." That was one of the first nights that Eddie had slept all night in his closet box.

V

The hedges were brimming with insects as Eddie crawled through, dark fast little things with thousands of legs. They got up inside his t-shirt and ran over his skin. Brushing them off in swoops, he heard something bigger in the hedge, something dark crawling through the branches. It jumped into a juniper just as he brushed past it, and he heard a faint chirp that sounded like a large game bird, thinking that it might be a pheasant or a stray mallard looking for a field or a pond. It had probably come from the donut pond, the pond that had been plowed over by the Caterpillars, the pond where all of the game-birds once converged in thick flocks. Game-Birds: they were just more victims of the subdivision, looking for food and water but trapped in hedges between houses.

Billy was sitting outside the shed as Eddie was flicking the last of the the chiggers from beneath his shirt. Dressed in a long-sleeved white shirt and an ironed pair of slacks, Billy had slicked back his hair and smelled like his father's cologne. He stood along the wall of the shed and held up the whisper finger, beckoning Eddie from the bushes.

"You're a little late dude," Billy said. "Looks like rain…supposed to rain all tomorrow. Another Phillies rain-out I bet." He stopped and breathed. "Listen we need to talk."

"You want me out, I can tell," Eddie said. "You got all dressed up to come out here and tell me I can't live in your tool shed didn't you?"

"My dad knows," he said. "Saw you this morning taking a piss on the trees."

"I swore I didn't see anybody at the windows."

"Dad's cool though…he told me he wasn't going to turn you in. He knows the Sheehans, and they told him all about your runaway. He was talking about Benjamin mostly, not you…he understood the whole deal, how you had to run away and all. He even said he might have done the same thing himself."

"Well then what's the problem with staying in the tool shed?"

"He just doesn't want to be responsible. He's afraid that if you get caught the news crews will come."

Eddie talked Billy into staying one last night in the shed because he didn't want to burrow through a hedge of bugs and game birds again. Besides that, the sky was looking like rain, and he could think of nowhere else to go except back to that dreaded construction site.

"Just get out before the morning light," Billy said. "My dad will coming running out in his underwear and his moose rifle if he sees you." Billy walked away, brushing some loose dirt from his pants leg. He moved into the darkness and across the dampened grass to the unlit house beneath the trees. He was unbuttoning his shirt as he disappeared, past the rhododendrons in a black blur. Billy: he was already in bed with his desk light off, asleep and forgetting about his holed-up friend.

Eddie figured that he might not see Billy ever again. He was going to have to sleep outside somewhere again, that was for sure, but now at least he knew that some money was coming in. He tried to envision some sort of near-future, a sprightly apartment maybe and a thick shag rug, maybe some Boston Ferns and spider plants like Billy's mother had hanging in her picture window. It would be after he got himself some paychecks that didn't bounce, after he'd stashed some money in a hole somewhere, dug it up, and slapped down a deposit for an apartment, maybe over in Valley Green. Maybe a pet, maybe he'd get a pet. In Willow Grove was "The Greatest Pet Store In The Civilized World." They had cheetahs and dwarf kangaroos and parrots from the Andes. Eddie especially remembered and liked the noise when he walked in, as all of them called in unison, spilling out their chatter in one screeching sound wave that worked his inner ear drums to a dull pain.

Eddie, in his earlier years—ten, eleven, twelve—went to "The Greatest Pet Store In The Civilized World" to see the reptiles. At that. time, reptiles were his life: all he wanted to do was be in the vicinity of things that slithered and crawled. He had shelves and shelves of Peterson's Guides and National Geographic albums and assorted other volumes given to him by his parents. His mother would drive him to Willow Grove on Saturdays and drop him off at the light across from the pet store. Then she would drive off to park her car down the block, and Eddie would have all afternoon to watch the reptiles while she shopped for lace curtains and took little Benjamin to look at the moving trees.

For the most part, Eddie stood over the lizard cages and dreamed of owning one of them. He especially liked the Monitor Lizard, a seven-foot dinosaur priced at six hundred dollars. The tongue hypnotized him with the way it shot out and then back in, cotton candy pink. He would time the intervals between the flicks: six maybe seven seconds if it was hungry, twelve or thirteen with its belly full. He counted three seconds on one visit, and he beckoned to the proprietor, a man who looked more like a librarian (always in a book of the "non-animal" variety) than a pet store owner.

"I think your Monitor Lizard is hungry," Eddie said.

The man looked up with glasses too thick to see eyeball. "Sheila is hungry again? She's on another one of her binges, I can tell you that." The librarian-looking man put down his book and grabbed a guinea pig from one of the glass aquariums spread on the floor behind the counter. He whistled in one sustained note to the back of the store, walking briskly into the reptile encove with the guinea pig held by its fuzzy nape. With his other hand, he fumbled for a key on a large ring that looked like a jail master's until he retrieved the correct one. Then he unlocked the little feeding door at the top of the cage, while Eddie paced and while the Monitor Lizard flicked its tongue like a pink flag flapping in the breeze.

Those next seconds were thorough entertainment: he watched as the whites of the guinea pig's eyes came out., as the man's fingers opened. The rodent fell to the stones, and then, as if expecting its doom, scattered to the corner behind a near-empty water bowl. Now Eddie moved closer to the front of the cage and pressed his face to the plexiglass. He and the librarian-looking man stood side by side, alone among the animals. The sounds rose around him, to a crescendo of squawks and chatters and buzzes and chirps and wails, as the lizard moved on it claws to the corner of the cage, sniffing out its kill. In a flash it struck, slamming the red bowl against the plexiglass and spitting up a spray of white stones and water. Eddie saw the pink cave of its mouth consume the guinea pig in one swallow and close around it with the force of a steel trap: then the crack of little bones, then a muffled squeal, then a flick of the neck, then stillness.

"Unbelievable," Eddie said. "Does she always eat that quick?"

"Not usually," the man said. "She doesn't usually attack that quick. Must be getting desperate, what with the meat cooler empty. She's developing a craving for live food, though. Hell, she's going through my pigs like butter. And I can't afford butter."

In a matter of a minute he envisioned taking that monitor lizard home. The vision became so complete and so plausible that he had asked his mother, who had just come from a frantic sale on housewares, if maybe he could have it as his next five Christmas presents combined.

"For God sakes, are you out of your mind?" she asked him. "You can't even get one of those pond turtles anywhere near me, let alone a seven-foot lizard. We've talked about this reptile thing of yours how many times?"

Eddie just stared out the window the entire ride home, angry at his mother and trying to pretend that she didn't exist. She had just torn down his perfectly envisioned world built and centered around a monitor lizard named Sheila, so he pretended that his mother didn't exist.

VI

Eddie first visited the donut pond with Brad Griggs, the reptile freak from Fergusonville. Brad Griggs had a garage filled with any species of reptile that could possibly be caught in the surrounding creeks and woods. He had Spotted Turtles and Fire-Bellied Newts and Black Snakes and King Snakes. He even managed to capture a twelve-inch Hellbender under one of the bridges along the Neshaminy. But the highlight of his collection was "Woody," the old Wood Turtle he had caught between the corn stalks on Miller's farm. Eddie was with him on the day he caught it, and he watched in envy from the end of the path as Brad hoisted it victoriously into the air: the Wood Turtle, the Holy Grail of reptiles.

His envy stemmed not from Brad's rare find, but rather from his complete freedom to capture and bring home whatever he pleased. He had pleaded with his father to take his mother aside and talk her into letting him keep some reptiles, some harmless turtles even, at the back of the garage. But she was afraid of their escape and that she might run across the things crawling across the yard or perhaps sneaking their way into the house. Eddie remembered the time that his father had dropped a pad of steel wool near his workbench and his mother had screamed (and had an eventual nightmare) because she thought it a small rat.

Brad and Eddie hunted painted turtles at the donut pond. Brad had taught him how to sneak up and wade along the shallow water where the reeds grew in towering clumps along the near shore, how to move the reeds and peek out into the clearing. There was a thick log there jutting out of the water with rotted wood fanning in all directions from its massive trunk. The dead tree lay on its side so that it was almost perpendicular to the water, extending twenty feet in the direction of the opposite shore. That was Brad Grigg's turtle log, his mother lode, and if he was quiet enough as he came around the reeds, he could fill up his burlap sack with a dozen or so turtles.

"It's all in the timing," he whispered to Eddie. "Like a cat ready for a kill. Cats, you see, move up dead quiet…they plant their feet, they look, they look, and bam…they strike."

On his first visit to the donut pond, Brad instructed Eddie to wait by the reeds and watch how he did things. Eddie pictured the leopards and such that he'd seen on the nature shows, and he saw Brad crouching and squinting in the same manner. Just as he got his entire body beyond the reeds, Brad dashed into the center of the pond. He kicked up a muddy splash as his feet sloshed rapidly toward the log and the water rose nearly to his waist as his eyes filled with the fire of capture. He lunged at one large painted turtle making its way, in a quick pedal of legs, down the length of the log toward the water. In a flash, his hand reached and grabbed it, and he opened the burlap bag and dropped it in. Eddie watched as the bag twirled in Brad's hand, as turtle after turtle plopped into the water, and as he expertly plucked the slower ones from the rotted log. He filled up his bag and gloated in fits of triumph.

Eddie would like to have had Brad's garage and owned that many reptiles. And the attention: he would like to have been called "Reptile King," just like Brad. How did it feel, that everything in the bag was yours? And that you had somewhere to display it? How did it feel to have a mother who petted your snakes and bragged to the neighbors about your wood turtle? Eddie's garage: only cars and tools and things in the way in the space where he might have kept his menagerie.

Brad cried on a rock on the day they came over the hill and saw the bulldozers plowing over the donut pond. They watched the Caterpillars rain a million pounds of dirt into the water, as the smokestacks belched black wisps, as the men shouted orders to each other, oblivious to the buried turtles. The log was gone, consumed by a field of fresh dirt. Some of the remaining reeds were crushed by the heavy tires and the game birds, frightened away by the grinding engines, assembled on the dirt mountains, confused.

"What are we gonna do,?" Brad asked. "What can we do?" Then he sat and cried on the rock, wailing about the fields they had plowed over in Landoff to put up more houses, about the buried frog ponds in his own Fergusonville, about the Newportville industrial waste, and now here they were again, snuffing out his mother lode. "You sons of bitches are killing all the reptiles," he screamed.

Since their excursions to the donut pond were the glue to their friendship, Brad fell out of interest to Eddie after the Caterpillars had come. Some years later, after he'd lost interest in reptiles (his books put away in boxes marked "Eddie's things" in the attic), he heard some stories about Brad, things involving the armed robbery of a Safeway, some years spent in the penitentiary, and then his disappearance over a church collection-basket fiasco.

Eddie wondered about Brad's reptiles. Did he lose interest and give them all away? Did he, in some drunken moment, release them into the neighborhood? More than likely, Eddie guessed, his pets had all starved to death. During the time that Brad went off in his souped-up Chevy to rob people and race down the straightaways and spend the church money on mind drugs, and as his father pushed his collection into the corner behind the mowers, the snakes stiffened up, the turtles rotted away in their shells, and the salamanders dried up in their bowls, assuming the consistency of stale french fries. Brad Griggs and his reptiles: just more victims of the subdivision.

VII

The thunder advanced, two or three miles distant. The shed, in all its blackness, was completely familiar to him now. He knew how to crawl in, how to latch it from the inside, how to avoid the rakes piled on the side. He knew how to feel for the indentation that his body had made on the dead sod, and he knew how long it would take to stare into the darkness and fall to sleep. His shed darkness was unlike his closet box: different and far away, a metal kind of darkness. The crickets made their noise, the occasional car would make its way up the road, and maybe he might hear a voice coming from one of the houses, a shout or maybe a long laugh. But this time he would not hear the voice of his mother and father, the cries from their bedroom, the whispers of consolation for their departed sons. He would not hear the Phillies losing below him night by night.

The thunder rolled closer, and Eddie thought about what Billy had said. It was going to rain soon, and it would probably keep on raining into the next day. He figured that he would probably have to leave the shed the same way he came—in the darkness of early dawn and in a downpour. Laying on the sod, he stared up at the invisible roof and tried to think of his next move. With money coming in soon, he would only need to hole up somewhere, find a place to get out of the rain. He could sleep under the Fergusonville bridge in the little "cave" there. He could cover up the entrance to the hole with some boulders and some tree branches and such. No one would ever suspect a thing: there would be no screened windows from which to watch him and no one to see him pissing on trees.

He decided to sneak over there in the morning. Maybe before he left, he could get some clothes from Billy, have him throw some things down from his window. It was going to be a week before his pay came in, and he didn't want to stay in the same "Power" t-shirt, the same jeans. Billy could toss down a sack to put the clothes in, and Eddie could use it as his pillow while he slept beneath the bridge.

The rain hit the tin roof of the shed. Eddie thought about the Phillies. There was going to be another canceled game if the rain continued into tomorrow. His father wasn't going to like it one bit, either. He was going to sit there with the TV on and watch the rain film, waiting for a let-up. He was going to curse the weather, maybe call up his Uncle Pete and bitch about the movie he was forced to watch instead of the game. He'd be drunk by late afternoon, that was for certain, with no one to curse: no misplayed balls, no botched suicide squeezes to hone in on, nothing to say to the television set as the alcohol filled his gut. He would just sink down into his easy chair, curse the rain and his misfortune, and fall to sleep.

After he put away the sound of the pitter-patter and drifted off, Eddie had another dream. This dream had him standing in water past his knees. He was at the donut pond perched among the reeds, their tips filled with red-winged blackbirds cawing him and eyeing him as he moved dead quiet into the clearing. There was the log again, the glorious log, filled with all the kinds of turtles he had ever seen, spotted turtles and painted turtles and soft-shelled turtles and wood turtles and musk turtles and sliders—on and on, species upon species, piled like polished stones. He drifted across the stagnant pool, approached his mother lode, now his mother lode. Brad was gone, off in a jail somewhere past the far shore, and now they were his for the taking.

Eddie held his sack and drifted on air over the water, suspended it seemed so that his feet made no noise as he slid into the dark murky pond water. He reached the log and grabbed. He grabbed them, just kept grabbing at the turtles as some of them tumbled into the water. But he was winning, he was winning and filling his sack as his hands worked nimbly to snatch the most prized of the scurrying turtles. Heavier and heavier became the sack, and he spilled out shouts of joy as they clawed and twisted. "Yeah spotted turtle…holy shit wood turtle…wow huge painter…wait until everybody sees…"

It must have been the escaping turtles, or perhaps, again as in his rake dream, the outside world reached in to poison his moment—for his joy began to fade. He could feel the walls of reality closing in to snuff his flame, to take away every turtle on the log, in the water, in his burlap sack. Eddie stood in his murky dreamwater and tried to hold on to his sack, as he closed it and raised it above the water. He held it with the strength of both his arms and waited for the thunder to wake him.

Lost Brothers

◆

I

The Fergusonville bridge rose with its massive concrete out of the flooded creek, soaked from the rain so that it spit waterfalls two hundred feet down from its railing. Some punks had scrawled their names along the cement face, indecipherable symbols marking their territories, coming to the bridge from all of the neighboring towns over a string of years, from Fergusonville and Milford and Hudson and Landoff. Some of their names had faded into almost invisible blacks and reds; the paint had soaked itself into the stone, names long forgotten, names of the now-dead, young scrawlers who'd met their violent ends in dark alleys with razors and guns, or in head-on collisions down on the boulevard.

Eddie found the cave, the little split in the concrete wall just below a spray-painted arrow pointing downward, as if some lost explorer was showing him the way to salvation. He removed some of the beer bottles littering the entrance, brown and green glass warnings shattered upon the rocks. He noticed the dark red blotches encrusting the rocks. Blood: there had been a fight no doubt, a swinging of fists and jagged bottles, the cursing of the messages left on the walls, the battle for some drunken superiority.

There had been several incidents with the McGrath twins over ownership of the cave mouth some years back and one twin had battered the other and ruptured his spleen. As ten-year-olds, Eddie and Billy had watched, from the other side of the creek, as the twins kicked and fought each other, as they bled and screamed, as each claimed ownership to the cave. Timmy McGrath wound up missing most of the school year because of the incident and needed spleen surgery. As he laid up in a hospital bed over in Hudson, the Board of Education arrived and wired his room with a Speaker-Phone and connected a line to the school. During his recovery, he was able to hear the nuns over at St. Anselm teach him the things that he needed to learn. Schoolday by schoolday they piped their religion into his hospital room and sent their tests over by way of Father Madrid.

Timmy, upon leaving the hospital, immediately smashed his twin brother Joseph in the mouth with a two by four, calculating that he would at least need enough stitches that would equal the amount running up the length of his own stomach. That was at the end of the school year. That summer the McGraths, all eleven of them, suddenly filled up a moving van and left. Someone said to England, another said to Idaho. In either case, Eddie figured that by now one of the twins was permanently scarred or paralyzed, maybe buried in a grave somewhere, while the other was doing time.

The cave was smaller than Eddie remembered, though he could still manage to squeeze through the mouth and slide in. There were some newspapers laid out on the little floor covering the damp earth spread to the crumbling wall at the back of the cave. The newspapers were wet, torn and yellowed from age, and he saw a sports page that told him, between the stains, the Phillies had won a game (It must really be an old paper, Eddie thought.) He looked for a date but found it torn away. Then he settled his head against the wall.

Billy hadn't thrown down the clothes Eddie was hoping for so he was still in his same t-shirt, which had begun to accumulate spots of dirt and sweat. It was going to be a warm humid day again. The early morning rain had done nothing to cool things off, and the damp cave offered little relief, even at seven in the morning.

Crawling out of the cave, Eddie brushed away the broken glass from the rocks and walked to the edge of the brown flooded Neshaminy creek. He dipped his t-shirt in and ran it along some sharp rocks, hoping to loosen the encrusted dirt and perhaps rinse the sweat stains from the sleeves. He would need to head over to Bingo's in a couple of hours and he didn't want to carry a foul smell. Squeezing the creek water out of the shirt—a diluted brown silt—he laid it over some of the rocks gathering the morning sun. Then he sat bare-chested and tossed some stones into a dark pool along the edge of the creek. He watched some minnows trapped there in the pool. They swam in a frantic circle about the edge, slamming into the stones that had walled them in. He removed the larger stones and then the smaller ones and forged a little canal to the creek. The minnows, by instinct, immediately filtered through their escape tunnel, one by one, tail on tail, and shot in silver flashes into the swell.

Eddie was hungry. He was hoping that Scott would provide him some toast or something when he went into the restaurant. Maybe he could warm up one of the frozen bagels from the walk-in or steal some shrimp cocktail from the left-over rack. The sun was beginning to knife its concentrated rays through the trees and he watched as the water trickled down the rocks from his drying shirt. He was going to have to wear it damp; the sun would never bake it dry by ten a.m.

"Hey you," came the voice from the top of the bridge. "Hey you."

Eddie looked up to the top of the bridge, where the stone facing arched over the trees. A man stood there in the center of the bridge, looking down, a dark silhouette moored against the green backdrop. It looked as if he were wearing a trench coat and Eddie's first instinct flared up a well of panic in his gut as he deduced that the man was a detective or someone looking for him. Perhaps it was the pale-faced man in the Cadillac hunting him down, or the green-jerseyed man finally closing in on him to avenge his grandmother's death.

"They lost a boy downstream last night you know," the man yelled down.

Eddie stared up, puzzled. "What?"

"A boy went in." The man pointed to the opposite end of the bridge. "Fell in along one of the muddy banks down near the sewage station. Slipped right into the flood. The cops, they just got done fishing his body out near daybreak. Drowned a mile or so further on."

Eddie looked out at the swollen creek and watched a thick log drift by, twirling like a baton, powerless against the current. The creek was deep, that was for sure. It could probably pull a grown man down and keep him there, trap him among the silt and the broken tree branches and the tumbling minnows. He edged his feet away from the bank, afraid of the realized power.

"Stay away from that muddy water if you know what's good for you," the man said. "Stay away." Then the man disappeared from the top of the bridge and walked on, leaving Eddie alone with the flooded creek as he sat quiet and bare-chested on the flattened grass.

II

The wet shirt began to itch him as he walked up Midvale. There must have been some microscopic organisms in the creek water, things out of the mud, and they were all moving around his shirt or something. He scratched and tugged at his shirt sleeves and saw an old woman sitting on her stoop watching him advance up the street. She must have thought him crazy with the way he was flailing his arms trying to get to the itch in the middle of his back. She stood up from the step and put her hands on her hips and with her pointed chin and her thick glasses she watched him go by. She moved down the lawn and watched him closely as he continued past her house and up Midvale until the thick foliage that drooped down divided him from her sight-line.

He didn't know what to think of her curiosity; perhaps she knew who he was. Perhaps she had seen his face on a milk carton or in the newspaper or something or heard some gossip about his run-away (probably from the Sheehans—the Sheehans had told everyone). He figured that everyone in Fergusonville still remembered the kidnapping and some of them were still keeping their eyes out for suspicious-looking people driving around in vans or people just walking along (scratching like mad). Some of these people had memorized that picture in *The Bugle-Dispatcher*, the one which showed his mother and father on the front lawn in frowns, with little Eddie in the background, right next to the tracks the kidnappers had left the day after they had taken Benjamin away. That was over two years back, and now this old lady with the telescope eyes (he could still feel her presence behind the thick foliage) looked like the type who would remember everything that came her way. She had that black-and-white photograph soldered to her memory cells along with all of the Shemanski stories: all of the truths, all of the lies. She knew what Eddie was all about, projected his growth right there on the step, calculated where he was coming from and where he might be headed. There was little doubt that she had already gone in to call the police.

Filled with urgency, Eddie broke into a sprint across Wellsley, tearing up some stones and watching the windows for movement. There was something going on: he saw no signs of life. That was unusual; this was the time that husbands should be on their way to jobs, pulling out of their driveways in their white shirts and ties, full of coffee. There should be joggers at least, a dog on a chain, some music or an alarm clock or some noise, any noise, coming from one of the houses. Nothing. Not a human sound and it scared Eddie. Well, there was a bird chirping in a tree anyway. He could hear the distant tractor-trailers out on the interstate, too. But Fergusonville was dead quiet of people, as if some rat-carrying plague had descended and wiped them all out in their sleep. Eddie became exhausted from running and he slowed down to a quick walk. He began to move up Holloway with his head down, waiting and hoping for some noise to pop up and relieve him. He hid his face from the houses, fearful of looking in any direction where a screened window might offer someone the opportunity of recognition.

He was certain, in a heavy dose of paranoia, that the thick-spectacled woman had gone and called them all, each and every neighbor, one after the other, house upon house. A phone rang from an orange-shuttered colonial, breaking the disturbing silence that had hung like a dense fog. It rang and rang and Eddie didn't know whether to slow and listen or to keep moving. He wanted to continue his sprint to a safer street, maybe Johnson or Klingmore or Barry, where there would certainly be the comfort of more noise. But Eddie's curiosity brought him to a stop as the phone continued to ring. He sat down on the curb with his face buried in his hands. Through his fingers, he looked at his feet, at the stones, at the house, and waited.

Someone answered, though he could barely detect the whisper coming out of the screened porch. A shadow moved across the wicker room and then disappeared into the darkness of the house, a man or a woman he did not know. He watched the orange-shuttered house carefully, listening all the while for a word that might rise up out of the whisper, something that might give him a clue, something that might confirm all of his fears. A curtain moved in the room above the garage; someone was watching him, something was going on. They were closing in, the old lady had made the call. It would only be a matter of seconds before they all came spilling out, out from the orange-shuttered house, out from every other house on Wellsley, out to nab him there on the curb.

There was a reward: that was it, there was a reward offered for his capture, five hundred, a thousand dollars, maybe more. His father had probably made some calls, put up some posters, placed some ads, offered the little cash he had left to bring his boy home. "Just get him the hell back here," he had probably said.

Eddie bolted from his seat on the curb. He ran toward the sound of the tractor trailers, up the long hill of Henry, across the open lots, over the muddied particle board and the scattered nails, through the skeleton houses. A sense of relief overwhelmed him as he scaled the medial wall, as he waited for the rush of cars to pass, as he fell into the briars on the other side of the interstate and caught his breath. Then, with his breath gathered, he pulled out his comb, removed the thorns and the knots from his hair, and cursed his panic.

III

"What happened to you, that's a bitch of a cut," Scott said as Eddie walked through the door.

"Cut what cut?" Eddie answered.

"Down your arm. Hell you're almost dripping blood on my carpet."

Eddie didn't even feel the pain, or rather, it felt only as sore as a scrape, certainly nothing worth looking at. But he twisted his arm around to see the long thin gash running down it, deducing that he must have gotten it in the thorns.

"You look like hell," Scott said. "You been sleeping under the stars or something?"

He worked quick to manufacture a lie. "Been helping a friend with his Camaro is all," he said. "Changing spark plugs."

"Well punch in and get on your whites. Night crew did it to us again."

He saw all of the bus pans as he entered the kitchen, stacked on the shelf and filled with the filthy dishes from the night before. Some of the dishes had spilled to the floor, probably after the restaurant had closed and after everyone had gone off to the bar. There was a pile of broken china, some shattered wine glasses, and a large chunk of pie spewed beneath the machine.

"Damnit," Eddie said. "This sucks." He was hungry and he felt weak and tired. He didn't feel like getting down on his knees and getting the piece of pie from beneath the machine; he wanted only to sit and eat a freshly cut piece of apple pie out of the dessert box.

"Here, fix your arm first," Scott said, bringing some gauze from the first-aid box and handing him a strip along with some white tape. Eddie stood among the broken dishes and fixed his arm. He rinsed his cut with the dish hose; it shot an explosion of hot water into his cut and made him jump back in a spasm of pain.

"You idiot," Scott called from the coffee machines. "Slow cold water. Take it over to the sink."

Eddie wrapped his arm and picked up the shards of china scattered over the floor. He wondered how night crew could leaving dishes and dirty tables night after night. He wondered if the owner knew.

"Who owns Bingo's?" he asked Scott.

"Freddie O'Hara," he said. "Comes in once a month or so and sits at the end of the bar and gets drunk. Fired three of my bartenders last year because they couldn't make a Mai-Tai the way he wanted. He's a real son of a bitch."

"Lucky he only comes around once a month."

"Yeah well he doesn't need to come around any more than that. He's rich and he doesn't care. As long as the place runs and doesn't lose money and he can come sit and get drunk, he doesn't care...unless you make his drink wrong. He inherited a ton of money from his sister. See, his sister had some scam going over in the church hall for years and years playing bingo. Seems she had a secret system where she won every game she played. "

"She cheated at bingo?"

"And got caught. Took them about twenty years to catch her, though. She had everyone going, insisting that a whole lot of praying was behind her winnings. She told the ladies, even Father Madrid, that she was going to the altar every day with her rosary and that she had some special communication with God. She heard voices in her sleep, she said. She was visited while she was driving, she said, while she was in the shower, she said. God just kept telling her how to win at bingo. She explained that she was just following through with His Plan."

"How'd she get caught?"

"Some of the suspicious ladies got her drunk off apple cider on one of the church picnics. They figured if they got her drunk she'd start spilling her beans. Sure enough, it all came out that day—the way she manipulated the cards, how she changed the numbers, everything. They couldn't really figure out all of the details, what with the way she was slurring, but she trashed God. That's the main thing, she just sat there at that picnic drunk off cider and laid into God, shocking the ladies and turning poor Father Madrid's face a pale white as she condemned Catholics and screamed at the idiot women praying to someone who wasn't there. 'You've all been taken in by an atheist,' she said. 'Don't you all know that God is dead?'"

"Wait a minute," Eddie said. "I think I remember hearing something about that. Wasn't that the lady that Father Madrid punched?"

"Laid her out right there on the grass. In fact, poor Mrs. McGrath, who wound up becoming a Mormon and moving to Utah…"

"I know the McGraths…I thought they moved to Idaho."

"No, Utah, right off the salt flats…anyway, poor Mrs. McGrath ripped her dress trying to pry Father off Mrs. O'Hara and got herself a bloody lip besides. It was a real mess."

"And nothing happened with Father Madrid? He wasn't excommunicated or anything?"

"To this day every one of those ladies denies the punching incident. It was Mrs. O'Hara against the Catholics. She walked away beat up, drunk, and screaming law suits, but she also walked away rich. Over those twenty years, the bitch stashed all of her bingo money away in some secret account. I don't know how much, Freddie wouldn't tell me that, but with the interest I'll bet she made herself a nice half million. She died just about three years ago of a brain tumor—screaming in her sleep, hearing voices of all things at the very end. And of course the church ladies ate that up, insisting that God was the culprit, getting her back for her bingo scam. She died with only her brother Freddie left alive as family. Left him a mansion over in Hudson and enough money for him to live comfortable and buy things—a couple of luxury cars…an in-ground pool…this restaurant."

"I can't believe he named this place Bingo's."

"Father Madrid still sends us a post card here every week" Scott said. "Religious post cards that he must buy by the dozen over at 'Catholic Things.' Post cards of Jesus, assorted saints, Renaissance paintings of the Old Testament with little messages on the back begging Freddie to change the name, and sometimes condemning him to hell."

"For naming the place Bingo's?"

"For naming the place Bingo's."

IV

It was a small world, Eddie kept thinking. Scott knew the McGraths and he knew Father Madrid, faces out of his own past that had now flared up and assumed full imaginative reality, crystal-clear photographs. It surprised Eddie that Scott did not recognize him or hear about him, Eddie the runaway, or at least had not gotten a little suspicious about his cut and his dirty creek-water-soaked shirt and wondered where he was from. He had to smell. Eddie smelled himself, stuck his nose under his armpit, but that didn't do any good. Someone had told him that you can never smell your own B.O., and he couldn't smell anything and figured everyone else could and didn't have the heart to tell him to take a bath. All of them—the manager, the waitresses, Chile, all smelled the sweat and the crushed bugs and the stagnant Neshaminy water that was soaked into his shirt and encrusted beneath his arms. He was sure that they were talking about him in the waiter holes. Maybe Scott knew about his runaway and he was keeping his discovery a secret. He was planning to get Eddie a couple of pay checks and fix up his life, get him on his feet and smelling fresh as a jug of pink soap. Maybe he was just waiting for the right time to call the police and collect his thousand dollar reward. Maybe Scott wanted to see how good a dishwasher Eddie was: if he kicked butt, he would keep him on—but if he went down in flames during one of the lunch slams, he'd call the cops and turn him in.

Eddie's stomach growled. He was tempted several times to pick at the half-eaten crab salad and fried haddock out of the incoming bus pans. The day busser hadn't shown up again, so Scott had to don an apron and bus the tables himself. He had smashed some things around in his office, kicked the telephone off the hook and knocked some plaques from the wall as Eddie approached him about getting something to eat. Eddie figured that it wasn't a very good time to ask for food, what with Scott's face so red, so he decided to wait until his employee meal at the end of the shift. He was starving, though, and he figured he might hit up one of the waitresses for some vanilla ice cream when Scott was too busy to notice.

He could ask Lisa, the waitress who was nice to him. None of the others had talked to him yet—not the tall blonde or the one with the horn-rimmed glasses nor the fat one with the pink jeans. He figured it was because he was just some skinny seventeen year old dishwasher

with greasy hair who smelled like the Neshaminy creek. But Lisa introduced herself on her way to punch the clock. Later, when she was busy
with a full station, she came back to the machine and made a comment
about a song on the radio ("Time Passages") and then mentioned that
some customers were complaining about cold soup and a tip she never
saw. She offered Eddie a cigarette out of her apron, which, for him, was
better than the ice cream.

"Thanks. I haven't had a Kool in a while" he said.

"Don't let Scott catch you smoking in the kitchen, though," she said.
"Go out on the dock if you want to light up. Waitresses can smoke out
in the waiter hole but Chile and Scott had a big argument over smoking
in the kitchen. Scott threatened to fire him because one of the customers found an ash in a steak sandwich. Seems he was smoking over
the grill, had it hanging out his mouth while he was flipping the meat.
And that was the end of smoking in the kitchen. Scott fired some dishwasher a couple months back for lighting up, poor kid, so don't become
a statistic."

After he had finished the last of the left-over dishes, Eddie went out
to the end of the dock. He took the Bingo's matches that he had found
on the counter and lit his Kool. He watched his puff rise and carry out
over the field of weeds as it dispersed into the trees. His mother always
watched her puffs as they rose, as they hit the ceiling and disintegrated.
That was the scenario that played itself out night after night in the den:
his father buried in the sports page or the television, his mother watching her puffs sail into invisibility. That was the way it was, and it was just
another reason why Eddie wound up storming up the steps, stealing the
cigarettes out of his mother's windbreaker, and taking them into his
closet box.

What were they doing right now at noon? His father was getting
ready to take his break at the plant, shutting off his lathe and heading to
the lunch room. He had all of his buddies by his side, the guy with the

beard from Sedgewick, Ernie the clown, and all of the others making their jokes about his father's growing bald spot and lambasting his beloved Phillies. He was going to go off and sit at a table by himself, eat the same lunch he packed for himself every day for twenty years: tuna fish and a banana. That's all Eddie ever smelled on those school mornings at the breakfast table, day after day, year after year—the pungent odor of those open cans of tuna squeezed over the sink, rising to his nose, hovering over his Cap'n Crunch. To this day, eating a bowl of cereal carried with it the disgusting and remembered aroma of tuna. Even now, as hungry as he was, Eddie hated Cap'n Crunch.

At noon his mother was crying or thinking about crying, just like any other time of the day. There were some days when she was just mildly sad after Benjamin's abduction, silent and introspective of things, of the news on the television, of the children playing on Midvale, of the dust gathering on the shelves. She would go about things with the sad but firm conviction of a woman self-contained by cleaning things that Eddie noticed were already clean, things polished an hour before—the heavy piano, the end tables, the old photographs in the ornate frames. She was occupying her time with the few things left at her disposal. But the crying was inside her and it always threatened to unleash itself at any moment.

Polishing the bannister one day, she made it halfway up the stairs before she stopped, stared away in some seconds of silence, and broke down. Contained no longer, she sat herself down on one of the middle steps and put her face into her hands. Then she cried and cried and muffled some unintelligible words into her cupped hands. Eddie's father wasn't there for that one; it was just him, alone in the living room with the television going and faced with the cumbersome task of consoling his own mother.

"It'll be all right mom," was all he had said from his seat on the couch. He squirmed and tried to pretend that some important information was coming to him by way of a commercial. "Things will turn out all right." He didn't get up during this uncomfortable interlude; his eyes had frozen themselves to the image on the screen, a woman talking about tampons or something. Sensing that her son wasn't about to come over and hold her in his skinny arms, she got up, left her polishing rag on the bannister, dashed to her bedroom, and closed the door. He sat for a minute in his solitude, then shut off the set and went out for a walk, out to the logs in the clearing to have a Kool. He sat there long after he had ground his butt into the wood, hoping that his father would not go to Fitzgerald's Pub or to Uncle Pete's on this particular evening, but instead would come right home from work to fix things for a little longer.

V

Benjamin Shemanski, Benjamin Shemanski, Benjamin Shemanski. The name wedged itself into Eddie's head and it stayed there as the dishes came in, as he ran the racks through the machine, as Chile cursed from the other side of the kitchen, buried in his tickets. Busy as he was, and as much as the steaming dishes burned the tips of his fingers, his little brother's name stood alone in his head and fixed itself there. Then the images came, soft like Vaseline on a camera lens, of the pale and smiling baby. Always in blankets, always with a smile that looked up to the mobiles, the counterparts of Noah's ark, pairs of pigs and giraffes and snakes and such, always spinning. The little sounds, the cooing, the attempt at forming words to speak, to say something, anything, to become part of the world of humans, reaching up to the hopeless white universe.

Everyone was infected with the smiling, hovering over the baby and putting on that same face. Aunts and uncles, cousins upon cousins, mother and father, even Eddie himself, put on that 'aw look at the cute little baby' face and plunged their arms into the bassinet to take his little fingers in theirs—fingers so little, so pink, fragile like tissue paper. "Gaaaaajaaaa," Benjamin always returned. "Gaaaajaaaa."

Eddie stopped in the middle of loading one of his racks. Right in the middle of washing the lettuce from one of the platters, he stopped and walked out of the dish area. He walked back to the dock again without a Kool this time and he closed the double doors behind him. He did not consider that Scott might be along with another full bus pan, that he'd call his name and demand his return to the machine to keep up with the dishes piling. The image of Benjamin had so consumed him that nothing else could now exist: not a moment of work, not another thought, nothing. It was Benjamin and only Benjamin, and it brought Eddie down. He crumbled to the dock in a burst of tears. Just like his mother on the stairs, in the middle of her polishing, here he was, in the middle of a rack of dishes, dissolved into an uncontrollable outbreak of sobs. Poor Benjamin. Poor, poor Benjamin.

He sat out there on the dock for the longest time, sobbing to the trees and the open field of weeds. As if by some miracle, no one came in search of him. Scott never called his name and never demanded his return to the world of teeming bus pans and churning water and angry shouts over the din of the exhaust fans. Eddie sat and cried, and he cried some more—about Benjamin, about his mother cleaning things already cleaned, about his father alone in the lunch room with his tuna sandwich and his banana.

Where could Benjamin be? Dead and covered by topsoil? Still alive somewhere? His brother, his lost brother, lost out there, lost in the eternal blackness of uncertainty. Eddie wiped away the tears from his face, which he assumed by now had become monstrously smeared by his dirty fingers. He considered, in a brief respite of hope, that his little brother was alive and well in some part of the world. This consideration helped greatly to stop his sobbing and helped him to move his vision from one of a baby to that of a little boy. Three years old—he would be turning three years old, ready to go into a nursery school the green-jerseyed man had enrolled him in. He was somewhere else, out on the great prairies of the Midwest, deep in the Minnesota woods, splashing about on a California beach. He was gone, perhaps never to be seen again, but he was alive, he was very much alive. Benjamin Shemanski: better walking and talking and growing than dead, that was for sure. Alive, there was a chance that he might turn up again, grow up,come running back home—after he had found his buried memory, his mental snapshot of the Shemanski home. And then maybe Eddie would pick himself up and go home, too.

VI

Lisa got into an argument with Chile just near the end of the lunch rush. Apparently, he had sent out a turkey sandwich with mayo even though she had specifically marked "plain" on her ticket.

"Every single time this lady comes in you do this to her. She's very nice most of the time and then she has to sit and wait while you make her another. By that time all the other ladies at her table are done eating."

"She'll live," Chile said.

"I won't if you keep it up. This nice little lady you keep testing blew her top on me just now. I could see the veins bulging out of her neck. It's not just the mayonnaise,Chile. You're torturing this poor lady and she's reached the edge."

"I guess she'll be needing therapy on my account. Me and my mayo…go figure."

Chile didn't much care about anything, especially the concerns of waitresses. He could cook, though. Eddie walked by the line a couple of times, helping Scott to retrieve some bus pans from the waiter hole, and he never saw anyone move that fast. Chile was turning steaks and slamming the oven and closing the steamer and opening bread drawers and walk-ins and reach-ins and pulling tickets and dropping fries into the oil and setting plates and firing up food, moving in a blur from one end of the line to the other. He was a good line cook, that was for sure. But he was a son of a bitch to work with and the waitresses let him know it at every opportunity. It quite often escalated into heated wars of words, and Chile, on this particular occasion, heaved a thick spoonful of mayonnaise at the swinging doors just as Lisa went out with her plain turkey sandwich.

"Here's the side order, bitch," he said. And Scott, who had pretty much established himself in Chile's corner, gave out a loud laugh, punched him on the shoulder, and then beckoned Eddie to clean up the mess.

"When you get a chance," Scott said.

"Sorry, bro," Chile said, winking at Eddie. "Hate to make you work harder. The bitches do it to me every time. No regard for my job."

Chile came back to the dish area a little later to wash his saute pans in the sink. Eddie watched him as he fired up a cigarette; he let it hang from his mouth while he worked the scrubby in a circular motion about the pans.

"I thought we weren't supposed to smoke in the kitchen," Eddie said.

"Yeah well fuck Scott and his rules," Chile said. "If I can wing mayo at Lisa, I can smoke, that's my theory." Chile hung the pans over the sink as he finished each of them and then flicked his cigarette into the garbage chute. "And if I can smoke in the jungles of Nam, I can smoke in a God-damned second-rate kitchen."

"How long were you there?" Eddie asked, not really caring, but figuring that Chile would appreciate his interest.

"Two God-forsaken years," Chile said. "Had me cooking in the hospital, you know, cooking the regular stuff that army hospitals dish up, mashed potatoes and roast beef, the same old powdered shit…" Chile edged closer, as if he were about to let Eddie in on a secret. "Let me tell you, though, while I was stationed there, about a year in, the Viet Cong went and shot down the relief planes that were supposed to bring in the medical and food supplies, shot them all the fuck down. We didn't know what to do because the food ran out and we had a hospital full of hungry people to feed. We had to go out into the jungles. The doctors, the nurses, the cooks, all of us—had to go looking for food. We were picking berries at first and finding citrus fruits, things like that. Then we went for the beetles. Giant things under logs, insects with a million fucking legs….hell, we were grabbing anything."

"And you cooked all of this up?"

"Have you ever had sauteed millipede, my friend?"

"Can't say that I have."

"Well nothing beats it….and nothing beat the most prized feast of all…monkey stew."

"Monkey stew?"

"Monkey stew, fried monkey brains, monkey salad, monkey-ka-bobs, monkey fucking everything. We had a doctor who knew how to catch the things by the dozen…apparently, they all went crazy over some sort of men's cologne. Yeah, Doc Jeffries…he'd go out and lay a little of the cologne in a trail through the bushes, right up to the traps and, bam, before you know it we were bringing them back in crates, little fanged gibbons screaming and howling and mauling each other."

"Who killed them?"

"Hell, me of coarse. I was the cook. Shut every one of them fuckers up." Chile held out his arm, which revealed a thick scar running up past his wrist that looked like a deformed vine. "Son of a bitch gibbon got me good just before I slit his hairy throat with a French knife."

Chile walked out of the dish area and back toward the line. "I'll tell you what though, bro. Those men never ate so good. They scarfed up that monkey and told me it was the best roast beef they ever had. And me, I never cooked so good in my whole life. If I could get me a crate of those fuckers over here right now, today, I'd wow the shit out of every-body. I'd write my ticket into chef history. I could write me a monkey cook-book and make me a million."

VII

Domingus came in early again, his left arm in a splint. He had pasted a band-aid to a cut in the middle of his forehead and its adhesive prop-erties had begun to dissolve, leaving it dangling over one of his eyes and revealing the deep gash that had just begun to heal. Eddie surmised that some sort of altercation had taken place over the stolen shrimp and Domingus had paid the price.

"I need to get extra hours," he told Eddie. "The hospital charge me two hundred dollars to fix me up. I need to pay for it. No insurance, no nothing."

"What happened,?" Eddie asked.

"My brother get me in alley. He get me with a bat."

"Why?"

"He say I take his girl. He say that the only love he ever know and I mess up his whole life for him. He say he can never forgive."

"Did you take his girl?"

"Margaret, she a very beautiful woman." Domingus smiled, which served to open up the cut on his forehead, forging a little droplet of blood. His band-aid dropped to the ground. "I can no resist a beautiful woman, brother or no brother." Then, donning his whites: "I think I go and get her name tattooed on my arm when it get better."

Eddie ate his burger in the break room, a cold piece of meat that Chile had slapped onto a burned roll. He did get some freshly cooked steak fries, though, and he buried them under a mountain of ketchup and shoved them into his mouth as the night waitresses came in and set up their stations. He could see the womens' movements as he ate: they were watching him, the skinny little day dishwasher with the tear-stained face, wondering what he was all about, shuffling about him with the pepper mills, the salt shakers, and the Bissell. He had spilled some ketchup on himself, as he came to notice; he saw the red blotch in the middle of his shirt and he could feel the wet ketchup drying on his face. He had to look like hell, what with the creek water and the tear stains, and now the ketchup. But he was hungry, and all that mattered now was that he finish everything in front of him, get out., and make himself presentable.

Lisa walked into the room and sat down in the booth with Eddie, who had by this time finished a mouthful of fries and picked up his burger.

"I see Chile made you one of his leftover specials," she said.

"Yeah well I take what I can get, being hungry as hell and all," Eddie said after the mouthful was washed down. "Besides, it's better than eating a monkey-ka-bob."

"A what?"

"Oh, nothing. Chile was just telling me about his time in Nam, how he went out into the jungles when he was cooking at the hospital there, and caught and cooked monkeys and stuff."

Lisa leaned in. "Let me tell you something," she whispered. "Chile never went to Nam."

"Sure he did," Eddie said. "That's all he ever talks about. I knew the guy before I even started here from my friend Billy and…"

"Hey, I dated him for a year," Lisa said. "He had me over his parent's house one Sunday afternoon to watch a Phillies game and I got to talking to his mother while he and his dad were buried in the game. She took me up into the kitchen to talk and I found out that Chile couldn't get into the military because of his bad teeth." Lisa looked around the room as the night waitress with the Bissell brushed by. She waited for her to move to the other end of the room, out of ear-shot and beyond the dividers.

"Why would he lie?" Eddie asked into his ketchup.

"Well, his mother starts telling me about his older brother Leo, who got sent over to Nam back in '68 or so. His mother, right there in the kitchen, starts crying and moaning about poor Leo, how he disappeared. His platoon woke up one morning and found his sleeping bag empty and his gun still there. They reported that he was acting strange that whole day before, whispering little poems to himself and carving crosses into trees. They reported that he just got up in the middle of the night and walked right into the enemy camp. His whole platoon, every one of them, thought that Leo went off the deep end, that the war snapped some circuit in his brain. He went and got himself shot up by the Viet Cong. War suicide, they call it."

"Did you talk to Chile about what his mother told you?"

"I tried to, but he went wacko on me. On the way home, he guns the car up over a hundred. He starts screaming that it's none of my damned business what his family is all about and that Leo is still alive somewhere and that his mother is crazy. He tells me no, Leo didn't head into the enemy camp but instead high-tailed it into Indochina where he went AWOL. Chile says he's living a care-free life somewhere with an Oriental wife and a couple of kids. He says one of his platoon buddies told him that in a bar one night, and that it was a secret never to be told."

"Did you ask him why he lied about being there?"

"He continued the crap about his mother being full of shit. He said that she didn't want to believe that only one of her sons came home and that she tells everyone that story because Chile was just a cook in an army hospital and he wasn't risking his life out there in the jungle like Leo. He wasn't gunning down the gooks like his older brother so he wasn't really there."

"Did you believe him?"

"Of course I didn't believe him and I told him that. That's when he opened the car door, took his foot, and shoved me out."

"At a hundred?"

"He'd slowed to forty or so. I landed in some bushes and wound up breaking my wrist. That was over a year ago, and I still hate the son of a bitch."

"I can't believe you can still work with him."

"It's amazing what you can do when you put your mind to it."

As Eddie went back to his burger, Lisa got up from the table to check on the late customers sitting in her station. He could hear her talking about the desserts—the different flavors of sherbet, the pies, the chocolate mousse, the rice pudding. Her voice sounded different, as if she had transformed herself as she entered the station, robot-like in her presentation. There was none of that anger there, none of that humanness that had flowered in front of Eddie at the break table. She was Lisa the waitress now, and she went about her business, working with her smile for the three or four extra dollars that might come attached to the check.

VIII

As the sun dropped behind the trees, Eddie walked with his shadow under the bridge and searched for the dark hole that he now claimed as home. A large truck rumbled over the bridge, shaking some dust from the cement rafters. Pigeons flapped out of the crevices, away from their nests and out the other side. Eddie looked downstream: the Neshaminy had lowered itself considerably since the morning overflow. There were thick logs, rocks, dead grass, and assorted paper products washed up beneath the bridge, caught in clumps that had formed into towering straw sculptures. He could see the creek as it curved around the bend out past the slanted elms. The sewage station was out beyond that bend, churning up the white foamy blobs and depositing them into the creek. Then the dark water, black like Coke, spewed non-stop out of the pipes and ran an ugly film a mile further on. He could smell the chemicals from beneath the bridge. Hot days did that. The heat carried a sour odor upstream with the wind and sometimes it would carry clear over to the houses on the other side of the woods and stink up just about all of Fergusonville.

They had found the boy down there, dead in the water. At least that's what the man on the bridge had told Eddie. They must have found him floating among the white blobs. They must have pulled him out of the stink, his corpse stained by black chemicals, his eyes glazed over by stagnant sewer water. Eddie figured with the way the creek was raging that morning that the boy had no chance at all. He must have slid right down the slippery bank just in front of the chain link fence and dropped into the churning chemicals. Logs must have come along, thick as his waist, spinning and clubbing him, beating him into the bottom of the swell. That poor kid never had a prayer, dragged down into the black hell of suffocation, pulled along the bottom and ripped downstream like some tumbling minnow.

Something told Eddie that the boy was not alone down there by the sewage station. Someone must have been with him, watched him go in, tried to reach his hands into the raging current to pull him free. But it was no good. The boy on the bank, whoever he was, watched him disappear and then went for help. He took off in a panic through the grass, across the stones and up the hill to the top of the bridge. Wet from the rain, he flagged down a car and pleaded for help. It might have been an old woman whom he stopped. The lady gave him a ride to the police station, where, in a burst of tears, he told his story. They all rushed to the sewage station, policemen and rescue units donned in yellow raincoats and armed with spotlights and thick ropes and bullhorns through which to call out a name. They searched and searched the swollen creek at the spot where the boy pointed and they followed the raging current down further and further until they found him, dead among the branches and the film.

Who was that someone? Who was that boy who had watched the other boy, in those frantic seconds, slide helplessly down the bank into the death-swirl? Eddie thought about that for a long time. He thought about it as he crawled into his cave, as he balled up his shirt in the corner, as he covered the entrance with some boulders and laid down on the newspapers to go to sleep. Laying in the dark, listening to the cars move across the bridge over him and then finally drifting off, Eddie couldn't help thinking that the boy standing on the bank was the boy's brother. From the top of the hill, he had watched, with hopeless and desperate eyes, as the black water took his brother down.

Circle of Saints

───────────◆───────────

I

Eddie went to cash his first pay check at Lincoln bank, and he had to hide behind the rubber plants because Mr. Sheehan came in to make a deposit. Luckily, Eddie saw him approaching from the parking lot with his hacking cough, and he was able to get himself behind the plants in time; otherwise, Mr. Sheehan would have spotted him, wrestled him to the ground, and dragged him home for the reward: a thousand, two thousand, three thousand dollars by now.

The armed guard, a large black man standing by the double doors, looked over at him. Suspicious, his hand moved to his holster. Eddie peered out from behind the thick leaves, watching Mr. Sheehan as he slid his check under the partition. The guard approached him, walking cautiously across the carpet. Mr. Sheehan waited and the Musak came to a stop, dropping the room into whispered echoes. The teller counted out the bills, and Mr. Sheehan began to look around the room. His eyes inevitably ventured across and scanned the rubber plants and the hidden Eddie, who waited nervously for his departure.

He felt a whirlpool of panic churning in his gut and he pleaded silently with his eyes for the teller to hurry things along. The guard closed in. Come on, come on, come on, Eddie willed across the room. Get done with the deposit, get done with it and get out, get out.

"Some kind of problem?" the guard asked. The big man in the blue uniform had squeezed himself into the little corner with Eddie, and his gun brushed up against Eddie's stained shirt. The guard glared suspiciously down at him, down at the filthy Eddie Shemanski and his much-needed pay check.

"Oh no," he whispered. "Just lost my check back here. It floated off the table and fell behind the plant. Got it now though thanks."

Eddie walked out from behind the plant, feeling the man breathing on him. The guard moved past, in a blue blur, to resume his place by the double doors. Mr. Sheehan stood at the window, still waiting for the teller to finish, and Eddie went to the table and picked up the chained pen. He had signed his name already, but now he pretended to sign it again, with his head down and between his arms, scribbling the air. He waited to hear the 'have a nice day' from the teller, for Mr. Sheehan to be on his way, for the coast to clear. The guard had moved back to his statue position near the door, and Eddie could feel his eyes burning a hole of suspicion through him. If Eddie had a gun on him, and if he could shoot another person, he might have pulled it out and dropped him right there.

Mr. Sheehan left without turning around, grunted a 'thanks' at the teller and headed off into the daylight of the parking lot. Eddie rushed to the window ahead of an old woman (probably from Hudson) who had just come through the double doors. He cut right in front of her as she headed up the roped-in walkway with her cane and her check.

"Hey careful," called the guard from his station. "No running in the bank and mind other patrons."

The old woman said nothing, but he could feel her silent scolding suspended in the walkway like a ball of stagnant smoke: "Damned kids these days."

After a long set of moments which Eddie watched tick off the bank clock, the teller slid the money under the partition. He grabbed the thick bundle and shoved it into his pocket. Money. Now he was going to be o.k. Now he was going to start on the road back to recovering himself, to getting the things that he needed to get his life in order. He headed over to the shops along Millcourt and bought some shirts, another pair of pants, a bottle of hand soap and some shampoo. Then he stopped into the diner and ate down an open-faced turkey sandwich and swallowed two big glasses of Pepsi. He figured that he would need somewhere to keep his money, so he went into the stationary store and bought himself a big metal box with a key. That would be his money box, where he'd put all the cash he saved, until he had just enough for an apartment.

Eddie felt a little uneasy with that much cash in his pocket, over a hundred dollars. He should have asked for twenties instead of fives. His pockets were small, and he could see the wad of bills sticking out as he walked. Guarding the cash with his hand to prevent it from dropping to the ground, he spotted two men, big and fat and smoking cigarettes, watching him from a doorway. They shut up when he got close, and they no doubt saw the bills billowing from his pants. He looked for a store where he might buy a wallet, a quick flash of eyes up and down the block, but saw nothing.

That was it. He went behind a closed-up tavern and took the metal box and opened it. He unloaded his pockets and put the money in and locked it, then hurried across Millcourt and into the subdivision. He risked getting spotted; a boy running with wide eyes and a big metal box would no doubt be noticed. He had to look like some sort of criminal with his bag of clothes and his hidden money, a stranger fleeing from the scene of a freshly-committed felony. He couldn't wait to get to his cave under the bridge, to change his shirt and bury his money, wash his face in the creek and look normal again.

Some kids were playing baseball in their front yard on Sinkler as he dashed by them. A whiffle ball came sailing out into the street, dropped to the asphalt, and rolled just in front of him. The boys stood and waited for Eddie to stop, bend down and retrieve the ball. But he was caught in a dead run, and another pang of paranoia flared up at him as he eyed the boys standing and waiting on the lawn. They had hit that ball over to him on purpose. They wanted him to slow and then stop to pick it up. It was all a set-up. When he came over with their ball, or even if he stopped and threw it back, they were all going to attack. They were going to grab his metal box and take off between the houses. They had seen him put the money in the box behind the tavern, and they ran ahead and devised their little 'game.' They were good, they were definitely good, right down to the perfectly placed ball and the way they formed their little circle on the lawn.

Eddie ran up the long street, faster now, looking left, looking right, trying to find the best place to cut through a yard and be free of them. "Hey thanks a lot goober," one of the boys shouted out. Eddie, clutching his box and his bag of clothes tightly against his chest, disappeared across the lawn of a shuttered house. There was no one to peek through the windows there, no one to shout out 'criminal' and come out, so he cut through to the safety of Perry Street.

II

Eddie began to dig a hole near the cave. He piled some stones, some of the blood-stained ones even, on top of his money box, and then sprinkled broken glass over the area, so that it blended in with the other rocks near the cave. Now it was safe. Now the baseball boys would never find it, and if they did, they'd get all cut up trying. He took the clothes out of his bag, the new pair of shorts and a t-shirt, and slipped into his cave to change.

Just as he got down to his underwear, he heard the voices coming up the Neshaminy. They were close, probably at the edge of the bridge. He moved the stones quickly over the entrance and peeked out. Two boys were wading though the middle of the creek in hip boots. One of the boys carried a large green fishing net. They were peering down into the murky water, looking for fish no doubt. They may have been looking for turtles even, though Eddie knew that all of the turtles were long gone, killed off by the sewage and the developments, the motherlode buried by bulldozers back at the Donut Pond.

The boys waded under the bridge. Eddie quietly slipped into his new shorts, hoping that the boys did not know about his secret cave just above them on the hill. He looked down as they came into view: it was Prettyman and Murphy from St. Anselm. There they were, out of their green ties and their white shirts, clad instead in tank tops and hip boots and searching for non-existent turtles. Eddie felt an impulse to remove the rocks from the entrance, to go sliding down the rocky bank and greet them. In fact, Eddie got as far as grabbing one of the boulders to move it before he changed his mind.

Prettyman's face out in the middle of the creek made it all come back: that little son of a bitch had turned Eddie in for flashing his pen knife at recess one afternoon in the sixth grade. Eddie was just playing around; he had worn his Scout uniform to school that day. Billy and his friend Martin, impressed with his uniform, had gone over to the trees and brought back some sticks, piled them in the middle of the school-yard, handed Eddie a pack of matches, and asked him to show them how to light a campfire. So Eddie got out his pen knife and had begun to whittle some of the branches down, instructing Billy and Martin on the proper way of piling the sticks, like a little teepee. A crowd gathered, some eighth graders even, and Prettyman and Murphy pushed through and saw Eddie there with the knife. Eddie, in a bit of a joking mood, went up to Prettyman and said, "And if any of you says a word about all of this, Pretty boy here gets it."

Then it all happened in a rush, as Eddie made his way in after recess, after the little fire had been stamped out, the crowd dispersed. Mother Superior threw him up against the wall and dragged him by his ear down to the office, past all of the filled classrooms. Eddie figured that he would get a little lecture about starting fires in schoolyards, at which point he would flash his Tenderfoot badge, throw out some kindling knowledge, and maintain that 'everything was under control, Mother.' But she had him stand up in the middle of the room and then she frisked him. On her way down the length of his pants, she felt the heavy chunk of metal at the bottom of his pocket, reached in, and retrieved it: KNIFE.

Eddie was sent home that day and fortunately saved from expulsion by a fit of sobs from his wailing mother. She explained to Mother Superior that Eddie just wanted to show off his Scouting skills, that he meant no harm to any one, and that he would come over and help out at the convent or something to make up for things. So, it was agreed, in order for Eddie to avoid expulsion, he had to paint the church rectory. It took him five Sundays to do it, and he made a permanent mess of the tiled floor, but Eddie got that giant room finished. All the while, up on the ladder with the roller, he was thinking about the harmless knife, that dull harmless knife, that he had used to whittle down the sticks, and that all he ever wanted to do was impress the eighth graders.

Now here he was, that sneaky Prettyman, wading down the creek in his hip boots. Eddie, in all the years following his knife fiasco, had never approached him with the blame, never cornered him or called him 'rat' or 'snitch' or 'stoolie.' But he knew he was the one that had gone barreling down to Mother Superior, whining that Eddie Shemanski had pulled a knife on him. And now Eddie's rage boiled up as he felt the pressing desire to remove the boulders and head down there, kick his ass right in the middle of the creek while his little buddy Murphy watched in horror with his empty net… He wanted to take Prettyman's head and dunk it forever into the water. "You want turtles? You want turtles?" Look for the damned turtles you little piece of shit."

Of coarse, Eddie would have to reveal his secret cave if he did all of that, reveal his presence as the runaway. Prettyman and Murphy were the last people he wanted finding out about the cave, about him, because they would head right to the police. Hell, Prettyman might even go back to Mother Superior for this one.

The boys moved out the other side of the bridge. "Wait I thaw thomething," Murphy said in his lisp. "A huge silver fith just took off, I think it was a pike."

"We'll never catch one of those," Prettyman replied. "Silver....too fast."

Eddie laid his head against the cave wall and waited for the voices to trail off. Then he went down to the edge of the creek, after the boys had disappeared past the slanted elms, and worked some shampoo into his hair. He dipped his head in at the place where the water ran over the mossy stones, feeling the water, despite its filthiness, cleansing him. He put his t-shirt on and headed up the hill, out to find some things to eat, out to sit in the sun in Kemper Park and think about things.

III

It happened while he was at the break table, eating another one of Chile's leftover specials. Lisa had just come from another late table and had to cash out. She sighed about something, though Eddie could barely make out her complaint, and was headed to the double doors of the kitchen to punch out. Then the night waitress came out from behind the partition with the Bissell and ran over her foot, trying to get the day dirt from the floor.

"Watch what you're doing, o.k.?" Lisa said.

"Let's get this straight," the Bissell waitress said. "*You're* in *my* way. That's the way it is...you're done and I'm on the floor...so you're in my way." Then she moved along, slowly, making sure to brush Lisa one more time.

During this slight altercation, and unbeknownst to Eddie, who was busy salting his fries, the day waitresses had come in from the kitchen door one by one, while the night waitresses, still busy with their set-up, had begun to file in from beyond the dividers on the opposite side of the room.

Lisa, who must have frayed her nerves already with a bad tip (or another argument with Chile), turned and slugged the Bissell waitress across her face. "You fucking bitch," she screamed. "You leave your shit for us to clean every night and we're tired of it. We spend half the morning cleaning you up."

Eddie stopped with the salt and watched as the night waitress, her nose bloodied, raised her Bissell into the air and brought it down squarely onto Lisa's skull. Lisa crumpled to the floor, and the armies converged, day and night waitresses, in a melee of angry shouts and finger nails and pepper mills, just in front of Eddie at the break table. Lisa, sprawled on the floor in a daze, dragged herself over to the divider and watched her fellow day waitresses grab and pull the hair of the nights, screaming and cussing them as they attacked with their weapons.

"You think you're so great because you're the night shift and you make more tips than us," the fat pink-jeaned waitress said. "Well here's something special." She swung her fist back and planted it directly to an older waitress's eye. "Die bitch die," she said, and the older waitress dropped her pepper mill and fell in a daze across the break table. Eddie had to quick pick up his meal to avoid her falling into it and squishing his burger. The old woman got up, turned, and pulled the fat girl's long brown hair and yanked her head down. She screamed and then tumbled over and fell with a thud to the floor, rumbling the tables.

Eddie took a bite of his burger and continued to watch the melee with a bit of delight. After all, he was just a harmless dishwasher who was neutral to the whole thing, the new guy who knew nothing about anything. Except for Lisa, he didn't even know any of their names. "Hey,

I'm Switzerland," he said to one of the angry women, and swallowed some Coke.

Scott and Chile came bursting through the door just as a high chair came flying from over the divider. It was Lisa, dazed and angry, searching with fury for the Bissell waitress. "Where are you Leslie?" she screamed. "I'll kill you."

"Whoa, Lisa, calm down," Chile said, grabbing her before she could get to the high chair. "Take it light."

"Who the hell are you to tell me to take it light, after you kicked me out of a moving car."

"Now let's not get into that." Chile pulled her by her arm through the double doors to the kitchen.

"I'm calling the police and pressing charges," Eddie heard her say before the doors closed off their voices.

"Let's all calm down," Scott said. "Let's all put down our pepper mills and talk this out, before there's a serious injury."

Scott walked nervously across the room, adjusting his glasses. "Leslie, tell the girls to put their weapons down."

Leslie whispered something to one of the other night waitresses and then began to collect the pepper mills. Eddie could see the fury still consuming her, the blood still rushing across her face. She was shaking too, as she took the wobbling tray of pepper mills away behind the divider.

"Scott you need to tell them," the pink-jeaned waitress said. "You need to put your foot down."

"Don't tell me how to do things, Annie," Scott said. "I'm pretty close to firing the whole damned bunch of you right now."

A tall man with a foo-man-chu moustache entered the room. He'd doused himself in cologne and slicked back his hair into a rock sculpture, and his pot belly swung like a lead balloon. "What's the problem here Scotty?, he asked.

"Oh hi Jackie," Scott stammered. "A little tiff between your waitresses and mine."

Eddie deduced that Jackie was the night manager and that Scott feared this big, imposing man. Scott's eyes widened as Jackie approached him with his big hairy hands. Eddie guessed that the two had had it out at some other point in time, and that Jackie, in that heated moment, had gotten the best of him. There had been some physical threats, no doubt, something to reduce him to his eyes of fear.

"A tiff?" Jackie asked.

"Tell him Scott," Annie said. "Go on, tell him what we're sick of…"

"Why don't you go punch the hell out," Scott returned in anger. "Get out of here. I'll see you tomorrow and we'll talk about this more."

Jackie put his arm around Scott and squeezed his bony shoulder. "Tell me what, gumba? You got something you need to unload on me?"

"Let's talk about this in private," Scott said, paler suddenly. The two men walked off through the double doors. Eddie could not hear what they were saying, but through the door windows he could see Scott's fear rising another level, as he readjusted his glasses and felt Jackie's uncomfortable embrace guiding him back to privacy.

Lisa came through the doors and slipped into the booth with Eddie, giving out a long sigh and rubbing her skull. "The police are on their way," she said. "I'm going to nail Leslie for assault, then I'm going to drive myself over to the hospital and see if they can't diagnose a concussion or something."

"Are you bleeding or anything?" Eddie asked.

"No blood. But I've got a mountain-sized bump, I can tell you that much. And I'm dizzy besides."

Eddie heard the sound of the dispatches coming from behind the partition, and then two policemen entered the room toting their night sticks and guns. Panic: Eddie the runaway squirmed in his seat as they approached the booth, his heart pounding in rapid thumps. This was it.

He could do nothing but wait now, wait to see if they recognized his face, the one that they had probably memorized from the pictures posted at the station that his parents had given them. If he ran they would surely suspect something, nail him before he got to the kitchen doors, fire off some warning shots if he got any further, shoot him by the time he made it to the dock. As they approached Lisa and her bump he just sat in fear, pale and trembling and waiting for the end to come.

Lisa explained the entire altercation to the policemen. She let them know all about the flying fists and the pepper mills and the high chairs, and about the Bissell that had made the welt on her skull. She inevitably let the policemen know that she had started the whole thing with her punch and her built-up anger.

"Well you can press charges for assault, but so can she," one of the officers said. "It'll be a lot of time and paperwork, and my guess is that it will all just make things worse. If I were you, I would best drop the whole thing. It's not worth all of the trouble."

The other officer had gone off to calm down Leslie and several of the other night waitresses (they had assembled behind the partition to listen to Lisa's complaint). There were some shouts rising up as Lisa sighed and agreed. Eddie knew she wanted to get up and slug another night waitress, though. She wanted to pound that Bissell waitress into the carpet and vacuum her the hell up, vacuum all of them up. In the ensuing silence, the officer looked across the table, right into Eddie's nervous eyes. Eddie looked away, down at his cold remaining fries and his half-eaten burger.

"Did you get involved in any of this?" asked the policemen.

"Oh no Officer," Eddie said. "I just tried to sit and finish my burger." Then he took some of the cold fries and casually swirled them around in the nearly-dried ketchup and put them into his mouth. "I don't like to fight with girls," he mumbled.

The officer smiled and got up, asking the way to the office. Eddie figured that he was safe now. In fact, as the officers left the break room, it was the safest he had felt in a long time, maybe since the nights back home in his closet box.

On his way to punch out, he saw the two policeman in the office, sitting in chairs and listening to Scott. He couldn't make out the words, so he moved closer and watched their movements. Eddie pressed his face to the glass: Scott's glasses were gone from his face, his hair had been mussed and a fresh cut had formed over one of his eyes. Then, in the far corner of the office, Eddie noticed Jackie, hair hanging over his face, his hands behind his back, cuffed to a chair and his belly drooping nearly to the floor. One of the officers turned and looked through the window, the same one who had eyeballed Eddie at the break table. Move along, his eyes said. This is none of your business.

Eddie punched out and wondered what had happened in there. He bet himself that Jackie was right in the middle of whipping Scott's ass when they had walked in. He had him down on the floor or up against the wall, wailing on him with his fists and demanding he apologize for the things his day waitresses had gone and done. Scott, at least by the look that had registered on his face through the glass, had no doubt given in to Jackie's request, in a whimpering stammer of 'I'm sorry it will never happen again sir.' And then, too late to save him from humiliation, the policemen had walked in and yanked that bastard Jackie up, out of his death-grip and into the cuffs.

IV

Just after Eddie had closed off his cave to the world, and in the pitch blackness beneath the bridge, he heard the sound of whispers echoing off the cement walls, from the other side of the Neshaminy. Eddie peered out from between the boulders, hoping for some light to reveal things to him.

Then it came: the striking of the matches, the fingers dropping the light to the ground, and the underside of the bridge bathed in a blaze of flame as a pile of sticks went up. Seven faces, he counted. Seven gathered around the sticks that they had piled in virtual silence. They must have added something to make the sticks go up like that…lighter fluid or fire-starters, gasoline maybe. The flames rose high into the air, illuminating the roof of the bridge, and the light became so bright that Eddie saw the shadows of his boulders elongate across the cave floor. The fire disrupted several pigeons as they flew out from their nests in fright, out into the darkness downstream. Eddie became nervous as well in his own nest, and he pressed himself against the side wall of the cave and watched his shadow flicker on the newspapers as the voices rose.

"Let's get started," one of the seven said. Eddie watched them from his vantage point. Merged with the fire, he saw older men, men in their forties or fifties. Their gray, drab clothes blended them, like chameleons, into the flickering concrete, so that only the glow of their faces existed in that confined universe on the other side of the black creek, suspended like balloons above the fire. They began to retrieve sheets of paper and bring them into the light, shuffling them about and passing them around the circle that they had formed.

"Everybody got a pen?" asked one of the seven, and the glowing heads all nodded. "Finbar, I believe it's your turn to begin, is it not?"

One of the seven stood in front of the fire, a tall balding man who bent down and peered into the flame, spreading his hands out over the fire as if it were some raging sea which he was about to calm. He passed them over the flames as the kindling cracked and as the other men sat silent and watched his every movement with wide expecting eyes.

"It happened when I was sixteen," he said, motionless. His voice resonated in a perfect acoustic cadence as it came across the water, as if he were standing in front of a microphone. "There were the usual things, you know, the suspicious whispers my parents made from their bedroom, the way I stood out different in the family photos. Hell, my skin was all wrong." The man held his arms out over the fire, and then brought his hands to his face. "You see, I'm dark. I'm dark as hell, and well, everyone around me, my two sisters, my dad, my mom, aunts, uncles, grandmothers, great grandmothers, all of the pictures of all of my so-called relatives......they were all pale, pale, pale."

In the brief seconds of silence that followed, Eddie began to gather some things about these seven men. They were here by design. There was no doubt that they had done this here before, assembled under the bridge around a raging fire to talk about things, united in some common cause. Eddie watched as they began to scribble on their papers, their eyes intent, as they focused on getting things down, looking and waiting for the man's next words.

"Anyway," Finbar continued, "it's late one night, after the news, after the TV's shut off, and my dad comes home late from work. It's a school night and they think I'm off to sleep. Most times I was at this time of night, but there was a big accident somewhere on the other side of town and the sirens woke me. So I start hearing the whispering again from their bedroom, and this time I can't take it no more. I have to find out what's being said, so I slip down and listen outside their door. It's a little open, and I can see them over by the big desk where the light is still going. Then I hear what I suspected from the day I looked at myself in the mirror." He paused, and the men stopped with their writing and moved their heads closer.

"My dad, he starts whispering that someone, a detective, had picked up a trail, a lead that he'd been following for fifteen years. He says that this detective comes to his office and starts asking questions about a kidnapped kid named Jonathan. He says the kid was taken right out of a baby carriage at a bus terminal in Reading, Pennsylvania, sixteen years back. No one had a clue who did it, and the mother of the baby, who began to scream hysterically, dropped dead right there in front of the carriage of some seizure. This detective told my dad all of this, and then my mother asked him what was going on."

Finbar stopped and pulled out a cigarette, stuck his face almost into the flame and lit the thing as the six pens worked furiously to get things down. "I can see my dad through the crack of the door," he puffed. "He's right there above the lamp. I see he's worried as hell, and my mother...well I can see her shadow bouncing around the room, her hand going to her head over and over. 'They're on to us', she says. 'They'll figure it all out before long', she says. 'They'll come to the house and have us assemble the kids together, and then they'll see how Jimmy sticks out. They'll want to see the pictures, especially the baby pictures, and they'll have their own and they'll whip them out and they'll match. They'll get us for kidnapping', she says. Then she dives onto the bed and starts bawling like hell."

A truck rumbled over the top of the bridge and shook more cement dust from the rafters. It rained down in a fine powder and lit up in a sprinkle of sparks above the fire. Eddie could not believe what he was hearing. He had now moved directly to the front of his cave, peering out through the boulders as he fixed his eyes on Finbar, his cigarette, and the other men gathering closer as the circle tightened.

"I'm still at the door but at this point I'm devastated," he said. "I don't know what to do, how to react to everything I'm hearing. I really want to burst in there and kill the both of them right then. But then my head keeps pounding the names back and forth at me like a game of ping-pong...Jonathan...Jimmy...Jonathan...Jimmy...Jonathan...Jimmy... that's all that's going through my head, those two names, and I get to thinking: who in the living hell am I? what is this hallway, this house, these people? I don't belong in any of this, I belong in the house of the woman at the bus station. She should be alive and raising me in Reading, or wherever the hell she was headed to on that Greyhound. I'm a Jonathan, from a family with dark skin. I might be Italian, I might be

Greek. Hell, my father might even be a black man…but he's my father."
Finbar sighed and flicked the end of his cigarette into the fire. "He's my
father, I'm thinking and he's somewhere out there…not his pasty
bloated son of a bitch criminal standing over the lamp."

One of the other men raised his hand. "That's when you took off,
wasn't it Finbar? That's when you saw no other way."

"My mind is spinning," Finbar said. "My identity is shot to hell. I'm a
kid in confusion, thinking suicide and murder, all of the horrible
thoughts they reduced me to. I go upstairs and I cry all night. I stick my
head in the pillow and I pound my fists into the mattress and I pretend
I'm killing them in their bedroom, whack whack whack, with one of the
kitchen knives. I'm mad as hell but I lock myself in. I make sure my pillow is wrapped around my head, and I scream as loud as I can into the
mattress. I mean I scream with all the power I've got in my lungs and
muffle it so it doesn't leave the room. I scream and scream and scream
until my throat burns dry."

" I'm up all night and I don't finish crying until morning. And then
I get up and act like I always do. I go down and eat my cereal, put on
my knapsack, and head off to school. The only difference on this day is
that I'm never coming back. I tell my mom I need money for school
pictures, thirty dollars. She gives it to me and I take off with a knapsack
of clothes across the fields of New York state. And all the while I'm
walking, hiking from town to town, as the days and nights pass, I'm
thinking about my name…and who I was, who I really was back there
in that house…Jimmy…God-damned Jimmy Milbourne. And you
know, guys, I came to realize it didn't matter. I was who I was, a kid in
a bedroom where I never belonged, with some son of a bitch father
that just took me out of a carriage for whatever demented reason. Hell,
maybe he took all of my so-called brothers and sisters for that matter,
the sick fuck. I decide I'm not going to stand around and watch the FBI
come barging into the house and tear up the family, take me away, send

me back to wherever it is I came from and cause all sorts of screaming and mayhem. Hell, I would be a stranger there…I'd have to live in some government housing project, and that's the last place a person should have to live." Finbar stood up and passed his hands over the flames, and then looked at each of the men huddled into the tight circle. "So now I'm walking the roads and I'm thinking I am who I am— someone in search of a name. And I've got thirty fucking dollars and I can be whoever I want to be."

"Hail to Finbar," the men said. They stood and they put down their papers and their pens. They stood and consumed him into their circle and they applauded him, they hugged him, then cheered him some more. They patted him on the back with thuds and let their noise echo across the Neshaminy as he hung his head and wept openly over the raging fire. "Hail to fucking Finbar."

The men disassembled after consoling Finbar on the logs. They whispered things into his ears, and made loud promises that they would take their papers and look into things. Two of the men doused the flames with creek water and the bridge once again fell into the darkness. Then they moved on into the night, out the other side and up the grassy hill to the top of the bridge, vowing to meet again.

V

Life is a river, Eddie thought. Everything comes from one source and flows into the same place, with backwaters and currents that pull things of equal weight together and carry them along. How else could he explain this remarkable assemblage that he had witnessed beneath the bridge? Could it be fate that brought him here to this cave? To the exact spot where these men had gathered for their ritual fire? That they were all kidnap victims, and he had a missing brother who was a kidnap victim? Was there a God that had designs on things, that put Eddie in this cave for a purpose, to hear what these seven men had to say?

The men with the gray clothes certainly had a purpose. Eddie couldn't sleep because he tried to figure out that purpose. They must all have stories to tell, just like Finbar. They all might be runaways or kidnap victims, gathered together after meeting each other in bars or at their jobs or through some personal ads in the newspaper. They arranged their meetings by some code, by secret phone calls or messages left in parks, and then they whisked themselves away from their families and friends and met here, Tuesday night under the bridge, to talk about their mysterious pasts.

Eddie knew he wasn't going to get much sleep. He had bought a little pillow and a bed sheet with his spending money, and he laid down with them in the dark cave. Certainly he was more comfortable now; he wouldn't awake with the imprint of the newspaper on his face anyway, and if it cooled off and a breeze came up, well he had the sheet. But the disturbing sight of the seven men and their fire blazed on long after the flames had died, and Eddie kept his eyes open and stared at the cave wall. He stared somewhere into the rocky blackness. The wall: it could be any wall in any dark room. Darkness did that, it made everything the same, turned everything to nothing, nothing to everything. It was easier to think in the dark, especially when the noises died away, leaving Eddie to believe he'd become his own universe. It was just like that in the closet box, in Billy's tool shed. Eddie wished he had a joint. A few hits off a joint really made the darkness a better place, filled it with possibilities, made ideas float about like wishies. Maybe he could ask Domingus for some joints when he went in tomorrow. Domingus would have the connections, that was for sure, what with the stolen shrimp and his reputation.

Like a feather, the word "saint" floated into the dark cave and landed on Eddie's brain. In the fifth grade over at St. Anselm, Sister John Rita had burned the word into him—that must have had something to do with the way it just landed there out of nowhere, out of the dark. Sister had pounded those saints into his brain after he didn't get the definition of "saint" right, after trying to impress Billy (and one of the girls in the next row) with his humor by saying "a football player from New Orleans." Sister pulled him right out of his desk and stood him up by the board and made him spout out the true definition, which, by that point, Eddie had laughed into forgetfulness. So, as punishment, he had to go over to the library and learn all about the saints, every one of them from A to Z, and write a one-paragraph report on each. It took him several weeks of detention to complete, and then Sister John Rita took his list and tested him on it, asking him about St. Bartholomew and St. Gregory and St. Alban and St. Cyril, Jerome and Philip and Clement and Agatha. On and on she went, and Eddie rattled them all off, one after the other. Fear had made him memorize that list. Fear. Sister John Rita was going to beat him senseless if he missed one saint, hang him from the coat room hooks by his collar and make him stay there. So he sat in the library and memorized over two hundred saints—Ninian and Daniel and Albertus Magnus and Francis of Paola, all of them—pound, pound, pound—one after the other.

Eddie drifted off to sleep thinking about Father Madrid. He was buying up all of those saint post cards over at 'Catholic Things' just to send them off to Bingo's, a priest on a mission, berated and angry at the evil Freddie O'Hara and his evil restaurant. Father probably couldn't even get the Mass straight, flustered beyond reproach by the name "Bingo's". He was dropping his Lambs of God and spilling his wine on the old ladies from Hudson and fumbling the words to the Homily because he wanted that name changed so bad that he could think of nothing else. Eddie figured it might be best for everybody if Father Madrid just quit the Catholic Church and got out before he lost it completely, before he went and tried to strangle somebody else and invalidate his platinum ticket into Heaven.

Eddie snapped awake from his half-sleep as the name "St. Finbar" flared up and took root in his black cave. That saint was one of the names that he had memorized for Sister John Rita out of the books in the library, out of his fear. Finbar, the Irish saint. Yes, he was a mysterious fellow, an illegitimate child who took off from his family, a guy who joined a bunch of monks and journeyed to Rome on a thousand-mile pilgrimage. He lived most of his life as a hermit, walled up in dark cellars and such, the bulk of his day in prayer. People would come from all over Ireland to surround his monastery, trying to get a glimpse of him as he ventured out for food, knowing that he was touched by God and hoping that they could get some of that magic touch, too. Little, fat, and pink: that's what Eddie remembered about the color plate in "The Big Book of Saints." St. Finbar was little, fat, and pink.

Then there were the miracles, the fantastic miracles. St. Finbar turned hair red and he crossed the Irish Sea on horseback and he did tricks with the moon. When he died, the sun refused to set for two weeks. Sister John Rita, who sat and listened to Eddie as she tested him orally, stepped in as Eddie rattled off the man's miracles and insisted that that was enough about St. Finbar, that it was all a bunch of Irish legend and those things never really happened. Jesus was the only one who could do the water thing, she said. And as for the sun, well, she told Eddie that even miracles have their limitations, and science tells us that the sun has to set every day in the west, and that was that.

Finbar the runaway: the man chose himself a new name; he shed the Jimmy and the Jonathan and he got himself an Irish saint. He sat by that fire, in that circle with the other men, proclaiming his anointment. Finbar was the name he searched for and found, the name that summed up his life: a saint on a pilgrimage of solitude, a man riding his horse over the sea into an eternal sunset.

Were they all named after saints? Had each of those seven men gone and chosen new names as well? What could their other names be?

Erasmus? Hilarion? Robert Bellarmine? Cajetan? All pushing on for their noble causes—that's what saints did all right, keeping a straight path on through the torturous wilderness. Saints died with nothing to their name except gray clothes and ashes, their identities obscured in the endless print piled on library shelves, only to be conjured up by the supposed holy, or by boys serving up their punishments on late afternoons.

Eddie tried to go back to sleep but the saints kept on. He heard the crows starting to caw downstream, probably roosted in the slanted elms as they beckoned the light back to the sky. There were some big ones down there, with wingspans of five feet or more—Eddie had seen them picking at the minnows just after the flood, and they scared him with their beady doll's eyes as they sat undaunted on the rocks.

He got up and removed the stones from his cave, feeling suddenly like Jesus coming out of his tomb, resurrected into the morning air. He saw the blueblack light delivering itself beneath the bridge, the light of five a.m. or thereabouts. Walking gingerly in bare feet to the edge of the creek, he noticed the same crows skulking beneath the bridge, near the ashes that the men had left. He picked up a stone and flung it across the creek, sending them cawing and flapping their black wings into the mass of trees downstream.

Eddie took off his new pants and, in his underwear, waded across the creek. The water was warm, with some sharp, slimy rocks that almost tipped him over. On the other side, amongst the stones, he walked to the ashes that the men had left. They had built a good fire, with the sticks piled just the right way, the logs crossed so that they burned long and even. Yes, they were fire-builders, all right. Some of them might have been Scouts in their day, Life or Eagle even, Scoutmasters perhaps in some other life.

In the ashes, Eddie saw a white slip of half-burned paper with a drawing. He reached between the wet crumbled logs and retrieved it : a smeared cartoon of some sort....a deformed man, with a long inky chin, seven eyes and seven hands, standing beneath a crude sun. Seven: a hand for each of the men around that fire, and an eye for each of them, a symbol no doubt for their mysterious cause and blurred by fire-water. Seven.

VI

When Eddie got to Bingo's, he noticed that Scott's beat-up red car was nowhere to be seen. Instead, alone in the empty lot, he saw the Rolls-Royce parked in front of the door, blocking the handicapped ramp. Freddie O'Hara: Eddie was finally going to meet the feared man. He walked in and saw him behind the bar stacking glasses on the shelf, a short man with a toupee and a thin moustache singing Sinatra to the empty dining room.

"You must be the dishwasher," he said as he broke off his song. "I'm Fred O'Hara." Then, after he'd finished stacking the glasses. "Sit down, I need to ask you some questions."

Fred sat Eddie at the end of the bar, came around and sat down next to him. Fred was shorter than Eddie, and that made him feel a little more secure, especially if he had to defend himself. He didn't know what the sit-down was all about, and he was ready for anything, what with the stories he had been told.

"I had to fire my day manager Scott," Fred said. "It seems he had a little fight in the office with my night manager, and they broke some valuables of mine in there." He looked at Eddie, who twitched nervously on the stool. "Jackie tells me Scott lost control and beat him with a picture of my dead sister. The cops walked in and caught Jackie retaliating, protecting himself, and they think Jackie was the culprit. Scott insisted that's not the way it happened, but I'm inclined to believe Jackie. The cops, they took Jackie downtown and booked him for assault."

Fred put his arm around Eddie. "Jack, see, he's been my main man for the last three years. And Scott, well, I never knew what to make of Scott. Tell me Eddie, you were there dishwashing yesterday. What did you see?"

Eddie didn't know how to react to this. From what he had seen in both the break room and in the office, Jackie had instigated the whole thing. He had taken the nervous Scott back into the office, put him against the wall, and beat him into submission there. Scott never had a chance, as he was hammered to the ground by punches and kicks and flying pictures of Fred's dead sister. Eddie didn't want to come out and say all of that, though. If he admitted to Scott's innocence, went and told Fred what he had seen, Jackie might come after him in much the same way. Eddie didn't want that; he had seen how Scott had gotten it good down there on the office floor, and defending Scott wasn't worth that sort of beating. Besides that, Fred didn't want to hear it. Eddie figured he might get so mad that he'd fire him right there on the bar stool. He didn't want that, either. He needed the money and he wanted an apartment. He didn't want to stay in that cave under the bridge any longer than he had to. He was tired of piling up the rocks.

"Well, I didn't see much," he told Fred. "I heard some scuffling in the break room while I was working, and then I saw the cops in the office when I was punching out."

"So you don't know who broke my sister's picture?"

"No sir."

Fred got up and then instructed Eddie to help him clean the office. That wasn't the most important thing at eleven a.m.; the dining room needed to be set up, the dishes needed to be cleaned from the night before, the floor needed mopping, and the food order needed putting away. But Fred was the owner, and if he said 'clean the office,' well he'd better never mind the urgent things and clean the office. Besides, Chile would be in in a little while to get the equipment going anyway, and hopefully the wait staff would be along.

He was afraid to ask Fred if he'd fired anyone else. Maybe the bastard had canned the whole crew, said to hell with it, he'd start over with a fresh slate. Eddie hoped that that wasn't the case. He liked Lisa and Chile, and the fat one with the pink jeans had said "hi" to him just yesterday. Besides that, he would need to do a lot of extra work, wait tables and seat people even, for the same pay.

Eddie picked up some of the broken glass from the office floor, and found one of the lenses to an eyeglass in the corner: Scott. The shattered picture that had enraged Fred, of his sneaky dead sister, was nowhere to be seen. A half-finished schedule lay beneath the desk and Eddie picked it up and placed it on the blotter. Then he noticed the post card propped up against the glass. It was of a saint, a woman donned in a purple and gold robe, holding a staff that curled at the top in an ornate design. She was standing on a hill that looked almost like a pitcher's mound, and there were dark clouds rolling in, the blackest clouds Eddie had ever seen, thick and ominous like lumps of uneven coal. The saint was holding her sceptre up to them, warding off some apparent apocalypse, endowed by God with the power to do that sort of thing.

Eddie flipped the card over. It was addressed to Bingo's, with a note scribbled in red ink:

> Fred—There is a God that judges such things as you've done. He'll send you down to Hell riding a lightning bolt. Redeem yourself and take that evil sign down.
> —Father Francis Madrid

Eddie read the little printed inscription at the bottom of the card. St. Margaret of Antioch, it said. St. Margaret herself stood on that apocalyptic pitcher's mound on the other side, warding off the end of the world. Yes, Sister John Rita had tested him on that one, and it all came back. She was the tortured one, the daughter of a pagan priest who kicked her out of the house when she turned Christian on him, a shepherdess who wandered around the countryside, lonely in her quest for God. Finally taken in by a man who tried to make sexual advances on her, she refused the man and angered him. In his seething rage, he took her and tortured her, tried to drown her and burn her over and over, but to no avail. He summoned Satan, who appeared in the form of a dragon. Satan swallowed her, but St. Margaret of Antioch took a cross down with her, and jabbed at the inside of the dragon's throat. The dragon spewed Margaret out upon the ground. She crawled away into the wilderness, away from Satan, steadfast with her cross to other tortures. Finally beheaded in the town square with all of her converts, St. Margaret of Antioch smiled and took her place in martyrdom.

She was the patron saint of safe childbirth, Eddie had told Sister John Rita, and he remembered how all of his memorizing had impressed Sister there at her desk. He impressed himself by recalling it all this many years later, and he stopped his cleaning, sat down on the swivel chair, and propped the post card back against the glass.

Safe childbirth. Eddie thought about that; it carried with him the rest of that day, through the dish slam that he had to bus and to the break table as he finished up another cold burger. It made him think about the film of his little brother Benjamin, taken in the delivery room on the evening that he was born. The film was made on one of those old 8 millimeter cameras, and his father had to carry bright, hot spotlights into the room to allow enough light. The doctors, the nurses, his mother even, as much pain as she was in, opened their circle and revealed him there, the newly born Shemanski child. They were all smiling because they had seen Benjamin come out of the muck of his mother's insides and into the spotlight of the conscious world. All so happy in the white room: they had brought another baby safely into the world, and they held it, red-faced and blanket-bound, for all to see.

Captions

◆

I

Four hundred thirty dollars. The box was nearly filled with money when Eddie dug it up again, though he did get himself on one of the broken beer bottles. Blood money, he smiled to no one. He buried another week's pay, and wrapped his hand in a piece of torn cloth.

He had accommodated himself quite well to his bridge cave. He had pillows and sheets, and down the hill beneath a large stone slab, he had dug a trench in which to store his food, a niche under some sod for cold sodas and snacks and such. It alarmed him one morning when he went to the creek's edge and he suddenly realized that he had fallen into habit. He was washing his clothes secretly in a dirty creek day after day; how many other people were doing that? He had done it for so many mornings that he had begun to drift off and think about other things while he was scraping the dirt away so that on this morning, Eddie had to sit in his cave and try to remember whether he had done his shirts the day before. Did he lay his things out on the rocks and let the sun bake them dry? Did he or didn't he? It was as if, in the unconscious act of cleaning his own clothes, he had ceased to exist.

He had enough clean shirts to get him through the week now, and he stored them in a plastic bag in the cave corner. Eddie was getting a little worried about his clothes, his food supply, his carton of cigarettes, and the access passers-by might have to his cave. There were no locks, only the boulders to protect his things. The cave was certainly no secret; it had its history of use, established itself as a punk landmark. Any one of those previous owners might return, at any time, to take it over—one of the older gangs from Landoff or Newportville, perhaps, with their knives and their drunken superiority.

Eddie figured he only needed another pay check or two before he could get an apartment. Two more weeks, he figured, and he could move in, just before the school year started. He'd already been over to Valley Green, which seemed like a suitable complex, but they insisted on references, and the woman looked at Eddie suspiciously as he inquired about the efficiencies. He couldn't give her references, he couldn't give anyone references, not as Eddie the runaway, unless he just made up some names and phone numbers and hoped they wouldn't try to call. He would need to start scouring the paper, maybe find something in there from a private owner, a part of a house or a room maybe, where they weren't so business-like in such matters, where they might just look at him and trust him on the spot.

Then there was the high school problem. He would be expected to show up at Newportville High for his senior year, so he was going to have to start manufacturing lies about his age. He'd already told the woman in the office at Valley Green that he was eighteen, but she wanted to see some identification, a license or a social security card or something to prove it, and he pretended to search his pockets and say that he'd be back. Eddie figured that Domingus would be able to help him out there; he had connections to stolen licenses and such (he had connections to everything) in case the truant officers hunted him down.

High School drop-out: that wasn't so bad, Eddie thought. He knew he was a smart enough fellow to get by, and he silently commended himself on his cave home. He didn't need all that garbage anyway, sitting there writing useless assignments and memorizing math problems and science facts that never meant a thing and never would. There was always going to be dishwashing, and if he kept kicking ass through the slams, well he would never have to worry about a job. Besides that, how many other seventeen-year-old kids had four hundred dollars to their name? Fuck science and math. Fuck facts. He was going to be all right soon, very soon. Things were getting better, and it felt as if he were coming out of the dark earth, as if his eyes were beginning to burn from the bright light that was his own near future, as the visions of apartments and new friends and laughter became more clear, more real.

II

Fred O'Hara learned of the mess that had descended on the Bingo's crew, and he decided to put a lot of time into the place to resolve the problem by working the day shift. Eddie saw him there just about every morning opening the place, as he had not yet replaced Scott. He fumbled around at first, searching for items on the inventory sheet, scouring the office for purveyor's phone numbers, searching the storage room for replacement silverware. But despite his apparent ineptitude, Eddie began to like Fred. He was certainly more friendly to him than Scott had ever been, patting him on the back every time he hurried by him with an overflowing bus pan or as he filled the machine. He even offered Eddie a beer one afternoon as he sat at the end of the bar with his Mai-Tai.

"Have a cold one, Eddie. You did a nice job today. You were all over the place with that bus pan, and I really appreciate your getting the barf off the floor of the ladie's room."

Eddie still felt queasy about that barf clean-up. He had to go into the ladie's room with a mop after a woman had gotten sick all over the walls, the floor and the two sinks. It must have exploded out of her, and Eddie was both disgusted and amazed as he walked in. He hid the smell away by some wet bar mops slung across his face, and he wondered how anyone could have that much power in their lungs—much less a woman—to spew their insides in so many directions at the same time and nail every piece of porcelain in the room. She must be pregnant or something of the sort, he guessed all along. His mother had barfed like like when she was carrying Benjamin.

Eddie sat down next to Fred and the new bartender, Manny, opened him a bottle of Molson. He was a little nervous about drinking the thing. He took a little sip and put it down, then looked at Fred stirring his new Mai-Tai.

"You know that I'm not twenty-one," Eddie said. "I'm just eighteen."

"I know that, but who in Jesus' name is going to know I gave it to you? The dining room is near empty, my boy." Fred reached over, patted Eddie and chuckled. "Besides that, I know damned well you've had beer before. All kids start early these days. Hell, I started myself at fifteen. And you wouldn't be asking for an imported beer if you hadn't."

Eddie nodded at that one. "Guess you got me there," he said.

"Eighteen, huh,?" Fred asked Eddie. "A good age, a damned good age."

Eddie was living the lie, and he raised his bottle, nodded, and took a swig as Fred finished another. He reminded himself to get to Domingus about the fake license.

"They found me dead drunk in a cornfield the day I turned eighteen" Fred said. "I have no idea how I got there, though my buddies told me I downed a fifth of Southern Comfort like a thirsty man in the desert with a canteen...I emptied the bitch in ten seconds flat. They said I took off in the dark across the fields, disappeared like a phantom...it was three in the morning and they just let me go. When the sun came up, the old lady from the farmhouse came through the field with a salt gun and shot me in the ass as I lay there on her stalks. I'll tell you what Eddie...there's nothing that cures a hangover more than salt in the ass. Poof, my headache was gone just like that. Of course, I had a hell of an ache in my butt. I had to crawl home, she'd put so much salt in that gun. She blasted it at point blank...never got it all out, either."

Fred reached down and pulled his shirt out from his pants and began to unleash his belt. Eddie couldn't believe it: he was going to show him his bare ass, right there on the stool, right there in the open. Sure enough, drunken little Fred hopped off the stool and pulled down the back of his pants for Eddie to see. There in the dimmed afternoon light, as Manny chuckled his way to the other end of the bar, the sun came in off the front window and shone a square of light directly onto his pasty white butt. "You see, forty-four fucking years later and there it is...salt in my ass."

Eddie focused and could see the little speckles. Fred wanted Eddie to touch it, to come over with his hands and feel the little ridges that the salt had left, but Eddie insisted on leaving it be. "Hey it's your ass, and I don't want to touch it. No offense."

"None taken," Fred said, looking back up. "It's not like I was going to fire you because you wouldn't touch my ass, though. You're a good kid, Eddie. I just wanted to warn you about having too many of these things." Fred got back on his stool, held up his empty Mai-Tai and beckoned Manny with a finger from the other end. "And if you felt all that bumpy old salt still stuck there, well maybe you'd think twice before you overdid it with the liquor."

Eddie convinced Fred that he never had more than one or two, and he walked out of the dimly lit dining room a little dizzy from his one Molson. He hadn't had a beer in quite a while, not since he had stolen some from his father's reserve in the basement, Schlitz in cans. He had taken four of the warm cans to his closet box one night and drank them there while his father watched the Phillies game and drank his own cold beer out of the refrigerator. Eddie had spilled one of them all over the floor, then got stoned and didn't clean it all up. For days his closet box smelled like stale beer, so he stole the air freshener from the car's rearview mirror while his father ran in to get some hex nuts in the hardware store. Eddie smuggled the little cardboard tree into his box, hung it there, and from then on in, the darkness smelled like a pine forest.

Eddie decided that he would really like to get drunk sometime soon-maybe off about ten of those Molsons-if he could milk them out of the drunken Fred. Despite the sight of Fred's pasty ass, Eddie still took a liking to him—not just because Fred liked him, but because he was a funny drunk who didn't take things too serious. He didn't seem to care that the place was slow most of the time, or that his employees were standing around in waiter holes or smoking and talking out on the dock or punching in late. He couldn't believe that Scott had called him a son of a bitch. Fred had his favorites, though, and Scott was not one of them. Eddie felt secure in the fact that he had firmly established himself in Fred's corner, his bar corner. He just hoped that the salt-gun episode would not come up again.

III

Chile came into a Friday lunch shift still angry at a driver who had cut him off on the bypass. His knuckles were skinned and bleeding, and he wrapped them with a gauze over the sink and then tied his bandanna around his greasy hair, cigarette hanging from lip.

"You know Eddie, you get really tired of the assholes," he said. "They think the highway is some sort of playground where they can race their cars around." He finished his wrapping and sighed. "This son of a bitch doesn't let me in as I'm coming up to the light. There's construction in my lane, so I figure I'll just get over and so I put on my blinker. Then this idiot in the Toyota decides he's going to floor it so I can't get in, so I'm stuck there in front of the flagman and the hole in the road. " Chile stopped and took the saute pans down from their respective hooks.

"So he's stopped at the light and I'm steamed, I mean really steamed. He knows it, the flagman knows it. I get out of my car, go up to his car, rip open his door, and pound my damned fist into his face. He's crying, the wimpy son of a bitch is crying by the time I'm done, down on his floor in his prissy striped shirt and swearing he'll never do it again." Chile walked away as Eddie set up the racks. "Lisa used to call me a highway vigilante. I think that about says it."

Chile's anger rose into expletives and shouts over the duration of the lunch slam, as he cursed the fried orders and the slew of well-done steaks on the fifteen-top. Things culminated in a shouting match with Manny the bartender, after he'd taken the kitchen mats and used them behind his bar. "I'm slipping back here damnit. If I go down on this floor, heads will roll, starting with yours my friend."

During one of Chile's tirades (over lunch platters sitting in his window), Fred came back into the kitchen, peeved that he had been distracted from his corner stool. "I'm getting a little tired of hearing your screaming way out in the dining room, Chile," he said. "I know you're busy, but that's no longer an acceptable excuse."

Just at that point, some grease splashed up out of the fryer as Chile was dropping a basket of chicken. Eddie had just come behind the line with a freshly washed stack of dishes, and he stepped back as the frozen drumsticks popped in the scalding oil. He saw a spray of grease rise up out of the vat like a solar flare, and it spit across Chile's hands and soaked into his freshly wrapped gauze. He watched his eyes blaze up in those suspended seconds, watched his face color up with total fury. Chile lost all control and lashed out with swinging arms, knocking the stack of china to the matless floor in one clean heave.

Eddie stepped back and shot his hands to his ears. The plates crashed and shattered with the decibel level of a plane taking off, one upon the other, and a million shards exploded to all parts of the kitchen, all over the line and under the equipment as the sharp projectiles shot like missiles to the walls. Fred jumped out of the path of one rather large spear that twirled end over end and embedded itself in the cork wall just beyond his pants.

"That's it you son of a bitch, you're fired," he screamed above the remaining breakages. "Get the hell out of my restaurant right now." ·

Chile had suddenly forgot about his burning hands and tried to stammer an apology, humbled by his own uncontained fury. He tried to come around and amend things, holding up his reasons in full view of the entire wait staff, the hostess, and Eddie. But they all knew, by Fred's purple face, that it was too late. Even the blistering grease burns and the dangling gauze would not save Chile this time around. Fred had seen him push those expensive plates off the side of the counter, and that was his last straw, the last of his maniacal outbursts. In the middle of his stammer—and sensing his imminent departure—Chile boiled over again. He gave a 'fuck this place,' stormed the length of the kitchen, flung open the double doors, and disappeared over the edge of the dock.

Eddie brought the broom out from behind the dishwasher and began to pile the shards in the corner, watching as Lisa gingerly placed a ticket onto the wheel, telling him with her eyes that her order might well go uncooked. But she smiled, too, she smiled at Eddie, at her sudden freedom, now severed forever from Chile and his Viet Nam bullshit. Fred approached Eddie, and he stepped in front of the shards, kicking some of them from out of the little mountain.

"Do you know how to cook?" he asked Eddie. "You said something about flipping some steaks over at King Arthur's."

Eddie didn't know how to react to that, suspended in silence while he considered his answer. He had told Fred at the bar one day about his emergency cooking back at King Arthur's, after one of the drunk cooks had fallen asleep on the butcher block table. That's when Eddie had to stop with his dishes and take the tongs, under the whispered plea from the concerned waitresses, and get through the rush. He had dragged that poor, fat useless cook into the walk-in refrigerator and let him sober himself up there on the cold metal floor. The tickets kept coming in, and luckily Lou was off visiting Candy in the hospital or else he would have fired that cook right there on the butcher block or as he stumbled over him on his way to the produce. Eddie threw the steaks on the grill and dropped the fried items and made the sandwiches, just the way the drunk cook had done so many times when Eddie watched him from his dish station. Later, after the slam, the waitresses came up and praised his ability (with only the one returned filet), just as Lou was coming back, and just as the drunk cook regained himself from his time on the floor. Eddie had to hold back with everything he had when Lou pulled all of the dupes off the spindle, counted them, and praised the drunk cook for his fine job.

Jeff, that was his name, Jeff. He had started as a security guard in the mall, and he caught a streaker during the Fourth of July parade, nailed him up against the fruit stand by running his genitals into the wall. Lou tucked Jeff in and hired him as his line cook on the day he saw him cooking a barbecue in the center pavilion of the mall. Jeff had cooked up the best ribs that Lou ever tasted, so he offered him a salary right there and showed him the way to his kitchen. What Lou didn't know, and as Eddie and the waitresses came to find out, hid itself inside Jeff's pants: a bottle of distilled gin, his nightly medicine.

Eddie figured he could step right in at Bingo's and cook just like Jeff, the sober Jeff. Everybody loved that guy because he never said much of anything, and when he did it was always with that friendly southern drawl, never angered, never bothered. The gin had severed most of his .

nerves, enabled him to handle the slams and the screaming waitresses and the burning heat. Eddie wanted that job, and he wanted those same friendly hellos, those same concerns if he fell drunk, where they all would drag him to safety.

"Yes, Fred.... I know how to cook," Eddie answered.

IV

Eddie got to his bridge cave with burn marks up his arms, long pink slivers running like highways on a street map. He had pulled out a sheet pan of baked potatoes and it got him on the arms on his way to the warmer drawer. Then he dropped the potatoes all over, burned a dozen steaks, and let the grease overflow out of the bucket as he was finishing his clean-up. "Don't worry about it," Fred said, after he'd seen the squashed potatoes and the charcoaled filets. "And be sure to rinse out the mop good after you've gotten up all that grease."

In his blackness he sat happy as the stinging left his arms. Fred was going to give him a raise, that was for sure, and there would be more money coming in. No more dark cave, no more flooded creeks washing things up, no more tractor trailers rumbling the ground and bringing down the cement dust from above. No sheds, no closet boxes, no pain. No darkness: just light—bright windowed light, light pouring in from all sides, light through the trees, light into his rented apartment, light.

It was Tuesday. The men would be back, all seven of them, to build another fire and huddle with their afflictions. Eddie closed off his world and waited for them to show. He kept a close watch with his ears to the stones. His new alarm watch glowed nine-thirty, just about the time they appeared the previous Tuesday. This time, he would listen for the whispers as the men began to gather the twigs and the logs, as they formed their circle on the dirt across the stream to exchange their identities.

Who would tell their story this time? Had they found Finbar's father? Which saint would stand over the flames? More kidnappings? More abductions? More tears? More promises of redemption? Eddie was determined to go out there when they came. He was going to roll the boulders away, wade across the black water, and pop in on them as they unleashed their pens. He had his own story to tell, and now he had found those who would listen.

Eddie waited and waited for the men to show, and he strained his ears long after his glowing watch had buzzed midnight. But in all that . time, he could only pick up the trickle of the water over the rocks and the cicadas gathered in the black trees. The saints weren't going to come tonight, he was sure of that. They had canceled their fire and settled for another day. Eddie moved his ears away from the boulders, pulled up his sheet, and went to sleep.

V

In all the dark spots of the world, Eddie's little space beneath the bridge held its own cement personality. He'd run a thick red magic marker all along the fissures, and, because the cave sloped downward at an angle with the hill, it came to look like the membranes of a womb. He'd removed the old newspapers, the "Phillies Win" page and such, from the floor of the cave. Now, it was lined with a sepia sheet (to blend in with the cave walls) nailed by sharp rocks into the earth. He had also fashioned a hook into the ceiling from which to hang his pen-light key chain. His key chain had no keys on it yet, only the pen-light. But that was o.k.—Eddie bought it so he could read the Daily News each night. Besides that, he would need the key chain for an eventual apartment key and maybe even a car somewhere in the future.

There was a little article on one of the inside pages of today's paper about "The Continuing Search for Eddie Shemanski." Some reporters had spoken to the Stigmeyers because there were phone calls reporting a boy sneaking in and out of their shed and pissing on trees. Someone from the "bush houses" had called the police and complained about some broken branches in their hedges (though it turned out later to be game birds). So the news crews came after all, and they took pictures and overexposed their best shot in the newspaper photo of Mr. Stigmeyer. Eddie could tell that he was pissed. In fact, he moved his paper up to the little pen-light, right up to the ceiling of the cave and looked close, and he saw some clenched hands in the bottom corners of the picture, around Mr. Stigmeyer's wrists, holding him back. With his teeth bared, the reflection off his fillings looked as if he were being given volts of electricity. The photo looked so familiar to Eddie and then he remembered: Mr. Stigmeyer had struck that same pose six years back, when the environmental groups had doused his leaf fire.

On the nights that Eddie couldn't sleep he would read the whole paper. Usually he just bought it to look for articles about himself, or at the real-estate section to hunt for an apartment, though more and more he found himself wandering toward world headlines. Those headlines were such things that he could never imagine, and if he did, it became too depressing. Today, he opened up the paper and read the story of a man held in a Turkish prison for seventy-three years. The Turks freed him, brought him out into the light and showed him the crumbling courtyard, a place which he hadn't visited for twenty years. He was a Russian fellow named Ivan Bolstryvik, amazed that he'd survived in his little cell that long, amazed that, according to his birth record, he had just turned one hundred. His present? Ivan, jailed in a cell for three-quarters of his life, died on the flight back to Moscow. The doctor got close and heard the man bleat out the terror within him as Ivan clutched the mans' neck in his last moments of life. "Tell me of this thing we are on, this thing taking us across the sky," he said. "Am I being taken into hell?"

On a lighter note, the Phillies won a game. Six runs in the ninth, the subheading read. The players all gathered around the plate in the big photo, names and faces Eddie didn't care to know. He did like the fat one called Luzinski, though. He used to like the way his father berated him every time he came to the plate. "Come on Greg, get a hit. You can eat all you want to…hoagies, cheese steaks, bags of chips, hell, my beer the rest of the night. Just get a hit this once." And then he would curse the man and wish him from the screen after he struck out. But on this day, on this sports page, Luzinski had done a good thing, hitting a game-winning three-run shot off one of the Mets pitchers. Eddie guessed that might have cheered up his parent's household a bit. His father was drunk and smacking the ceiling, and William, home from Washington by now, had probably clapped his hands in a craze before the set. When the win had settled in them and after the beer had disappeared and the television shut off, they went on to talk about more serious things no doubt— about Eddie's runaway, about the undertaking of another search.

Eddie tried to remember if William had ever talked about the bridge cave. He seemed to remember his involvement with some hippies when he owned his Harley, though by then, now that Eddie thought about it, he'd moved clear over to Bristol to live with eleven of them. He never remembered William talking about the cave, never a whisper. The fact was, he and William never really talked at all, except in his last days, after he'd moved back home the first time and before he took off for the Northwest Territories. It wasn't even talking, really, just playing with the hamster William had given him as a going-away present. William would hang Elvis in the air over a mountain of cedar chips that he'd piled out of the spare bag, watch it paw the air in frantic swoops, and then let the thing fall. He had to tell William to stop doing that, not because the hamster might have been harmed, but because the cedar chips kept spilling out from the pile and falling into his shag carpet.

Eddie piled the Daily News in the corner with all of the others. He'd accumulated a nice knee-high stack now, almost to the ceiling of the back wall. He'd fallen into the habit of buying a paper every day at the convenience store over the past month (along with handfuls of Smarties) and all the old news had begun to mildew from the damp earth. He calculated another three inches, ten more papers or so, before the newspapers reached the ceiling of his bridge cave. Ten more papers: just about the time left before he could move out, before he could dig his cash box out of the earth, dig it out for good.

VI

Fred beckoned Eddie to the bar one afternoon, after he had successfully cooked the lunch slam, and bought him another Molson. Eddie thanked him and sat on one of the middle stools and read an Apartment-Shoppers Guide that Lisa had picked up for him in the supermarket. He sipped away on his Molson and searched for efficiencies, up and down the columns, hoping that this time around, Fred would buy him a second beer, and that he might see something cheap and interesting.

"Apartment hunting, Eddie?" Fred asked.

"Yeah, for a little place," Eddie said.

"I might be able to help you there," he said. Eddie put down his paper as Fred stirred his drink and stared for a time at the warped bar top. "If I recall…I think I've got a vacant basement apartment over in Hudson." He looked over at Eddie. "Would you be interested in a basement apartment over in Hudson? Someone broke a lease there, some French guy. He moved out in the middle of the night and the son of a bitch took the refrigerator with him…I'll have to replace it before you move in. But the place is yours with a little cleaning up….say, two hundred a month?"

"Sounds good," Eddie said without a pause. "When can I move in?'

Fred finished his Mai-Tai and offered Eddie a ride over to Hudson to see the place. Eddie liked to call Hudson "Rancherville" because those were the only houses there: white ones and beige ones, white ones and beige ones. Ranchers—what a terrible thing to build. Row upon row, street upon street, squared off and set back by little green lawns, and most of the time bordered by forsythias that blossomed in a dizzy yellow symmetry each spring.

Hudson. Nobody young lived in Hudson, nobody. Eddie's brother William used to drive over there on his Harley and make tracks on the lawns after rainstorms. The grass was damp and fragile then, and so it would come up easy when he spun his tires. He'd spit the chunks of sod into the air and land them on the cement porches and the telephone wires, hoot, and drive away. The old ladies kept calling the house, swearing to brow-beat him and send him to prison. That's when Eddie's mother went off on William with a broom handle to the knees, screaming that he should have more respect for old people.

Old people: Eddie was going to have to come and go quietly in Hudson. He knew that on the ride over, he knew that as the homes descended to ranch level, as he saw the wrinkled faces coming and going up the sidewalks. Nonetheless, he would have a toilet now, he would still have his privacy behind a closed door, and there would be no more stones to pile.

"Now you have to understand that this is a little ranch house," Fred said from the driver's seat as they pulled up Small Road. "There's this old woman who's been living in the house for centuries. She won't want to be hearing any of that loud music or parties and things coming from below. This woman likes her silence. She's got the white hair, the cane, the whole bit, and she likes her peace and quiet."

The basement apartment was small, and the little windows, two on each of the "longer" walls, had been boarded up by sheets of plywood. There was a blue strip of carpet running the length of the room, exposing a few feet of old faded tile on either end, warped and bubbled. Fluorescent lights hung over the washboard and extended over a tiny sink and stove. The kitchenette, flickering in and out of existence, looked more like a child's play set than the real thing.

Eddie wasn't so sure now. He had certainly envisioned things differently. For one thing, he at least expected some natural light. There were always large picture windows, hanging plants, huge trees and sunlight in his apartment visions. Now he saw only the plywood shutting out the world, nailed in, a variation of the same theme that had personified his closet box, the tool shed, his bridge cave. Cabinets: he wanted plenty of cabinets, yet here there hung the lone-doored metal thing in the corner of the kitchenette. He wanted room for a long couch, some end tables, he wanted a wall for a stereo and a television—but all of those things would never fit into the room. He wanted one of those big stoves, like his mother had, to cook up all of the things he'd learned how to make over at Bingo's, a stove where he could have the room to flame up and saute and baste and maybe even roast a pig if he got up the energy or the company. He wanted space, but now, here in front of him in Fred's basement efficiency, he saw his vision crumbling down, torn from him like that day in the pet store when his mother had said "no" to the Monitor Lizard. No—another dream deferred.

As he walked to the middle of the blue carpet, the floor doused his dream entirely, as it brought up a stench not unlike his half-dried clothes. Mildew: the apartment had apparently flooded at one time or another, and he couldn't help thinking of the most recent rainstorm. "Now does this place get the rain in?" Eddie asked.

"Not that I can recall," Fred said, checking the cabinets and finding some jars of marmalade labeled in French. "Mrs. Haas would have called me if there was flooding, believe me. See, this basement extends beyond that far wall, and it would have flooded over there, too. On the other side, past those vents, there's a washer and dryer, which you're free to use by the way. Just go up the stairs and knock, and Mrs. Haas will let you through. There's a trap door in one of her bedrooms that takes you down to the other side of the basement. She'll leave the door open for you if she's not home."

He tried to remember some of the other apartments he had read about in his Apartment-Shoppers Guide. There were a couple of nice ones over in Landoff, upwards of three hundred dollars. He could probably afford one of those if he could pick up some overtime and find a way over there until he bought a car. But there would be applications to fill out as well, and suspicious faces poking into his personal life, digging him out of obscurity and revealing him to the world. He didn't want any of that—too much of a price to pay to satisfy his vision, especially now that he had what he quickly began to believe his destiny staring him right in the face.

"All right, I'll take it," he said. "I guess you'll be needing two months rent and a security deposit?"

"Don't worry about the deposit. Just give me the first month, and we'll worry about a lease later."

That suited Eddie perfect; it made up for the sunken dream. He had more than enough to cover the rent. He had spending money to buy some things now, and his mind worked excitedly to unearth the material things he would want right away: card tables, chairs, a television, a boom box, some plants, some food, a pet. Food to fill the cabinets, beer to fill the refrigerator that Fred would deliver, chairs and chairs to sit upon. Then people: people to fill the room, people to fill up his cushions and his blue carpet, people to fill up his life, a girl friend, more than one girl friend, more than enough of everything, more.

"Fine. I'll change the locks and get you the key tomorrow," Fred said. "You can move in tomorrow if you can stand life without a fridge for a few days."

VII

Eddie went back to his bridge cave to collect his things and to spend his final night. Evening had settled in, and swarms of mosquitoes had gathered over the stagnant pools formed along the Neshaminy. Eddie was going to head down there to clean his dirty laundry, but he knew the mosquitoes would cover him in seconds, and then he would lie awake all night smashing them. He'd rather not wash a single shirt tonight, that was for sure.

Nonetheless, he was a little worried about the scout mosquitoes. They were going to send their blood-sucking patrol up to his bridge cave. With all those millions of needle-noses down there by the pools, there was no doubt they smelled him lurking, he, a warm-blooded human feast on the hill.

He piled the boulders careful for the last time and closed off the underside of the bridge. He could hear the whining buzz of the scout mosquitoes entering his cave, though it had become too dark to see them. Then the sound stopped, and he waited for the bites that never came. He estimated that the mosquitoes had headed on back down the hill and had somehow signaled the others, the billion others, the trillion others, about the warm blood in the cave. They would all be on their way up in a matter of minutes, after the signal had gotten around to the various swarms, as they rose up from their pools in a gray mist. They would be attacking his cave soon, so Eddie tried to arrange the boulders so that it would be more difficult for them to get through. He pushed them snug, and he took handfuls of dirt and stuffed the dirt between the cracks. He fumbled through the darkness, turned on his pen-light, and listened.

Not a mosquito. Not a sound. Nothing floating about the light. The coast was clear, and Eddie gathered his Daily News and laid down beneath the swinging pen-light. It cast a thin shadow across his paper as it swung on its short chain, and he fumbled through the front pages to find something interesting.

"Viet Nam Vet Loses Control," the headline said, and it grabbed Eddie's attention as he crawled to the center of the cave and let the light shine upon the words. A short little article, tucked into the corner of the second page without an accompanying picture that read:

> "Duluth, Iowa—A scraggly bearded man came out of the woods near Duluth on Sunday brandishing an arsenal of guns and knives, spouting poems, and shooting wildly into the air. He began to shoot passers-by in the knees as they scattered on the town square and it took several patrolmen to coax the guns from his hands and surrender. Because no one recognized him, authorities believe that the man was a stranger in town. He is being held without bail at the County Sheriff's Office for further questioning to determine his motive,his identity, and his sanity."

The article ended there and it got Eddie to thinking about Chile. Iowa rang a bell: Chile was talking on the line one day about Iowa, talking over the exhaust fans about a farmhouse he had holed up in during the seventies and how he used to bring corn to town and cook up chickens and such on Saturdays in the town square. It was one of those murky stories of which Eddie had heard only bits and pieces over the rinse cycle, fragments of words and sentences booming out from behind the line that he tried to glue together during the slam. Chile always talked on and on like that about different things that he had done or supposedly done, sometimes to the waitresses, sometimes back to Eddie, but mostly to the walls, to himself. Eddie never took Chile's banter seriously, but now, in the light of the article, and after he had convinced himself that Chile was that Duluth madman, he began to believe all of the stories. He really had been to Viet Nam after all, and he had seen some things there. Some loose screws rattled themselves around in that brain, and it could only have come from war, from hearing the explosions over hospital roofs, from watching a brother disappear into the jungle. Chile went on a rampage in Iowa because all of those things exploded to the surface with that grease burn. No wonder he pushed the plates over the edge of the counter. No wonder he took out knee-caps.

Eddie snapped off his pen-light. This was it, the last night in his bridge cave. He could hear a truck engine whining up the road toward its destiny across the bridge. It would be over him soon, and the damp earth would tremble and the dust would fall from the roof and lay into his hair. He couldn't sleep again—that was only natural because the next day of his life held so much change. He'd be digging out his cash box from the rocks, packing up his clothes and his toiletries, and moving on to a safe, clean little apartment. But something else crept in, as things always crept in, and it disturbed Eddie so much that sleep became an impossibility. It came in like a floating scout mosquito, pestering about his ear and his brain, and it wouldn't leave him alone, not for anything. The little story in The Daily News: it sank beneath his skin and into his blood and drew a little life from him. Chile was in that cell somewhere in Iowa, locked up without an identity. It was dark in Iowa, too, it was dark everywhere now. But especially for Chile, it was darkest of all. He had nothing left. They'd taken his life away a little at a time, little by little. His ugliness, his yelling and cursing, his tantrums, his kicking Lisa out of the moving car and his pushing of the plates to the floor, all peeled itself away now and revealed to Eddie the fragile, human day cook, poisoned by the events of his life. His war, his brother, his mother, Lisa, Fred, they had all chipped his dignity away a fleck at a time. He took out all those knee-caps because no one wanted to hear him any more; they'd all shut him off as a ranting bullshitter, Eddie included. So Chile did the only thing left he could think to do: tell them all, in his own violent way, "Look what the hell you've done to me."

Eddie squirmed and he laid on his side, then on his back, his stomach, his other side. He sat up after a time, and watched his alarm watch glow to 4 a.m. The cave had gotten stuffy from the wedged boulders, so he removed the packed topsoil and one of the smaller rocks. A little breeze came up off the black Neshaminy, and the cool air hit him in the face and he breathed in the chill. Eventually, because he couldn't sleep at all, he removed all of the boulders and walked down the hill to the edge of the creek. The water had gotten suddenly cold, so cold that he had to remove his bare feet, and he went back into his cave and retrieved his long-sleeved shirt and some fuzzy socks.

He sat on a flat rock and he thought: "Things won't nail me the way they nailed Chile…the way they dragged him down and sent him off to the corn fields…no…I won't ever have my senses fried like that. I'll keep my hands away from the hot grease, they won't be burned like that, blistered to make me scream and snap. I won't ever get some guns and go off, shoot out kneecaps and such, lose my job, my identity, my head. It won't build up for me like that, never, never, never. I'm Eddie Shemanski. I've been sleeping in a cave beneath a bridge, I've spent some time in a tool shed, and I hid myself away in a closet box because I was afraid that men were coming to get me. I've probably killed a woman, and here I am, on the run, running still, maybe always running, who knows. I only know it's time to move on again, move up, that someday the running will stop, that light will finally come into some windows. Past, after all, is past, present present, future future."

The sun lightened the sky enough for Eddie to see the shrubs and stones scattered on the dark hill that ran to the foot of the bridge. He removed the rocks from his bank vault, retrieved his cash box, and stuffed the bank, and then his clothes, into his knapsack. He could see the hill clearly enough now. Now he wouldn't trip on one of the boulders wedged into the ground there, or on the thick vines growing and running into the woods just beyond the crest. He shook off the cement dust from his duffel bag, slung it over his shoulder and grabbed hold of one of the vines. Pushing up on a boulder, he scaled the hill to the road and moved on past the rumbling trucks.

Salao

◆

I

Domingus surprised Eddie, he surprised everyone, when he carried his pet Andean parrot on his cast through the kitchen and propped it atop the service rack. He dishwashed the night shift, and throughout, the parrot squawked and squawked and froze its eyes onto the machine. Fred came back and made some jokes about the sound, how it sounded, from his bar stool, just like Chile used to sound going off on one of his tirades. The waitresses fawned over the parrot, at every opportunity between tables, as they walked back and looked at the thing, listening and laughing as the parrot belted out its Spanish squawks. "Salao salao salao." The bird spouted that word over and over, and even the rinse cycle, the whirring of the ovens, the talk of the busy waiters and the slamming of the plates could not drown the thing out.

Eddie punched out after his break, and he turned to admire the colorful bird before he left the kitchen. Blue and yellow and red and green: it kept ruffling the feathers on its head, making some of them rise so that it gave the impression, as the feathers came down in a slant across its beady eyes, that something had angered it. It might have been the spray coming off the top of the dish machine, the fine mist rising over and falling on it—or the echoes of the waitresses coming and going through the swinging doors under the buzz of the fluorescent lights. "Salao," it belched out again, this time in a screech not unlike blocks of styrofoam rubbing together. "Sally sally salao."

"Hey Domingus what's that mean, what's your parrot saying?" Eddie asked.

"That his name," Domingus said. "Salao—that his name." Then he took his hand and pressed down the bristling feathers, put his finger out, and the parrot jumped from the service shelf and slid down his cast to its fleshy perch. "Salao…that mean…how you say…'bad luck' in English. It the worst kind of luck you can have, like a bad disease that infect you and leave you dying in the bed with no medicine to help. Salao…it take happiness out of you like air out of balloon and there nothing you can do except keep saying salao over and over until it go away."

Domingus told Eddie that he was afflicted with salao. Bad luck had pursued him and run him down. It started with the shrimp theft, the simple deal he had made with one of the sous chefs in a restaurant over in Landoff. He had made the deal by phone, so he didn't know what the sous chef looked like. They were to meet in Kemper Park on the swings, and, at the appointed time, Domingus approached the man in the chef coat with his fifty-pound case of stolen frozen shrimp slung over his shoulder. The man, rising from his swing and reaching into his pants, whipped out his badge and revealed himself as a detective. Domingus, caught off guard, dropped the case and shot across the creek. He sliced up his bare legs as he tore through the sticker bushes on the other side, got his foot on one of the long nails in the open lot, and lost his wallet somewhere across the gravel.

"I find out later that the man not really a detective, he really a chef after all, out to get my shrimp and pay no money. He get me good. He chase me anyway, how he chase me, I don't know why. He chase me in those shiny shoes, he chase me through the water. He chase me and chase me until he cut himself up in the sticker bushes just like me. But he—he tear his pants to pieces and he curse me because I make his legs bleed. And I yell back and I curse him—because he make me bleed too, plus he make me lose my big box of shrimp, and he get to go back to his restaurant and he use it all up with his Saturday special."

"Salao start then. It come some more when my brother get me with the bat and break my arm and slice me up. He cry that I steal his girl, he cry and he beat. Margaret, I thought she love me, she feel sorry for me maybe because I stay overnight in hospital and come out and work overtime in my—how do you say—cast—to pay the bill. I work twenty-four hours and thirty minutes one day, you know that?"

"Twenty-four hours and thirty minutes?," Eddie asked in disbelief.

"I punch in at nine o'clock Sunday morning. I punch out nine-thirty Monday morning. I help Fred count things and I clean behind dishwasher and sweep parking lot and fix gutter, and I take a long break."

"Wow...all that overtime," Eddie said.

"Yes, but I lose it. I run my car through stained glass window of church over in Hudson. I fall asleep at wheel. Women praying in church come out and call me the devil. I see Jesus statue run over by my tires. It broken in ten places—head broke off—hands gone—body cracked—some of it dust. I try to get to holy water to bless myself, but the priest—he tackle me at altar. He beat me with his fist and tell me police are coming to get me and make me pay for new stained glass and new Jesus. He tell me I a real son of a bitch. Then he take my money from my pockets, two hundred dollars, and I get away from him and run out of broken church."

"You must have crashed into St. Anselm," Eddie said. "I went to school there."

The parrot squawked 'salao' again, and Eddie, despite the distracting noise, completely envisioned Father Madrid, his madness unleashed, pounding relentlessly onto Domingo's head, face full of blooded fury, fists injected with rage. Bingo's was going through his mind—the name of the restaurant, the well-lit sign, little Fred laughing at his post cards. And through his fists? "you're one of those sons of bitches over at Bingo's…and you've just wrecked my church."

"Margaret, she go back to my brother," Domingus continued. "She say she can no make love to man with broken arm because I cannot hold her strong. She want big hugs—she no want a one-arm devil who knock down church wall. I get mad at her I get, very very mad, Eddie. I spit in her face I so mad. She run off and I know she tell my brother. My friend Hector….he tell me just today that my brother looking for me with his bat again."

"Do you live together?" Eddie asked. "You and your brother I mean."

"No I live in Newportville," Domingus said. "Maybe not for long though. I two months behind in rent, and Fred will no let me work long days, get overtime. He say he can no afford."

"He's rich, he can afford," Eddie said. "I'll talk to him for you, see if I can't get you more hours." The parrot had climbed halfway up Domingus cast, and its beady doll's eyes cocked themselves at Eddie as he talked. It spread its feathers for him to see, a blue-yellow-red—green winged panorama that fanned the air and breezed his face. "I love that parrot," he said. "Would you be interested in selling it? I'm looking for a pet for my new apartment."

"Oh no I can no sell Salao. He a bird, a bird bring luck. He have to keep saying his name for me. He have to keep saying it to make my salao go away, to make good happen, good luck. No, no, Eddie, I can no sell. But I can get you another parrot. I can get you any pet you want. What you want?"

"Any pet? How can you do that?" Eddie asked. "You steal from zoos or something?"

"Oh no. Salvadore, he my father's friend. Salvadore work on boat that come up from South America and Africa. They bring many things on that boat, fruit and chairs and animals. I just ask him to get things for me and he get them cheap. He get me wicker seats for my apartment and a big bird cage….he get me Salao. It no cost much. I can get you something cheap too. Salvadore, he have a way of getting things off that boat. He have a—how you say—connection."

"Come to think of it, there is something I always wanted…a pet…and it comes from Africa," Eddie said. "A monitor lizard…you ever hear of a monitor lizard?"

"I have to ask Saladore," Domingus said. "I see what he can do." Domingus raised his casted arm and lowered it quickly so that Salao flapped his wings. "Mon-e-toor lizard," he said. "I remember that." Then he raised the bird to the shelf and brushed it to the metal as a fresh load of dishes arrived. Domingus walked away from the parrot, he closed the dish machine and then he disappeared into the steam.

II

Eddie's little basement apartment had nothing at all; the room emptied into echoes when he walked in, and he closed and locked the door behind him. Only the knapsack: Eddie laid it in the middle of the shag carpet in his petty attempt to fill the room. He opened the knapsack, removed his dirty, balled-up clothes, and retrieved his cash box. He emptied the contents of the box into the middle of the floor. He spread the money out, edge to edge, and the bills stretched like a paper carpet the length of the room, sporting Lincoln and Hamilton and Jackson heads in even rows and accumulating to five hundred dollars to the paneling on the back wall.

What was it going to be? A couch? Some nice cushioned chairs? Certainly a kitchen table, some plants, appliances, a bed. A mattress: now that was something Eddie hadn't slept on since his old bedroom, a big, comfortable mattress. He wanted a nice foamy one, with some soft sheets and such, some giant pillows and a quilt for the winter time when the ground above him froze solid. Lots of things to keep him comfortable, that was all that mattered, so he wouldn't wake up in the night. He would need to figure out a way to get it to the apartment, though. Maybe somebody somewhere delivered such things.

As Eddie did his mental inventory of the things he needed, his sights suddenly shifted. Before anything, he decided, before the comfort of tables, couches, stereos, there would be the pet., there would be the Monitor Lizard. Even if it took up all of his paper carpet, there would be the lizard. He looked at the rows of money stretched to the back wall and he wondered how much he would need. He wanted a six-footer, a seven-footer if he could get it He wanted it to rule the room, to climb his soon-to be furniture. He wanted it roosted on the wall. Domingus had planted the possibility within him hours earlier, seeded his brain with the vision that had been snuffed out by his mother so many years back in "The Greatest Pet Store in the Civilized World." Now renewed, his vision, just like it had done so many years before, seized him so that he could think of nothing else. Lizard, lizard, lizard: he began to remember the books, the color plates, all of the species of monitor lizards around the world, long and green and leathery, the giant African ones crushing through the jungle in search of their scurrying meals. Nile Monitor, that was the one in the cage in the pet store. Eddie glued many hours of his afternoons up against the wire mesh of that cage, watching every move the giant lizard made, getting to know it like a brother, like his very own blood.

Yes, it was a water monitor from South Africa, and in its natural habitat it dug burrows into the river bank, long tube-like tunnels into which it would slide. It ate little rodents and such, and it especially liked the taste of crocodile eggs, sniffing them out with its long pink tongue, finding them gathered in their nests along the shore. One of his favorite television moments came during one of the nature shows, when a Nile Monitor confronted a female crocodile protecting her eggs. The two giant reptiles, like something from a dinosaur movie, began to fight, and the dirt kicked up, bits of weeds and chunks of earth flew into the air and their leather bodies entwined with a series of exotic grunts. A flash of jaws snapped out, angry rows of teeth from the mother crocodile, and she tore into the overpowered lizard. It tried helplessly to bite back, tried to penetrate the thick crocodile skin, but to little avail. It succumbed to the angry crocodile, torn apart finally and swallowed in football-sized chunks. Eddie's mother had him turn the station at that point. He was disappointed because he wanted to see the rest of the program, because his favorite lizard had been swallowed up. So he left the living room and headed up the stairs again, up to his room to smoke cigarettes and brood about things that might have been, to imagine only possible endings (perhaps a band of lizards would come to retaliate.)

The pet store was asking six hundred dollars for their lizard, and that was some years back. "The Greatest Pet Store in the Civilized World" closed just last year, mostly because it just wasn't doing the business any more, though Eddie had heard a story about an anaconda they'd sold to a couple from Landoff. Apparently, at least according to Billy Stigmeyer, the snake had escaped from the rabbit hutch they'd built for it. The hutch had been sitting in the rain for years, and the husband had built the thing with untreated lumber that began to rot away, little by little, in the legs. One hot day, while the couple were both away at work, the legs gave way, and the rabbit hutch and the anaconda crashed to the ground. The cage splintered open, allowing the snake, which had grown to twelve feet, to escape into the subdivision. It made the news that night, that much Eddie remembered, and some herpetologists from the coast drove into town to begin a search for the thing, looking with snake sticks between the houses, in the hedges, under porches, along with a look of worry in their eyes. The snake went unfound all summer, and then a little girl from Landoff disappeared one day, out from her rubber pool in the middle of the afternoon. The news crews descended again, poking about with their microphones in an attempt to blame the snake, asking the herpetologists if anacondas ate little girls and showing graphs of the snake's digestive system on the evening edition. Then they converged on the pet store, pointing out to the thick-spectacled man that some of his pets were illegal to sell, that some, like the ocelot, the badger and the anaconda for instance, could stalk and kill humans if they escaped into peaceful subdivisions.

They closed down the pet store after all of that. The anaconda was never found, and most people figured it died over the icy winter, froze up like a dead log. The little girl, however, did turn up several days after she'd disappeared. They found over by the interstate, lost chasing a "pretty butterfly."

Eddie rode by the pet store one day with his mother some months after it shut down. The place had been boarded up, with a sign pasted over the wood promising "vitamin shop coming soon". He gave up hope of ever getting one of those lizards that day as he watched his mother smile. Now revival: Domingus raised the possibility again, raised the Monitor lizard up from the dead, raised it with his 'connection'. Now, Eddie had the money to buy the thing, he had a basement apartment all to himself, and he had no crying mother to stop him.

III

Eddie heard the car start up in the driveway: Mrs. Haas on her way out for groceries or something. The ground rumbled as the tires crunched backwards down the stone incline, and her engine gathered power and then trailed off down Small Road. He gathered his laundry and stuffed the dirty clothes into his backpack and headed up the stairs. Giving the door a jiggle, he entered her home from his below, stealing into her kitchen. She had a big stove with six burners far across the white linoleum, with a covered pot full of something still warm; he could feel the extinguished heat lingering in a patch just in front of him. Shelves cropped up from out of the nooks like living things, stocked with little statues of ballerinas and elephants and such, all conspiring together with their painted eyes to watch him as he moved through the room. Pictures, pictures of people in black-and white, of places, long brown rivers and tall office buildings, old city streets with low-burning lights, and a life-sized oil portrait of herself studded the living room, hanging above the velvet red furniture in measured proportions. Eddie could smell the polish in the air, the familiar Endust that infected his brain through his nostrils, bringing back Billy Stigmeyer in his desk in the first, second, third, fourth grades—and buffing the tables at Bingo's. He hurried through the infection, made his way down the carpeted hall to the bedroom, and picked up a pair of his underwear after it had dropped from the knapsack.

Mrs. Haas had enshrined a man in her bedroom, hanging his portrait over the trap door. The picture, another life-sized oil painting, hung in the thickest oak frame Eddie had ever seen, borders thick as trees, squaring off a man in a tuxedo who sat back and stared, emotionless, into his black-painted universe. Two candelabras sprouted out from the sides of the frame, gripping white half-burned candles and leaving the smell of wax still lingering over the trap door. She had been thinking of him recently, Eddie surmised—she had burned the candles for him in a solemn remembrance. He studied the man briefly before he searched for the trap door handle, and he noticed the peculiar color of yellow paint the artist had used on his moustache—it almost glowed. In fact, Eddie was half-tempted to peer behind the canvas to see whether a night-light powered the moustache, but he decided he'd better look for the handle.

He grabbed the brass ring cut out of the carpet and lifted. A section of her white rug rose up in a five-foot square, raising a thick beam from down below and flicking on a bare bulb attached to a chain.

Eddie carried his laundry down the wooden steps, just catching the same pair of underwear before it slipped between the steps and floated off into the darkness. He could see the white machines as he got to the basement floor, with a basket of dresses and bras and such resting atop the dryer, folded in order. Mrs. Haas might be along soon, Eddie suddenly feared, and she might come right into her bedroom and down the stairs to finish her laundry. He feared that she might scream at his strange presence under the bulb, he holding his knapsack and his escaped underwear.

Eddie quickly dropped his clothes into the machine. He did not care that his whites were going into the mix with jeans and red shirts and dried creek water. He just wanted to finish it all and get out. He shook in some Tide in a pang of worry: he did not want to surprise the old lady—he would rather meet her out on the driveway or knock on her front door and introduce himself there, with a smile and a limp handshake and an "I'm your new downstairs neighbor." If she found him here, in the bottom of her house, she might do anything, call the police, scream and die, get him with a broom handle or a gun. None of it was good, either, none of it could be: discovering a strange boy in your basement was cause to take measures, especially in Hudson.

He went upstairs and peeked out the window to see if she was coming. It was going to take about two hours to finish his laundry, and he went to the picture window and peered out from behind the thick curtains that had been drawn to darken the room. He could see Small Road as it rose on the little crest to the stop sign five hundred yards beyond the house. That was the direction he had heard her car go, so he looked for her blue Impala and her knotted hands on the wheel as they pulled up to the sign. He waited and waited with an eye peeking, careful not to be seen by the neighboring ranchers and listening to the washer as it swooshed his clothes. The bright light coming through the glass made him turn away after a time, and he turned to the dark living room and tried to adjust his sight.

The scene developed like a photograph in a bath of chemicals, as the dark forms inked into existence like wooden monsters coming out of a fog. What furniture, Eddie thought, what old things she had collected here. They looked too formidable to sit upon, to touch even, what with their ornate carvings, grape vines and morning glories and figs snaking around the wood, sofa to wing-backed chair to cedar chest to hutch.

Did she have guests over? Did they sit in her polished chairs? Did they gather for tea within the wooden vines to talk about all of the dead ones, the long-buried ones? Eddie moved away from the window and moved closer to the pictures lining the walls, one black-and-white photograph after the other, of wedding parties, of people next to pools, of crowds gathered into diner booths with their burning cigarettes. She had organized them by the same faces, the same places, the number of years distant. All dead no doubt, decades removed from the living, all buried in the same cemetery, in even rows just like her photographs. Eddie glanced at the far wall: the pictures there contained only places, buildings and bridges, rivers and parks, peopleless in their compositions. He peeked again out the curtain to the stop sign and saw no Impala. Then, as he heard the spin cycle engage itself below, he moved across the room to the far wall and looked closer at the photographs that spread frame-tip to frame-tip to the doorway.

All of the pictures here were taken of Philadelphia, and some of them had places and years scrawled in their lower corners, 1932's and 1944's, 57's and 63's, Chestnut Streets and Sansom Streets and Lombard Circles and Rittenhouse Squares. All of it looked the same from a distance, from half-way across the carpet, blending into gray geometric forms rising and slanting into the countless black frames pressed together across the wall.

Eddie got closer in the subdued light, and he focused on some of the details, the empty streets and the rising buildings, the expanse of steel bridges, the thickly flowered parks with the slatted benches, and finally the old ball yards vacated after long-forgotten Phillies games. She must have been from the city, lived most of her life there, taken these with a camera of her own. All of those people on the far wall came from Philadelphia as well, and as they died one after the other, and as her friendships emptied into a peopleless existence, like her places on the wall, she settled down in Hudson to pass her last days. Hudson: a vast wasteland of ugly ranchers.

Eddie heard the washer click off, and he made his way down the steps again and put his clothes into the dryer. He must have stared at the photographs too close and too long; the bridges and parks and booth crowds merged together in a montage of gray blotches as he stood beneath the bare bulb. He thought only of the woman young again, Miss Haas, with an antique camera slung over her shoulder, making her way thirty years back through the deserted streets of Philadelphia, perhaps holding the hand of a young lover and wearing one of those dresses, now folded, in her basket atop the dryer.

He heard the crunch of the stones from outside the wall, and he could feel the walls rumble as the car advanced above him. She was home, she had come up the driveway in her Impala, and he heard her click the thing into park. What now? Eddie moved up the stairs in three leaps and moved across her carpet and up the hall. Through the side window he saw her shadow enlarging on the walk and he bent low and dashed into the kitchen. He reached for the door leading down into his dungeon. Just as she opened the front door, he closed his own door, and he crept in the dark down his steps. He wondered how he was going to retrieve his laundry, and when she would be leaving again.

IV

Fred booked a party of thirty for lunch, and Eddie had to get in early to portion some extra hamburger patties, defrost and cook an extra ten pounds of cocktail shrimp, and weigh more flounder. Fred had gotten a good deal on some soft-shelled crabs as well, and Eddie opened the crate to something he had never seen before: live soft-shelled crabs crawling over each other, fifty brown ones piled like wet leaves. The bottom of the sopping box had begun to fall away, so Eddie spread his hands beneath it and carried it into the walk-in. He put the box down on the metal floor and lifted one of the crabs with his finger. It folded in the middle like a used tea bag. The claws hung limp and heavy, and the legs, with the little power they had left, pedaled the air in a flurry of strokes. The sudden movement of all its legs at once scared Eddie, and he dropped the crab back into the fold.

"Batter dip them live," Fred said before the doors opened. "Three to an order. We'll go with five on the dinner menu."

The first order came in just after twelve, and Lisa asked to see the live crabs before Eddie dipped them into the batter. "They're still alive," she said, noticing them flail as Eddie dredged them in the flour. "You mean you have to drop them into the fryer and kill them there?"

"That's what Fred told me," Eddie said. "Apparently, when you dip them in the egg, and when the oil fries them up, it catches them just as they're struggling to escape, it freezes them in terror in the batter. But they look oh so very pretty on the plate," he said.

Lisa walked away with her head down, scolding Eddie on killing the poor defenseless crabs. "That's got to be the most horrible way to die," she said, "frying the way they do."

"Lisa, don't you know crabs are invertebrates?," Eddie asked.

"Meaning?"

"Meaning that they have no central nervous systems or a cerebral cortex, meaning they feel no pain. Meaning they don't really feel terror, meaning I don't feel guilty."

"No pain?"

"No pain. The damned things don't even know that they're alive."

"How do you know all this?"

"Nature shows, Lisa," Eddie said. "From watching the nature shows. They ran a special on crustaceans, and that's what the man said." He dropped the order of dripping crabs into the deep fryer and watched as the three of them bubbled and twirled about the black grease, spinning into each other like bumper cars. The batter hardened around them into a thick yellow shell, and Eddie took his tongs and plucked them out one by one, placing them gingerly on a leaf of romaine.

Fred had to come back and bail Eddie out when the thirty-top rolled in; Lisa had gone and recommended the soft-shelled crabs, and explained to the party, just as Eddie had done to her, about the nature of a crab's existence. She had also pointed out to them that cows and chickens and such could feel themselves being slaughtered—they knew what was coming—but the lowly crab was incapable of such a thing. "I got almost all of them to order the soft-shelled special," she said with a smile as she pinned the long ticket to the wheel. "I sold them all for you Eddie."

Eddie made her go out to the bar and get Fred up off his stool. Leslie had slammed him with an eight-top at the same time, all club sandwiches, and things were out of his control: too much toast, too many crawling crabs. Fred came back with several Mai-Tais in him, and he wobbled and dredged the crabs, a handful at a time, through the flour. "Die fuckers," he slurred, plopping them into the vat and counting the orders as they congregated. "Die."

Later in the day, after the parties had gone out, Eddie found a stray crab crawling beneath the fryer, powdered from the flour and making its way blindly over the thick cables. Either that poor crab had fallen from the pan, or the drunken Fred had dropped it between the cracks, Eddie didn't know which. He only knew that a wave of pity overtook him as he saw the white thing crawl. No, he kept telling himself, they can't feel pain, they're invertebrates with no cerebral cortexes and they simply don't know that they're alive—they can't tell the difference between the sea carrying them through columns of plankton, or the deep scalding oil smoking them up in a deep fryer—the man on the nature show told me so. But now this one didn't know where it was going. It grappled blindly with the little power left in its quickly softening legs to get over one more cable, and it just didn't know anything at all.

V

Domingus punched in with a smile because the doctor had finally removed his muddied cast. He stood in his whites by the dish machine and scratched and scratched the length of his arm. He had, by the time he walked in, dug long pink lines where his nails had scraped away the dark skin. "That cast…it make me itch for so long…I want to scratch for so long…I can no stop since doctor saw it off," he said. "I scratch all the way over here and now I can no do nothing else. I no think I can wash dishes even." Domingus pressed his nails into his skin,gritted his teeth, and dragged his fingers upward one more time.

"You really don't want to overdo it with the scratching," Eddie said. "Your arm might end up worse than broken."

"What you mean,?" Domingus asked.

"I mean that there have been documented cases of people scratching themselves to death. Not only that, I heard that most of those deaths occurred from people who just had their casts removed. Seems they couldn't stop their itching until they got down to raw bone…and by that time of course, they'd bled to death all over the place and even the paramedics were no good."

Domingus could see the pink of his skin deepening across the dark surface. His eyes widened in stunned disbelief, and his fingers dropped limply to his sides. "I should think about something else," he said. "I try not to scratch. I try to think of dishes, many many dishes…or how to get rid of my salao."

Eddie had fooled him again with another bullshit, the way he always fooled him. But it got Domingus to stop his scratching at least, so he figured it was a good bullshit, a benefit for the poor luckless dishwasher and his bleeding arm. All he needed was a few lies, something to help him along, something to stop the onrushing salao.

"Hey have you heard from your boat friend?" Eddie asked.

"Yes yes," Domingus replied. "I see Salvadore at street party. I tell him you want moneetoor lizard. I tell him you want big one, five six feet. He see what he can do."

"When will he know?" Eddie asked.

"When he go on his next boat trip. He leave tomorrow, he come back next week. They going for wicker mostly…to the Ivory Coast, chairs and tables. But they always bring back animals. Salvadore, he love to hunt in the jungle. He make the captain wait, he make him wait extra two days sometimes so he can hunt things, birds in trees mostly but sometimes animals on ground. Salvadore love to climb. He go out on long branches and he catch birds and monkeys. He catch them and sell them to the captain. The captain, he skinny man. He sell them for more money when he come ashore. He make money this captain, he make money from selling Salvadore's animals. And Salvadore he happy because he can go to different jungles and catch different things."

Salvadore worked on a boat out at sea, free of the land, docking on different continents to catch all of the animals in the world in their jungles. That must be the life, Eddie fantasized: nothing to hold you down but the promise of another port, the promise of more exotic creatures, the promise of brilliant green jungles to take you into their infernal power and hold you there. And then you came free, free with the brightly colored things, birds and monkeys and giant beetles and reptiles upon reptiles, squawking and chattering in cages, stacked and rolling through the jungle to the ship. Salvadore: one lucky son of a bitch.

"Well you tell your friend I'll personally give him four hundred dollars if he can get me a five-foot monitor lizard." Eddie said. "Tell him I've got the money right now. Tell him the sooner for me, the richer for him."

Domingus walked away from that one, trying to register the command into his head in Spanish, forgetting about the pink streaks the length of his healed arm. "You have it soon," he said into the steam. "You have it soon, you have it with four hundred dollar."

VI

Eddie had worked himself into a fever over getting that Monitor lizard. Back in his little apartment, he mapped out a section of the carpet where he might build the cage. He wished that he could get back into his father's lumber in the attic: those two by fours, that plywood, some of that chicken wire, if he could find it, would all build him a nice-sized cage over in the corner. He thought about his closet box again, empty now of his presence, his eternal secret preserved behind the hanging sweaters. He had done a nice job sawing and fitting the plywood into the space between the walls and hammering the pieces snug along the beams. He had measured the way his father had always measured by drawing his line in pencil across the wood; then he mounted the little hinges so that the door would open out and close out the light behind him. They would never find it, never. They'd tear the house down before they found his closet box.

Eddie heard some thumping above him, and he guessed that Mrs. Haas was moving something heavy. The sound rumbled down from above the far wall, just below where he calculated she had enshrined the moustached man. He made his way across the small room and stood

beneath the sound, which had now subdued itself into a mere scratching upon his ceiling. What could she be doing up there? His curiosity
flared, as he shut out the sound of the humming refrigerator that Fred
had installed, shut out the cars making their way up Small Road, shut
out everything but the woman in her room. He listened as the scratching ended—he could hear the mumbles then, slow and monotonous
and just out of the range of decipherability. Sounding like the slow
drone of some exotic chant, it seemed to seep down out of the ceiling
like dripping wax, deliberate and constant, filling the basement room
suddenly with its humming cadence.

Eddie wanted to see what she was doing in that room, barge up the
stairs with some laundry in his bag and catch her there, or perhaps go in
and tell her that he was getting the laundry he had left in the dryer. He
wanted to see her shriveled beneath the glowing moustache, there on
her knees with her hands up, her lips going, spewing out her haunting
tribute to the dead man on the wall. He searched the room for his
assorted dirty clothes in the consideration of getting them together,
though he never wrested his body from his spot beneath the chants. He
could never go through with it; he could never expose her naked like
that to a soul out of nowhere, what with the room darkened and the
candles burning, her head caught buried in her cupped hands. It would
be much too cruel to inflict such a scar across her grayed brain, so he
forgot the idea and turned his attention back to the corner, blocking out
the dripping whispers and envisioning his cage hammered snugly into
the corner.

Eddie noticed the phone jack below the heating vent. He'd never
considered it before: perhaps he could get himself a telephone.
Everyone had a phone, and he figured he could afford the thing because
he made so very few calls. But then he would have to worry about
revealing himself again; perhaps someone at the phone company had
been tipped off. Runaways were probably tracked down and caught like
that, kids who decided to get their own apartments and a make a new

go of things. Eddie figured that's how most of them got caught—not by the police or by their searching fathers—but by the telephone company. He had seen a documentary once about tracking devices, though the memory of the show had become too muddied to recall any one single thing, just bits about phone signals and hunting people down. They had gotten a man, some criminal, that much re-registered. They had gotten him at gun-point on his rotary phone moments after he'd made a call.

The chanting above him stopped. He listened as she walked from her bedroom, down her hall, through her living room and into her kitchen. Clack clack clack, her heels hit the tiles and then her breath sighed against his top door, magnified beyond its hush into Eddie's dampened room. She rapped ever so slight with her withered knuckles, and it drew him to the foot of the stairs as his neck hairs raised up in alarm.

"Excuse me young man, are you home?" came the voice. "Are you down there?"

Eddie's heart tingled against the fabric of his shirt as his legs took him up, until he unlatched the chain, until he was there in the open doorway looking right across at Mrs. Haas. The whiteness of her hair, perhaps coming on off the subdued light of the lace curtains, blinded him for a second to her pale powdered face. The whiteness sprang up like a fire upon her head, not unlike the glowing of that moustache in the back room, powered by some unseen electrical source wedged in her skull.

"I'm Natalie Haas," she said, extending her cold bony hand across the partition. "I understand Frederick purchased a new refrigerator for you. I saw the movers taking it down sometime yesterday."

"Yes, I left my back door key for them while I was working."

"You work under Frederick."

"Yes, I cook over at Bingo's on the lunch shift."

The woman stood silent on her tiles. Behind her spectacles, Eddie could see her eyes working, perusing his frame in the doorway, sizing him up and drawing her secret conclusions.

"It's olive."

"Olive?" Eddie asked, unsure of whether she had lost sense of things, whether he would have to prepare himself for a flood of gibberish.

"Your refrigerator. I saw the men, they had it on the dolly. I saw that it was olive. I like olive refrigerators personally. I had an olive one in my old place, but when I moved up here I saw the white one, and I guess I just settled for it." She sighed, as if the very notion of accepting white refrigerators became a symbol for a dwindling life, a life robbed of choice and dominated by necessity.

"Where did you live before Hudson?" Eddie asked, careful not to let her know that he already knew the answer to that one, that he'd already gone past the kitchen door and snooped around her living room and eyeballed all of her pictures and still had some of those black-and-white images floating in his brain.

"Why I'm from Philadelphia. I'm surprised that you didn't notice all of the pictures on my wall when you were doing your laundry."

Eddie's neck hairs went up again, and he caught himself speechless against the wood. "Oh my laundry," he said finally. "No I just went down without looking."

"Well the reason I knocked and disturbed you was to remind you to close the trap door when you're done in the basement. Sometimes I do it myself, and if I go into my room in the dark, well I could fall. And at my age, that's a little frightening."

"I'll be sure to close it next time," Eddie said. "I need to come and get my clothes anyway, if you don't mind."

Mrs. Haas moved away from the doorway and let Eddie pass into her kitchen. He could feel the heat still hanging in a ball in that same invisible spot, eternal almost.

"So why did you move up here?" he asked. "From Philadelphia." He followed her through her kitchen and then she stopped in the living room and guided his view to the framed photographs.

"You see, it's all here on the walls, all I was, my past, my days there. It got so I got tired of it. Things got so expensive down there with the rent and the electric bills. I had myself a little efficiency down off South Street, and the kids they came and made their ruckus on Saturday nights and they left their beer bottles broken on my pavement and their graffiti—always their damned graffiti—painted to the building."

Mrs. Haas had folded all of his laundry and put it atop the dryer in even piles—pants stacked, shirts stacked, underwear and socks stacked.

"You put your whites in with your colors," she said.

"I was in a hurry."

"Well you can take your time and have white underwear," she said. "Or you can hurry and have pink underwear." She walked over to the stacks, picked through, and pulled out a pair of BVD's, stained obviously by one of his red shirts. She held it along the waistband between index finger and thumb and waved it like a little pink flag. "Is this the sort of thing you really want to wear?"

"No I guess not," Eddie gave in.

"Well take your time." Then she smiled, put the pair back and clacked up the stairs.

VII

Eddie wrestled with his sheets as the minutes piled into hours and the night dragged on into an eternal unsleep. He would be hearing the birds start up soon, the ones hanging from invisible trees behind the hammered plywood. Their little chirps and squawks would come at him and remind him that he had not yet slept, that the beginning of the long day had already delivered itself with the first seepage of light over the ranchers. Eddie peered across the room at the shuttered window, waiting for the inevitable cracks of light to form visible squares, waiting for the sounds to begin. He strained his ears for any kind of sound, a bird, a car starting up, a movement above him in the woman's bedroom. But the silence thickened in a blanket over him, and he closed his eyes to bring on sleep.

Billy Stigmeyer had told him once, after a freshly smoked joint, that there was no such thing as silence. He sat and talked about sound, always present, only a careful listen away, and all you had to do was strain your ears a little bit and the sound of the world would come rushing in, the sound of everything happening, things miles and continents distant. "The trouble," Billy had said as he finished the roach, "is that it takes some practice straining your ear muscles just right. You have to work at it every day, exercise them so to speak, in any minute of quiet you might get." Then Billy contorted his face, opened his mouth, stretched his jaw, put up an index finger, and listened. "You see, I'm working my ear muscles, opening the canal, letting in the distant sounds." Billy sat there stoned and let the noises of the world come rushing in (or at least he said so). Eddie wasn't inclined to believe that Billy could hear the Chinamen in the market square a half a world away, or the cars traversing the suspension bridge a thousand miles west, or the crickets even, dying in the grass just over the next hill. But Billy insisted he could hear each distinct sound as they arrived and touched his eardrums. "I can taste them like flavors of ice cream," he had said.

Now, Eddie stretched his jaw in the dark, and he thought he could hear the crows starting up on the Neshaminy. That was at least two miles away, out past hundreds of scattered ranchers, out across the interstate with a million noises in between. But he swore could hear the cawing as it echoed through the glade just past his vacated bridge cave, and that those very birds were delivering their sound to his basement apartment as they sat picking at minnows, undaunted on the rocks.

And then 'salao.' Domingus' parrot, as if it had entered the room through one of those cracks of the shuttered wood, began its lamenting of poor Domingus and his terrible luck. Salao, salao, salao, salao, salao, Eddie kept hearing through his opened canals. Perhaps it was as Billy had said. Perhaps the parrot was speaking from its perch in Domingus' apartment somewhere over in Newportville, and Eddie had simply tuned in, snagging the sound out of the air like a radio antenna. Perhaps he had tuned in for a reason—his ears beckoned this particular sound from behind his silent wall because that's what his brain wanted him to hear.

Salao: it infested Domingus, and Eddie, despite his pity for him, never really gave the affliction much thought. It was just one of those Puerto Rican things, something he would never understand because it was something that sprouted out of some distant culture a thousand miles south, brought on by generations of terrible superstition and carefully whispered warnings. But now here he was, at five o'clock in the morning, alone in the blackness once again, trying to figure out salao, and whether he too, had fallen under its spell.

The string of incidents played themselves out again, merging and fluctuating until they attained new realities, festered by the expanse of time and strung with the cobwebs of shrouded memory. Now they came back again, and Eddie saw the men standing in the hall light, standing beneath a bulb that never existed, save for the burning light in Mrs. Haas' dim basement. Nor could Eddie have ever seen the men standing there in his bedroom doorway, for his head all along had been buried in the quilt deep under his bed. But now they came back, unearthed like walking zombies, and their masked faces breathed the steam of the cold winter air, as if the house itself had suddenly froze up in a deliverance of horror. Now he exposed his face to the cold air, now he let himself up from the floor, albeit invisible to the masked ones. They, in their thick coats and their stomping boots, moved in black flashes to the next room, plucking the baby out of the crib, sliding

Benjamin beneath one of their overcoats and exposing the green jersey there, the number sixteen that now glowed white. The flashes blurred beneath the light with their stolen parcel, and they leaped amidst shadows down the darkening stairs.

How could it be? How could these memories take on such a new life as this? Should they not now have begun to fade out and return only as murky shadows? Should not the happier present snuff these things out? Everything was a mistake, life out of order. Everything might have been o.k. if only he hadn't thrown that soda into the air and tried instead to learn something about the baseball game going on below him, stuck his face into his father's scorecard and questioned the markings in the columns. He might have learned a thing or two about the game right then and there. His father might have guided his hand between the columns, pulled out a little yellow pencil just for him, while William, on the other side of him, learned likewise how to mark the double-play grounder to third to shortstop to first. And then the revelation of baseball might have descended upon him, and the beauty of the game would have come at him from the Astro-Turf below, and he would have finished chomping the ice in his cup and placed it gingerly beneath the seat.

But he threw his cup into the air, and now that moment returned to replay itself: he threw it with all his might, with his teeth clenched in a volcanic rage, because it was William and only William learning those things, the one holding the little yellow pencil and receiving the glow of revelation from the plastic grass. All Eddie had to do was ask if he could give the scorecard a try, and the chain of events would never have begun themselves at that moment, and he would be home right now, at this very moment, sleeping in his own bed, or getting up early to help Benjamin with his homework, or dreaming of the Phillies making the playoffs.

Now, here he was over in Hudson, watching the visible squares form along the far wall. Deep in his distance, Eddie could still hear the "salao," no longer a parrot but Domingus now, his thick Spanish accent lingering like pollen in the air, floating into his opened eardrums. The whole chain of events was nothing but salao, nothing but the snow-balling of one vast mountain of horrible luck, from the moment that cup came sailing down to kill the old woman in her seat to the runaway to now, he in his perpetual darkness.

Now the full list of dark places played themselves out, strung them-selves out like lanterns across his brain. The closet box, the smell of pine, the sobs coming up the vent, the cigarette burns in the buckling wood, the drone of the game, the crickets out his window, the crickets on the lawn near his ears, the crickets just beyond the tool shed. Billy Stigmeyer walking away dusted, completely dusted and smelling like his father's cologne, shielded from the particles of the world. The interstate and its oil trucks, the opened lot and the jutting nails, the bridge, the massive bridge of metal and stone that sprung out of the trees, man and nature crushed together, cracked only by the red-veined womb behind the fissure, the newspapered floor, the papers piling, the mosquitoes massing for an attack. Hudson, the rancher wasteland, fading in black rows, always evenly and full of the old and dying ones, into nightfall.

Darkness had followed Eddie everywhere, and he looked angrily at the plywood nailed into the cement, as if it were thick metal bars pre-venting his escape, as if he had been mistakenly sentenced behind it. He had never thought about taking those boards down before, never thought about their presence. He just always assumed that they were there for a reason, that the basement apartment should remain hidden from the world, hidden from Hudson, from all of the nosy neighbors walking by, neighbors who would surely be drawn like battered moths to the curious light between the forsythias.

But Eddie wanted daylight. It didn't matter that they saw him; he had to bring some of that sun in, he had to have his outside coming in. He had enough. He got up from his bed and walked over to the wall, climbed onto the little cement ledge and reached up for the edges of the wood. He fitted his thin fingers along the cracks and felt the cold draft of the outside air. Then he pulled. He pulled the shuttered plywood with all his might, with the mighty force of a thousand subdued grunts, a thousand years of darkness bottled within. He leaned back with all of his weight and gritted his teeth as a stinging pain shot through his fingers, and then he could feel the board giving way.

In an instant, he exploded from the cement ledge, as if some invisible hand had pushed through the window beyond his reach and shoved him back. He fell and seemed to always be falling, as if, in the course of the nails freeing themselves from the cement, he had become suspended in the stagnant air of his apartment, beholding, from invisible strings, the oncoming light. Then he fell, and the thick cement below the carpet shot one long injection of pain the length of his body as he dropped with a thud. He held the freed board, nails jutting skyward, over his head. Partially dazed by the blow, partially enamored by the light, Eddie lay there on his carpet for some seconds and finally put the board down. A cool rush of autumn air came flowing down through the broken window panes. Old and dusty, encroached by spider webs and such, the window had obviously been boarded up to save Fred the cost of replacing the broken glass. But dust, spiders, and dirt-thickened panes could not keep out the light now, the light that crept groundward with the dew.

Eddie felt a sudden chill envelop his little apartment. The broken windows had done that, all in the moments that he lay on his shag carpet looking skyward. It had dropped twenty degrees or so and it had gotten downright cold. He looked around for some rags, some old clothes perhaps, to stuff into the broken windows. He considered hammering the board back into the cement to wait for the replaced glass. No, he decided, there was light finally, light coming into his little place beneath the ground, and having that was better than anything. All of his salao was tied to darkness—that he knew now—to shutting himself into his own private universes, to shutting out the rest of existence, place by place. Well, no more. Domingus had his parrot to help him rid him of salao, and now, Eddie had his daylight.

He crawled along the floor and climbed into his bed in a long shiver, then he grabbed the extra sheet at the foot of the mattress. He wrapped himself tight, made certain that his feet did not protrude from the bottom, and laid down on his pillow. For some time he watched the blueblack light delivering itself downward between the forsythias. Finally he closed his eyes and drifted off to sleep, hearing in his waning moments of consciousness, and then in a opening of a dream, the sounds of the world come rushing in.

Jude

———————◆———————

I

Eddie saw a baby in a car seat that reminded him of his stolen brother Benjamin. Alone in the back with the open windows allowing the breeze, the baby turned this way and that, and mumbled some words that sounded nothing at all like baby murmurs, but rather like that of an adult perplexed into speechlessness. Just like Benjamin: he had the long white hair, the wavy bangs coming down the front, and the teeth coming in along the top gums, chiclets dripping slobber. The baby shook a crumpled fast food bag in his hand, something that he had no doubt picked from the seat. He rattled the bag in short, manic jerks, and it spilled out cold fries, falling like Brad Griggs' dead salamanders into the garbage encroaching the floor. The baby, whom Eddie gawked at through the open window, turned around and noticed him, dropping the bag and his two-toothed smile and stopping his eerie garbling.

Eddie stood and awaited some half-hearted recognition, struck by the sudden hope that perhaps Benjamin, in the time since his kidnap, had not grown at all, and now he sat bolted into the seat before him, a victim found. But the baby screamed, a piercing screech that carried out in a shot across the open window and echoed into reverberation down the macadam on Wellsley. Eddie watched the rapid movements through the window of the hardware store across the street as a sweatered man peered out with widened corneas and then gathered his bags in a hurry at the counter.

Eddie moved on down the street, the man, thin and weighed down by his twenty pounds of mulch, nearly missed being hit by an oncoming car as he called out "Joey joey daddy's coming joey" across Wellsley and over his hurried footsteps. Finally, the man plopped the heavy bag atop the vinyl roof, reached in, and patted his son's white hair down. Eddie turned back and saw him standing there still, his hands rested upon the roof, ready to do something with his bag of mulch, something like club someone if they tried to reach in and unbuckle his little son. The man looked right at Eddie as he turned the corner onto Holloway, and he could still feel his glare—the glare that said 'keep away from my kid you little son of a bitch'—and could still hear the piercing scream of the baby as he disappeared behind the brick.

Haunting, Eddie thought, to see a baby so much like Benjamin, held in a prison of time like that, with the same white wisps blown across his eyes, the same mangled voice painting abstract strokes of sound. In the course of his brief vision, everything came back: the memories unearthed themselves and delivered again his only brother to behold, a photograph on the wall. It blended in with the other photographs he had remembered from Mrs. Haas's living room, merged with old ball yards and expansion bridges, with people gathered by in-ground pools and mashed into diner booths under the hazy fog of cigarettes. Now, framed in black and white and tucked somewhere across the old woman's wall, the little boy, white hair caught hanging, mouth caught open, tugged at Eddie's brain as his past converged like some colliding train into the present, as his memories mixed into a hazy delirium of cityscapes and faded colorless decades and portraits of dead men with glowing moustaches. He brushed his face, ran his fingers through his hair as if he had passed through a spider web, for he could feel the tingle of something against his skin, though he knew, in his quiet contemplation, that the physical world held nothing to explain it.

Later that day, in the evening after he had finished cooking another shift, he heard the same piercing scream several streets distant as he made his way toward Hudson, just as the darkness descended with its elongated fingers across the subdivision. The baby kept on and the wailing seemed to keep coming, like a siren through traffic. Even after the sound had vanished entirely from the physical plain, he could hear the echoes about his head, and he became quite certain, in one such spasm, that the crying might keep on coming every minute for the rest of his life.

II

Eddie took off his whites from another busy lunch. He had spilled marinara sauce down his chef coat, and Lisa had made some jokes about his "bloody" appearance and how he looked like a mass murderer at the end of a rampage. The night waitresses began their set-up at the service rack, and he could hear the chatter from the break room, so he knew that four o'clock had come. He balled up his bloody chef coat and tossed it into the bin. The t-shirt that he had worn underneath had picked up the stain, a faint red spot in the center the shape of a heart.

"You get shot?" came the voice. Domingus had come in off the dock as Eddie punched out. "Somebody get mad at you today?" He looked back from the open door, as if he were watching something there, something hidden by the piled crates. "I have something for you out on dock," he said.

Though it had been two days since Eddie had seen the white-haired baby in the car, the phantom scream still kept flaring up in his head; he had, during the slam, stopped and pushed through the swinging doors to the dining room, looking into the booths for the skinny man and his son, or another baby even, to ease his mind. But he found only the low mumble of faceless lunch patrons and the inquisitive Fred on the other side of the room behind his Mai-Tai. Now, at exactly four o'clock, he thought he heard the baby wailing from out on the dock, muffled by the half-closed doors, behind piled crates or hidden in the dumpster, perhaps even wriggling under some empty boxes. Eddie thought that Domingus had gone and stolen that baby out of the car seat, snatched it from the open window and brought it back for him. Before he reached the dock doors, in fact, he felt quite certain that Domingus had figured it all out—his whole life story right down to the bridge cave and his new apartment—and now here he was helping him to fix things in his own Spanish way.

"I tie it good with heavy rope because it strong," Domingus whispered. "Everybody look at me when I bring it over in back seat of my car."

The monitor lizard propped its brown paws upon the crate and lifted its head into full view, and Eddie fell back against the double doors and slammed them shut with his back, surprised by the reptile's size—at least five feet in length—and by its long forked tongue that flickered the air. The lizard craned its neck and tried to squirm from the thick rope burning into its scales, and it grunted though its nostrils and knocked the top crate over the edge of the dock.

"He make that noise all the way over," Domingus said. "He whip his tail around the car and make me drive crazy. Some lady she crash her car when she see monster lizard in my back seat. She run her car into guardrail and make sparks."

"I can't believe it...Salvadore came through," Eddie said, closing the doors entirely.

"Yes, he come through—but he want five hundred dollar."

"I thought you said four hundred?"

"Yes but Salvadore he tell me he have a hard time catching this lizard. He run through rainy jungle and get cut badly on his face and lizard's claws scratch him all up and he need—how you say—many stitches." Domingus beckoned Eddie to the lizard, which had now calmed itself considerably and stared statue-like into the mass of trees beyond the back lot, probably at some birds carrying on there that it wanted to stalk and kill. "Salvadore jump on it and stab it. He think he going to die when he fight it in jungle. It get on top of him." Eddie could see the open wound lining the side of the beast, a long thin slash partially obscured beneath dried green blood, patched by sloppy gauze and duct tape.

"Who bandaged it?" Eddie asked.

"Salvadore do it while captain hold down lizard. Captain very strong. He skinny, but I see him one time and he have biggest hands I ever see, hairy hands. Salvadore tell me he almost break lizards neck. Lizard very very angry while Salvadore put bandage on."

Eddie reached out his hand and petted the reptile, its beady eyes still frozen on the trees. He touched the crest of its skull, feeling the large smooth scales molded perfectly into a taut coat, ridged in little hills over the eyes. The lizard turned its head in a slow cock and tasted the air with its tongue again, baring a wall of the cave of its mouth, oblivious to Eddie's strokes.

"How am I ever going to get this thing home?" Eddie asked. "I have to go all the way to Hudson. I'll have people watching me the whole stupid way." He never considered the problems that might arrive with a five-foot lizard lizard. The size, the sheer mass of reptile, overwhelmed him. It rose off the concrete on legs thick as dining-room table legs, tasting the air and watching a swallow take off above the treetops.

With a jingle, Eddie turned to see Domingus holding his keys over the edge of the dock, wiggling them in the air like a just-caught fish.

"I let you take my car," he said. "I have green Falcon, nine teen seventy one." Domingus pointed out to the edge of the asphalt, where, parked slanted under a tree, his car sat with its oversized tires. The particular color reminded Eddie of Crayolas, of Spring Green, of the marks on the nursery walls. Benjamin again: even through the sight of a spray-painted Falcon under some trees, even in the presence of a monster lizard, his little brother rose again, trailing his pink little hands in brush strokes across the drywall. Out from his crib came the green lines, some straight and dug in just above the brace, some arching in great swirls like galaxies over the bars, testaments to his found possession and grand in their scale of possibility. Eddie had laughed at all of that on the day that he walked in on his mother with her sponges, and he watched her smear the wall into a hideous mess that would need two coats of paint. 'Damnit', his father said on the Saturday he had to go in there with the roller. 'Damnit.'

Domingus offered him the car to drive home, so that he could take his lizard back to his apartment with a little more peace. Eddie wanted to take it, too. Despite his never having driven before (except for Driver's Ed), walking that lizard home was simply more dangerous: the huge reptile, untied, would drag him across the lawns all the way through Fergusonville and into Hudson. The leather tail would whip him and the claws would puncture him. And Eddie knew that he would be seen. Bleeding, helplessly tugged about, eyes wide, he would be seen by every car that happened by, through every window, and his presence would spring out in an echo across the subdivision, he walking along, the runaway with the giant reptile. Phone calls between the houses, calls back to the Shemanski house, calls down to the police station. The tracks: his father, his mother, William, the police finally, would only need to follow the reptile tracks across the dirt lots to Hudson, to Small Road, and finally down to his little basement apartment hidden so nicely away from the world of recognition. And then they would nab him among his bandages, get him there through the splintering of doors and the shattering of windows, and shoot his lizard dead on the carpet, because it was too big a reptile, and his mother hated reptiles.

"I'll take the back roads," Eddie said. He grabbed the keys as Domingus dangled them, careful not to divulge his many secrets as he jumped from the dock. "And I'll try not to scare any ladies into guardrails."

III

Eddie had Domingus pull his car up to the edge of the dock. "I'll drive real slow," he said. He didn't bother to tell Domingus that he was only seventeen and without a license, that he had only driven once on a serpentine course over at St. Anselm, and that the instructor had flunked him because he plowed over a row of orange cones and then he told the man that his permit had expired. Mr. Walsmith: that was the same instructor who had flunked him in Archery after Eddie had shot an arrow into the ground between his feet...

He took the keys as Domingus opened the passenger door and pushed back the seat, clearing some shredded paper bags from the back floor.

"That leezard, his claws very strong," he said. He held the destroyed bags in the air, then carried them to the dumpster and tossed them in. "I hope he not get too angry and wreck my seat."

Nervousness descended: now it was time to unleash the reptile from its mooring on the dry dock, put it into the car, and drive for the first time alone. The lizard cocked its head and looked right at him. "It must know," Eddie said.

"I no understand. Know?"

"Yes, it must know I'm coming over there to get it and put it in the car."

"Yes, it a smart leezard. It have a big brain, that for sure. It have a big everything."

His pale hands shook as he reached to untie the rope. The tongue flickered, sniffing Eddie as he worked to free the thing. "I hope lizards aren't like dogs and they can sense when a person is nervous. If that's the case, this thing might go crazy."

Domingus had tied it tight, and Eddie had to pick at the strands of rope with his nails to unravel the thick knot.

"I want to make sure it no escape," Domingus said. "I tie that five hundred dollar lizard tight."

Eddie took the freed rope and tugged his lizard in the direction of the car. The lizard advanced in a sideways motion down the cement incline as he pulled the rope from below. At the level cement, it pulled away toward the trees like an untamed dog, yanking the rope with all its reptilian might. Eddie had to ask Domingus for a hand as the lizard dragged him toward the open lot, where the birds suddenly had begun a loud banter among the falling leaves, ascending finally in an upward rain of beating wings. The lizard struggled to free itself from the rope, flicking its tongue in manic flaps and scaring Eddie as it opened its mouth to reveal its massive pink cave, straining all the while toward the hopelessly airborne birds.

"It look just like one of those monsters in movies," Domingus said, and he grabbed the bottom of the rope and helped Eddie to drag the thing to the open door of his Falcon. Eddie and Domingus worked the lizard's head into the back seat, guiding its leathery body as it sucked in the air and contracted its stomach. The tail whipped Eddie across the legs. He cursed the thing as he felt the sting travel up his thighs, and in a surge he shoved the lizard into the seat and closed the door.

"It do that all the way from Salvadore's house, all the way over here. It whip and whip," Domingus said. I no think I make it alive." Domingus rubbed his arm again, his fingers ready to scratch. He looked at Eddie and remembered his warning. "You have money soon?"

"I'll bring it in tomorrow," Eddie said. "I didn't know that you were bringing the lizard today, or I would've brought the money in." He walked nervously around the side of the car, knowing for certain that he was the first person in the human race to drive for the very first time with a five-foot monitor lizard thrashing away in the seat behind him. He mentally mapped out his trip home—picturing the near-vacant streets of Holloway and Crestine, Sinkler and then the short stretch of interstate over to Hudson. The interstate worried him the most, what with the trucks rumbling, their cargoes of flammables barreling along at seventy. It would take just one glance into Eddie's back seat from one of those drivers, one long stare out from the cab of one of those dangerous flammable trucks, and it would be all over. Eyes off the road, the driver would lose control, the big steering wheel would jerk and pull the truck out of the lane and tip on its side, smashing down in a fiery ball of destruction.

"Maybe I can put something on the windows," Eddie said. He looked over to the dumpster, noticing the cardboard boxes piled like building blocks. The lizard had begun to thrash about the inside and its tail smacked against the window while the car rocked on its springs. Eddie ran to the dumpster and grabbed some of the empty boxes, tearing them along the seams and flattening them with his sneakers on the hot cement.

"That lizard he going to break my glass," Domingus said. "he no like riding in car. He know he going to go somewhere again."

Eddie lined the inside of the windows with the flattened cardboard. All the while he had to avoid the tail whipping about him. He feared that perhaps the lizard might give a try at swallowing him while he remembered how to drive.

He got into the car and drove slowly from the dock. Domingus mumbled some Spanish things as he pulled away, though Eddie was more concerned with driving a straight line than deciphering the trailing words. He didn't draw too much attention as he crawled along the side roads, along Midvale and Sinkler, Buttonwood and Crestine, pegging the speedometer at twenty all the way. Out on Holloway, a large blue Cadillac passed Eddie in the roar of a missing exhaust. It shot by in a blur and sent a wall of air into the car, whereby the lizard, in the melee of sound, sprung about the back seat in a spasm of panic and tore the cardboard curtain from one of the side windows. Eddie braked as the light poured in from the side, and he suddenly remembered, despite his fiasco, the broken window in his own apartment. He wondered if perhaps the lizard could escape through that broken glass, and how he might need to fix it the first thing back. He watched the blue Cadillac disappear over the hill. It looked much like the one that had followed him in the rain so many nights back. The man with the white bony face might have whizzed right past him, on to stalk and kidnap another helpless victim walking down the road.

Out on the interstate, Eddie watched nervously at the yield sign as the tractor trailers and the oil trucks and the speeding cars shot by him at seventy. His lizard snapped its leather jaw and flickered a tongue at the passing forms, and then Eddie stepped into the onslaught as the traffic died briefly away. The cardboard-less window worried him, and he already saw the faces begin to peer through and see the giant lizard crouched upon the seat, some kids in a station wagon as they passed in the other direction, a man with glasses who smiled and slowed. Three exits up, three exits up. Come on Hudson sign, come on. Eddie could see a large tractor trailer, with upright exhausts, approaching at high speed from the other lane. He had played this scenario out already, and it seemed to be unfolding like a bad dream realized. The man driving that rig was going to look down and see the lizard, lose control of the wheel, slide into the oncoming traffic, and spill over. It was going to happen just like that, and Eddie was never so certain of anything, because the image of the truck, with the upright exhausts, the black cab, the smoke billowing up, was exactly as he had imagined.

He stepped on the gas, gunned the car above seventy, and shot past the first exit, "Newportville." Domingus' parrot had to be going crazy in that apartment, shut in alone on a perch and calling for its master, or perhaps lamenting its displacement from the thick green jungle where Salvadore had snatched it from the tree. Eddie worried about Domingus' car. He felt the steering wheel begin to shimmy, and he let off of the gas a little. The truck kept coming in the other lane, and Eddie put on his blinker and moved in front of it. If the truck was going to pass him, he figured, he'd have to get into the other lane, and there the man would see only the cardboard, unless he really crouched low and looked back through the windshield. Eddie steadied the car and watched the lines on the road, careful to guide his tires straight. Mr. Walsmith had yelled at him about that on the serpentine (comparing his driving to his drunken aunt on her way home from a New Year's Eve party). So Eddie made sure about the straight driving, and he brought his speed down to sixty, and now he looked nervously as a police car shot by in the oncoming lane. He passed the second exit, "Landoff," and figured he'd better get back into the right lane. He saw the truck there as the bulk of it vanished into his blind spot, so he slowed to get behind it.

"We'll be home soon," he said to his lizard. "Off this highway in a minute."

The truck rumbled past as Eddie braked, and then the traffic was upon him, a thousand different cars passing him, trying to get through him and the truck in a flurry of metal. Eddie craned his head to see if his blind spot was clear. He put on his blinker again, fearful that the exit was coming soon, that he wouldn't get over in time and that he'd have to take the interstate clear down to Jamison and find a way to turn around. He didn't want to have to do that, and he cursed, not so much at the frustration of not being able to get over, but because he, in his paranoia, had moved into the other lane to begin with. The truck of his nightmare had now moved well ahead of him, though he could see other nightmare trucks approaching in the melee of cars. Not a car slowed to look into the back seat, though. None braked, no one pointed, no one screamed. Eddie looked into the rear view mirror and panicked when he didn't see the lizard. He craned his neck and noticed that the lizard had laid down on the floor. That was good. He figured that the thing was afraid, and maybe it sensed human fear, that being seen in such a fast place as this could kill it in a quick ball of fire.

The exit appeared over the roof of the tractor trailer, and Eddie slowed and traversed the ramp. The lizard, as if knowing that the danger had passed, lifted its cold black eyes into the boundaries of the rear-view mirror and let loose a forked tongue to taste the suddenly tranquil air of the imposing ranchers, of Hudson. Now it would be only the old people, and Eddie slowed to twenty as he rolled up Small Road, and his heart raced as he saw the Impala sitting upon the stones. Now he was going to have to smuggle the thing in, walk it along the bricked path to the back of the house and down to his little door. He saw a car approaching as he pulled to the curb, and an old man slowed and watched his moves as he downshifted and shut off the engine. The lizard snorted a ball of air, and, as the man passed, Eddie waited for the curtains to move, for the woman's face to appear among the alabaster figures conspiring on the ledge.

His chance: the street emptied of sound, and he saw the path and clicked open the door, careful to grab the leash as it swung about the interior. The lizard pulled inward, as if it didn't want to escape the confines of its back seat. Eddie had to tug the thing with all his might. He wished that Domingus had come along to help him, though he quickly realized that a Spanish kid in Hudson would be more out-of-place than even a five-foot Monitor lizard.

"Come on," he whispered. "It's just around the bushes up there…so be good for me." The lizard must somehow have tuned in to Eddie's request—with some reptilian sixth sense—for it walked right along side of him down the brick path, toe to toe, clicking the hard brick with its mighty claws. Its tail lashed out and knocked over some chrysanthe-mums, and it sprayed the mangled petals into a yellow explosion across the topsoil. "Shhhh," Eddie whispered—pulling and pulling some more as the burning rope reddened his fingers. Then it was over: he unlocked the door, pulled the lizard in, and closed off the threatening world.

IV

Mrs. Haas had some music going, and it rumbled down the walls in a sonorous dripping of notes that reminded Eddie of the piano coming out of the church basement ten years back. It was not unlike the particular key in which his mother wailed—over the patter of the raindrops—in the weeks after Benjamin was stolen, and the way that it, too, rumbled through the duct to his very ears. The echoes tranquilized the lizard and subdued it into a restful repose. Eddie latched its leash to the refrigerator door, mindful of the broken window and its shaft of daylight. The air had warmed considerably from the early morning chill, and with the spiders gone, he considered what could be done in order to prevent his pet's escape. He stared up at the daylight, as if expecting the arrival of some cosmic answer, watching the lizard as it gazed up too, its yellow eyeballs fixed on the square of light. It flickered its tongue (smelling possible game birds trapped between the hedges) and emerged from its repose to tug at the refrigerator door.

Really, the only option would be to secure the plywood again, to hammer the jutting nails back into the cement from where they came. He would need to wait on the new glass, until Fred had the time and the sobriety to replace them. Eddie would need to go back into his darkness for a spell. When Fred did visit, he would have to hide his lizard. (But where to hide a five-foot lizard? Under the sink? Behind the shower cur-tain? On Mrs. Haas' side of the basement?)

Eddie tried to fix the board back into the wall but the nails had been bent from his earlier yanking, and he realized that new nails were in order. He heard the floorboards creaking above him in the living room: Mrs. Haas was pacing again, probably examining the photographs and reminiscing, pondering her fate in the rancher wasteland. She probably had that man on her mind, the one they buried underneath the shiny marble slab, he of the white hair and moustache that glowed above the trap door.

The lizard grunted full force and opened the refrigerator door with one fierce tug, and the little light bulb shot a bar of light across the shag carpet. Startled, Eddie turned to see the thing flicking its tongue in manic bursts as it clawed the linoleum in a struggle to get free. Its head cocked skyward toward the natural light, Eddie's new pet swung the door completely wide and a ketchup bottle, nearly empty and perched upon the door shelf, jerked out of its holder and fell upon the floor, spinning like a rotor and finally coming to rest at the base of the cabinet.

"Whoa take it easy girl", Eddie said, jumping down from the ledge with his failed shutter. He approached the lizard as if he were a cowboy trying to calm a horse in the face of a rattlesnake, and the lizard snapped its mouth to reveal the pink cave. "I'll bet you need something to eat." He pondered and stared at the unbroken ketchup bottle, remembering the guinea pig swallowed up by that monitor lizard in the pet store. He would need to get some rodents and such, keep them in little cages somewhere else in the apartment, then feed the thing when it flicked its tongue in short intervals. Eddie felt for the bills in his pocket, calculating at least ten of them, one of which definitely was a twenty. That would be enough to get him at least five guinea pigs from the K-Mart, back in the pet section where they sold only rodents and parakeets. He could get them on the way back to drop off the car at Bingo's.

Eddie lashed his lizard's leash to the door knob with a double bow-line before he left the apartment. He was certain it would hold: he had taught so many of the scouts that knot during the meetings, on jamborees and on hikes. Two loops over, one under, two around, one through: it was as good as a padlock. He could hear the lizard tug from behind the door as he locked it in. The knob rattled and Eddie half-expected it to come ripping off, half-imagined himself peering through the vacated hole to watch in horror as his freed lizard shot across the room, scaled the cinderblock wall, and squeezed its long leather torso up and out the broken window. He half-expected it to come dashing across the lawn as he made his way, past the exploded chrysanthemums, up the walkway.

V

On the ride over to K-Mart, Eddie decided to call his lizard "Jude." The name just came to him, just floated down and stuck there on his brain as he merged onto the interstate. Just a short little name with a nice sound that his lizard might eventually learn and respond to. "Hey Jude," he said aloud. "Don't let me down." He hummed a little of the song, and thought about his Beatles albums in his old room, and then about putting on the radio. His eyes darted to the dashboard; he didn't want to take either hand off the wheel. Not on the interstate, not at sixty. Not with the trucks advancing in the rear-view mirror. So he just continued to hum, thinking: "You have found her, now go and get her. Remember to let her under your skin and then you will begin to make it better better better."

Eddie got off at Landoff and traveled two lights up, where he pulled into the K-Mart parking lot and parked near the auto service entrance. They kept the pets right near the rows of motor oil, and he wanted to be close to the swinging doors so wouldn't draw attention carrying a load of animals back to the car.

They only had two guinea pigs left so Eddie bought them, along with ten gerbils. The fat saleswoman looked at him suspiciously as she rang up the total and searched for some empty boxes. One by one she fished the gerbils out of a cage of fifty with a pair of plastic tongs, sending the parakeets into a chatter. She swung her monster hips and cursed the rodents as they deftly avoided her clampages. "Fuck," she kept saying. "Sons of bitches." Finally she squeezed her tenth and dropped it into an empty box labeled "Valvoline Motor Oil." She closed it up as the frightened gerbils scattered about the bottom, and Eddie saw some tails drop out of the little crack in the center of the box.

"You're sure they won't get out of that box?" Eddie asked. "Those gerbils…they can squeeze out of little cracks like that," he said.

"Honey I've been doing this for eight years," the fat saleslady said. "I had a parakeet get away from me just about five years ago. I had to climb the damned curtain displays over in Fabrics to get it. If I didn't have that little boy and his mother following me around and watching me break my fucking neck trying to get to the thing, I swore I would have torn that little fucker feather from feather right there on the valance." She tonged the guinea pigs and they squealed in terror as she dropped them into another empty oil box. "But other than that, nothing's ever escaped me." She adjusted her tight shirt around her bulging stomach. "I make sure nothing ever escapes me."

The lingering image of the fat woman sent a chill through Eddie as he made his way out the automotive department door, and suddenly he felt some pity for those K-Mart pets, albeit rodents and parakeets, mindless creatures that could barely perceive the notion of existence. That woman was a monster. She must have tortured those poor things that tried to escape. She squashed the poor scurrying hamsters, the white mice and the gerbils as they maneuvered the floor to seek the asylum of stacked tires. She reached into the rows of anti-freeze and squeezed her tongs upon them until their eyeballs exploded all over the shelf. In some other life perhaps, she might have been a prison warden—she might have caught the girls trying to scale the fence and strapped those poor delinquents to their beds and lashed them with a whip in a barrage of profanity.

Eddie carried the guinea pigs on bottom, and he could feel their heavy bodies as they moved in unison about the darkened box. Their feet scratched the cardboard and their little claws protruded from the crack and dug into his hand. They squealed, and they squealed louder as the cold air hit the sides of the box. "You think you're scared now? You don't know what scared means until you meet Jude," he said as he opened the passenger door and placed the boxes on the seat. "And wait till we get moving on the interstate."

He picked up his humming again—nah-nah nah-nah nah nah nah—nah nah nah nah—hey Jude—and decided to go back to Hudson to feed his lizard before returning Domingus his car. He considered the gerbils that scurried about the box. They seemed to all push against the one side and nearly banged it from the seat before he stopped it with his hand. Would Jude eat them? Were they too small and insignificant for a five-foot lizard to stalk and kill? Would he need to dangle them over his lizard by the tails? And what of the guinea pigs? Could he really go through with sacrificing them to Jude, snuff out their lives as if they were insignificant crustaceans like those soft-shelled crabs he had fried up? He had bought the lizard, and now he had to feed it. He never really considered the ramifications until now. He was going to have to figure out a cheaper way, because this huge reptile would need an appetite to fill, and that would mean more money and more guinea pigs, more squealing guinea pigs.

Jude had scratched through the coating of white paint on the door, depositing long thin lines running well over Eddie's head. It must have been up on its hind legs with its nose nearly to the top of the door, Eddie surmised, sniffing the cool breeze delivering itself from the walkway. It must have tasted the gamebirds coming off the draft and wanted to hunt them down in the forsythias. The lizard pulled on the leash as Eddie walked the boxes to the kitchen, flapping its tongue in manic bursts and snorting through its scaly nostrils.

"Yeah you know what's in here don't you girl," Eddie said. "Well let's see how hungry you might be." He opened the flaps and grabbed one of the guinea pigs by the nape, holding it aloft just like the spectacled man in the pet store had done so many years back. He held it just like that and tried to drain himself of emotion, tried not to attach himself to the furry thing he held squealing above the lizard. This, after all, was the circle of life, the food chain, the great way of Nature. No shame here, no remorse, no sympathy, no victims. He was just a mediator in the life-death struggle. The lizard must eat, it must sustain itself and go on, and whether it choose to eat plants and such, or decide that the flesh will do more nicely, well then so be it. The monitor lizard needed the guinea pig right now, for Eddie knew that it might come after him if he didn't comply. The guinea pig must be lowered.

The animal squealed in terror as Eddie dropped it to the ground in front of the lizard. He stepped away as the lizard lunged on its leash, unsure at first where to point its snout, searching maniacally in the poor light with its dwindled eyesight. Finally it found the thing as it ambled toward the crevice beside the refrigerator. And then it was over: the lizard snapped it up in one clean jerk of its neck, and Eddie watched the jaw muscles click into gear as the serrated teeth tore into the terrorized guinea pig. It must have tore the thing up in its mouth, and Eddie watched its cold remorseless expression as it finished the thing in two swallows. The tongue slowed its flickering to a stop, and the lizard came to a rest on the linoleum. No remorse: Nature's way.

VI

Fred had spilled a fresh Mai Tai just as Eddie came around the end of the bar. The drink had dripped all over his pants and the glass cracked clean in half as if cut by a sharp tool. His eyes spelled anger, and he called the new bartender from the other end with a very loud and slurred "hey." The skinny man, whom Eddie had never seen before, put down his polishing rag and submitted to Fred's request, eyes wide in nervousness as if anticipating some level of demise.

"Now this drink here you just gave me exploded before I could even stir it," Fred said, sighing. "Now why do you suppose a drink would do such a thing of its own volition?"

"I dunno," the skinny new guy replied, shifting on his feet. "One of those things?"

"This glass just came out of the machine didn't it?"

"Yes sir. I thought I'd give you a nice clean one."

"Well tell me young man-and you don't have to be Mr. Science to answer this—what happens when you pour cold liquid into a hot glass?"

The skinny man looked at the puddles as Fred picked up a bar towel and dried his pants. He seemed perplexed by the question, not because he didn't know the answer, but because he knew that his ultimate answer would certainly vindicate him for his stupidity and cause an unpleasant reaction from the drunken owner.

"Cracks?"

"Cracks exactly." Fred began to mop up the mess in front of him before the new bartender could get to it himself. Calmly, almost in a whisper, Fred delivered: "I'd like you to get out from behind my bar. Your Mai Tais suck, and you've got zero sense about you. I won't be needing your services any longer."

The skinny man was about to reply, and got as far as raising a finger before his surrender. He hung his head and walked away from Fred and exited beneath the bar top at the other end. The man disappeared into a gathering of night waitresses, and Eddie knew he would never be seen again. Just another inept bartender who couldn't deliver, washed away in a tide of failure.

"Jesus deliver me a Mai Tai man," Fred said, looking skyward with a roll of the eyes. "Give me some son of a bitch who can bartend."

" I know this isn't a good time," Eddie said. "But if I can have a minute to talk about a broken window."

"A what? Huh?"

"I took the board down, see, in the apartment. I needed daylight for plants and things, and the windows they were all broke. I need some new glass in."

"Can't you live with a boarded window?" Fred shot back. "What's the big deal?"

But it was a big deal. To Eddie, putting the board back up meant a surrender to the darkness again, a return back to all of the other places from which he sought escape, from the closet box, from the darkened tool shed, from the bridge cave, from the thoughts that suspended themselves there in his private universe, his own conscious fears, his dead woman at the ball game, his prevailing paranoia. He wanted daylight and a lizard, that was all. Daylight and a lizard. That would be enough, and then he could go on.

"Well I need to get over there this week anyway," Fred said. " Natalie has a problem with her driveway. Called me just yesterday, something about washed-away stones. I try to save myself money where I can, see, and I don't see the point in hiring a guy when I have a lot of stones myself." Fred got up from his stool as a couple sat down at the other end of the bar. "Well it looks as if I'll have to don the old apron again," he sighed. "And put an ad out for another bartender."

Fred brushed by Eddie and he could smell the spilled Mai-Tai coming off his pants, and then he could see the wet spot dominating his crotch.

It looks as if he peed himself, Eddie thought, and the daylight filtered in through the half-closed blinds and exposed his wet spot there behind the bar as he reached for the bottles on the rack. Eddie watched a couple, seated at the other end of the bar, engage in whispered laughs as their eyes shifted to Fred's stained pants. He caught the last of their subtle pointing as he swung around with the freshly-made drinks. He saw the woman's eyes watching his pants, and thought perhaps that his fly had come undone. Then he saw the wet spot delivering itself in the afternoon light for all to see, and Eddie turned to see the night waitresses assembled in the south station working up chuckles as well. When Fred was able to deduce the chain of events, he paused in the sunlight, speculating on how to react. Eddie waited at the end of the bar with the most serious face he could muster, anticipating a flare-up of unconscionable fury into which Fred would begin firing the entire staff. He waited for Fred to take the couple's drinks away and ask them, in a restrained moment of seething anger, to kindly leave the premises.

But Fred chuckled at his wet crotch. He chuckled and he put his hand to his chin and looked out through the half-drawn blinds. "You know this reminds me of…well some time back…second grade to be exact," Fred said. He moved closer to the couple and explained the spilled drink and the fired bartender, then continued his story at a higher volume so that it reached the south station and Eddie in particular. Fred opened him a Molson and walked though the shaft of sunlight to deliver it. "Anyway, I'm going to St. Anselm and we've got this monster nun by the name of Mother Phoebe. She's got this face like leather, like she's been riding horseback through the Sierra Nevadas her whole life. She's on a tear because she's giving us May Procession practice and the tall boys are having trouble turning, so much so that she's had to take the yard stick to them time and again." He paused to make himself a drink, filling the glass with its respective ingredients. "Can't ever make the damned thing right myself either. I need somebody to make the damned thing right."

"Anyway," he continued, "I'm the littlest in the class…and as you can see, not much has changed." The couple sipped their drinks and smiled. The waitresses whispered as Fred balanced himself upon unsteady feet. "Well I'm at the front of the line and I've got to piss like nobody's business, so I raise my hand and ask Mother Phoebe if I can't be excused to the lavatory to relieve myself. 'You most certainly can not, Mister O'Hara. You will stand in this line until we get this thing right. And then maybe I'll let you go to the lavatory,' she says. Then she goes to the very back of the line and starts laying in on the tall dopes, smacking them around because they can't carry the wreath of flowers and put it on the Mary statue the right way. I mean she's back there forever spewing out physical threats and extra homework assignments and meanwhile I'm bursting my kidneys at the front of the line. I think I'm in control, I think I can make it….and then I let loose with what I think is just a little pee, just a little to get me through the next few minutes. Except that you can't just pee a little if you have to go real real bad. I learn this. It explodes out of me, and I feel the warm piss soaking my pants. It just keeps coming because my damned dam has burst."

"Catholic school," the man said, rubbing the woman's back. "Had it seen it done it."

"Well here I am scared. We're standing in rows of two, and I'm next to William Robinson. Now he's seen me shaking my leg the whole time, so he knows what's coming. He gasps when he sees the little stream start up, right there on the hill, right out of the cuff of one of my pants legs." Fred stopped and downed his Mai-Tai in one swallow, and reached for the refill bottle in the shaft of sunlight. "I suppose I can laugh about it now. I suppose when a little kid pees his pants no one will ever take it too serious. But I'll tell you, I was never in such a state of horror as when I watched that little yellow stream foam its way down that God-forsaken hill right toward Mother Phoebe. Now I'd never really prayed before, I mean the kind of praying where you concentrate all your energy and try to reach God, try to will your thoughts upward and all that. But I did at that moment. I put my hands together and shut my eyes tight and thought as hard as I could 'God make that yellow river go away. Make it go the hell away.'

The torment registered there beneath Fred's smile and reflected itself in the quick swallows of alcohol and the rapidly deteriorating stride upon which he delivered himself. The laughter echoed out of the south hole, where the waitresses had relaxed themselves as if assembled in a night club to hear some lounge act. The couple continued to sip their drinks and listen. Eddie formulated a mental picture of a little frightened Fred on the hill, eyes closed and hands done up in prayer. That little boy was anticipating and envisioning, in some unconscious manner, his distant future as a wobbling drunk.

"She saw it Mother Phoebe did. She saw the stream. She started to follow it to its source, walking slow up the hill, so damned slow-an eternity-as the line got dead quiet. I panicked. I tried to brush the piss over to William's leg, ready to say 'he pissed he pissed.' But then the shadow was over me. Old leather-face with her cold black eyes was looking down at my wet crotch and the trickle that was still coming out my leg. And then she grabbed me by my hair. That monster nun pulled me up off the ground by my hair and she smacked me forever across the face and screamed into my ears about what I was doing to the asphalt." Fred refilled the couple's drinks, and Eddie watched as the waitresses disbanded from the station. "Had red welts the shape of a hand for a week across my cheek. Had to apologize to the eighth-graders who hosed down the hill. Had to write a ten thousand word composition on life inside a ping-pong ball and had to apologize to Jesus. Over and over, rosary after rosary, I had to apologize to Jesus."

VII

Eddie got some long new nails and hammered the plywood back up, shutting away the sunlight dropping over the forsythias. Really there was no other choice until Fred came out and replaced the windows; he would need to spend a little more time in darkness, and he would need to keep away the cold air gusting up in bursts now across the lawns of Hudson. Winter was coming and Mrs. Haas had just taken in her withered chrysanthemums from along the walk. The heater clicked away in rapid bursts that sounded much like a toy machine gun, and Eddie pulled the extra sheet from beneath the bed and shivered at the remaining draft.

Jude laid down on the linoleum and ran his tail up the length of the cabinet. He seemed to like it there, what with the refrigerator motor humming and the warm floor just outside the vent. He had fed the thing three gerbils, though one had momentarily escaped and he had to take the broom handle and fish it from behind the refrigerator. It shot in a panic across the floor before the leather jaws came down around it and swallowed it in one snip. The remaining gerbils worried him; he could hear them in the box beneath his bed, scratching away at the sides. They had nibbled away at the previous box, and now this box was going to get it, probably some time in the night, and this time they would probably get through the holes. He thought briefly about just letting them all loose. Jude was going to eat them eventually anyway, so what was the point of keeping them boxed. But then some might escape. Some might make their way up into Mrs. Haas' apartment or Jude might eat them all up in one day and he couldn't afford any of that.

Laying down in the night, he listened to the clicking of the heater and the intermittent bursts of air coming out of Jude's nostrils. He looked across the darkened room and could feel the reptilian eyes watching him from the tile, little yellow moons reading the darkness. They were planning, always planning. Those eyes were figuring on how to escape the rope, how to find the scurrying rodents, how to get through that plywood nailed into the cement. His lizard wanted out, he could sense that as he lay there. It wanted back to the jungle among the dripping plants and out of his basement apartment. Hudson was no place for a Monitor lizard. Hudson was no place for anyone.

Eddie smiled at the thought of Fred again, the little Fred at the front of the May Procession line, his eyes closed tight, his hands folded in prayer, his piss foaming up a river snaking down to old Mother Phoebe. So many years back Fred had that awful embarrassment on that hill, and it sunk in and poisoned him for life. He carried that incident with him all the way through school, and years later it surfaced when his sister willed him all of that bingo money. Then his revenge erected itself in the sign for all to see: Bingos. That sign really said that he hated being Catholic, that he hated his life, and that hate flowered up from that moment when Mother Phoebe wouldn't let him go to the lavatory. And he continued to wash it away, always with a thousand Mai-Tais and a thousand drunken nights, always washing it away. How ironic, Eddie thought, that Fred's kidneys failed to hold back that pee, and now here he was, teetering behind bars and destroying those kidneys with strings of Mai Tais.

Jude let out a long sigh and jumped up from the tile in a start. Then the lizard relaxed itself again, and Eddie figured that some reptile dream had jolted it awake. Perhaps it remained haunted by Salvadore, if lizards dreamt such things. Perhaps it had just re-lived its capture in the dense jungle, the thick-armed man lunging at it from beyond the palm fronds, knife in hand. And perhaps if his lizard could think such things, perhaps if its eyes could form tears, human tears, it would have cried itself back to sleep right there on the tile, longing for its nest beneath the wet trees. And it might have thought, in its own primitive fusion of synaptic thought, 'I want to go home.'

Eddie hummed a little and closed his eyes. He hummed "Hey Jude" again, the song that had persisted on his brain like a festering mosquito the whole of the day. It came out and absorbed everything else, and he could think of nothing but the recurring chorus as it formed an ellipsis around Fred, around his lizard, around the distant raging fires of his missing baby brother. And then Jude became another saint unearthed, dug up out of the throng of saints that had been indelibly tattooed to his memory in the quiet afternoons of library tables. He re-kindled that memory, blew air upon it and fanned the flames, and then the saint came to life right there in the dark: Jude, the patron saint of hopeless causes.

Yes, there was no doubt that the Beatles song had nothing to do with his naming his lizard "Jude." The name had come from his buried saint, and now the man that Matthew had called Thaddeus in his Gospel—St. Jude—beckoned him. Eddie whispered his name in the dark. "Jude," he said. "Jude." He believed at first that he was simply calling to his lizard across the room as he spoke, talking to his new pet in the hopes that it would understand and warm to his voice. He wanted to believe that, but he knew, really, that he had begun to pray, in the manner in which Fred had done at the front of his line so many years back, a prayer that had gone unanswered.

But Fred did not know about St. Jude. He did not know that the faithful avoided seeking his help in fear that he would be confused with Judas Iscariot, the saint who betrayed Jesus, the thirteenth saint of the Last Supper. Very few prayed to St. Jude—only those who knew him as the last resort, the one to turn to in desperate situations, when prayers to all of the other saints, to God, to Jesus, to Mother Mary, failed. Fred might have been saved that day, Eddie figured, if he'd concentrated all of his energy on the patron saint of hopeless causes. Perhaps Mother Phoebe might have walked up the other side of that line instead, guided the tall boys with their flowered wreath along the path and down the church aisle and never looked down, never to see the yellow stream.

And Fred would be somewhere else now, sober and happy and saved, instead of wobbling as a helpless drunk beneath his neon legacy.

"St. Jude look down on me," Eddie whispered, feeling the words come alive like no other words he had ever spoken, words that hung suspended in the dark like parts on a mobile. "I'm here in a basement in Hudson. I'm here to ask your help because I'm really scared about things. I can't sleep nights thinking about who I might have killed, about the old lady, about my little brother. Is he still alive? I don't know what I'm doing running away from home, I don't know what I'm doing with a five-foot lizard tied to my refrigerator door. I'm just doing it. I need your help, Jude. I need you to help me find my baby brother, Jude. I need to wake up in sunlight. I need you to point me the way to Benjamin. Jude...please help me find the way to Benjamin."

The cold air blasted against the plywood and he feared that it might give way, that the long shiny nails might remove themselves from the cement and the board would come floating down like an apparition. And then his fear vanished, for Eddie believed that St. Jude was giving him a sign by forcing the wind through the forsythias like that. Saints could do those sorts of things with the elements, especially a saint such as Jude. Something was going to happen, and he closed his eyes and waited for it to arrive, on the wind, in the whisper of some cosmic words, on a shaft of light patterned, by a miracle, from the night molecules. But as the hours tumbled he finally tired of the wait. For the board held steady, the wind died considerably, and the room remained dark and silent around him. He pulled up the extra sheet and sighed "Jude" once again. Then he folded his hands beneath the pillow and shivered his way to sleep above the gnawing gerbils.

Waning Gibbous

◆

I

Just after Mrs. Haas rolled down the stones in her Impala, Eddie carried
another load of laundry up the stairs She was headed to the Farmer's
Market one more time—the place she headed every Saturday morning—to get her cooking things and her fresh fruit and perhaps to find
another sale on picture frames. Several times, Eddie felt compelled to go
and talk to her, especially when he heard her walking the expanse of her
living room, to find out more about her sepia past. Those old photographs, that city, continued to intrigue him every time he traipsed
through to the other side of the basement and it drew him like flypaper
to the walls.

Mrs. Haas sounded pleasant when she talked on the telephone and
when she had her friends visit her in the evenings. Even alone, she sung
in low hums amidst her cleaning and sometimes mumbled sentences
to herself that Eddie came to figure were jokes. She would probably
welcome some conversation from below to take her from her solitude.
However, Eddie still became frightened at the prospect of advancing
up the stairs to knock on her door. She might be in the middle of
something very private, reciting her incantations to the white-haired

man above the trap door or something, her eyes glazed over in a milky trance. Or she might catch a whiff, with her acute sense of smell, of the giant reptile harbored below, and then she'd want to come down and have a peek into his personal life. He continued to keep his distance as he waited for the sound of the car to pull away, so that he could carry his laundry in solitude through the top of the house.

Today, Eddie smelled the odor of Boysenberry permeating the entire floor, something she had no doubt purchased to freshen her living room. The smell wafted from the pine cones and the wood shavings piled in a ceramic bowl in the center of her coffee table and he stood and stared at the variety of textures blended together in a magenta mountain.

Taking his laundry down the wooden steps, he loaded the washer and walked back up the stairs to snoop. Starting in the kitchen, he opened the drawers to inspect the forks and such, observing the vines etched into the metal and the bunches of grapes carved at the tops of the handles. Antiques again, antiques everywhere, frames on her walls, tables on her rugs, spoons in her drawers, ornate carvings everywhere. Even the appliances, Eddie came to notice, reeked with age: twenty-pound toasters and mechanical juicers and a contraption that Eddie stared at for a good twenty minutes before he deduced had something to do with the de-boning of whole chickens. It must have been something created by some crackpot at the beginning of the century which he had sold to her over a display table at some World's Fair, he surmised. He even searched her refrigerator for a chicken that he might hook into the prongs so that he might give the thing a try. But then he thought he heard the crunching of the stones, so he closed the door and made his way to the window in a rush of heartbeats.

Nothing again. He thought: how many times have I done this? How many times have I thought I heard sound of the stones? What is making me think I hear the sound of the stones? The sound of rubber tires crunching two thousand pounds of metal down upon the driveway? Is there something else, some other sound coming at me from somewhere on a sea of sound waves that sounds just like those crunching stones? Is it perhaps the humming of a refrigerator, the distant swoosh of a washing machine, the even more distant scratching of a Monitor Lizard's claws, the traffic on the interstate, the shouts of children, sirens wailing, doors slamming, men yelling—is all of it blending together into a soup of sound that resembles a crunching of the stones?

He was reasonably sure that some part of his brain was manufacturing the sound. Nothing from the outside world could imitate the sound of crunching stones just like that. Instead, some chemical emanated from that excess fluid within and from all of the paranoia flooding his synapses and seeping into his conscious universe of sound. People hear voices like that, he'd read somewhere. Voices in their heads, coming and going, turned on and off like electric switches, like faucets. The crazy ones swore that someone was speaking to them from out in the real world, from around corners, from behind bushes, from beneath their beds as they tore away their sheets. He had read all of that some time back or he had heard it off of the television, he couldn't remember which.

He dropped the curtain back again and stood in the middle of the boysenberry. He didn't care that she might come home now. After all, he had every right to be up here—he was simply waiting for his laundry to finish itself. Besides that, she had encouraged him to snoop. 'Haven't you seen my pictures?' she had asked, and she had opened her arms to the expanse of the living room. That gesture was an invitation: go ahead and look around, peer into the pictures and see what I'm all about, get to know me because I live upstairs from you and you've got every right to find out all about me. Just go ahead and take yourself a look-see.

Eddie pulled open her dresser drawers and found an assortment of bras and underwear, and he quickly closed it and moved on. After all, he surmised, there were some things he shouldn't investigate further, things too personal and feminine and none of his business. He moved to the closet on her far wall. The washer had finished its cycle, but no matter—his mission to snoop had now assumed control over his roving fingers and he peeled away lid after lid from the shoe boxes piled at the back of the closet. Shoes, shoes, shoes, all black with special heels, some tall with laces, two pairs of boots eventually, all spewing the odor of boxed leather. He had hoped for some hidden letters, some secret photographs that could never be displayed by frames and nailed to walls— ones that told tales of some secret life, perhaps of Nazi prison camps or outrageous sex parties or occult rituals over open flame. But Eddie found only shoes, and then he squatted and searched the closet walls for a hidden door that might lead to a secret room, to a closet box just like he had constructed in his parent's house. During his long stare his knees began to ache. Soon he sighed and got up from his squat. Then he closed the closet door and moved down the basement stairs to dry his clothes, still smelling the leather of a thousand shoes.

II

Lisa smelled like pot during the lunch shift. Eddie figured she had been out on the dock smoking a joint or toking one up on her way from the lot.

"Got any left?" he asked as she picked up two orders of scallops.

Her eyes widened, bloodshot as they should be. "Any…?"

"You know," Eddie said. "Smokables. You reek"

"Do I really,?" she asked, surprised. "I've got this cold and can't smell a thing. "

"Well you'd better douse yourself with perfume or something. And you'd better give me a little of what you've got left so's I don't hunt down Fred and snitch on you," he joked.

Lisa reached into her apron pocket and retrieved a fat roach and slid it across the window. Eddie felt the heat still registered on the tip. "You just got done smoking this, didn't you? It's still going I think."

"Oh no...I might have burned a hole in my apron." Lisa searched with her fingers for a burn. "I don't want to be dropping change across the dining room."

"Hell you could stick your nose down in there in that apron and get another hit I bet."

Lisa returned a stoned smile and moved her bloodshot eyes into the darkened dining room. "I'd better go freshen up in case Fred comes near," she said.

Just after the last of the lunch rush, after fixing the re-cooks for the old ladies of a large party, Eddie took the roach and a pack of matches and walked to the edge of the dock. He had planned on torqueing up right then and there to get himself a buzz while he finished the night prep. He wanted to ease the stress from the slam and to numb the stinging of his grease burn. But then some birds started up in the trees across the lot, twenty or so of them he surmised by the chattering, and it got him to thinking about the noises of the world, and he drifted off without the aid of pot.

The fact was, Eddie didn't really want the thing. He'd only gotten high once since the runaway, with Domingus on the cinderblock wall some weeks back after he'd filled in for one of the line cooks one night. Domingus kept lighting up joint after joint, pulling them out of a gold cigarette case, each one perfectly rolled (like Billy's joints). One after the other: they smoked until daybreak, until Eddie's lungs tickled from overload, until his head floated in a sea of smoke. They didn't talk much during those hours—Domingus knew only so many words in English and had pretty much forgotten them all after several wicked hits. So Eddie just listened to him talk about Salvadore as the Spanish slowly seeped in and took him over completely. Then he walked home in the morning light, just as the traffic started up, and just as the old ones from Hudson were making their way down driveways and sidewalks. Some of them had enough of their sight left to notice his red eyes and smell the pot lingering, and Eddie slammed his basement door and said to himself 'never again.'

But now here he was with the match pulled from the pack, his hand already cupped to ward off the wind. He stared at the thick roach and became enticed by its smell and by the feel of the end twisted between his fingers. He should have lit the thing and brought it to his lips, inhaled as much of the smoke as he could muster. He should have stood there on the dock holding in the smoke until he felt the blood churning in his face and the marijuana high come easing into the recesses of his brain. He should have let out the remaining smoke in one long coughing gasp. Instead, he flicked the roach into the dumpster and rubbed away the encroaching stains from his fingertips, then opened the dock doors to return to the line.

No, he wouldn't put himself through that trip though Hudson high again. They'd be on him in a second if he dared venture past with his red eyes. Those nosy ones in the yellow rancher especially, always on their porch, even on the frigid mornings would be waiting. They would be across their lawns to sniff him and the cops would jump out of their rhododendrons, with cuffs ready and waiting, to click shut around his wrists.

Besides all that, what was the point any more? Pot didn't do anything for him now that Billy Stigmeyer was gone. Eddie wished for a moment where he could be back in that tool shed again so that he could reminisce with Billy one more time and toke up. Then he could drift off brain to brain with his friend and talk about the days in the school hallways, about the parties under the green bridge, about the grapefruits over his eyes. But the police were waiting for him there—they were all gathered about the steel shed awaiting his return, eyeing the movement of the bushes, waiting for some sign of his re-appearance. So there was no going back, and there was no point in getting high if he couldn't enjoy it. Besides, with all of his new responsibilities, he wouldn't be able to think as clearly. He had rent to pay, he had a job to perform, he had a five-foot Monitor Lizard to feed. And he had Mrs. Haas and the rest of the old ones surrounding him, watching him, conforming him. Living in Hudson had molded him, grayed him into submission, and Eddie felt seventy years old.

Later, while he prepped a tub of flounder, Eddie watched Lisa come and go through the swinging doors, in and out in a series of erratic spurts filled with forgetfulness. He pitied her. With her reddened eyes and her glassy gaze, she seemed almost sub-human, powerless against the foggy forces encroaching her brain, swatting away the high like some wasp she had let into a room and which she now wanted out. She headed for the darkness of the dining room, slipping silently through the doors, introspective of her fogginess.

III

"I've got something for you," came the voice from the top of the stairs just as Eddie dropped a guinea pig in front of Jude. Mrs. Haas spoke to him through the door, her voice flush against the wood: "Something you might like," she said.

His heart motored along as he watched Jude stalk the rodent across the linoleum and as the lizard snared it with its patented swallow. "You be quiet girl," he said. "You digest and I'll be right back." He headed up the stairs and watched as the knob turned. The woman opened the door in one jerk. He had left it unlocked after bringing down another load of laundry earlier in the day. Though he had made certain to close the trap door and leave no discernible trail from his snooping, he had forgotten about his own door. Now, there she stood in the kitchen light, donned in one of her flowered dresses, the hair glowing white, the smile emanating downward as he climbed towards her. She held something in her left hand, something cupped within, and Eddie watched as the bony knuckles unfurled to reveal a brown tattered baseball.

"I don't know whether you like this sort of thing," she said. "But it's something old with a little history."

He moved past her into the kitchen, invited himself in, and closed the door behind him. He could hear Jude whipping his tail against the wall and he needed to be careful and close off the sound. "A baseball," Eddie said, taking the ball into his own hands and inspecting it. "It looks a little old. Is this an antique?"

Instantly, his mind raced to establish some facts about the game that endeared his father through those nights on the couch; he retrieved bits and pieces of teams and players and statistics, tried to recall the names of the teams and other things that he might need in case she asked and to separate her from her curiosity of the goings-on below.

"Eighteen ninety-five," she said. "That ball you're holding was given to me by my father. It's from the deadball era."

Eddie scrutinized the worn leather casing. The ball did seem heavier and smaller than the modern balls. Apparently it had been re-stitched, as the laces that wrapped around the ball emanated a brilliant red against the brown backdrop. He could barely make out two names scrawled across the surface in faded ink. "Two autographs," he said. "Can't make them out."

" One would be my father, Nig Cuppy. The other…a pitcher that you might have heard of by the name of Cy Young." She stood and smiled, as if expecting astonishment and disbelief from Eddie.

Cy Young: now he had heard that name a hundred times coming out of the room downstairs in his parent's house, belched out by his father, his Uncle Pete, his father, his Uncle Pete, during their trivia tirades. The name had some sort of award attached to it, he remembered, and Eddie deduced that the ball he weighed in his palm held some special value with that faded signature. Indeed, the smile which persisted on the old woman's face bore further testament.

"Oh sure Cy Young, of the award." He inspected the ball without looking up, hoping that she would not test him on the name any further. "He was a good one all right."

"Have you ever heard of the Temple Cup?" she asked him.

He racked the recesses of his closet box memory cells to retrieve that one, but nothing came. "Can't say that I have," he said.

"Well I wouldn't expect that you would….the boys played that as the championship before they named it the World Series…." She stopped and peered toward the living room. "Why don't we go into the living room and sit down. I'll tell you a little history of that ball."

Empowered by her pull and still nervous about her hearing the tail whipping below, he followed her into the room, into the scent-laden Boysenberry air, and sat upon the chair from which he had spent many laundry hours gazing at the photographs. Now the room seemed different, as if the presence of the woman imbued it with the life it richly craved. She sat and folded her hands on her lap. Eddie continued to cup the ball, feeling the sweat beginning to accumulate like morning dew.

"Be careful holding it," she said. "It's fragile from age you see. Things and people…they become fragile with age and sometimes they fray at the seams." Eddie placed the ball in the center of the table, as it took its natural place among the other things, and it blended like camouflage into the ivory light.

"You sure you want me to have this ball, Mrs. Haas?" he asked. "It must be pretty valuable."

"I want you to have it.," she said. "Boys should have things like that. Boys should have old baseballs and history, things to tell their friends, their brothers, their sons." She paused and unfolded her hands, opening them to Eddie. "I want to tell you about that ball, about some history."

Eddie thought of his father as she began. He would have loved to be sitting right where he was sitting with that ball in his possession, with another baseball story about to be absorbed. He would love to have some morsel that he could fire across the room at his Uncle Pete, one mighty stumpage in his arsenal.

"My father played on a team called the Cleveland Spiders," she said. "Pitched for them at the end of the century. Changed his name...he was born George Koppe, but got himself a name change after the nickname caught on. Nig Cuppy the boys came up with. He thought it sounded good alongside Cy Young, I suppose...never really asked him. He wound up asking my sister, my two brothers, my mother, me, to all take up the name Cuppy as well. He told us we were all going to be remembered as Cuppies."

"Did all the players do the name change back then?" Eddie asked.

"It was a fad I suppose, among the players. I like to think it came from the Indian tribes...you know, like Little Horse and Sitting Bull and Lone Wolf. The nicknames were supposed to reflect your personality—Dizzy and Gabby and Pud and Ping—they told the other team something, that you were kind of crazy, out of your element."

"So what was the meaning behind 'Nig'? Eddie asked.

"It's short for 'niggardly,' " she said. "My father was a cheapskate, there's no denying that. He never claimed to have any money and wound up getting drunk every night after the games off Cy's earnings or mooching off some other member of the team. I don't think he ever spent a penny on anyone, and it got to a point where, after he was given the nickname, he was actually proud of that trait. He never bought a damned thing for anybody, even after the Spiders won the Temple Cup. God knows where he put that money."

"Anyway, my father won a few games in his day...twenty-eight his first year with the Spiders, a couple of twenty-win seasons after that. The Spiders were the talk of Cleveland, winning all of those games between him and Cy. The townspeople went crazy rooting for that team, and they'd pack themselves in like sardines in those wooden bleachers. Nig, he took me and my sister and my brother and sat us along the first base line, on a wooden bench just for us, and the players would pinch our cheeks and rub our heads for luck." Mrs. Haas smiled, and then the smile vanished and she grew silent, and her hands resumed their fold and her eyes grew dim and vague as she perused the distant photographs.

"That son of a bitch Frank Robison," she said in an angry tone. "Frank owned the Spiders, but he also owned the St. Louis Browns. You could do that back then, own two teams in the same league. You could do that back then. Can't now, cause of what Frank went and did. You see, Eddie, in 1899 Frank decided to put all of his eggs in one basket, so he took all of the best players on the Spiders and sent them to the Browns, my father included." She sighed and let the memory come pouring back, the bitter taste of things long ago. Her hands clenched tight as if some electrical shock had enveloped her system.

"So what became of the Spiders?" Eddie asked.

"What became of the Spiders......what became of the Spiders. Well let me tell you, Eddie. We had ourselves a nice little home in downtown Cleveland, and friends, and a nice school, and things were right with the world. And when my father got moved to the St. Louis club, he sat us down and asked us what we wanted to do. And of course we all voted to stay in Cleveland, which was fine with my father. He figured he would just do a little extra traveling. Well, the Spiders had been decimated of their good players. The fact was, they were terrible. The fact was, that 1899 club turned out to be the worst baseball club of all time. They won only twenty games that year, lost 134, and finished 85 games out of first place."

Eddie found some of this interesting, still thinking that his father and William and Uncle Pete would be more enamored by the story. If he could retain her story and someday return home, well, they would all be mighty impressed. Maybe the story would take off the pain of his run-away a little. But now, as his mind began to drift, he was hoping that she was finished. He wanted to get back down to tend to Jude. Then he noticed her eyes welling up with tears, and he looked uncomfortably away to the brown sphere resting upon the coffee table and took in another long whiff of Boysenberry.

"If we'd only moved to St. Louis," she said. "You see, the city of Cleveland was so angry at Frank, so angry at all of the players who left. They felt betrayed—their beloved Spiders were ripped apart, the very fabric of their lives torn asunder. Many of them threatened the remaining players on the team, threatened to kill every one of them. So those poor players took to the road for the last eighty games of the year and never came back. They played the rest of their games in other ball parks because they feared for their lives."

Mrs. Haas moved to the edge of the couch and leaned in. "The townspeople torched our house one Saturday evening. There must have been forty or fifty of them out there in the dark with jugs of kerosene. I'll still never forget the leaping flames as we ran into the summer night, the smell of the burning wood. I'll never forget the angry blathering as they threatened to tar and feather us and ship us to St. Louis on a cattle train. "Get out of our town, traitors,' old Mr. Otterbeck kept screaming. Old Mr. Otterbeck...the nicest storekeeper I'd ever met—he used to give us the licorice every time we walked by, the sourballs—and now, on this horrible night, he held up his blazing torch and told us never to come back."

Eddie didn't know how to react to the sudden flow of tears that started up across the room. It reminded him of his mother's frequent outbursts over his stolen baby brother, and he felt, for several suspended seconds, like crying himself—not for Mrs. Haas so much, but for the sudden unearthed memories of Benjamin's baby face and the despairing aftermath of his abduction.

"So," he said, walling his emotions. "Where did you go?"

Mrs. Haas stopped her sobbing. "You know, the worst thing was that my father never came home. It must have been the guilt. He tried to strangle Frank. A news report out of St. Louis said he had him on the floor of his office and it took three other players, including Cy, to pry him off. It must have been the guilt, Eddie. He was traded to Boston the following year along with Cy, and we never heard from him again. My brother was playing baseball in a semi-pro league some years later when an old man came up and handed him twenty dollars, then got into a big car and drove away. My mother cried when Johnny came home and described the man. And though she never told us, I really believe that was him…Nig Cuppy…digging up some of that money and giving it back, just his way of saying I'm sorry and just forget about me and buy a little something for the family."

The afternoon sun found its way through a crack between the curtains and shone a square directly onto old Mrs. Haas' head. Eddie came to notice a peculiar mark on her forehead, what he guessed was a birthmark. It almost formed a perfect circle, pale and glowing like a dimmed flashlight, as she sat and composed herself. He stared at her birthmark for several seconds. With the subtle pock marks gathered within, the mark reminded him of the moon, a moon in the day sky, barely visible, yet nonetheless there.

"So remember your history, and remember this baseball story when you look at that ball, " she said as she got up, handed him the ball from the table, and guided him back to his door. "Eighty years ago that ball saw it all happen. And if that ball could contain a brain instead of cork, if it could think and see and feel the way Nig saw and felt, it might tell you some things. It might just tell you some things."

Once downstairs and safely harbored away, Eddie placed his gift on a saucer atop the refrigerator to prevent Jude from snatching it up into his pink cave. He felt suddenly that he'd become a part of the woman above him. She had opened her soul for him to peer in, and it held more secrets than any shoe box or silverware drawer ever could. He wondered why she had an interest in a sport that had torn her life apart. And he couldn't help thinking about that moon birthmark. It had seemed to suddenly materialize on her forehead in that patch of sun just as she finished her story. Not quite a full moon: Eddie remembered Astronomy class and Mr. Delpino lecturing about the phases of the moon, about the gibbous moon in particular: it was a phase beyond half, but not quite full. Yes, that was a gibbous moon birthmark there upon her head. Natalie Haas was born a moon child, born with the mark upon her, and it hung, barely visible, over her torment.

IV

"I'll be over tomorrow to fix that damned window of yours," Fred said between drinks. "I ordered a whole new window because it's easier than replacing the panes. The panes are a pain." He chuckled as the new bartender carefully delivered him his next drink and laughed along with Fred for his own sake (in the event that his Mai-Tai was not up to par).

"Be sure to knock a couple of times," Eddie said. "I'm working a double today, and I won't get home until after two. I'm a pain in the ass to get up in the morning after   I've been up all night."

Later in the evening, after the dinner rush had slowed to a crawl and when Eddie had more time to think, he suddenly realized that he would have to reveal Jude to Fred. Though Fred had never told him 'no pets' when he moved in, there was no doubt that he would be appalled at the sight of his large reptile crawling upon the linoleum; he might just flare up in anger and order it removed from the apartment. Eddie didn't want any of that—he had worked too hard to endear himself to Fred and he didn't want to destroy that bond. Besides that, he didn't want to give up Jude. He had gotten quite accustomed to feeding it and he had established a routine of stopping by the K-Mart and buying up new batches of gerbils and hamsters and guinea pigs. He had even begun to take home meat scraps. He heated the meat in the oven just to get it warm and tossed them into the air for Jude to swallow. He had formed a special bond with his lizard, talking to it, petting it along the bony ridge above its shifting moon eyes, listening to it snort in the apartment air and watching its long torso expand and contract in a ripple of scales. Eddie had devised a game of avoiding the whipping tail and he came to believe that his lizard was playing right along, and that it was trying to nail him as he maneuvered his feet in rapid skips.

To ensure that Fred would not see Jude, Eddie would need to take measures. But where to hide a five-foot lizard in such a small apartment? His mind worked as he dropped a late order of fried shrimp, as he wrapped the remaining batter and sifted the flour of dead fish parts and prepared the grease buckets. He would need to take Jude out of the apartment and hide her somewhere in the bushes of Hudson. There were several large conifers across Small Road, ones in which a Monitor Lizard could safely be secluded. Eddie thought about the night; it would be safer to take it out there in the dark so that the old ones would not spot him. He could walk it across the street after the porch lights and televisions were shut off and after they had all gone to sleep. But the cold of the night would kill it—the weather report had said it would go down well below freezing. The biting air of ten degrees would freeze it to the ground between the trees. That would be no good, either.

Eddie walked out into the dining room to search for Fred. He was going to tell him to come another day, after he had more time to find a haven. He would tell Fred that he could get by in his darkness a little while longer, that the light of a window could wait a few more days. But Fred had gone home, and Eddie stood at the edge of the empty bar and pondered his next move. Call Fred at home? That was no good—he'd wake him from a sound sleep and piss him off. He would just need to take his chances now.

He went home and scanned the apartment, the cabinet, the flimsy couch, the unmade bed, the assorted clothes piled into cardboard boxes. There was no foreseeable way to hide Jude, that was for sure, not in this little place. She would need to be smuggled out, hidden somewhere beyond the walls, if he was to have his daylight. He would either need to take his chances with the neighbors spotting him, or he would need to work up a lie—tell Fred that he was keeping the thing for a friend or something.

Eddie twisted and turned in his bed the whole of the night, unable to sleep, unable to foster a way around his predicament. He might be evicted. He might have to take Jude to a zoo. He might have to find another job. He might have to start all over again. Everything that he had built might come tumbling down because of his desire for daylight. He wished he had gotten Fred's number before he left; even though he didn't have a telephone, he could easily have gotten up and walked down to the gas station., made the call and settled things for a few more days. But now the daylight was coming as he tore in frustration at the tangled sheets, as he anticipated Fred's arrival and the beginning of his own demise.

Then, just as the morning light appeared around the edges of the nailed plywood, Eddie heard the Impala start up in the driveway, and the distinct crunching of the stones stifled every other sound. Mrs. Haas had gotten up early, and she was headed somewhere. She was probably going out for the day. And then the answer came to him and he jumped up excitedly out of the bed and slipped into his jeans: he could hide Jude upstairs in Mrs. Haas' part of the house. Then, after Fred had fixed his window, he could bring it back down the stairs. Yes, it was all so simple—things had a way of working out simple. Mrs. Haas was now providing him with the perfect gateway. He was certain that she had left for the day and it would only be a matter of hours before Fred arrived. And how long did it take to install a window? He would be gone and the lizard would be safely back into his basement lair without anyone suspecting a thing, and he would finally have that light that he wanted all along.

Eddie untied Jude from the refrigerator door and tugged her up from the linoleum. "Come on girl. We need to hide you away or you'll be lizard meat in some exotic restaurant," he said. The lizard, sensing Eddie's fear, complied and followed him up the narrow stairs. Jude flicked the new air with its tongue and its retinas widened within the yellow moons as it eyed the odd assortment of antiques and memories draped about the room. Eddie thought about tying Jude to her refrigerator door or to one of her many cabinets or to some heavy piece of furniture in the living room. Then he considered that the lizard might make a bowel movement on one of her rugs or her tiles in the manner that Jude had done so many times on his own tiles Then she would smell the odor as soon as she walked in the door. Besides that, Jude might scratch and claw some things up, knock some frames from the wall, and create a ruckus to which Fred would respond.

Eddie opened the trap door and walked Jude down the other side of the basement. This was the safest place, away from the possibility of discovery. He tied the rope around the legs of the sink at the far end of the basement and shut off the light. Then he made sure to close the trap door. He paused in the living room, where, less than twelve hours before, he had listened to Mrs. Haas tell her baseball story. Now it was an empty church without its priest. Eddie could still feel the spirit of her words hanging in the air, echoing off the imaginary buttresses, coming down in a fine powder between the photographs. He thought again: why did she give me the baseball? why did she say nothing except for the baseball story? why did she dump her torment down on me?

That birthmark kept tugging at Eddie. He tried to piece together fragments from what she had said, tried to imagine the Cleveland Spiders hiding in hotels and scurrying down alleys, tried to picture her father holding out a twenty dollar bill to her brother, their house ablaze, their lives gone to ash. But the glowing moon on her forehead kept returning and completely absorbed his interest. Was it really a birthmark? Or was her moon some sort of scar?

What could make that sort of scar, round like the moon? Something circular, something forceful, no doubt. Then Eddie became seized by a moment of sublime revelation, and it pulled him down into the same chair in which he had sat listening the night before. That Phillies game, that cup that he threw into the air with its rocket-ride downward and its blow against the old woman's head. That stretcher which carried her out through the tunnel. All along he figured that the old lady had died on her way to the hospital, what with the way the blood was gushing and the manner in which all of the worried eyes roamed, ten thousand upon ten thousand eyes spelling the air with death. He had figured that the boy in the green jersey, the woman's mysterious nephew, had seen him and fostered his revenge by kidnapping Benjamin, that he had formulated a plan to nab him next. Now, in this room, in this house, in this divine moment, that entire string of theories disintegrated before him. Eddie realized that that same woman, Natalie Haas, was here, living in this very house. She liked baseball and she had that round scar on her forehead, a scar the exact dimensions of a hard paper cup. And of course she had the photographs of Veteran's Stadium posted on the wall, a further testament to this revelation. Eddie sat and absorbed the new possibilities, and he basked in a glow of relief as his walls of paranoia came tumbling down and he thought: the woman is alive.

V

As Fred pulled his truck up the stones, Eddie heard the heavy sound that made him believe, without looking out the window, that this was not an Impala and that the woman had not come home. He peered out to see the blue truck and Fred unlatching the tailgate, retrieving the window for which he had waited an eternity. He watched as the old man carried it down the walk and then as he guided it between the hanging pine boughs. Eddie walked calmly across the room, filled with contentment, and opened the side door. "See you remembered me," he said.

"Got me a hangover," Fred said. "Sure hope I won't need hammering on this sunbitch." He leaned the window against the outside wall, walked back to his truck, and retrieved a large rusted tool box. "I'll need to get in and take down that plywood and screw this window in from the inside."

As Eddie sat on the couch watching Fred screwing and cursing, screwing and cursing, he considered the timing of his new window. It all seemed too perfect: at the very moment that his inner darkness had receded, here came Fred with the window. That perfect, clear window through which the light, the glorious light, now filtered down into his basement. The woman was alive and his joy rode the shafts of sunlight pushing through the trees past Fred, and he stared and smiled at the patches running across his floor.

Light coming to him, just like the light filling the moon, a gibbous moon unfolding into a full moon in the night sky. The astronomers called that a waxing gibbous, as a moon approached a full moon, as the light, slowly, night by night, revealed more and more of the lunar surface. He had gotten that one on the Astronomy Final and passed the course, and now he smiled at remembering it. He smiled, too, because that very sort of moon had glowed on Mrs. Haas' forehead. That moon-scar now told him that she was alive. That moon-scar told him that he would need no more closet boxes to shut him in.

In his rapture, he must not have heard the crunching of the stones. Perhaps Fred's cussing over the stripped screws had drowned out the sound and the shadow of her car had not impaled itself upon the pencils of light running across the floor. For he abruptly heard the woman's voice from just beyond the window, and then she leaned down into her shadow and peered through the open hole to greet Fred. "Well look who decided to make an appearance," she said, her voice suddenly amplified, her face and her white tuft obstructing the sun.

Eddie's heart raced. Then his euphoria vanished. Now, in one blazing second, the lizard weighed upon him like a falling boulder. Now his thoughts rose and shot to the other side of the basement, to the far end, to the sink, to Jude tied to the post. Now what? Now what? Now what? Jude was waiting there to be seen with eyes roaming and tongue flicking. His lizard was whipping her tail and waiting for the light from the trap door, waiting, just waiting, to reveal herself to the woman, to Fred, to all of the curious old ones strewn across Hudson. Now it was over, and Eddie suddenly felt trapped, divided from his lizard by the cement walls and helplessly mired in worry.

Mrs. Haas got down on her knees, moved to the open hole, and ran her eyes across Eddie's room. She scrutinized the apartment and smiled at him as he sat upon his cushions masking his fear. "It's about time you got yourself some light down there," she said.

"I won't be burning the lamps up in the afternoons any more." Eddie looked to the open sky just past her head. " Maybe I can get me a spider plant or something."

"Oh why don't you let me give you some snippings from one of mine," she said. "I've got some geraniums that would look nice on the ledge here as well. I've got some clay planters…"

Mrs. Haas moved out of the sunlight and suddenly bathed Eddie, who had moved across the room to the open hole, in a shaft of brilliant light. There he stood below the window watching the woman advance between the pines, up her walkway with the keys jingling. Then he heard her enter from above as the resilient clack of her heels moved along the linoleum. She was going to find that lizard as soon as she found a reason to enter the basement. Eddie searched the room with his eyes, expecting some answer to materialize. Fred inspected him for a moment before he went on screwing the hinges into the cement, perhaps sensing his sudden change of complexion. Eddie brought his hands together and kept them folded on his lap, and whispered, just beyond Fred's earshot, a little prayer to Saint Jude.

"Keep her out of the basement. Keep her busy with other thoughts. Keep her from doing laundry until I can get my lizard back safe. Keep her from screaming, St. Jude, don't let her see it, don't let her see it, don't let her, don't let her."

"Well your window's ready to go," Fred shot down into Eddie's solemn moment. "She swings open, not in, so don't try pullin'. The cement might give way if you try pullin'. Swing her out like so..." Fred pulled the window with his fingers and the bottom swung out, and his knees kicked up some moist dirt and sent it showering in through the open hole. "She'll close tight for you and should keep out the rain....let me know if she doesn't keep out the rain."

He watched Fred retreat down the walk with his rusted tool box and listened as his truck drove off. Now his fear re-awakened as he heard the thumping above him, as his universe closed to the parameters of the woman and his lizard. His heart raced as he thought that he heard the sound of the trap door lifting, thudding down from the far corner of the ceiling. She's going down: he tore up the stairs in a flare of panic and rapped loudly on the door. He rapped again. The woman approached; he could hear her as she moved through the living room, as the heels began on the kitchen tiles. Eddie worked to manufacture something, to dredge up anything to say to the woman, fixing his face into a furtive calm.

"Um, I was wondering about the baseball," he said as she opened the door. "What I was wondering was…was why it was called a dead ball."

"Thought you might have known that. Thought all boys knew baseball history." She opened the door wide again, just as she had done the previous evening, to invite him in. Eddie stepped nervously into the room, listening for any little sound, a scuffle, a panting, the snap of a tail, any sound that might reveal a lizard below her. He began to tune Mrs. Haas out as she explained about the deadball's heavy center, its absence of a rubber casing, and the manner in which the balls smacked meekly off pine.

"Can you believe they called him 'Home Run' Baker?" she asked, moving close, aware suddenly that he had drifted off.

"Huh?"

"Have you been listening?" Baker….hit only twelve home runs in his best year. A home run was as rare as an eclipse. Dead balls didn't carry you see."

"Oh sorry. I was just trying to remember whether I left some laundry in the dryer. I….have some shirts missing and I was wondering…"

"Well feel free to go check if that's what's pressing you," she said. Then she stepped aside and gestured him to the back room. As he passed, Eddie glanced at her temple, searching for the faded cup scar, the waxing gibbous moon that had emerged in that patch of sunlight. He flashed his eyes away, for he did not want to get caught staring. He felt compelled, for a brief instant, to tell her about that day at the game. He wanted to pull her into that very room where she had divulged a secret from her past just yesterday, sit her down and tell her his own secret, that he was the one. He wanted it all purged from his soul, every last bit of paranoia, every fragment of every memory of every dark place in which he had shut off the world. Cry as he might, he wanted it all spilled out there in that very room for her to hear, where he would fall to the carpet and ask her forgiveness. But then he thought he heard a thump from below, and what sounded like the scraping of metal, the legs of a sink pulled across a cement floor. So he shuffled down the hall and, in a flash, opened the trap door. My paranoia acting up again, he thought. The sounds starting up again inside of me.

Then the disquieting satisfaction of the sound realized: indeed, the sink had been moved. He saw it as he flicked on the bulb; it jutted out at an odd angle from the far wall, with one of the legs bent so that the sink itself seemed to be collapsing to the floor. The rope? it dangled from the bent leg, frayed at the end and empty of his lizard.

"Jude," he whispered, careful to look up the steps for the woman's presence in the room above, and then louder, "Jude." Frantically, his eyes scanned the dimmed basement, finding only the inanimate washer and dryer, the long work bench, the wood beams stacked horizontally along the wall. No movement, no lizard. He stood in disbelief, not because Jude had escaped its leash, but because a reptile of such a size could utterly disappear like that. He looked up and noticed the broken window above the stacked lumber, its frame ajar. He had never noticed that window before, that light spilling down the cinderblock wall. It was as if Fred had slipped it in there on his way out. Now the hole beckoned him, letting him know full well that Jude had found it and crawled up that wall to freedom. Jude was somewhere out there and whisking between the ranchers.

Eddie took the length of the cellar stairs in three long strides, and brushed past the living room, where Mrs. Haas had seated herself with a thick book. "Did you find your shirts?" she asked him.

"No, I think they're at work or something," he shot back. He moved down the stairs to his suddenly quiet apartment. Now what? Jude was loose. He was going to draw the attention of the nosy old ones in no time flat, get every one of them out of their living rooms and to their front lawns. He opened his window and tried to peer between the for-sythias, looking for a lizard that might have encroached upon some unsuspecting sparrows as they chirped away in the branches. He looked for the long brown tail crossing the road, the head reared, the leather sides breathing in and out, the tongue tasting the tranquil Hudson air. He listened for the screams of disbelief. He watched for shotguns and brooms to come pouring from front doors. Nothing.

Eddie locked his side door and walked between the pines, whispering 'Jude' along the walkway, watching for the moon eyes behind the boughs. He carried an extra piece of rope in the event that Jude revealed herself, and he suddenly remembered the story Domingus had told him of Salvadore. He was going to have to stalk and capture the Monitor Lizard just as Salvadore had done. He was going to have to walk slowly behind Jude, crouch like a cat, and then pounce on her before she had time to take off. He was going to have to wrestle her to the ground and somehow get that leash around her neck, cut and scratch and fight her with all of his might, bleed and curse and draw attention to himself.

He walked nervously up Small Road, trying to hide the long piece of rope dangling from his hand. He had never walked past these houses beyond the yellow rancher. It was a lucky thing, he figured, that his own rented apartment was at the bottom of the street, close to the interstate. He never drew much attention walking home from Bingo's or carrying his groceries back from the convenience store. It was a nice thing to avoid those eyes behind the curtains. But now he had no choice. He was certain that Jude had made his way into the heart of Hudson among the bushes lining the road. The forsythias must have been its only solace, the closest, with its narrow vision, that came to the jungles of the Ivory Coast. Much like the snakes, the turtles, the game birds that had been displaced from the donut pond, here was another lost animal looking for some natural harbor.

"Jude," he yelled. He didn't mean to call out quite so loud, and nervously fumbled his rope so that it fell to the street. An old woman, picking some letters out of her mailbox at the bottom of her driveway, looked over at Eddie as he bent down and picked up the leash.

"Lost your dog?" she asked.

"My dog…yes my dog," he said.

"You're the boy living under Natalie aren't you?" the woman asked. She had begun to move up the sidewalk toward him, and beneath her glasses Eddie could see the eyes, the curious eyes, working to fix his image to her brain.

"That would be me," he said. Now that was it. This woman was going to go to Mrs. Haas and tell her that he had a dog, and that it had escaped. Then he was going to have to lie to Mrs. Haas and tell her that he had a dog.

"You don't seriously keep your dog on a leash like that……that's a hanging rope you got there…"

"Well this was all I could find. My dog…"

"What were you calling it? Did I hear you calling it Jude?"

"Yes her name is Jude"

"As in Saint Jude, the patron saint of hopeless causes?"

"No…well, yes but you know the Beatles song 'Hey Jude'? It's my favorite song, so I decided to name my dog after it."

"Well I'm Mrs. Crawford…"

"I'm Eddie." They stood silent for some seconds, as if the woman expected more information, a last name at least.

"You look so familiar. I know I've seen your face around before."

"Well I come and go." Eddie began to move down the street and past her mailbox. He didn't want her inspecting him further, making the connection to that newspaper photo stuck on one of her memory cells, the one next to the runaway headline, or the one of his standing on his lawn two years back after the Benjamin kidnapping. She was going to piece it all together any minute now. Things were clicking inside of her, so he began to move on. "Well I really need to be looking for my dog. Don't want him getting too far away."

"Well I hope you find poor Jude. I'll say a little prayer to Saint Anthony. He's the patron saint…"

"Of lost things," Eddie finished with a shout back. He continued up Small Road and looked between each of the houses. He brushed his hands through the thick rows of forsythias and whispered his lizard's name again and again. He began to ignore the curtains as they opened in the windows of each rancher that he passed. He paid no attention to the eyes, a hundred it seemed, watching his every move, the young boy so out of place in this wasteland for the aged. They were wondering no doubt what he was going to do with that rope that he carried, and he was sure that each set of eyes recognized him as 'the boy below Natalie Haas'.

The darkness began to descend on Hudson. A stiff wind carried through the pines and chilled Eddie as he walked along Charles Street, down Euclid, over Worthington, and across Belmont. No lizard, no lizard, no lizard. Jude was gone, and now the prevailing cold front that had enveloped Hudson whispered to Eddie that it was going to kill his lizard by daybreak. Wherever it had gone, there was no escape from the Arctic air mass coming in. This sort of weather had never touched down on Jude's native jungle in the Ivory Coast. Jude was going to freeze solid to the ground.

Through much of the night, Eddie laid in his bed listening to his last guinea pig squeal in the box beneath him. The squeal was different this time, a cadence lower, as if, in guinea-pigese, it was muttering relief that the monster lizard had vacated the room. The guinea pig, among other things, was keeping him awake, so he went to the refrigerator and broke off a chunk of romaine, slid his hand over the box, and dropped it in. The guinea pig chattered in gratitude as it gobbled the chunk up. Watching from the dimmed light coming from the window, Eddie petted his final rodent along its skull and down the length of its backbone. He whispered for it to be silent and yawned his way back between the sheets.

VI

He must have been sleeping soundly, for the sound had all but trailed off by the time he sat upright in his bed. It was a scream, there was no question, yet it seemed to linger for a moment and then pass, as if it were the floating spores of a dandelion blown by a gust of wind. He thought it a dream as he sat and listened, as only the distant cars on the interstate came and went, as the clicking of the heater spattered the room with sound. He looked to the window, now filled with early morning light. It must have been nothing. It must have been only the lurking remnant of some nightmare, now wiped from memory, from which he had just escaped.

Then he heard the muffled cry coming from behind the wall. For several seconds, Eddie tuned in and became certain that someone had been trapped within the wall, like that black cat in the Poe story. Someone was stuck within the cinder blocks crying to escape. Then the cry softened to a low wail, and it began to pass out of earshot, fading like a passing car on the interstate until it became barely audible. Then he realized that the sound came from the other side of the basement, from the laundry room, and he crossed the room and listened with his ear to the wall as the sound completely died away.

He dressed nervously and flicked on the lamp, listening in on the wall for the sound again, hoping that it was just another distant sound that had crept in and fooled him into thinking it a scream. Perhaps it was all in his head, inner noises coming out of those excess fluids. Or perhaps the woman was chanting to her long-gone lover again, wailing in agony over his passing. She had gone down into the basement to lament his loss, and now she had stopped and would, at any moment, make her way back up the stairs. The silence crept in. The cars all died away and the heater clicked off, leaving Eddie to dead quiet. And then he shivered, as if a cold shaft of air had made its way between the cracks of his newly installed window and brushed over him. But this was no chill from the morning air. This was unlike any chill that had ever gripped him and he thought: something has happened on the other side.

Eddie walked up the steps and rapped on the door. Please, he whispered. Please come to the door. Please with your footsteps, vibrate the floor boards, click-clack across the linoleum, and open the door. Open the door. Saint Jude, please make her cross the room and open the door. Eddie turned the knob and opened. "Mrs. Haas?" he called. "Mrs. Haas are you in there? I thought I heard you calling me. Are you there?"

He walked across the floor and into the living room, hoping that at any moment she would emerge from the shadows and reveal some new artifact from the palm of her hand, ready some new story from her lips from the comfort of her couch. The smell of Boysenberry had suddenly ceased, and the room had taken on the encroaching air of a coffin, the subdued light of a funeral parlor. His breath quickened into manic bursts, and he made his way down the hallway and into her room.

"Mrs. Haas....I'm worried....I thought I heard you calling...." The trap door had been propped open, and he could see the light shining up from below. He called her name again, and again, and again as he advanced nervously down the stairs. And then in a flash and in a sudden jolt which nearly knocked him off the steps and into the darkness, his lizard lunged upward. Jude's head shot out from beneath him and hovered just in front of him, face to face. The moon eyes came down all around him and the long pink tongue tasted the warm air seeping down from above. Eddie lunged for the nape of its neck. He reached and grabbed, but Jude dashed off the edge of the steps and into the darkness. He saw the long tail move swiftly in the direction of the washer and dryer. As he advanced to the bottom of the stairs in pursuit, he watched as Jude disappeared behind the dryer. It tucked itself neatly away in the warmest place that it could find. That was where Jude had been hiding all along—it had not escaped through the window and between the houses. It had sought the warmth behind the dryer.

As he lunged for the space behind the dryer, Eddie stumbled over the woman's body. She had just materialized there on the floor. He was so intent on capturing Jude that his vision had blocked out every other thing in the room, including the obstacles in his path. Mrs. Haas lay there in a pile of white clothes. She was draped over her own bras and underwear, her long white shirts, her pillow cases, her sheets. She lay face down with her arms spread, her legs twisted beneath her dress. Her hands had frozen into tight fists, as if enclosing some secret messages never to be revealed.

"Mrs. Haas? Mrs. Haas?" he called in a quivering whisper. And then, in an eruption of realization, Eddie was back up the steps and staring down at the bare bulb. And then he was closing the trap door and running the length of the house, and opening his door and slamming it behind him and screaming the pain of his moment down upon the walls. He sat down on the stairs and envisioned the old woman's face as Jude had jumped out at her from behind the dryer. If he had bent down to turn her over, he might have seen the terror still cemented there. He might have seen the expression of a woman caught by surprise, her eyes frozen open to a sight she had not witnessed in her eighty-some years of life: a giant lizard staring her down.

The face wouldn't go away. It burned into him beneath the bright bulb. Eddie's hands trembled as he brought them to his face, as he muffled his anguish. "What am I going to do? What am I going to do?" he wailed. He waited on those steps for an answer to come, as the bright morning sun revealed his room for the very first time. Everything seemed so different as he stared across the room from his vantage point on the stairs. Nothing seemed to belong, not the couch nor the chair nor the empty red bowl nor the lone guinea pig, quiet and filled with romaine beneath the bed. Amidst his tears and through his fingers, it looked as if he were looking down a long tunnel flooded by rain. These things were not his any longer, this place was not home. He had no couch, no chair, no guinea pig, no Jude. He did not even have himself, the self which had finally found the light of day.

Eddie spent the entire day sitting on the stairs. All the while he hoped for a sound, a resurrection from the other side. He was scheduled to be at Bingo's by nine, but no matter—he was not going to go back. Everything was finished. The neighbors would come snooping when they saw her Impala unmoved upon the stones. They would come knocking to no answer, and they would let her telephone ring and ring and ring, and they would get themselves in through the side door and call her name and they would walk down the basement steps and scream and find her dead on her whites. Then the police cars would swarm the house, and they would discover the lizard behind the dryer and the boy on the other side of the cinder block wall. He had caused it all, he and his lizard. He had tried to kill her once at the ball park, and now he had done it again. And there was no doubt this time: he had killed Natalie Haas, and now he was going to have to pay.

The day was a long, bad dream, and the night came down between the forsythias and dropped the room into darkness again. In all that time, Eddie had not moved from the stairs. Finally with the coming of night he stood up and walked to the middle of the room. He fumbled about in the dark room, and without turning on the lamp he gathered some of the clothes from the stacked boxes and stuffed them into his knapsack. He pulled the thick blanket from the top of his bed and draped it over the top of the pack. He made sure of his wallet in his pocket, then flipped through the bills and counted them in whispers. Just before he stepped from the room, he plucked the old baseball from the top of his refrigerator and slipped it into the side of his pack. He walked out the side door and closed off his apartment behind him. He knew he wasn't going back in there. He knew that he was leaving it all behind.

In the advancing cold front he walked down Small Road. Despite the darkened porches, he could see his way ahead quite clearly, as the thick branches of the bushes cast dim shadows on the road. The moon was doing that, he could tell. It had risen high in the night sky just behind him. Eddie didn't look up. He had seen the moon several nights before on his way home from working a night shift, a brilliant full moon rising over the interstate. Now he calculated that the moon was no longer full. It had gone into the phase of waning gibbous, which meant that it was creeping, little by little, towards total darkness.

Grow Light

◆

I

Eddie had every intention of going home. He walked along the interstate and pictured the opened arms of his mother and the shouts of joy from his father; he pictured the cumulative tears soaking shirts and dresses and carpets as he walked in though the foyer. Home: he was going to sleep in his own bed tonight, he was going to stare off across his old ceiling tonight. He was going to divide himself from the cold front approaching with those clouds gathering in the night sky just over the groves of bare trees. The clouds rolled across the sky—over Eddie, over the road—and rolled across the gibbous moon.

He just wanted to close off the runaway as if it were a dream. His reawakening would be just like any other emergence from sleep; he would brush it all away, go on and on and brush it away. Brush away the terrible lizard, brush away the dead woman on the laundry. Brush those things away into one long pretended dream as if they never happened at all. Who would know, who would ever know? He was just a mysterious boy come to Hudson, a shadow on the aging memory cells that would vanish into another curious fragment of the past. Lost and gone, those brief snippets would all slip away by the time they found her down there, dead in her basement. Who would put it all together? Who would figure out the identity of the boy on the other side, the one behind the cinderblock, the one with the escaped reptile? The lady with the mail? The curious ones watching from their porches? And so what of Fred O'Hara? So what of Bingo's? He would be gone and forgotten and Fred might get a call from the police and he would sit in his office and scratch his head and look through his file and find only a name: Eddie Stillwell, a mysterious boy come to Bingo's, now just a fictitious name inked upon an application. So there was no worry there; there would be no trace, no identity, and he would be home soon. His new life would dissolve back in to the old one, forever diluted into the well of his life.

He tried to fix his mind on the happy faces which would greet him as he came back home: his mother, his father, William, the neighbors running, the endless phone calls sending messages of relief, and finally the news crews descending with their blinding spotlights. He tried to keep all of those good things there and fix a cheerful future in his thoughts. He tried to force a smile even. He could not, however, overcome his immediate past and conquer the festering image of the dead woman down on her freshly dried clothes. And the only word that recurred faintly upon his lips, as he walked block upon block towards home, was 'damnit.'

Eddie followed the wide shoulder of the interstate and walked beneath the "Fergusonville" sign. He should have kept going straight ahead to the next exit, past the middle school and through the maze of orange construction barrels. Two miles down he should have kept walking down to Newportville, down the dip in the road to the older developments, down past the plowed-over frog ponds to the street on which he lived. But the thoughts of the day had absorbed him so that his unconscious now carried him up the exit ramp towards Fergusonville. He kept envisioning the great reptilian leap from behind the dryer as he walked, as Jude's long tongue flickered across his brain and the lizard's moon eyes kept an unblinking stare through the woman's fatal scream. It kept on and on, whipping at his every thought like some long leathery tail swinging dangerously away. When for one brief remission that lizard-image tapered off, Eddie turned and looked up in the cold night air to notice the massive Fergusonville bridge looming above him. The sounds of the interstate had drifted into the subtle passing of a car or the occasional rumble of a truck. Now, as if by design and surrender, he made his way down the grassy embankment to his bridge cave.

They'll catch me, he thought. When I go home and when the news crews descend, my face will flare up on all of the television screens across Hudson and they'll catch me. The old ones will point to my face and pick up their telephones and call the police and report me as the murderer. Fred will call up and admit that it was me, Eddie Shemanski, and then he'll fire me. And my mother, well she'll break down and admit that she had never let me buy that monitor lizard so many years back. It was all her fault, she'll tell the police as they cuff me. And as they put me into the back of the car, she'll take off bawling to the back bedroom.

II

The cold air came up off the Neshaminy creek in a series of gusts as Eddie removed the rocks he had carefully placed to hide away his cave. The clouds had now moved across the sky in thick clumps, blotting out the moon and creating such a blackness beneath the bridge that Eddie could not even see his hands as they worked to remove the invisible rocks and get himself inside. It reminded him of the tour he'd taken at Crystal Cave some years back with his father. The tour guide had flipped a switch that shut off the overhead lights fixed in the cavern's ceiling. Eddie stood there in the dark with his father and fifty other tourists in the pitchest black he had ever witnessed. He had listened to the echo of the tour guide as she told them all about going blind in such a blackness where eventually insanity set in. Frightening: months of pitch blackness would do that to a person, she said, just months. That was all it took.

The chill had settled into the floor and among the rocks. The dankness was unlike the air that gusted along the bridge walls, for it carried the smell of dampened newspapers. He could feel the ice forming at the crest of the cave walls in sharp ridges, almost like knives in their compositions, down between the cement cracks. Eddie figured he had better watch himself in the night, especially when he drifted off and started squirming. He didn't want to wake up and find himself bleeding all over the cave floor.

It was cold enough to snow if the clouds let loose, and the wind whistled through the piled rocks and made him shiver. He unzipped his pack in the dark and felt for the blanket. This would have to do him the night, this would have to get him through. Even if he had decided to go home, it was too late now anyway. By the time he scaled the hill and got down the exit ramp to the interstate and walked the last two miles, his mother and father would be sound asleep. He would startle his father if he walked in the door that late. That sort of late entrance might make him reach for his bat at the bottom of the bed. and before Eddie could explain it was his own son come home, his father would wail on him right there in the foyer. None of that: he wrapped the blanket around him and balled up some of his shirts and laid down on the cave floor, quite sure that he was never going home.

Eddie tried to work up a good cry. It seemed to him that his circumstances dictated a good cry and that a good cry should come naturally as the rumble of one lonely truck died away and left him in his black silence. He shivered and pulled the blanket tighter and closed his eyes. He knew that several hours would pass before sleep, but he tried anyway. It was as if a light had been turned on, for with the closing of his eyes, the myriad of images flashed through him like a slide show. A montage of wrenching memories spliced back through time, from the walk along the interstate to the long stare across his basement apartment to the discovery of the dead woman to Jude jumping at him from beneath the steps to the long walks home from Bingo's to the orders piling up to the soft-shelled crabs bubbling away in the deep fryer to the drunken Fred falling one more time from his stool to Chile screaming from behind the line to the long hot nights in the tool shed to Billy Stigmeyer to the bony-faced man in the Cadillac to the runaway in the rain to the droning of the ball games from the living room to the wailing of his mother in the back room to the night the masked hoodlums came in and stole Benjamin from the crib.

Benjamin was fading. His absence had made Eddie begin to forget about him now. Now his little brother flickered as some out of focus Instamatic shot that was part of some other life that had receded to foggy obscurity. So much had happened since that night two and a half years back, so much. No longer did the haunting images return to tug at him and pull him down. He could not bring himself to tears for his brother any longer. He tried to cry for him there in the dark the same way that he had cried out on the dock at Bingo's and through so many sleepless nights, so many nights of prayer. But nothing forced itself to the surface, not a single drop of sob.

St. Jude probably had a lot of orders to fill, Eddie figured. Those requests were shooting in from every part of the globe, from icy Antarctic metal shacks to steaming jungle huts. There was a line formed: thousands upon thousands of prayers were piled and waiting to be opened, waiting for the gentle breath of the patron saint of hopeless causes to unravel them into the light. Eddie's beckoning the return of his little brother might very well be buried under pleas for drowned sons to return to life, for rocks to stop falling down mountainsides, for legs to heal and untwist, for whips to die off, for diseases to fade, for abrasions to go away, for minds to clear themselves of pestering insanities.

Perhaps there was no invisible hand of Jude at all. Perhaps no saint at all came down and fixed hopeless causes. Maybe faith was just a word for believing something that wasn't really there. If that were the case, Saint Jude was a fable, a fairy tale like the Easter bunny, like Santa Clause, like the tooth fairy. Hope for hopeless causes was just as ridiculous as flying reindeer and bunnies carrying baskets and money left magically beneath pillows in the night. With no Jude, the mad ones would always remain mad, the whips would slash and slash until the screams fell into a death quiet, the diseases would spread like ravaging fires until all of the life was burned away, the crippled would always crawl, the landslides would crush, and all of the living sons would drown and be carried into the pull of the current, down among the tumbling minnows. And Benjamin would remain forever lost, out among the living, or reduced to some brittle skeleton beneath the loosened earth.

The chill of the cave carried a sudden stabbing terror as it worked to crush Eddie, and he wrapped his thick blanket completely around him, drum-tight around his arms and over his head. He shivered in his cave and stared ahead through the fibers of the blanket, trying to detect some light from a half-moon that might venture out from behind some clouds and shine beneath the edges of the bridge. But the moon stayed away and the darkness persisted, and then the sobs arrived. They blistered forth from beneath the blanket in one long, uncontained wail.

III

In a dream Eddie walked behind his father and he took his hand as they ascended the steep path to the mouth of Crystal Cave. They followed the tour guide as she beckoned them forth with her hand, and she led them down to the place where the sunlight disappeared. Come in, she said. Walk through the entrance-way and make your way down.

And so they did, and Eddie carefully watched his father and stepped along behind him as they descended into the mansion of caverns.

Lights planted high in the ceiling, hidden somewhere among the forests of stalagmites, bathed the spacious rooms in an eerie yellow glow. The imposing rock walls came down all around him and Eddie looked back to see from where they had come. The entrance had vanished as they foraged deeper into the cavern, far removed from the sunlight, the trees, the open sky. A mile of rock tunnels snaked into an intricate maze beneath the earth, narrower and narrower, shutting them in like boxed gerbils. They followed the tour guide every step as she made her way around the wicked bends beneath the lights. She made her way down, and now the earth seemed to come alive and breathe a soft rumble through the ground as Eddie walked along in his unsteady dream-sleep.

And further and further he went down, and he seemed to go down forever, deep and cold and silent. And then in a sigh, his father was no longer there to follow. Eddie looked around the cave; he looked behind him and through the fissures between the stalagmites but could not find him. He continued to follow the tour guide as she walked. The lapse of time in the dream seemed to carry on into weeks where the sun came and went and came and went in its arc across the hidden sky. Finally, in her elongated shadow, the tour guide stopped, and the trickling of cave water overcame her footsteps.

"And now I will show you something," she said. And as her hand reached up to switch off the overhead lights, she turned around and looked back at him. Eddie came to notice her wrinkled face beneath the hidden bulbs, the waning gibbous etched into her skull, the face of Natalie Haas. With her white hair glowing, in her flowered dress shining, she stood there beneath the lights and smiled back in that last bright moment, as if she was letting him know that she had somehow survived his lizard. Then her hand came down upon the switch, and she threw the room into darkness. And she said, "When you live in a deep black darkness like this, after a couple of weeks you go blind. And when you live like this for a couple of months…well then you go insane."

Then she wasn't there. Eddie groped through the blackness of his dream-cave in search of something to set him into the light, trying to remember where she had reached to shut off the lights. But he couldn't find the switch, and again the hours seemed to carry on into days, and then weeks, as he fumbled along in his blindness. He needed to find that light was all he kept thinking. He wished only for the end of the dream. He was going to go insane if he couldn't locate that switch or get himself out of the dream.

Then the sound of the ball game: he could hear it coming from somewhere below, a distant muddled drone which became clearer and clearer as he walked down the incline into suffocating passageways, deeper and deeper into Crystal Cave. He was trying to find his father's living room. He was trying to look for the light of the television, for the broadcast of another ball game.

"If Hobose gets aboard,…if Hobose gets aboard……if Hobose gets aboard…it's a sure steal" were the only words that kept on, as if he had come across a skipping record that he was condemned to hear over and over in his father's voice. Just beyond the rock walls he could hear it crackling, and he felt along the rock face for some sort of opening that might lead him down to the light of his father's television. A sudden urgency welled within him: he had to find his father. In his dark dream, the only escape, the only way to make up for not finding the switch was to find the source of his father's voice. He hoped that, with every corner he turned, the blue light would come flooding over him, and then across the emerging carpet and the worn couches, the image of Hobose taking a long lead off first base would flash out of the television set and settle his eyes back to sanity. He was going to ask his Uncle Pete to slide over when he reached that lighted cavern, so he could sit with them and watch the pitches come in.

"Dad," he called out, "dad." But Eddie had taken a wrong turn in his dream-cave. Now the sound of the game began to fade. He could barely hear the announcer and soon no voices at all shot up from below. His father was gone, lost down there among the million rooms. Eddie fumbled through the blackness, alone and without a guide. The switch, the television, the trees, the open sky were a cavernous maze, worlds removed from him and hopelessly woven beyond discovery. Now the walls closed in tighter and tighter, now the rock face pressed against him from all sides.

IV

Eddie must have cried himself to sleep, for he could feel the thick layer of dried tears pulling at his face as he awoke and brushed away the terrible dream. The blanket had soaked some of the tears as well and had stiffened from the cold cave air. Suddenly beneath his cocoon he could see that some light had entered, as the fibers gave way to some invading brightness stabbing in from somewhere beyond the rocks. Daylight? It did not feel like daylight; it felt as if only minutes had passed since his drift into cave sleep. Besides, it was not enough light to come from the sun. He peeled away the blanket and knew for sure that this was no daylight, as orange light flickered bright and died, flickered bright and died, all along the walls. The fire had returned to the other side of the creek. Sure enough he heard the voices, whispers off the concrete walls beckoning his ear to the piled stones. The saints had returned; Eddie could see them gathered around the fire, clothed in gray jackets and wool hats. Together again, those same faces gazed intently into the interior of the raging flame.

Speak someone, someone speak, Eddie willed across the Neshaminy as he gazed in a half-sleep through the cracks. But the men remained silent and stared away, as if conjuring up some spirit from the burning logs. Eddie breathed in short gasps through the cold rocks and he could see his breath steaming out and rising among the shadows cast by the fire. He pulled back from the rocks to keep his steam in the cave, just enough so that he could peruse the hunched forms. Seven, he counted. He looked for Finbar but did not see him. He deduced that he was gone and that a new saint had taken his place.

He scanned the other men, the same ones as before, and found the new arrival, who rose and passed a look over the others. This one had a thinning beard and a patch of flesh adorning the crest of his skull. Forty-five years old, Eddie guessed as the man passed his hands over the flame. Studying him, he came to notice the man's enormous head, with a face mottled by red blotches. His body, in its thin condition, had to work to keep the massive skull aloft. He was about to tell a story, just as Finbar had done some months back when he spoke of his own kidnapping. The man pulled his hands back and stuffed them into the pockets of his drab jacket, and the other men looked up at him to study his eyes and to await his voice.

"Well in case you didn't notice I've got this monster head," he said. "I've got this monster head." He steadied himself on his feet, as if a build-up of tears had suddenly sloshed against the walls of his gigantic tear ducts and swayed his head like a water balloon. The men gathered their papers again and began to scribble. They watched the movements of the man and began to write about him, just as they had done with Finbar.

"My father was a gullible man," he said. "You could tell him just about anything and he believed it. He read the chicken little story when he was six and really believed the sky could fall. He ran around afraid for about four years, never calmed by my grandmother until he learned some science that told him the sky couldn't fall like that. But my father kept on believing everything else, and the kids of the neighborhood needled the hell out of him and fooled him about everything." The large-headed man stopped and raised his hand to his temple and smiled.

"This has something to do with your head, doesn't it Garrison?" one of the men asked. It was the same man who had consoled Finbar some months back, and the man clicked his pen open and pointed in the direction of Garrison's skull.

"The National Fucking Enquirer," Garrison said.

"I'm sorry," one of the men said as the large-headed man stood and gazed into the flame. "The Enquirer, what about it?"

"My father subscribed, got it weekly in the mail. It was unbelievable the things they printed in there, well you all know some of them I'm sure, the unbelievable headlines. Three million copies a week they print. Three million readers a week. Now that I get to thinkin', I guess there are a lot of people out there who believe everything they read, just like my father. And I guess I can't blame the Enquirer for trying to make money. If there's anybody to blame, it's those three million readers."

Again the man stopped and looked into the flame, as if he didn't know how to continue.

"If you're uncomfortable talking about it…." came a voice.

"I'm here and I'm telling it, aren't I?" Garrison shot back. He pulled his hands from his pockets and lifted them to the sides of his massive temple, rubbing. "Just let me get to it. Just let me work my way through it." When he sighed, long and loud, Eddie could see the steam rise from his mouth and nostrils, the steam of anger. The other men squirmed as they waited for Garrison to continue. Eddie reviewed the names in his head, the names of the saints mired there: no Saint Garrison. Eddie sat and breathed out his steam into the cold cave, confused now about the circle of men. Perhaps they weren't saints after all. Perhaps they had huddled for some other mysterious cause.

"My father, just about the time that I was born, he reads this article in National Enquirer about these light bulbs some agricultural graduate student invented to help crops grow. This graduate student, and mind you I've memorized his name—Aaron Shagcropolis—this student contends that these lights can make anything grow. He works it out so that he gets plants going, all kinds of flowering things mashed together in greenhouses under these grow lights he's got going night and day. And then, according to the article, it says that he's tried it on a batch of kittens—stuck it right over the little box where they were born—and before he knew it he had himself a load of thirty-pound cats."

"Did you read this article? Did your father show it to you?" came one of the voices. The men scribbled their thoughts, his words, perhaps other things, as the man looked into the flame in silence again. Eddie had crept back to his spot in front of the piled stones, quite unable to believe this science fiction. He removed one of the smaller ones to get a better view and a new batch of firelight entered the cave. Better watch my movements, he thought.

" I was a baby when this article appeared. I wasn't yet a year old, still helpless in my crib. I'll tell you I only found that article recently over at Landoff Library. They got one of those microfilms over there and a whole metal drawer full of reels and I was surprised as hell when I pulled out the "N" drawer and found boxes and boxes of National Enquirer, going all the way back. I pull out all of the boxes from the year of my birth. It took me hours to go through them, but then I finally hit pay dirt just near closing time. I find the headline, "Magic Light Grows Anything." I read the article and it chills me because it's all about me. Aaron Shagcropolis, I read and I memorize. Aaron Shagcropolis, the inventor of the 'Ultra-Grow Light.'"

One of the stones slipped from its place on the pile and rolled down the hill. Eddie pressed nervously into the shadows along the wall and listened as the stone splashed into the icy black water. They were going to find him now. They were going to look across the creek and up the hill and spot the bridge cave. All seven of them would be across the water and up that hill in a manner of seconds, and then they would seize him there and pummel him with stones picked from the night hill.

"Must have been one of them painted turtles," came a voice. "Didn't think there were any of them turtles left in this polluted water, what with the developments…. Anyway, go on, Garrison. Go on." Eddie breathed relief steam and found contentment within the rock shadows.

"From my very first memory—two years old—three maybe—my dad told me about these special lights. Secret lights, he called them, magic lights. He must have looked this guy up, talked to him, bought some of the lights from him or something. I don't really know how he got them, how he made his connection. But I saw the pictures of me in my crib. I saw me and I saw the lights hanging, six lights lined up above me hanging from wires, warming me as if I were some germinating seed. And by the time I could walk and sleep in my own bed, well dad had gone ahead and fastened lights into the ceiling above me. I never slept in the dark until I was twelve. Every night I laid down to the glare of light bulbs pouring down on me."

"How could you sleep with the lights on?" questioned the man on the opposite end of the fire. "I can't sleep with a hall light on, much less a light over my bed."

"Well I suppose you adapt to things like that," Garrison said. "I don't think I could do it today unless I was real tired. But that was all I knew back then. I slept under the lights and that was all I ever knew."

Eddie couldn't help looking out again. He wanted to see Garrison's head as he talked, so he peered around the shadows toward the light and he saw once again. The monster skull bobbed as it breathed in the smoke and gazed with watery eyes into the fire.

"My father," Garrison continued, "told me that if I slept under the secret lights every night, I would get strong, I would grow at the bones, get myself bones as thick as logs. My father you see was a skinny man— you could see the bones through his skin. I remember the one day when he was standing in the field playing baseball for the company team at SPS. He had these little shorts on and no shirt, all bone. He was standing there and a warm wind picked up and blew against him, and it pushed against his skin so much that I could see just about every bone on his body coming through, ribs and sternum and arm bones and it made me sick and then worried that I was going to grow up looking like that. And that's when I figured out why he put those grow lights over my bed. He didn't want me turning out like him."

"Why didn't he just make you eat your vegetables and potatoes?," asked one of the men. "And how did he know that the grow lights would work?"

Garrison paused again. His face turned a brighter hue of red as the flame captured the blood churning furiously within. "My father didn't like anything. He didn't like steak or hamburger or milk or cheese or any kind of green vegetable. Corn on the cob and hot dogs was about all he ate. Hot dogs buried under half a jar of mustard, corn dredged in salt. That was all that my father ever ate really and that's what kept him skinny his whole life. But he wouldn't hear any of it. He swore that if you were born with big bones, you would be big and strong no matter what you ate. He was born thin and frail and that was the end of him. And he swore that Aaron Shagcropolis had found the answer…not for him because he was too old and it was too late…no, Aaron had found the answer for his son."

"So your head…"

"My head, my fucking head," he shouted. The echo came across the bridge and carried over the water and sailed into the cold black night, down among the bare trees. Garrison's eyes spread across the whole of his face; the corneas came out like white sheets and absorbed the dancing flames as his teeth clenched, as his body tensed, and the men grew closer with their pens waiting. "Those grow lights, I think only two of them worked. I can't be sure of this now, but I really believe that the bulbs over my head were the only ones that had something in them, the special filaments or secret teaspoons of plutonium or what have you. I'm thinking now that maybe my father was right. I mean, if he had gotten six bulbs that worked, who knows what I might look like today?"

Eddie couldn't believe, in the ensuing seconds of silence, that the lights had actually made this man's head grow like that. If there was anything that he had inherited from his father, it was his gullibility, and that this particular man's sky really was falling.

Garrison began to weep, some little sniffles followed by thick tears that ran the length of his face like a trickling waterfall off a steep cliff. He cupped his hands and tried to fill them with his face, failing. "The kids laughed at me and called me 'head' all the way through school. You think my head is big now, you should have seen me in high school. I swear it was hard to lift up my head in the morning and carry it through the day. When I figured out that it was the lights that were doing it, I told my father. But he just laughed and said the growing was working from inside my bones and then he stuck his wrist next to mine to show how far along I'd come."

"So where is your father now?" asked one of the men. "Do you need us to find him as well?"

"I know damned well where my father is. He's dead and buried over in Fairlawn. Didn't need much of a grave either, the son of a bitch. Just a skinny little ditch dug in the earth for his skinny little casket."

"We're sorry to hear about your father," said one of the others.

"Yeah well you're the only ones then," Garrison said. "I sure as hell know I'm not. He broke his own pencil neck falling down the basement stairs one Saturday morning. Two of my uncles had to haul me from the funeral when I wouldn't stop spitting down into the hole after they lowered him. That was the only time I ever cursed in front of my mother, and curse I did, one 'fuck you' and 'son of a bitch' after the other until I had every relative looking away in shame. They couldn't look at me because they knew I had every right to curse like that. They couldn't look at me because my bulbous head had suddenly become my father's tragic legacy."

The quiet settled over the circle of men again, as they all worked to get the story down, to mark their comments and offer possible solutions. Eddie's curiosity had gotten him again as he edged closer to the piled rocks. Here they were again, in their mysterious way, working to fix Garrison's problem, to bring some order to his turbulent life.

"What is it that you want, Garrison?" asked one of the men. Is it revenge that you want? Do you want the head of Aaron Shagcropolis? Is that what this as all about?"

Garrison smiled over the fire and wiped away a remaining waterfall from the cliff of his face. "Revenge no," he said. "I'm only bitter at my father for abusing the invention. No, I just want to find Aaron if he's still alive. Perhaps he's found some way, some way…"

"To shrink your head?"

A low mumble of chuckles came over the men and Garrison's massive face flared in anger. "For God's sakes don't any of you believe this? I've done library research, I know what my father did to me. It's the grow lights, I believe it now and I'll believe it to my dying day. And I know this Aaron Shagcropolis is the only one with any sort of answer. No, he can't shrink my head, but maybe he's developed some sort of light to make the rest of my body catch up to it. Maybe I can get big-boned just like my son of a bitch father hoped for…"

The pile of rocks suddenly gave way during Garrison's tirade, as if the added decibel level of his voice had risen across the creek and knocked against the side of the bridge. The rocks tumbled down, one by one, in an avalanche down the hill. Each of the boulders crashed into the water, leaving Eddie exposed at the cave entrance. The firelight revealed him there, blanket-bound, on the other side of the water.

Now they noticed. Each of the men rose from his seat on the stones and gazed across at Eddie in his blanket. Garrison's face sank into a dull white and his eyes flashed in confusion about the circle. "Who is that…it's a boy. Who is that boy?" And for several long silent seconds the men stared up at Eddie in disbelief.

And then, in an epiphany, Eddie suddenly saw the tumbling stones as the beginning of his destiny. He thought that he might have unconsciously knocked against the flimsy wall because he really wanted them to tumble down and to be revealed. He wanted those seven men to discover him there across the creek so he would be forced to explain everything. This was his destiny now: to walk across the Neshaminy creek and explain everything.

"What are you doing up there boy?" one of the men asked, as the seven men walked to the edge of the water. "Come on down from up there."

So Eddie obeyed, the way he was meant to obey, and he saw suddenly the unfolding of a vision he had had so many months back as he laid in his dark cave and anticipated their return, a vision in which he sat among them and told his story. Despite the night and the rock-strewn hill, he walked down unfettered by the obstacles. His feet carried him nimbly down the embankment, and he reached the icy water and, without hesitation, immersed his feet. Eddie didn't speak a word as he walked across the slow-moving water, as he felt the numbing cold pierce his feet and his ankles. He just kept walking, and he stepped upon the stones that he had remembered from the summer. He thought that he must have looked magical coming across the water on the hidden stones like that, as if he were walking across the surface of the water toward them. He thought, by the looks of bewilderment fixed on their faces, that he must have looked like a saint performing a miracle before their eyes, or perhaps he reminded them of Jesus Himself as he stepped towards salvation.

V

"I heard you back in the summer," Eddie said as he stood in his wet sneakers before the men and stared nervously into the flame. "I was living in the cave up there all summer and I've come back just tonight. I have a lot of things that I'd like to tell you."

The men only stood and looked around at one another, puzzled by the cold wet boy before them. Eddie turned from the flame, daring to look at each of them. He passed his eyes around the circle, gray coat to gray coat, scruffy face to scruffy face. The men had completely surrounded him now as his feet carried him slowly toward the sitting stones. The circle of men moved with him.

"Things like what?" asked one of the men. This one wore a thick moustache and a wool collar that came up around his neck. One of the other men broke from the circle and retrieved a blanket that had been spread upon one of the rocks. Eddie could see the steam rising from the blanket as the man broke back through the circle and placed it over his shoulders. Eddie felt the warmth radiate down through the wool and into this body, though the sting of the cold creek water persisted through his sneakers.

"You need to get out of those wet things," suggested the moustached man. "We'll dry them over the fire for you." They guided Eddie to the rocks and he sat down and removed his sneakers and socks. He placed them carefully along the edge of the fire. "They should dry off a little anyway," he said.

The men introduced themselves as Jonathan, Charles, Pennington, Grover, Bart, Ian (the moustached man), and finally Garrison, whose face had suddenly sunk into a pale white and seemed to harbor a silent resentment at this boy who had sat on the other side of the creek and heard his terrible story, a boy who had encroached upon his private territory.

"My name is Eddie," he said as they finished. "I'm wondering why you come here, why it is you sit around this fire." He knew that these men had not named themselves after saints, yet there was a mysterious purpose in their gathering.

"We help those who can get help nowhere else," Ian said. "We place a little ad in the personal column of the Landoff Dispatch and the Fergusonville Bulletin."

"Don't forget the Philly papers," Jonathan said. "We've been placing ads in The Daily News and the Inquirer."

"What does it say again exactly?" asked Charles, who unbuttoned the top of his shirt over the flame.

" 'Hope for the hopeless' the ad runs," Ian said. " 'We'll find who you've lost,' and then our number. Short and simple and effective. We've helped many to find their lost ones. We have our ways of finding the loved ones."

A chill ran through Eddie. He was convinced that the circle of men were sent to him by Saint Jude. A circle of saints after all: Jude had answered his prayers, and here he was delivering the answer in The Men of the Fire. They were magical agents of Saint Jude sent to find his lost brother. Just like the Neshaminy, they were drawn together in a current of destiny, disparate debris washed up upon the shore, side by side beneath the bridge to carry out Jude's plan.

"So you find kidnap victims?" he asked. "I was here the night you listened to Finbar."

"Yes Finbar," Ian said, who Eddie came to believe that he was the leader of the men. "Finbar had some problems but they're fixed now. He's back in Reading with his real father. We found his real father living in a townhouse and working in a paper mill. Finbar is happy now and he's working in the paper mill with his father."

"Well I hope that you can help me," Garrison said, bobbing his head in and out of the circle again. "Try to find Aaron Shagcropolis, do what you can for me." He held his head aloft as if a great weight had suddenly made it that much heavier, as if he could barely endure the burden of carrying on. "My neck is so tired…I don't think I can go on with my pain much longer."

"Well Garrison we'll do what we can," Ian said. "We'll look for this man and we'll tell him your story. But I must say, we all must say, that you've got to go on no matter what. Your head might not be as heavy as you might think."

"It's hopelessly heavy," he returned. "Like carrying a boulder."

"One way or another we'll help you. But you've got to make it lighter in your mind. You need to think that it is lighter."

The men turned away from Garrison and now looked fully at Eddie as he thawed his toes before the flames. Their silence beckoned his story.

"We don't usually take more than one at a time and we usually work by appointment," Ian said.

"But we usually don't have boys hidden away in caves listening in on us either," Charles said.

"It's unbelievable but you're exactly who I need to help me," Eddie said. "You may have heard my story. I'm Eddie Shemanski, brother to Benjamin Shemanski."

Eddie waited in silence for some response. He had fully expected the men to leap up in recognition, to recite his story for him, but nothing came. Instead, only the silence, save the crackling of the firewood, pervaded the circle. "Doesn't sound familiar but go on," Ian said.

"Well almost three years ago, on a cold night in January, we were all sleeping, me, my mom, my dad, my little brother Benjamin. Some men came in, broke in I should say, came in through the cellar door. Now I remember I was scared. I remember laying in the bed as my mom and dad tip-toed down the hallway wondering what the noise could be. Then I'll never forget my mother's scream, my father's shouts, the sound of a lamp breaking, the sound of strange voices coming up from below. 'Face down damnit' was what I remember one of the men saying, while my father pleaded for them to just let us all be."

"Shemanski...now I remember. The little boy taken from the crib," Ian said. "In Newportville wasn't it?"

"Yes, my little brother Benjamin," Eddie said. "They came up the stairs, two men in wool masks. One of them wore a green jersey, the other a trench coat. I didn't see them really. I had crawled under the bed and hid beneath a quilt. But I heard them go into the nursery and I heard them march down the stairs and I heard my mother and father yelling and crying as they slammed the door behind them. The men took off into the night.with my little brother."

"Why are you here in this cave on a cold night like this? You've run away haven't you?" asked Grover.

"It's very long and unbelievable but I took off last summer. I was afraid that someone was out to kidnap me, those same men who got Benjamin. I couldn't figure out why they had taken a baby, it didn't make any sense."

"Things like that never make any sense," Pennington said. "It's the nature of the crumbling world."

" I was so paranoid that I built a box in my closet and I would go hide there. And I fell asleep in that box one night and my parents thought that I had run away. Well I didn't want to come out and tell them about my box because they would have found out about my paranoia and they would have thought I needed mental help and sent me to all sorts of doctors. So I ran away, over to this cave for a while, and I got a job and rented a little apartment over in Hudson and bought this pet monitor lizard which escaped and scared the woman living upstairs to death." Eddie caught his breath as the men drew closer in disbelief. They had all gotten out their pens and had begun scribbling away.

"I'm sorry, did you say a monitor lizard?" asked Ian.

"A Nile monitor, about five feet long, something I always wanted. I loved reptiles growing up and I always wanted to collect them but my mother was afraid and wouldn't let me keep any. Brad Griggs, he had so many reptiles and I just wanted one or two because I thought reptiles were so cool. And then they plowed over all of the ponds and killed all of the turtles, and then the sewage station took care of all the ones living in the Neshaminy. So I made up for all of my frustration by buying this monster lizard…and it goes and scares a woman to death."

"So now you feel like a murderer don't you?" Ian said. "You think the police might be hunting for you."

"Yes so I can't go home. I want to go home but they'll find me." Eddie felt the tears welling inside of him but could not bring them to the surface, not with seven strange men eyeing him there in his bare feet.

"Perhaps the authorities would understand," Ian said. "Your mother and father no doubt miss you. You can't live in a cave, not with winter coming."

"Maybe soon I'll go home," Eddie said, though he did not really believe that. Rather, he saw some murky future where he might go somewhere else, some place different and far away, some new job, some new apartment, another universe free of pain.

"So how would you like us to help you Edward?" Ian asked. "You would like us to find Benjamin?"

"Yes," he replied. "I want to see Benjamin again. I want to have a little brother again."

For several moments the men sat silent with their pens, as if conjuring up solutions to Eddie's problem. They sat and stared into the flames, and Jonathan retrieved some thick logs from the edge of the creek and laid them on the fire. A stiff wind came up and blew a million brilliant sparks into a funnel that swirled up and splashed the roof of the bridge.

"Well the first thing we need to do is to get a description of the boy," Ian said.

"The last I saw him he was just a baby," Eddie said. "He had this long blonde hair, thin and long. He had eyes round and blue like marbles. He'd just be turning four, so I guess he's walking now, talking now. He probably doesn't much remember anything about his life before the kidnapping. He won't recognize me, or my mom or my dad for that matter. He's a stranger now, my brother's a stranger now."

"Do you know if the police had any leads?" asked Charles.

"No, my mom and dad always yelled at the detectives over the telephone and as they sat together at the kitchen table because they couldn't find a trace. The police didn't do much good at all. Those sons of bitches won't admit it, but I think they pretty much gave up."

"How about you? Do you have any suspects?" asked Ian.

Eddie didn't want to have to divulge the root of his paranoia, but he was certain that his truth would serve to bring Benjamin back to him. "Well I'm paranoid, and this is probably nothing, but there was this baseball game, Phillies-Padres, about five years back, before Benjamin was born. My dad took me and my older brother William. William, he took off for the Northwest Territories a little after that, came back after the kidnapping. Anyway, I was a little kid then, and I was mad when my dad didn't pay any attention to me at the game. Shit, he just ignored me the whole time. He was sitting there talking baseball to William, showing him how to fill out a scorecard and talking about losing streaks, things like that. I was mad because they were ignoring me. I was so mad that I threw my cup of soda into the air. Came down like a rocket right on this old lady's head in the level below, right on her forehead. The old lady, she fell between the seats, bleeding all over the place, and her relatives started screaming in terror." Eddie watched as the men worked to get the story down.

"So you hurt this woman pretty badly," Ian said.

"Worse, I thought I killed her. They came with a stretcher and took her away, and she wasn't moving when they disappeared down the tunnel. And one of the grandkids, he must have been a few years older than me, he looks back and sees me standing there over the rail. He had these eyes I'll never forget, eyes that were telling me 'I'll get you you son of a bitch. It might take some time to find you but I'll get you.' And he was wearing this green jersey, with the same number, the same damned number-sixteen-that one of the men wore the night that Benjamin was kidnapped."

A hush fell over the circle, and even the fire itself seemed to contain the crackling and burning noises from out of the burning wood and let the silence give way.

"But it couldn't be," Charles said. "How could a boy find you, how could he know?"

"Well like I said, I'm probably just paranoid," Eddie said. "But the green jersey, it's just such a…"

"Coincidence," Ian finished. He rubbed his chin and poked at one of the logs, stirring the flames into higher leaps. "Something we have to consider, no matter how improbable."

"But then this woman over in Hudson," Eddie continued. "Talk about coincidence, this woman, Natalie Haas who was living in the upstairs part of the house."

"The one frightened to death by the lizard?" Jonathan asked.

"Yes."

"You've got some problems killing old ladies don't you Eddie?," said Pennington, and he chuckled a little, and the others tried to contain their laughter. Eddie didn't want to react in anger at that, afraid that they might not help him then, so he went on. "Well this woman Natalie was a baseball freak, had pictures of old stadiums on her walls and everything. I look at her in the light of her living room bay window and I see this scar, or at least it looks like a scar, on her forehead the shape of a circle."

"You're not saying that you think that this was the woman at the ball game," Charles said.

"That's what I'm saying. I was going to ask her, too. I was going to ask her if she'd ever been taken out of a ball game on a stretcher, cut with a cup, had her head sewn up. But Jude never gave me a chance."

"Jude?" asked Ian, marking down the name.

"My lizard. Jude jumped out from behind the dryer just as she was putting in a load."

"Where is Jude now?"

Eddie sat and pondered that one. His lizard might well have found her way out of a window and was now busy scaring all of the old ones in Hudson back into their houses. "It's probably still down there in the basement. Lizards don't like cold weather, so she probably took refuge behind the dryer, or maybe found her way up to the top of the house."

"You've got a little more to worry about than finding your brother Benjamin," Ian said. "You need to straighten those other things out…If I were you, I would go home and explain everything. And we'll do what we do."

Eddie thought into the flames about Ian's advice. "I would like to go home with Benjamin," he said. "Going home with Benjamin would make up for things. Please…if there's a way that I can go home with my little brother."

The men, except for Garrison, excused themselves from around the fire. They moved off beyond the bridge, along the edge of the creek where the trees massed along the shore, to talk in whispers of Eddie's plea. He could hear them vaguely from out of the darkness mulling over his request, and then he felt the pull of Garrison's massive head beckoning his eyes back. He passed a glance over the fire and his eyes moved into contact.

"I sure hope they can help us," Garrison said. "I know this guy Aaron is out there somewhere with some sort of cure."

"I'm sure he's perfected a light bulb by now," Eddie consoled him. "I'm sure he can find a way to make the rest of you grow."

"These men are very good, you know. They helped a buddy of mine find his father. His father walked away from a beach party with amnesia. No one could find the man for ten years and these men came in and found him in ten days. My buddy thinks that they're psychic or something. They harness some special powers to find the lost ones, they have some secret ways about things."

"Maybe they're agents of God," Eddie speculated.

"Well let's not go overboard and bring religion into this," Garrison said.

The men returned from the darkness, bringing the chill of the black creek with them on their clothes. Ian put his arm around Eddie and passed his eyes through the other men. "We're going to try to get you your brother back," he said. "But you need to stay somewhere else besides that cave. We need to find you somewhere to stay."

"He can stay with me," Garrison said. "I've got an empty attic and a fold-down cot over in Landoff."

"That would be better than the cave," Eddie said.

"Then it's settled," Ian said. "Garrison, we'll begin a search for Aaron Shagcropolis, and Eddie, we'll search for your little brother Benjamin." The men got up from the fire. "One more thing," Ian said. "When we deliver, the only thing that we ask is that you don't ask. Don't ask how we accomplished our mission, don't ask us where we come from or where we go. Just walk away happy is all that you need to do. We'll get you what you ask for."

Charles dowsed the remaining flames with a bucket of creek water and Eddie put on his socks and sneakers and followed Garrison up the dark, boulder-strewn hillside to the top of the bridge. Then he remembered his knapsack.

"I need to get my things from the cave," Eddie said. He walked across the top of the bridge while Garrison waited beside a parked car. He stumbled down the hill and reached into the dank cave for his things, pulling first the blanket, and then his backpack from the dark hole. He hurriedly stuffed the blanket back into the top of the pack. Just then his souvenir baseball from Mrs. Haas popped out of the side pocket and went rolling down the hill. In a desperate lunge, Eddie tried to reach the baseball before it dropped into the darkness and continued its fall into the creek. He slipped on the steep hill and went falling himself, taking rocks and loose dirt with him as he slid toward the creek. And then, as if by design, the baseball was in his hand. It had somehow stopped its fall and his hand had snatched it out of the dark. He drew his feet together and splashed into the cold creek. Holding the baseball aloft, he moved safely away from the current and made his way back up the hill toward Garrison and his parked car.

Stained Light

◆

I

Garrison's car smelled like mildew, like something extracted from a cesspool. "It's the trunk, it takes in rain water," he said. He drove out across the interstate towards Landoff. "Two years back a deer came crashing through the back window. Out of the blue, out of the woods it came one night. Scared the bejesus out of me. I wound up in a ditch with a broken arm and the deer wound up decapitated. Found its head on the back seat floor, almost a perfect cut across the neck. Could have had it stuffed if I wanted, mounted over my pool table or something. Anyway, the back window I replaced was never installed right. Still leaks along the molding and the water runs down into the trunk. When I stop hard at traffic lights, you can hear the sloshing of water trapped between the seat and the trunk. Hell, there might be fish in there by now. The car's a good one hundred pounds heavier lugging around that trapped rain water."

Eddie could feel the blast of the heater coming out of the dash and it warmed his wet toes. His feet began to itch, so much so that he wanted to take off his sneakers and his socks right there in the car and scratch away. He remembered Domingus and his cast back by the dish machine at Bingo's, his bleeding arm and the nail marks. "I wonder how they do it," he said.

"How they…do it?" Garrison said.

"The men under the bridge, how they find the lost ones?" Eddie asked.

Garrison drove in silence for a time, flashing his eyes into the patches of trees that rolled past, searching perhaps for a sudden animal that might dart into the road. His massive head filled the driver's side and it bobbed to the side as the car made a sharp turn up the exit ramp. "I asked Ian that on the telephone the first time I called." he said. "He told me they almost guaranteed success, but told me they could never divulge their secret. Like I said, I've been told they've got some special powers, and they all pull those powers together to find the spirits of the missing."

"They're a strange bunch, that's for sure," Eddie said. "I wonder if they have day jobs."

"No doubt, and they most likely have families and mortgages and such. They don't charge a penny, though. Damned if they don't charge a penny."

"So they're moonlighting as good Samaritans?" Eddie asked.

"Good what?"

"You know from the Bible, the story of the Good Samaritan, the man who does good deeds and doesn't want anything in return."

"There you go with your religion again," Garrison said. "I haven't got time for religion."

"You're an atheist?" Eddie asked.

"It's not that exactly," Garrison said. "There might very well be a God, but I'll worry about that when the time comes. The way I figure it is, I'm in charge of my own destiny. I'm in charge of getting things together and I shouldn't have to rely on silly prayers and looking to the sky for some magical interlude." Then he paused and smiled. " Come to think of it, these men are sort of a magical interlude."

Nodding in agreement, Eddie turned away and sat quiet as the dark trees rolled by. The car made its way up the exit ramp and into the lighted streets of Landoff. The subdivision came out of the dark woods like a cancer, with its cheaply-built bi-levels strung like fence posts along the painted curbs. A man came out of one of the houses and followed his elongated shadow across the grass to leave two heaping trash bags at the side of the road. He dropped the bags and eyed the car as it rolled past him. Garrison gave him a slight wave and an embarrassed smile in the dimmed street light and moved his head to the center of the car as if to hide Eddie from the man's view.

Eddie was going to ask Garrison if taking a seventeen-year-old boy home might look a little suspicious to his neighbors, then realized that it did in fact look very suspicious. After all, what would a forty-five-year old man with a giant head be doing with a strange young boy? Garrison must be lonely and desperate, a man in need of friendship or perhaps more. Eddie knew nothing about this man except for his tormented childhood nights beneath the grow lights and his desperate quest to rid his aching neck of that massive skull. He grew edgy in his seat at the prospect of this man's strangeness and tried to hold off the wall of onrushing paranoia. Where a month ago he might have, in a spasm of fear, opened that car door and fallen to the road, he now relaxed and watched the dark road unwind. Perhaps, he thought, his paranoia had waned because the death of the old woman had forged little consequence of anything else. Perhaps nothing else mattered now that the poison was gone.

"Do you live alone?" Eddie asked.

"Now I do," he said "Wife and kids left me and….well, I really don't want to talk about that…". He pulled into a pothole-ridden driveway and stopped the car. Eddie could see the dark bi-level house moored against a backdrop of towering hedges. The massive bushes rose twenty feet out of the grass and surrounded the house from all sides, walling it in like a prison. Garrison fumbled for his keys in the darkened car, finally switching on the interior light to find his house key, as Eddie worked to establish the image of some woman who had fallen in love with this large-headed man and bore him children.

"Wow you've got some giant hedges here," Eddie said nervously. "They must have taken years to get that high."

"Bought the house fifteen years back and planted the things when they were no more than three feet high." Garrison got out of the car and Eddie followed him up the dark walkway. "Little by little they grew up the sides of the house. Little by little they began cutting off the light from the windows. The windows, they're hidden now. We trimmed the hedges for the last time 'bout four years back. But they just kept growing faster, getting thicker. To tell you the truth, I kind of like the look of them. Makes me feel secure here."

"So you're telling me you get no sunlight at all in this house?"

"Almost none at all."

"Incredible," Eddie said. "Incredible. Every place I've gone, no sunlight. It's really unbelievable, if you think about the improbability of it. No sunlight anywhere at all, every single place since I took off."

"Yes, you were saying at the fire," Garrison said, and he opened the door and turned on the foyer light. The foyer opened up into a larger tiled room, shiny and polished and empty except for a chair and a small television set and several piles of books strewn like islands across the floor. Eddie again wondered about the man's past, how he had come to have nothing in such a large room as this, a room that he conjectured had, at some time back, more furniture than this and peopled by family as well.

"Well as a matter of fact, the room you'll be staying in has the only sunlight in this house," he said, as his voice echoed across the piled books. "You've got some of that light coming in over the hedges." In the wake of the echo of his footsteps, he led Eddie up the darkened stairs and switched on the hall light. He walked up another set of stairs and opened the door. "I'll have to open your cot. It's been folded against the wall." He turned on a floor lamp, filling the room with shadows.

Cardboard boxes consumed the attic room and were stacked in piles against the walls. Nails stuck out of some of the sheets of cheap ply-wood hammered into the beams and the dust swirled in a circle beneath the lamp. Garrison rolled the cot into the center of the room and unhitched it. It sprang open like a flower, and the metal legs shot to the floor with a resounding thud. Another storm of dust rose from the floor. "The mattress, it's a little yellow and seedy, but you won't contract anything from it. I'll get you a sheet," Garrison said, and then he pointed to the opposite wall. "See the colorful window?"

A round stained glass window, holding the black of night against it, reflected the lonely lamp bulb as it glared along the ridges like ripples in a pond. The night pushed in on the window with its wind and its cold biting air and Eddie walked the distance of the room to inspect the hidden colors. Reds, blues, yellows and greens all wove themselves between the strips of grooved lead that ran like highways across a road map. Eddie could see the doves wings, the fruit bowls, the flowers, a seven-branched candelabrum and an urn of oil all obscured by the night. The elaborate design reminded him of the church windows in the way they sported the heads of assorted saints and miraculous feats, of ascensions and divine acts of God. Yet there were no saints or ascending figures on this glass. Eddie tried to understand the meaning of the images merging in the circle.

"It's a beautiful thing," Eddie said. "Must look so much better in daylight."

"Yes it's impressive," Garrison said. "Too bad it's stuck up here in the attic. Too bad it's the only light I've got, this pretty light here in the attic. Too bad I don't understand what the shapes are all about."

"Well I can tell you I'll enjoy it while I'm here," Eddie said.

Garrison went down the steps and brought back some sheets and a thick blanket, then rolled the cot up against the wall. He gathered some of the empty boxes and moved them to the other side of the room. "It's late. I'll be up tomorrow after work to get rid of some of these boxes for you. I'll be leaving early in the morning. I'm in construction, so I got to get to the sight by 7 a.m. to get the houses going. So make yourself some cereal or something out of the kitchen when you get up. I'll talk to you when I get home."

"Thanks for letting me stay," Eddie said. "I might have frozen to death in that cave."

"Well this attic can get drafty sometimes too, so I'd use these heavy blankets. There's no way you could stay up here in the summer. It bakes up here in the summer."

"Don't intend to stay that long," Eddie said.

Garrison smiled and walked down the steps. He flicked off the hall light, still engulfed by the shadow of his massive head. Eddie could hear the echoes of his breathing and an occasional cough coming from the bottom of the house, as it finally trailed away to one of the empty bedrooms.

What happened in this house to give it the echoes it now held? Eddie wondered about Garrison's family, his wife, his kids, a possible dog or cat roaming the hallway. Some great mysterious incident must have come down here, some explosion of anger that had built up through carrying that monster head day in and day out. It must have come down in an uncontrolled outbreak of violence, shouting and smashing things, shoving and punching wife and children, crying and running to telephones and cars. Now they were gone. The furniture was removed and they all moved somewhere else, to somewhere not so plagued. Now, Garrison was left with only a vacant house encroached by monster hedges, left only to ponder his father's legacy reflected in the medicine cabinet mirror and in the echo of his own footsteps.

II

Eddie awoke and heard the scream from below, certain for several suspended seconds that he was in that basement apartment again and that he was listening to the old woman dying on the other side of the cinderblock wall. He moved off the bed and halfway across the wood floor before he realized, before the stacked boxes materialized in the dimmed stained glass light and placed him squarely into the consciousness of Garrison's attic. But there was that sound from below, that same lingering scream, and he thought perhaps that he had heard it in a dream, the distant crying of children down bricked alleys or the wailed muffle of a fallen woman one more time or his own bottled desperation crying out for reprieve. He went to the top of the stairs anyway and looked down into the blackness, listened for a sound that might echo up.

"Garrison?" he called out. "Garrison?"

"Yes. Yes, Eddie. Sorry to startle you. I…must have had a nightmare," came a voice out of the darkness, from out of the back room. "I'll close my door then."

Eddie moved across the room, which had suddenly gotten very cold from a draft coming through the roof beams. He crawled back beneath the covers, then laid there and tried to close his eyes and drift back to sleep. Intermittently, he flicked open his eyes and watched the light coming back to the sky through the stained glass. The thought of Garrison, alone in the dark below him entering another dream, weighed heavily on him and prevented his return to sleep. He must have had nightmares about the grow lights, he must have awakened screaming in the dark room because he thought his head had swelled more and more under a whole new set of lights fastened above him by his father's ghost. He must have been strapped down in his dream, as the lights penetrated his skull, as they worked to expand his head and stretch the skin on his face so that it filled the bed and overflowed over the pillows and the headboard until he could no longer lift it. He must have screamed because he could no longer lift his head in the dream. He could only lay and stare up at the ceiling at the glare of the lights that offered him no relief, with no cool darkness to ease him into slumber.

No wonder he let the hedges grow. Garrison was his opposite really, because he didn't want any light at all. He'd had enough of those nights, enough forced light, so he just sat back and let the hedges consume his windows, let the sun vanish from all of his rooms. He sought solace in the shade of himself, the prison of his being. The highlight of his day was to close that door, bolt it tight, and sink into a sunless existence.

The quiet persisted from below without even the echoes of heavy breathing. Garrison had closed his door, so Eddie couldn't hear his body wrestling with the sheets or hear the sound of his long sleep-induced sighs or another nightmare that might flare up and rouse him into a sitting shout.

Eddie laid awake and watched the window fully. The day seeped through in reds and blues, and he could see the shapes bursting through as the window brightened. Like a photograph developing in a dark bath, he saw the fruits materialize in the bowls, bunches of thick blue grapes, brilliant naval oranges and solid red apples. The roses and morning glories unfurled out of their vines, and the candelabrum, wick by wick, flickered on. Then the doves rose out of the glass as the sun inched above the trees. Their perfectly balanced wings tipped into a redeeming white glow. He felt as if an apparition was at hand, as if one of his memorized saints had ridden in on a beam of light and entered the room. For now the sun, hot and glowing just outside the house, forced its thick beams of red and yellow and blue upon the wood floor, and Eddie walked across the room to bask in them. Imbued by this long-sought light, finally the light, he sat squarely into the middle of it. Right there on the wood floor in his underwear, Eddie felt the warmth enter the room and penetrate his chilled body. But it was more than a warmth, for the light carried with it an epiphany, a glow that transcended that pattern on the floor, and a deep satisfaction settled over him in his solitude. Just outside of his reach he could almost feel the hand of Saint Jude reaching with invisible fingers through the glass and clasping him, and he could almost hear the voice whispering in his ears, "Benjamin will be coming soon."

III

Eddie heard Garrison as he opened his bedroom door below him and as he made his way in a string of yawns to the bathroom. He didn't want him to know that he was awake, so he sat in the light of the window and breathed quietly, staring up at the doves with their winged glow. He was thinking of Benjamin and how long it might take the men of the fire to find him and bring him back. He was waiting for Garrison to leave him alone in the house.

The telephone rang and Eddie heard Garrison turn off the faucet in the bathroom, walk quickly to the back room, and answer in a low mumble. He couldn't hear because Garrison had closed the door behind him. He talked for nearly twenty minutes with that mumble, and Eddie guessed that the woman who had left him might very well be on the other end, or perhaps one of his children calling to hear his voice one more time. Finally, Eddie heard the door open as Garrison's footsteps approached the bottom of the stairs.

"Are you awake up there?" came Garrison's voice. "I need to tell you something."

Eddie moved across the room and slipped on his pants and shirt, then made his way to the top of the stairs. "Yes, I'm awake," he said.

"Ian told me to tell you to not leave the house," he said. "There's no reason for you to leave the house is there?"

"Well, no. I was going to try to look for a job, another job maybe...."

"Well Ian says you should cool it for a few days. He said that they found the woman. He saw it in the morning paper. They found her dead in the basement. They found the lizard, too, and they're looking for the mysterious tenant who disappeared. They've described you, Eddie. Some of the neighbors gave a pretty good description of you."

"Do they know it's me, Eddie Shemanski?" he asked.

"Well Ian didn't say that, so I guess not, at least not yet," he said. "There's no doubt they're out looking, though. They'll figure it out sooner or later. If you stay in the house you'll be all right."

"Well what about the guy taking out the trash last night?" Eddie asked. "He saw you bringing me home. Don't you think that looked a little suspicious?"

"Oh, you mean Willie Fulwiler," Garrison said. "No, I built an add-on kitchen for Willie. He wouldn't say anything even if he figured it all out. I did Willie many major favors, so don't worry about Willie." Garrison moved away from the bottom of the steps and toward the bathroom to finish washing. "I'd better get me a move on," he said. "Go back to bed and get some sleep. And help yourself in the kitchen when you come down."

Eddie walked away from the doorway and moved back into the patch of light, listening as the water ran down the drain and as the toothbrush swirled away in Garrison's mouth. Now he was trapped here, now they were looking for him. All of the eyes of Landoff would be shifting from their morning papers to part the curtains of their windows to see what they could see. The world would be upon him, peering and peering: there was no escape from the inevitable capture the moment he walked out the door.

He moved across the room and tried to look out through the window to see the world beyond the distorted glass. He put his face up against the colors and looked down from his lofty perch at the top of the house but the shapes of the trees and cars only merged into fluid black masses. There was no way to tell whether he was being watched or whether the police cars were advancing into Landoff to surround the monster hedges or whether the neighbors were advancing with shovels and rakes and brooms with the hopes of turning him in for a considerable reward.

The door slammed and locked below him as Garrison made his way out of the house, to his car, and off to his construction. Suddenly alone, suddenly locked within a stranger's house like some kidnap victim, suddenly a prisoner: now the house, with its walls of hedges, closed in on him and suffocated him in a blanket of fear. He felt the presence of the bushes all around him, living entities which seemed to rise all at once as the sound of the car engine died away. Now the hedges could think, as they conspired to close in on the windows and strangle the house.

Eddie walked down the stairs, free to roam where he pleased. He moved to the windows to check for light. Garrison was right: a wall of thick evergreen branches pressed against the glass and entirely blocked out the sunlight. Eddie noticed that some of the branches had come through the molding along the windows and encroached upon the sill. Garrison had apparently twisted off most of the growth, for he could see the fresh green breaks where the branches had been torn away.

He moved around the empty room and surveyed the little remaining furniture. The old red chair had begun to lose its stuffing and the television set had a crack running up the side of the plastic walnut casing. Assorted piles of books were stacked around the room. Garrison had fashioned one stack, right next to the chair, into a table, which held a small crystal lamp. He bent over, flicked on the little lamp, and read the titles, most of which were incomprehensible terms dealing with land surveying,electrical maintenance, and zoning law. He picked up the drinking glass on the top of the stack (still containing a bit of milk), and read the title beneath it. "Dealing with Deformity" by Noel S. Schmidt., Phd. Eddie took the glass and placed it on the floor, sat down into the red chair, and flipped through the book. He was hoping for some photographs or illustrations, perhaps of other men with large heads in other spots of the world, or women with extra breasts or children covered in hair, but there were only words. Eddie tried to decipher, with his limited vocabulary, some of the sentences that spilled across the page, but terms like "onanism", "polymorphous perverse," "infantile etiology of the neuroses," "Dementia praecox," and "sublimation and reaction formation" roadblocked his comprehension, and he finally closed the book and placed it back beneath the lamp, carefully replacing Garrison's milk glass back within its white circle.

Eddie sat in the red chair and perused the empty room, including the other stacks of books. He wondered if Garrison knew what those words meant in "Dealing With Deformity," or whether he had bought the book because he was enamored by its title, bought it without opening it, certain that it held, somewhere in its five hundred pages, his solution. Perhaps the frustration of reading that very book, the roadblocks of those impossible terms, had impelled him to go on his rampage, his angry thrashing out at the world, at his wife and kids. That very book may very well have emptied his house.

This house was not at all like Natalie Haas' house and its emptiness overcame him as he became aware of his isolated breathing. He heard the refrigerator click on. The sound of the compressor rattled though the house and beckoned him out of the red chair and to the kitchen, where the warmth of the oven radiated across the tiles. He clicked on the light, opened the refrigerator and found some milk. He rooted through the cabinets until he found a fresh box of Wheaties. He searched and found everything—the silverware, the bowls, the drinking glasses—almost immediately. Eddie figured that all of that snooping in Mrs. Haas' house had somehow paid off, for he was now proficient at rooting through a stranger's things. It was a skill that came in handy, he convinced himself.

Sitting at the little table and finishing his Wheaties, Eddie dumped an extra helping of sugar into the sea of milk and stared at the photograph of Garrison and a marlin mounted on the wall. The sun was in Garrison's eyes and his skin was reddened from the sun, and he could see the veins along his arm as he held the heavy fish over the dock. Eddie got up from the table and inspected the photograph closer. He could see some people in the background, some children further down the dock, and the fragment of a woman's dress blowing into the corner of the photograph. His wife and kids, he deduced, and he went back to his cereal.

After another bowl, Eddie suddenly grew tired, as if the milk had tranquilized him. He hadn't slept much over the last three days, and he realized a good long nap was in order. So he washed the bowl and placed it back into the cabinet and put away the cereal and walked upstairs to the attic. The room had brightened considerably, as the colors on the floor had expanded to the base of the bed, a brilliant circle that looked like Jupiter. It was warmer, too, and Eddie wondered how warm it had gotten outside. It frightened him that he was locked in this house and that he could not find out about the air outside or see the world through his muddled glass. But he was too tired to care, too tired to try to find a possible escape route. He laid down on the bed, looked at the bright doves and the fruit bowls and the candelabra again, and fell into a deep sleep.

IV

It was the sound of a shotgun that woke him. Eddie turned and looked at the window, which had again fallen into darkness. He must have slept through the day, and then he remembered the sound and jumped up from the bed. He was certain that a gun had gone off, though he was not quite sure that it came from below. Rather, it seemed to have come from somewhere just outside, just below the window, possibly from across the yard. Footsteps echoed below him as the front door slammed shut.

"Garrison is that you?" Eddie called down nervously.

"Yes," came the familiar voice. "I looked in on you earlier but you were dead asleep. Been home for a couple of hours."

"What was that sound I just heard?" Eddie asked. "It sounded like…"

"A shotgun. It was a shotgun. Come on down and I'll show you what I've got."

Eddie walked down the dark stairs, apprehensive of what might suddenly be revealed at the bottom. Would Garrison be standing there bloody, holding the shotgun aloft? Who would be there on the floor? His wife? One of his kids? Some intruder who had broken through the hedges? Eddie stopped in the middle of the stairs, fearful of the strange man with the giant head. Perhaps he was ready for another rampage. Perhaps he had tried to read more passages from "Dealing with Deformity." Now, out of his frustration, he was packing a loaded gun.

"Did you…shoot something?" Eddie called out from his dark post on the stairs.

"That I did," Garrison said. "Come see."

Eddie advanced with pale skin to the bottom of the stairs, where Garrison, still in his heavy gray coat and wool hat, held aloft a dead Mallard duck. He held it by its neck, and some of its feathers had dropped to the floor about his feet. Eddie saw the shotgun hole just inside of the duck's left wing. Its eyes had already glazed over with its beak frozen open, caught dead in mid-breath.

"Nailed it in one of the hedges," Garrison said. "Damned things get into the hedges all the time. Hell, they must nest in there. Don't know why they don't migrate south in this cold weather."

"What harm was it doing?" Eddie asked. "It probably had nowhere else to go."

"Scared the bejesus out of me, that's what harm it did," Garrison said. "Damned things have been scaring me for too long. This one won't be doing any more scaring, though." Garrison walked across the empty room and took the dead Mallard into the kitchen. "Wish I knew something about cooking these things," Garrison said. "I could make us up a real nice meal."

"Well I wouldn't know either," Eddie said. "It's just such a shame you killed it."

"Hey ducks don't belong in hedges," Garrison shouted from the kitchen, and his echo vibrated the floor. "They should all be swimming."

"You know, I used to go to the donut pond, this pond over in Fergusonville, some years ago," Eddie said. "There were hundreds of ducks over there, happy ducks. They had a place to swim and nest and eat."

"Yeah, I remember them sitting on the dirt hills when we were plowing that pond over," Garrison said. "Creepy, like they were watching us, like they were plotting something against us, just like in that Hitchcock movie."

"You?" Eddie asked. "You were one of those men who plowed over the donut pond?"

"We were contracted for the Deer Run development," Garrison said. "Investors from Philly bought the land off the farmer who owned it, Miller I believe was his name…he sold it outright. We plowed over a good two hundred acres. A pond, some woods, some corn fields. You got hundreds of people living over there today, hundreds of happy people. I'd say that was a pretty good trade-off."

"But you killed all of the reptiles," Eddie said sadly.

"Reptiles?" Garrison said. "Look, I know you like reptiles and all that, what with your giant lizard story. But…"

"Not just me," Eddie shot back. "My friend Brad Griggs, reptiles were his life. He lived and breathed reptiles, wanted to be a herpetologist.

When you plowed over that pond, well he went nuts. He didn't have anything else to do with his days and he started getting into trouble. Got arrested a couple of times, spent a few years in a correctional institute." Eddie sighed and looked angrily across the room. "I can't believe you plowed over the donut pond."

Eddie looked at Garrison as he stood in his tapered shadow, as he plopped the dead Mallard on the counter and considered it. He suddenly looked uglier in that harsh light, his head more massive and tilted like some mutated gourd.

"Well I should decide what to do with it before it stinks up the house. Should I try and de-feather it…. pop it in the oven, see what happens?" he asked.

"Why don't you just bury it?" Eddie asked.

"Grounds frozen," Garrison said. "Trash night isn't until Tuesday. She'll be ripe by then. Guess we should try and cook her." He walked down into the living room and got down on his knees before one of the stacks of books, then crawled over to another stack. "Ah ha, here we go," he said, and pulled a thick book from the middle of the stack. "New York Times Cookbook."

"Are you sure it's O.K. to eat Mallards?" Eddie asked.

"You mean is it legal? You mean can the duck police come and haul me off?"

"No I mean are certain ducks like Mallards poisonous?"

"Ducks aren't mushrooms," Garrison replied as he chuckled his way through the index. "Meat is meat if you cook it all the way through."

"Well I cooked in a restaurant so I know that some meat can be bad, can have diseases and such."

"What sort of disease do you think that a game bird in a suburb might have? This is as clean a place as any."

"I don't think that has anything to do with it."

"Duck, here we go duck, 273," Garrison said, and he flipped through the book to a list of recipes. He perused the list as his massive head cast a shadow over the words. "Hmmm, nothing about de-feathering here," he said. "You'd think they'd put something in about de-feathering."

"Maybe they're assuming you're not going to go out and shoot your duck in a hedge," Eddie said.

"What's your problem?" Garrison shot back in anger as he slammed the cook book upon the kitchen table. "I let you stay here in my damned attic and you're getting on my case about a lousy duck."

"I'm sorry," Eddie stammered. "I was just trying to make a point. It's a little unusual is all, your shooting the duck like that."

"What's unusual is that the duck is there to begin with. Ducks don't belong in hedges, they don't belong where people belong. Get them all out of the suburbs is what I say. And shooting them is one good way."

"Yes. you're right. They don't belong in hedges, they belong in ponds," Eddie said. "Ponds."

"And if you're going to get on my case about plowing over your sacred donut pond…"

"Look I'm sorry," Eddie said. "I know you were just doing your job. It's just that, well, that I can't ever forget Brad Griggs screaming that day when he saw the turtles being buried by the bulldozers. I still can't forget that, o.k.?"

Eddie and Garrison stood silent in the kitchen and both of them stared at the duck with its wings out and spread upon the counter, its mouth still agape. Garrison rubbed his monster skull.

"I guess you just cut them off," Eddie said.

"Cut…?"

"The feathers, when you remove them. I never cooked anything with feathers, but I had to scale some fish back at Bingo's. Had to slice the skin off trout and tuna and bluefish. I guess it works the same way."

Garrison picked up the book from the kitchen table and flipped back to 273. "Well I guess we can try. I got some sharp French knives. And one of these recipes sounds pretty good if we get through that. 'Duck L'Orange' it says. I got some fresh oranges in one of the produce drawers, I got some brandy in one of my boxes somewhere. Butter, got it, parsley, sage, coriander, got all of them." Garrison propped the book open with a salt shaker and retrieved two long French knives from the drawer. "Let's make us some duck, Eddie," he said.

Eddie walked into the kitchen and took the French knife offered to him. He took it and began to work on the feathers as he sliced them off in clumps, wondering about the dead duck's mate. It was somewhere—in one of the hedges, perhaps—awaiting its return. He dug beneath the skin and strained his ears for the sound of a distant quack.

V

Garrison overcooked the duck, and except for the oranges, it was bland and bristly and went hard down the throat. Eddie tried to force down a few swallows and finished the boiled potatoes and string beans that Garrison had prepared, saved finally by Garrison's dropping of his fork and then his contention that the bird could not be eaten. "This duck sucks," he said. "I really thought we had something there after we got the feathers off and had that recipe going, Eddie."

Eddie pushed his plate away and agreed. "At least now it won't rot and smell your place up." He got up and helped Garrison empty the hardened Mallard into the garbage.

"Let's finish the brandy in any case," Garrison said. "We'll get us a load on."

Eddie sat beneath the flickering fluorescent light as Garrison retrieved two heavy glasses from a cabinet, watching as he filled the both of them with brandy and then as he sat back down with a heavy sigh into his chair, a sigh that told him another long day of holding his head aloft was drawing to a close.

"Had to fire one of my workers today," Garrison said as he swilled the glass. "Johnny can't run a dozer after he's smoked a joint."

"You mean he was getting high on the job?" Eddie asked.

"Warned the son of a bitch when I caught him in the trailer. He was passing it out to my other men. Our work lags when they smoke that shit. I don't mind them toking away after a shift, but when my projects run behind, well that screws me."

"Don't blame you there," Eddie said. "Gotta get them houses up." He raised the glass to his lips, quite sure, despite his never having drunk brandy, that the taste would impel him to cough it up across the table. But he kept it in, and then he wiped his mouth as the burning liquid shot down his throat.

"More sarcasm?" Garrison asked as he refilled his glass. "Just like the duck…"

"No I'm serious," Eddie said.

"You've smoked a little weed, haven't you?"

"Never on a job," Eddie lied. "And my jobs don't include driving five thousand pound equipment."

"Try ten thousand," Garrison said.

"That'll crush a turtle in nothing flat," Eddie said before he swigged again.

"Really didn't see any turtles that day you know," Garrison said. "We just plowed over the cattails and pushed the dirt down into the water. Didn't see nothing but birds, those red-winged blackbirds and those creepy ducks on the hill."

"There were turtles there, believe me," Eddie said. "Hundreds of them on logs. Painters, sliders, spotted, musk, wood……"

A knock came at the door and startled them. They looked at each other and then across the room, waiting again for the sound. The knock came louder and Garrison shot up out of the chair.

"Expecting someone?" Eddie asked. "Girl Scout cookies for dessert?"

Garrison walked down the stairs and opened the door. "Well, Ian," he said. "An unexpected surprise."

"Eddie is still here?" Ian asked.

"Yes we just finished an attempt at duck," Garrison said. "You have some news already?"

"I do," he said. Ian walked up the stairs behind Garrison and Eddie watched in anticipation as they arrived at the table. Ian removed his long gray trench coat and slapped it over the chair.

"News for the both of us?" Eddie asked.

"Yes....we've done some overtime on the both of you," Ian said. "Found some startling things."

"Like what?" Garrison asked. "All good news I hope."

"Well, the good news for you Garrison is that we found your Aaron Shagcropolis. Unfortunately, he's buried in a grave in northern Minnesota."

"How in the hell is that good news?" Garrison asked. "My only hope dead and buried…"

"Ah, but Aaron is not your only hope. His son Louis has taken over the grow light research. Charles and I flew out to Seven Woods this morning."

"Seven Woods?"

"Minnesota wilderness. He's got a research facility that rises out of the water and it's got everything. State of the art equipment hidden in the woods there."

"Has he got a solution for me?"

"Louis wants you to go out there. He says you need to get to the plant because he's got these enormous lights that can't be transported. He's going to put you under those lights and try to fix you, Garrison. He says that he's improved on his father's invention but can't market the result because of the size and because of radiation restrictions."

"Radiation? I'm going to be nuked?"

"Nothing alarming. He uses microwaves and x-rays in his filaments is all. He sounded confident, Garrison, looked like a real scientist. Why don't you get on a plane and get out to Minnesota?"

Garrison sat silent in his chair and ran his hands the length of his skull. Then he wept and excused himself from the room. Eddie and Ian sat and listened to the wails echoing from the bottom of the house, from out between the stacks of books.

"Why is he taking the news so hard?" Eddie asked. "I would be happy if I were him. That is good news, isn't it?"

"Well I think he is happy, Eddie. I think he's thinking about his life that's about to change, that's all. You see, when he goes out to Minnesota, everything will change for him."

Eddie finished his last bit of brandy. "What about Benjamin, Ian?" he asked.

Ian sighed and picked up Garrison's glass of brandy and swigged the remainder, offering a smile across the table. "We've found him," he said.

Eddie sat stunned, partially by the sudden dizziness that had rushed through his blood by the alcohol, but mostly because the words had come across the table and hit him like a freight train. They were the words he had been waiting to hear for so long, and now the moment was upon him, and he let those words, 'we've found him,' swirl about his brain and ferment. Saint Jude's deliverance was at hand.

"You found Benjamin…already?" he stammered.

"We did what the police couldn't do in three years," Ian gloated. "To tell you the truth, I'm quite proud of this one. The Men of the Fire, they really came through." Ian sighed and his smile vanished as he rolled the empty glass around in his hands.

"So when can you get him? Is he all right? How did you find him? How did you know it was him?" Eddie asked in a rapid fire.

"Remember what we asked you by the fire. We asked that you don't ask," Ian said as he put down the glass. "However, I must let you know that we've got a bit of a problem with this one."

"Problem?" Eddie asked. "Everything's all right with him, isn't it? You didn't find him buried like you did Aaron…."

"Benjamin is fine. He's a cute kid. It's just that his family, not his real family—not your family—but the family he knows, well they made sure to cover their tracks. They got birth certificates, school records, a social security number for him even. There's no way to prove that he's not theirs."

"Well maybe he is. Maybe you've got the wrong kid."

"We know what we're doing Eddie. Believe me, this is your little brother."

Eddie felt helpless in not being able to ask all of the questions that were rising to his lips. He wanted to know who this mysterious family might be, where they lived, how Ian had managed, in the expanse of two days, to figure it all out. So many questions. But the mysterious men of the fire had their rule, and he would have to abide by it to get Benjamin back, to bring him home, to be hailed as a hero and erase the long nightmare that had led its trail from the closet box to the Stigmeyer's tool shed to the bridge cave to the basement apartment in Hudson, erase the image of the fallen woman at the ball game, the fallen woman on the laundry, the escaped lizard and finally the man wailing away in the next room, his massive head buried in his red chair.

"So what will we do?" Eddie asked. "How will we…"

Ian reached across the table, clasped Eddie's hands, and whispered, "We're going to have to kidnap him right back."

Eddie roamed his eyes about the room, settling finally on the photograph of Garrison and his marlin. "Kidnapping is illegal, though. How will you..."

"That's the problem, it is illegal. Now you can go to the police if you like, give them your story, bearing in mind that you keep us out of this. You can go home if you like, tell your mother, your father about this family out there somewhere that has Benjamin safely sealed away as their son. Any way you look at it, though, you're talking about people believing you. And even if they do believe you, the police, your mom and dad, well then you'll have investigations...and if they do manage to track him down, lawyers and loads of money paid out and years and years of waiting..."

"So you're telling me that kidnapping is the best solution here?" Eddie asked as he eyed the corner of the woman's dress in the photograph. "You're going to have to sneak in and snatch him?"

"I don't see any better way," Ian said. "The kidnapping itself isn't the problem, we can do that for you. We can deliver Benjamin to you. Charles is an expert in those matters."

"The problem is that I'll be arrested as soon as I get caught with him," Eddie said.

"Exactly," Ian replied. "And the police are already looking for you because your lizard killed that woman in Hudson."

"Is that what the paper said...that I killed her?"

"Well, they figured it all out after one of her grandsons found her down there, and then the lizard popped out from behind the dryer."

"Grandsons? Did you say grandsons? This is too creepy....I really didn't mean for that lizard to do that you know."

"Yes well I'm sure the police know that. But they're still looking for you, at least according to the report. You're not supposed to have a lizard of that size was what it said."

"It's illegal to have a monitor lizard?"

"Of that size I guess…they said five feet is illegal."

"Just like kidnapping," Eddie sighed. "I got myself in a hole, didn't I, Ian?"

"Yes, but holes can be covered over."

"Meaning what?"

"Meaning we can cover you over and get you a new life."

Eddie suddenly felt a chill overcome him, as if the room had dipped several degrees or as if a draft had suddenly blown through. He thought of the grandson advancing down the basement stairs and of his terrible scream at the discovery. He wondered if it might be the same grandson who had looked back at him at that ball game, the one with those furry eyebrows. Perhaps he was even wearing that same green jersey.

"A new life?" Eddie asked. " I don't know if I like the sound of that."

"Again, we're talking about viable solutions here, Eddie. You want Benjamin, do you not?"

Yes, but what about his feelings? What's he going to think when you get Charles taking him away?"

Ian stopped for a second and searched the room, possibly for another bottle of brandy, resting his eyes on the cluttered counter and then shifting to the doorway as Garrison came back into the room and sat down on a chair. The tears had stained his face and his lips quivered as he raised his index finger toward Ian.

"I want to thank you Ian." he said. "I want to go to Minnesota tomorrow. I'm going to call the company and tell them I'll be taking an emergency vacation and I'll fly out there. Any idea how long this will take?"

"Well Louis didn't say exactly. Don't think it'll happen overnight, though, Garrison. You might be out there for a while. The fact is, you might be under the lights for a while."

"Well the important thing is I'm going. I might have to quit my job, start things over. But hell, I'm going. As long as it takes, well, as long as it takes. My head is the important thing."

Ian took some paper and a pen out of his jacket and drew directions to Louis's plant. "Fly into St. Paul," he said. "And take this road north for about two hundred miles to this dash, this unfinished road that runs between the lakes. You'll see it through the trees. It looks like a gigantic tool shed."

"I've been waiting a lifetime to get head and body together," Garrison said as Ian finished the map and slid it across the table. "I want to get started." He took the map, folded it into little squares, got up from the table and made his way up the stairs, where Eddie guessed he was dragging out suitcases for his long trek into retribution.

"So you were saying?" Ian asked, passing his eyes finally back to Eddie.

"About Benjamin," Eddie replied. "Ripping him away from his family like that. Don't you think that's going to upset him?"

"Well we've got that one taken care of, too, believe it or not," Ian said. "Pennington will get the boy to forget about these people who have him. Pennington will get him ready for his new life."

"How can he do that? The kid will be screaming for the mother and father that he knows, won't he? How will he make Benjamin forget?"

"Remember the 'no questions' rule."

"Yes but I can't believe you can do all of these things. I would like to know a little at least, how you can make a little kid forget like that."

Ian sighed and passed his hands over the table, once again enclosing Eddie's. "Know this," he said. "Know that they'll be looking for you, the police, the people who took him to begin with, the FBI eventually. Know that you can't stay here long in this house and know that you've got to begin a new life somewhere else. It's the price you'll have to pay to get your brother back. You can't go home is the price you'll have to pay." Ian got up from the table and put on his coat. "If you don't want us to go ahead, I'll understand. It's a hell of a price. I'll understand if you want to forget all about it."

Eddie looked at him as he made his way to the kitchen doorway. He turned and looked into the empty rooms beyond. "I want my brother back," Eddie said. "Nothing else matters now."

"Then we will begin the operation," Ian said. "Things will happen quickly from here on out."

Ian turned for the doorway just as Garrison came down the stairs with a load of laundry. He extended one of his hands beyond the soiled clothes to shake Ian's hand good-bye. "I'll never be able to thank you enough, you know. At least let me pay you something for your time."

"We don't take money. I told you our policy when you first contacted us. Go start yourself a new life now," Ian said. Then, silent like a cat, he slipped out the door and beyond the towering hedges, a mystical saint walking into the night.

VI

Garrison had rummaged through the boxes in the attic, knocking over several of them in his haste to pack. One of the boxes, containing an assortment of ceramic figures, had spilled upon the floor because its cardboard bottom had given way. Eddie stood over the spilled things and noticed several cracked vases, a broken dish of potpourri and a minia-ture Jesus statue scattered upon the floor. He picked up the statue: one of Jesus' arms had snapped clean off and had skitted across the room; he could see the limb glimmering in a cobwebbed corner. He inspected the little smile that Jesus was giving him, and then the little black painted eyes that reflected the stained glass window. The eyes held a fire it seemed, red and blue swirls of life, and the fire burned a spirit into the attic air. The statue, which he gripped tight like a promise, had become imbued with some force that now pulled his eyes into a hypnotic contact with the alabaster, whereby the remainder of the world shut itself away so that he and the statue stood alone in a vacuum. Eddie couldn't help but murmur a silent prayer at that very moment, a little plea that carried with it the hope that some spiritual shaft of light had in fact come in through the stained glass and had settled into the broken Jesus. He stood in the middle of the shattered things, held the statue for a little while more, and prayed for Benjamin to arrive soon. He prayed some more for his own life to settle into peace, and he prayed for his mother and father, buried in their torment. He put the statue down among the shards, walked across the room, and sat down on the edge of the bed. Ian had told him that he could never go home, and now, as his prayers drifted up like spores to their Receiver, it hit him: he might not see his mother or father ever again. He had made up his mind that he wanted Benjamin back, and now this would be his price. No more mother, no more father, the eyes told him from among the broken things.

He wondered if his parents were moving on with their lives and whether his father was driving to work the same as always in his blue Chrysler, coming home with the Daily News and waiting out the long winter for baseball season to arrive. Beer upon beer: baseball was as much on his father's mind as his own absent sons, if not more so. Would the Phillies have a winning season this time around? Would they make the trades to take them to the top? And might Eddie and Benjamin come home, too? There was probably a lot of silence now between his parents, in the long wake of the runaway, after a string of hapless Phillies games had played themselves out and opened a canyon between them over those frozen nights. Evening by evening, as things whittled away, they had checked the newspaper for some ray of hope. They had read that front page article about the dead woman in Hudson. As soon as his mother had read about that big monitor lizard, that same awful lizard which had repulsed her in the pet store, she must have known that it was her own son who had done the deed in that basement apartment. She must have soaked that newspaper into a soggy mess with her waterfall of tears and slammed her bedroom door in a fit of guilt. 'Don't worry honey, it wasn't him', his father must have whispered through the locked door. 'It couldn't have been him.'

Garrison's footsteps echoed just below him and Eddie got up from the bed, anticipating his march up the steps. "I'll be leaving late tonight," he said from below. "Real late. Catching the red-eye into St. Paul and taking it from there. You can stay if you like. I'll leave a copy of the key for you on the table down here. I might not be back for a time and you'll be gone for sure by then. Be sure to lock up when you leave for good." Garrison smiled weakly, extended his hand, and patted Eddie on the shoulder. "Lots of luck with your life by the way." Then he crossed the hall one last time and made his way to the back bedroom, where he closed his door and, Eddie guessed, worked himself up a good afternoon cry.

Eddie laid down on the bed. He could smell the potpourri wafting from out of the broken ceramic things and across the attic floor. The smell haunted him with its familiarity, for it took him back into Mrs. Haas' living room, to the seat on the couch, to her story of the Cleveland Spiders and the way the sun came through the curtains to reveal the waning gibbous on her forehead. He closed his eyes as the smell continued to drift through his nostrils, permeating his memory. Billy Stigmeyer had told him off of a joint once that smell evoked memory more than any other sense. Eddie didn't give it much thought at the time, high as he was. Now, as the Boysenberry drifted all around him, he knew that Billy was right, because the images on Mrs. Haas' wall came back, photograph by photograph, as clear as if he were standing back at that wall.

Then the frames disappeared with the closing of eyes, and the image blurred into one thick montage of black and white, just as it had done beneath the bare bulb in Mrs. Haas' basement. The city came alive; the smell of Boysenberry must have ruptured something deep within his brain and let loose the buildings all at once and mashed all of those photographs together. For now, with the closing of his eyes, the structures merged and the names tumbled back in one crystallized vision: St. Augustine's church, Arch Street Friends' Meeting House, Carpenters' Hall, Lemon Hill, Fairmount Waterworks, Head House Square, the Cathedral of Saints Peter and Paul, the Walnut Street Theater and Independence Hall, and then the ballparks—Connie Mack Stadium, Baker Bowl, and Veterans Stadium. He could see each of them clearly as if he were standing right at that wall again, or better yet, as if he were standing in the middle of the city itself and was afforded a panoramic view. He could see the stuccoed facades, the louvered shutters, the crafted double doors and the intricate carvings of bearded men etched into the stone. He could see the circular amphitheaters, the slabs of towering marble, the checkerboard bricks, the elaborate balconies, the mosaic floors. And then, as he turned with eyes still closed to the brilliance of that stained-glass window in Garrison's attic, the city came alive suddenly with color: like the sun rolling out from beneath a blanket of clouds, the black and white vision gave way as the streets flared with the life of the city-dwellers, strolling down sunlit sidewalks beneath steel and glass monuments, along quiet tree-lined streets and unified block-long facades of elegant row homes. Eddie opened his eyes and stared fully into the brilliance of the white doves. He saw himself there among the city-dwellers. He was there, right in the middle of all of it, working at some busy restaurant, obscured by the masses, his identity happily lost. Then, closing his eyes once again, he saw Benjamin by his side. He took him by the hand as he walked him home, up one of those sets of concrete steps and into one of those row homes. Benjamin was smiling as they climbed the stairs and the sun filled his face with possibility.

Eddie could not sleep as the city-vision persisted over the course of the afternoon, as the hours tumbled into evening and turned the outside world to silence. Finally, the light left the window and the images sank back into their pastoral grays and began to fade, dissolving beneath his weary eyes as he dropped into a wonderful dream.

VII

Eddie awoke in the dark room as he heard a car start up: Garrison was on his way to Minnesota to fix his head. The car roared down the street where Eddie guessed that Garrison blew several stop signs on his way to the interstate. The engine faded, the silence crept back, and then he was alone. A sudden chill crawled beneath his blanket as the attic materialized out of the darkness. Here in this empty house, surrounded by hedges, he felt the uneasiness of loneliness and darkness overcoming him, trying to reach down and tug at him once again. But the smell of the Boysenberry and the images of the city returned and saved him, for he knew that despite the blackness, this time was different. Now the long wait was nearly over and now he had a plan. Soon, very soon, he was going down to Philadelphia, down among all of the people there, to a well-lighted row home. He would find a job in a restaurant there, meet some people, get himself a girl friend. He would raise Benjamin in that row home and he would assume a new identity. No one would even find him or Benjamin and he would have the city—all of the beautiful buildings rising, the new faces, the new experience—to guide him to salvation. He would learn the street names, the places to see, all of the light coming down all around, and he would show it all to Benjamin. He would be father, he would be brother, he would be guide.

He would need to shed his past and those long nights of torment and the memory of that lizard and the dirt raining down upon the turtles as Garrison buried them for good. He could easily forget the ugly subdivisions, the dying ones in Hudson, the oil-slicked Neshaminy. But could he easily forget his mother and father and William? Could he simply shut out that part of his life as if it had never been? How could he ever forget the sound of those wails coming out of the vent, or the image of his mother hunched in grief on the stairs? How could he ever forget the times before the kidnap, before that baseball game, before the thrown cup?

His father was always trying to get him to play baseball back then. In his earliest memories, his father had him out on the side yard with a little red glove throwing the ball in the air and instructing him to catch it. Perhaps it was his father's impatience that impelled him to hate the sport, because all he could remember was the dropping of the ball, time after time, and then the persistent yelling, 'squeeze the damned glove,' 'watch the ball,' 'get your arm out', followed by long, vocal sighs and a return to the house in disgust. One day, in a fit of anger, Eddie had tossed his red glove over an embankment and his father forced him down the hill and into the weeds to retrieve it. Down there in the undergrowth, seven-minute itch leaves attacked his bare legs as he reached for the glove, and he cried his way in blistering pain back up the hill. In the footsteps of his red-faced father he returned to the house, sent to his room with the needles of pain running the length of his legs, where he cried into his pillow until the sun went down.

After that, he came to hate the sport. He came to detest every walk through the living room when a game was on, he came to detest the voices of his father and his Uncle Pete as they got going on the trivia. He could never figure out why anyone would want to watch a team that had losing season after losing season, why they would sit there and get themselves worked up into a lather of fury over what he saw as inevitable: the Phillies were going to lose, the Phillies were going to always lose.

Perhaps all he ever needed was some guidance, just a little more patience, a bigger glove, a little more talent or a little more time. He didn't hate his father for that; they had done so many other things together and enjoyed each other's company. His father had accompanied his Boy Scout troop to an Indian Jamboree one summer and had even dressed as an Iroquois with loin cloth, war paint, and mallard feathers. John Burke had run Eddie's pants up the flagpole and his father had laughed at that and had even made some sexual jokes about half-mast. They had washed his car together and he had taken Eddie for ice cream cones on numerous occasions.They had even wallpapered the bathroom just last year. But it was always the baseball that returned when he thought of his father, from the Phillies dropped balls to his own dropped balls. Perhaps his father had looked at him and saw those Phillies, an eternally hopeless mess that would never resolve itself. Perhaps his father's frustration at his son's ineptitude was just a venting of his anger at his beloved baseball team. If only the Phillies would have had a winning season, maybe that would have made things better. Maybe it would have been o.k. to drop those balls and toss that red glove down the embankment. If it wasn't for those God-damned Phillies…

Alone in the empty house, Eddie had a sudden urge to telephone his mother and father, to go right down those steps in the dark and call them up. Eddie guessed it was near five a.m., but it didn't matter. His mother was awake, he knew that. She was restless to begin with and the news of the dead woman in Hudson was certain to keep her wide-eyed with worry for days. She had to be a mess by now, her hair stringy, her dentures fermenting in two-day old water, her nightgown dragging the dirt of the carpet behind it as she shuttled the hallway. She probably didn't bother with the make-up any more because it would just drip down her face every time she bawled. She was struggling to get through each day now, and she probably had just about enough.

Eddie got out of his bed and walked down the steps and to the back bedroom, to the place where he had heard Garrison's footsteps retreat. He flicked on the overhead light, noticing another monster hedge barricading the light from the window. The room was painted a sterile white, its walls empty. On the floor of the room lay a mattress with rumpled sheets and hundreds of papers scattered upon it. Next to the bed he saw the phone tangled in a web of wire. He sat down on the bed amongst the papers (receipts for building supplies, tax forms, a wedding certificate, many blank pages) and picked up the telephone. 645-2109: he slammed down the receiver before the first ring and then looked at the bare walls. This would be the last time, he promised himself. No matter what the reaction on the other end, this would be the last time he would ever call. Never mind the pleads, never mind the wailing in the background. He firmly implanted that city image into his brain, wedged it there, hand in hand with Benjamin walking along the side street, and he dialed again. 645-2109: his father answered on the second ring with a groggy 'hello'.

"Dad it's……it's Eddie."

Then the silence, interrupted sharply by a 'my god, my god.'

"Dad, please listen…"

But his father wouldn't listen at that very moment of contact, for he had bolted from the bed (he could hear the rustle of sheets) and began to scream, "Eddie, it's Eddie, honey it's Eddie, pick up the other receiver."

"Eddie, dear God, where are you?" he asked finally.

"Dad listen…"

"Eddie please come home Eddie," his father said.

Then the click of the other line broke his pleading, followed by the familiar whimper of his mother. "I knew you were alive. Oh, Eddie I prayed and prayed and I knew you were alive." She quickly drowned herself out in a static of sobs.

"Please, please listen," Eddie said. "I want you to know…"

"Tell us you didn't kill that woman in Hudson," his father said. "Your mother is certain…"

"I'm going to hang up if you don't listen, I swear to God, dad," Eddie said, and then silence.

"Why are you angry at us?" his mother asked in a dull whine.

"I'm not angry, I just want to tell you….I want to tell you I won't be coming home soon. But I don't want you to worry about me. I'm seventeen and I can take care of myself, you see. I've learned to do that. And there's something else…."

"Go on," his father said (and sniffles on the extension).

"I've found Benjamin."

Eddie could not make out the words coming out of the receiver, for it became a mishmash of his parents' voices shouting into the phone, male and female epithets hurled at him from the other end. He deduced that they wanted him to explain.

"Some men helped me, they have this secret way of finding people. They're delivering him tomorrow."

"Delivering? Are you joking?" his father asked.

"Are you on some kind of drug?" his mother asked. "This doesn't sound like you. Is this you?"

"Of course this is him," his father shouted through.

"Look, I called to tell you that Benjamin and I will be taking off somewhere. I can't come home because I've done some things…"

"That was you in Hudson, wasn't it?" his father asked. "That damned lizard was yours, wasn't it?"

"Look I don't want to get into things," Eddie said. "I want you to feel better knowing that Benjamin and I will be alive and well somewhere. I'll be getting a job, and I can take care of…"

"A three-year-old?" his father asked. "You've got to be kidding."

"I'm begging you to come home," his mother wailed. "Please think about all of this insanity. Something's got into you, Eddie, some insanity."

"You've got to have faith that we'll be o.k.," Eddie said. "You've got to stop the crying and the worrying, mom. Get on with your life. I've been praying, too, you know, praying to Saint Jude. Prayer works, mom. I wouldn't have found Benjamin without Saint Jude."

In the ensuing second of silence, Eddie hung up the telephone. He imagined the anarchy on the other end, then stared at the gnarled mess of wires on the floor and fell immediately to the mattress. A bird from somewhere out of the obscured trees chirped of morning, and he let loose an uncontrollable burst of tears that soaked the sheets and the scattered pages. "I won't go home," he cried over and over. "I can't ever go home."

VIII

The light in Garrison's attic is such that, on a particularly brilliant winter morning, when the trees are bare and the sun is afforded a full burst upon the side of the house, the stained glass projects a most beautiful pattern on all of the walls and floor at once, magnified ten times its actual size. It is a marvelous thing to behold, as Eddie discovered upon waking that next morning, for he never remembered a morning so bright and colorful as this. The light from the window had come full across the bed with its brilliant reds and greens and yellows and covered him like a blanket, and he felt as if some cosmic force had descended with its magical hand and that he had become the center of the universe.

As if by design, for Eddie was certain that design was carrying him now, he heard the latch of the door below him, and he closed his eyes as the footsteps moved across the downstairs rooms, as the breathing advanced upon the foot of the stairs, as the sound of the shoes ascended toward him. They were soft steps, almost inaudible in their approach, but there nonetheless, growing closer to the top of his attic room. When Eddie opened his eyes, he saw him standing in the light, as the projections of the doves came down upon him and engulfed the little boy in the middle of the floor. The boy looked back to the top of the stairs, uncertain of his place and mesmerized by the colored light in which he had become ensconced. His blond hair glowed white as he turned to the bed and addressed Eddie with a weak smile, as he raised his hand to ward off the blinding white doves.

"You're Eddie," the little boy said. "You're my brother."

Then Eddie jumped from the bed, startling the boy so that he stepped further into the light. He walked across the floor and inspected the little boy, his blond hair, his brown eyes, his little sweatshirt and sneakers. He was surprised that the boy was not frightened as Eddie's arms reached nervously into the stained glass light, as they came down all around him into a loose hug.

"I am Eddie," he said awkwardly. He released his grip and stared at the child, who had passed his own stare to the stained glass window. The boy inspected the shapes coming down, wondered about them perhaps in much the same way that Eddie had first wondered about them. Benjamin had grown so much, Eddie thought in his silent interlude. He was no longer that baby in the crib that he had held, that he had tickled, no longer that helpless creature reaching up into the white universe. An uneasiness overcame him, a sudden feeling that the boy might not be Benjamin at all, but rather a stolen child who was merely a stranger. His hair glowed too white, his hands were too large, his mouth looked wrong. And his eyes were brown, not blue. Was this really the boy?

Eddie heard the heavy breathing at the bottom of the stairs and then the footsteps advanced. Ian appeared at the top of the stairs with a content smile and Eddie got up from the middle of the floor as the child turned back from his stare at the window, puzzled suddenly by his bath in the colored light.

"Everything all right?" Ian asked.

"Yes," Eddie said. "You got him. I don't believe you got him so soon." He turned and stared back at the child, forcing a smile. "You like the pretty window?"

"What are all those things on it?" the boy asked. "Are they birds?"

"Yes, there's birds," Eddie said. "And there's flowers, and candles, and…"

"Fireworks on the floor," he said. pointing at the projection of light. "How come there's fireworks on the floor?"

"Well the sun does that," Eddie said. "When the light from outside comes through the glass, it makes all the colors on the floor."

"How come they don't make all windows like that?" the boy asked.

"He's a smart little kid," Ian said. "Asked me why water was wet on the way over. Didn't know what to tell him."

"Listen Ian," Eddie whispered. "This is unbelievable what you've done…"

"Well thank you," Ian said. "That's what we do sometimes, the unbelievable, that's what we're known to do. Charles got him calmed down and believing in you in nothing flat."

"You're certain it's him?" Eddie asked, turning to the boy, who was stretched out on the floor in the light of the doves.

"Yes, why? Aren't you sure?"

"Well, it's a little strange, but the eyes especially, they…"

"They're brown instead of blue."

"Yes, how did you…?"

"It happens to many children. They're born with blue eyes and they turn brown as they begin to grow. Genetics."

Eddie turned to look at the child again, waiting for some sign of familiarity to move across the stained glow, for a saintly hand to reach down and touch him into recognition.

"It's him, it's him," Ian said. "You need to believe that…and now we need to move the both of you out of here. You can't go home now, you know."

"I gathered that," Eddie said.

"The police are probably already looking for the boy. They'll scour the neighborhood, they'll have the forces out." Ian stopped and placed his hand on Eddie's shoulder. "Pennington wants to re-locate you to Seattle."

"Seattle? No, I would like a choice of where I can go," Eddie said. "I would at least like to choose my spot."

"Well it can't be around here. If anyone recognizes you…"

"Philadelphia. I want to live in Philadelphia. I 've been thinking about it, and it could work. I know I could get a restaurant job there, pay rent in a little apartment, find a way to look out for Benjamin."

Ian pressed his hand into Eddie's shoulder blade. "Do you know how much effort it will be to raise this boy?" he asked. "Part of the plan to move you to Seattle was that you would have some help raising him there. Pennington has family there and…"

"I want to give it a shot," Eddie said. "On my own. Besides, I don't want to move that far away. No one will recognize us in Philly, and I think we'll be happy there."

Benjamin had come across the room and now stood next to them listening. Ian grew silent and paced the attic floor, moving in and out of the colored light. "We could get you a cheap room until you found a job," Ian said. "You would need to lay low."

"Yes, that's exactly what I planned," Eddie said. "Then later on, a little apartment when I was getting along."

"We can't hel p you out with money," Ian said. "We don't have the resources for giving away money."

"You got my brother back. That's more than enough." Eddie watched the boy as he climbed upon the bed and sprang up and down on the mattress. "I just need to convince myself it's him is all."

Benjamin had begun to jump on the bed as the rusted springs resounded across the room. His little body fell in and out of the stained light like a feather touched by the wind. He smiled and almost laughed. It amazed Eddie that the little boy had forgotten his past that quickly, that efficiently.

"Let's go then," Ian said. "Gather what you need and let's go."

Eddie smiled weakly at the boy, moved around the side of the bed, and retrieved his blanket. He balled it up and shoved it into his backpack, then zipped it closed.

"Look how high," the boy said. "I'm going all the way into the light."

Eddie smiled and watched him rise and fall into shadow and back into light. Then he felt Ian's eyes burning with urgency from the top of the stairs. "We've got to go now," Eddie said to the boy, still apprehensive of calling him Benjamin, or of thinking of the boy as his little brother. He slid on the backpack and waited for the boy to come down from his jump. Then, with both arms, he picked him up off the bed. He held the boy and followed Ian down the stairs, past the monster hedges, and into the sunlight beyond Garrison's house.

IX

Now the road became highway and the car maneuvered into the fast lane as the cityscape developed like a photograph from out of the distant haze. Eddie could see the pointed skyscrapers barely visible on the horizon: City Hall, Society Hill Towers, the PSFS building, Penn Center Complex, as the sound of the cars gushed by. He took in a burst of air as his hair flew all about his face. He did not look behind him, for he knew that his past was receding there at seventy miles per hour, where all of the dark places were fading to specks. Looking straight ahead at the unfolding buildings and the way in which the light settled between them, he could feel the ease begin to sink into him, as if vise grips had been loosened from his skull. He wondered about the pull of this place, this city spilling on the horizon and settling peacefully into him. What drew him here to Philadelphia, what impelled him to come? Was it simply those photographs on Mrs. Haas' wall? Did he perhaps want to live the life of the woman, walk the streets as she had done so many years back, live the life which he had twice taken away? Or did he just want to get away from the sprawling wasteland of subdivisions, from dwindling nature, from the memory of buried turtles and escaped lizards and ducks shot dead in hedges?

The little boy, whose blonde hair had blown back as well, tugged Eddie on the shirt and pointed to a huge factory that had risen suddenly from the other side of the interstate. The factory, gray and imposing with its stacks and ramps and pipes, spread several hundred yards across a paved lot, where hundreds of cars had parked in uniform lines.

"What is that?" the boy asked.

"A place where they make things," Eddie answered. "They make metal things there I think, bicycle parts and screws and bottle caps."

"Like Santa's elves? Is that how they make things, just like the elves make all of the toys at the North Pole?"

"Something like that," Eddie said, fumbling for a parallel. "Except the people in there make things to pay for their houses and their food and…"

"I got lots of toys from Santa last Christmas when I was staying with that man and lady," the boy said. His eyes suddenly glazed over, inhibiting some faraway expression, perhaps recalling bits and pieces of a past that had been vanquished by Charles. Eddie looked to the front seat, where Ian had cast a wide eye back through the rear-view mirror. It looked as if he were expecting an outburst of terror from the boy or a forbidden question from Eddie. Instead, a silence prevailed from the back seat and then a sadness descended on the little boy as the factory dropped into the distance. He sat quietly and watched the traffic grow thick.

Eddie realized that he was not ready for all of this new responsibility. He wondered what Charles had told this boy, what churned in his brain as the skyline loomed, as the buildings grew tall and imposing. What would a little boy think of a city so large, of people so massed together, of everything new, of a past wiped away? Then Eddie realized that he felt the same way himself, that they had all of that in common. As their hair blew and twisted in the wind he realized: they were shedding their pasts and heading into a void together, a universe of steel and glass and brick, uncertain of anything at all. They were two boys headed for new identities.

Deep down, down where he dreamed at night, down in his dark well of thoughts, Eddie was sure that the boy was not Benjamin. There was no hint of familiarity, not one physical trait that made him believe that this boy was that same baby who had cried himself to sleep in that crib, who had smiled his smile at the peering faces, who had made those crayon marks, those swirling galaxies of possibility, on the nursery walls. Those crib bars had become a prison for Eddie now, holding and suspending those happy thoughts of baby Benjamin in front of him, back when the world was small and delicious, when the yellow squares peeked through the bedroom curtains. No hints of darkness then— only the perennial sunlight plastered upon the nursery walls. No cries of anguish, no stolen children, no crying mothers closing bedroom doors. No hopeless causes. Now the crib was gone and only the bars remained. Eddie wanted to go back. He wanted a return to that simpler, uncomplicated past, to a Benjamin he knew, to the warm sunlight that could forever bathe him. But the past was gone, seventy miles an hour, a million miles an hour behind him. The past was dust.

Consciously, he did not allow himself to believe that the boy sitting next to him watching the city rise up was not Benjamin. He couldn't allow that, not now. He had to make the boy Benjamin now. He had to make him his brother because he was headed for his destiny and there was no way to stop. Under the guiding hand of Saint Jude and now filled with the faith of the hopeful white universe, he had committed himself to never going back. The road only lie ahead now, and he would take that road to the end with the boy by his side. He was going to take all of those old photographs and project himself into them. He was going to make it work. He was going to be brother, he was going to be father and guide.

"I have a toy for you, Benjamin," he said. The boy snapped from his glaze and turned to watch Eddie reach into the side of his knapsack and retrieve a very old baseball with faded signatures and a shabby casing. He handed it across.

"It's a hundred years old," Eddie said. "It's a baseball."

Benjamin examined the ball, took both of his little hands and turned it like a globe. His eyes followed the road of bright red stitching as it went around, and he smiled and continued to turn the old baseball, as the city rose all around them and the buildings cast their shadows into the back seat. Benjamin was too enamored by the stitching to notice the looming buildings, though. He just kept turning the old baseball over and over with his little fingers, fascinated by the line that just kept going around and around, into eternity it seemed.

From Benjamin's Diary

◆

—I had another one of those dreams last night, but this time I didn't carry on like a baby and run from the room. I dealt with it, and before I knew it I was up and putting on my shirt and shorts and heading out the door. I decided I wasn't going to tell my brother about the dream— though I was getting tired of keeping my dreams to myself and I knew that one morning I was going to let him know. It was the same old thing over and over, of men coming to get me in a white van. Besides the fact that I wasn't afraid any more—(most times now I wake up in the middle of the night and laugh right out loud and say 'is that all you've got? is that all you've got?')—the dream was getting to be downright irritating. It's like I'm standing on the corner and I start counting down the seconds as I wait for the van to come. Sometimes they come out the back, sometimes out of the cab, sometimes out of the sliding door. One time it got real strange and they were getting me when I was lying in a crib. But they always look the same, arriving in those ridiculous ski masks, running at me and grabbing me by the elbows and tossing me in the back. I keep trying to tell myself, before I go to sleep, to just laugh at them in my dream, or to try to rip off one of their masks, or to stand on a different corner, or to bring a big Doberman Pinscher with me. I guess I haven't been trying hard enough. Tonight I'll make sure to concentrate on the rabid dog before I zonk out.

—Bernie brought in a Phillies program from a game his dad took him to over the weekend. We got in trouble for talking in the back of the class about how good the Phillies were, how they were going to the World Series for sure this year, but it wasn't my fault this time. Bernie showed me some autographs he got after the game and started telling me how to do a scorecard. He got to telling me about the numbers you mark for all nine positions, about the three slashes you form to make a "K" after a strikeout, about the "E" for error. "See, I marked E-2 here in the fourth," he was saying. "That's when Boone fucked up." Of course, that was just as recess was quieting down, and so Mrs. Culp heard Bernie with his curse word and ordered us to stay after school. We had to memorize the capitals of the world, and she said she was going to test us on every one of them. Eddie was pissed because the buses stopped running and he had to take the subway out to pick me up. I didn't want to tell him about all of the memorizing I had to do. I know he would just laugh and tell me I was getting what I deserved.

—Mrs. Culp told Eddie about my memorizing assignment, and sure enough he told me I was getting what I deserved. Went down to the dinner table and told him I had the capitals memorized and he didn't believe me and said I needed to spend more time with the books. I bet him that if I could rattle them all off right then and there, he'd have to take me to a Phillies game the next weekend they were home. He said that he didn't like baseball very much but that he'd do it if I won the bet. So I rattled them all off, every single country he could think of, and won the bet. Then he started in on another 'when I was a kid' story and told me he had to memorize all of the saints when he went to Catholic school. I knew what was coming—sure enough, I had to sit there and listen to him rattle off every single saint—must have been seventy of them. Afterward he told me that they were stuck in his head forever and he would die an old man with saints on the brain. He started humming some old Beatles song and that's when I excused myself. Eddie gets weird sometimes

—Went to the zoo today. Boring place, I don't get why people go there. We had to wait in line in the hot sun forever and when we got in there the whole place smelled like one massive shit. Eddie insisted on taking me around, on telling me every little thing about every elephant, gazelle and gorilla. Most of the things were just sitting in their cages, miserable as anything, miserable as most of the people gawking at them. What a thoroughly miserable place for everybody. If it smells like shit, stay away is what I say. I admit the reptile house was cool, though. Eddie seemed to know more about the snakes and turtles than anything, kept telling me about where they lay their eggs and where they eat and which ones were poisonous. He told me that he hunted for turtles when he was a kid, that he was going to make reptiles his life when he was my age. He said he was going to take me to look for salamanders in Fairmount Park some time. He got kind of funny when we went past the Komodo Dragon, though. I asked him a couple of questions about the thing and he changed the subject and headed for the tree frogs.

—Eddie's going to nail me stealing his smokes one of these days, especially if he finds this diary and reads this entry.

—Phillies-Padres game today. Pretty good one, ninth win in a row for the Phils, and now they're fifteen games up on the Pirates. Looks like they're going to win the East. A funny thing happened at the game, though. I did a scorecard the way Bernie taught me and as I was doing it I showed Eddie. I figured he would be surprised that I knew so much about filling out a scorecard and that he'd even be proud of me, even though he didn't like baseball very much. 'What are you doing?' he asks me after he buys me a program and I ask the vendor for a pencil. I tell him I'm going to score the game, and he looked at me kind of funny, and he looked at me real funny when the game started and I started filling in the blocks, 6-5-3, E-7, 9, HBP, inning after inning. He kept looking over my shoulder every time I made a mark, and then I realized he didn't know what I was doing, so I sat there and explained every mark I made. I taught him how to fill out a scorecard. And then, right there in the middle of 45,000 people, Eddie starts crying. I thought maybe a bee stung him somewhere or something. Out of nowhere he starts bawling and then he says he always wanted to learn how to fill out a scorecard, and something in his sobs about our father and a game a long time back and how funny life was. I told him to stop crying because it was pretty embarrassing, that older brothers shouldn't cry, that younger brothers should cry. But he said he couldn't help it, and he cried and cried and couldn't stop, and everybody in the row beneath us and behind us and everyone in our row started looking, even when they all stood up and pumped their fists and cheered, even as Hebner hit a bases-clearing triple into the gap.

About the Author

---◆---

Tim Wenzell lives in Garwood, New Jersey and teaches writing at Bergen Community College in Paramus, New Jersey. Much of the subject matter of *Absent Children*, from Catholic school to restaurant work to baseball to collecting reptiles to living in suburbia, comes from Tim's own experiences. Even at forty-two, Tim can still be seen hunting turtles with his son Ryan and driving the length of the New Jersey turnpike to attend Phillies games in the hopes of watching them win.

About the Novel

❖

Absent Children is set upon the backdrop of generic suburbia and centers on Eddie Shemanski, a seventeen year old boy whose baby brother Benjamin has been kidnapped from his crib. Eddie, in a growing sense of paranoia, has built a box into the wall of his closet to hide from the men he is sure will return to abduct him as well, and finally runs away to avoid what he percieves to be his dark destiny. This sets in motion a bizarre journey through suburbia, where Eddie encounters many odd characters and homes as the novel rushes forward to its stunning conclusion.